Mr Scarletti's Ghost

A Mina Scarletti Mystery

Mr Scarletti's Ghost

Linda Stratmann

To
Auntie Marc

Cover images:
Top image: ©iStock
Bottom image: Medium Eusapia Palladino, 1890. ©GettyImages

First published 2015

The Mystery Press is an imprint of The History Press
The Mill, Brimscombe Port
Stroud, Gloucestershire, GL5 2QG
www.thehistorypress.co.uk

British Library Cataloguing in Publication Data.
A catalogue record for this book is available from the British Library.

ISBN 978 0 7509 6050 2

Typesetting and origination by The History Press
Printed and bound in Great Britain by TJ International Ltd.

One

On a sparkling June day Mina Scarletti gazed out across the dipping waters of the Channel, thinking about ghosts. They were pirates and murderers with the coarse burn of the noose still on their sinewy throats, smugglers endlessly searching for lost cargoes, and lovers driven by grief or shame to seek cold peace below the waves. Their images, scored in wood and glistening with thick black ink on cheap paper, rolled and pocketed, torn and soiled, were, she thought with no trace of regret, the only children she would ever have.

Mina had awoken that morning to find that a narrow line of pain had drawn itself down the right side of her neck, darting over her shoulder and plunging into her back. She was usually free of pain but every so often it would return like an old friend needing to be soothed, and then she would go out and rest her palms on the railings of the King's Road esplanade, and lean there for a while, looking at the sea. Two worlds met and fought here, worlds where life in one meant death in the other, and hungry wavelets hissed as they scrambled for purchase on the pebbled beach where ribbons of black weed gave off a sour rank odour.

Stiffly, awkwardly, Mina turned for home, walking with her odd, limping, lurching gait, like a small dark bird with a broken wing. She was composing a new story about a haunted jewel that had been flung into the sea by a cursed and dying man, but was found again in the maw of a great ugly fish. Mina wondered, not for the first time, what her nervous mother would think if she knew that her daughter occupied her hours with writing not wholesome stories for children, as the family had been led to believe, but tales of almost unimaginable horror.

The quiet season was drawing to a close, and Brighton, freshly painted and varnished, its gardens invitingly in bloom, was awaiting its first flood of visitors. It was the best part of the year, when the town was bathed in a warm clear glowing light that glittered off the sea. In a few days the seafront would be crowded with noisy families; women in their gaudy holiday clothes, men chasing hats that had been whipped from their heads by the unaccustomed breeze, children scattered like frilly scuttling crabs over the shingled beach, while overhead from early to late, cliff-top bands boomed and blared under snapping flags. Vehicles of every size and kind would rattle back and forth along King's Road, which became a kind of Piccadilly-by-the-sea. Contemplative visitors, who read novels or simply wished to gaze at the sea in peace, turned to the old Chain Pier in the east, but fashionable promenaders, who had come to see and be seen, flocked to the bazaars, exhibitions and wide walking deck of the new West Pier.

Everywhere the smiling sunny faces of strangers would suddenly darken and turn away when they saw Mina. Sometimes a helpful gentleman, not seeing her face, would hurry up and offer his arm, and as she turned to smile at him he would recoil in alarm to see the head of a woman of twenty-five on what he had assumed to be the body of a shrivelled ancient.

If Mina Scarletti had not had a twisted back she would have stood just over five feet in height, but as it was, her spine, curving treacherously first one way and then the other like a bony snake, had crushed and shrunk her to the size of a child, tilted her hip, forced her shoulder blade and ribcage out of their proper places, and made her into a cruel parody of womanhood. Medical men, after their accustomed fashion, had given the affliction a Latin name, *scoliosis*.

Shock, pity and embarrassment were the landscape of Mina's daily life, but the one ghost she never thought of was the ghost of what she might have been.

Mina hobbled up the slope of Montpelier Road, a long narrow street prettily carved with the forms of seashells and ammonites, which lay on the western side of the town where the breezes were kinder than in the gusty east. The Scarlettis had moved there two years ago, when her father's declining health had forced him to retire from his business of publishing stories for the Scarletti Library of Romance, and leave the choking fogs of London. Brighton, he had been assured, was in itself a doctor, and his best hope of recovery. Their new home, with its gracefully curving bay windows that welcomed in the healing light, was – like everything that was best in Brighton – tall, like a plant reaching for the sun. It was hard enough for the maidservant, Rose, a strong young girl, who tackled the stairs from basement to attic with a permanent unspoken grumble on her lips, but for Mina, every step was a hill.

Henry Scarletti had not expected to die so soon, indeed he had rather expected to live, since the most successful doctors are those who only have good news for their patients. In his last few days, choking on the tumours in his swollen throat, he had been unable to eat or speak, but he knew that Mina was beside him. There were those who claimed to have seen the spirit of a dying person leave the body and rise up to Heaven like a soft transparent wisp of light, but at the moment of her father's passing, Mina saw nothing.

After Henry's death, Mina's mother Louisa retired into a state of melancholy and Mina took the entire management of the household upon herself. Her first act had been to engage Miss Simmons, a quiet, dutiful person, as a nurse companion to her mother, and the second was to let the upper-floor apartments to a fifty-year-old widow, Mrs Parchment, who had retired to Brighton for her health and pleasure. This energetic lady enjoyed brisk walks, sunshine and sea breezes, and thought nothing of basking in a cold east wind with a cliff-top picnic of bread and cheese or watching gales sweep in from the sea bringing heavy waves crashing on to the esplanade. Mina hoped that Mrs Parchment might do what she had failed to achieve; take her mother out into the light to breathe sea air and see the moving colours of fashionable visitors, but found to her disappointment that the lady was not disposed to enjoy any company other than her own.

There was a black iron railing by the side of the three tall steps to Mina's front door, which assisted her climb, and she energetically clutched and swayed herself to the top. Many people, seeing her ungainly rocking walk along a flat pavement, concluded that she was unable to use a staircase, either up or down, but there were few obstacles she could not negotiate unaided if she set her mind to it.

She was looking forward to a busy afternoon, composing her new story and writing letters to her brothers and sister. Her older brother Edward had been preoccupied with business in London since their father's death, and her sister Enid, the beauty of the family, had escaped the house of mourning to marry a Mr Inskip, the dullest solicitor in England, and became the mother of twins within a year. Enid had once confessed that marriage and motherhood were not all that she had expected them to be, and neither, it appeared, was Mr Inskip. There was always the hope that Mina's younger brother Richard would descend upon Brighton, as she had not seen him in several weeks. Richard, with a cheerful optimistic nature and confidence that the future would somehow take care of itself, was constantly about to make a great fortune in ventures which he was only able to describe in the vaguest terms. It was impossible not to like him, but every time he came home, lifting his mother's spirits with his extravagant promises, and borrowing money, Mina suspected that his generosity was chiefly benefitting his gambling friends.

As she took off her bonnet in the hallway Rose came up from the kitchen, carrying a laden tea tray, which she took into the parlour. No doubt, thought Mina, her mother was entertaining one of her church visitors, ladies whose sole occupation in life was to call on the sick and miserable, and make them even more painfully aware of just how sick and miserable they were. Mrs Bettinson was a particular connoisseur of misery in others – she fed on it and it made her fat. Her visits gave Louisa free rein to dwell on her many reasons for unhappiness, one of which Mina felt sure was herself. When Mrs Bettinson departed, leaving Louisa in an even more melancholy state than before, she always seemed a little fatter. Mina often found that lady, sitting like a mountain of black frills with an inhospitable summit, in command of the parlour. She was, like the queen, in a permanent state of mourning, although in her case it was not for one adored husband, but a series of relatives who had followed one another to the grave with such regularity that she had hardly been able to trim her gown with lilac before the next funeral plunged her once again into night. Unlike Mina's mother, however, Mrs Bettinson was able to manage her grief with equanimity, soothing herself by contemplating the distress of others. In particular she continued to assail Mina with stories of this or that wonderful doctor who had achieved the most marvellous cures. During the last ten years Mina had been subjected to every kind of treatment: deportment classes, shoulder bandages, a plaster of Paris waistcoat, and a steel brace, none of which had assisted her. She had been accused of causing the condition herself through bad habits of sitting and standing, accusations she had always denied even when threatened with surgery to cut or stretch her muscles. The final diagnosis, that the condition was incurable but would not get any worse, had come as a relief. She was four feet eight inches in height and there she would remain.

Louisa made no efforts to contradict Mrs Bettinson's implied and sometimes outright declaration that Mina's refusal to consult yet another medical man was only adding to her mother's unhappiness. Their visitor's latest enthusiasm was for a Dr Hamid, who she said was very handsome looking, and who had come all the way from India with some mysterious herbs and opened an establishment where he did something unusual with steam. His special baths had helped so many to regain their health that he had been dubbed 'Dr Brighton'. Mina, who had had her fill of medical men, did not want to see Dr Hamid or Dr Brighton or any other doctor, even to please her mother, which it most probably would not, and informed Mrs Bettinson of this with a firmness that only just stopped short of insolence.

That afternoon, Mina, having no wish to spend time in the company of someone who found her defiant contentment so intolerable, decided to retire to her room and pursue her story of the jewel discovered in an ugly fish, a fish which, now she thought about it, was very fat with glossy black scales. The story had written itself a little further during her walk, and the jewel was now haunted by the ghost of a lovelorn lady, the dead betrothed of the cursed man who had thrown it away in a paroxysm of grief, but it would keep returning to him until he was able to break the curse, and be reunited with his beloved in death. Mina needed to commit the story to paper before she forgot the details, and started to work her way up the stairs.

Rose emerged from the parlour. 'Excuse me, Miss, but Mrs Scarletti says she would like you to take tea with her.'

Mina paused, wondering if she could plead a headache or a backache or any sort of an ache, but the streak of pain that had pinched her into wakefulness that morning had been warmed by the sun and was gone. Rose stood awkwardly shifting from one foot to the other, as if there was something more she wanted to say but dared not.

'Thank you, Rose,' said Mina, accepting that *The Cursed Emerald* would have to wait. Rose looked relieved and hurried away. Mina limped downstairs, opened the door of the parlour, and paused there in some surprise, for she was met with an unusual sight.

Louisa Scarletti was one of those fair, thin, frail-looking women, who always seemed to be on the verge of some terrible illness but was actually in perfect health. She had been favoured with an opalescent skin, vivid blue eyes and a cascade of blonde hair so pale it was almost white. It was now more than a year since Henry had died, sufficient time for most widows to begin participating in at least a few activities in which widowhood was not an essential feature, but she had become enamoured of the life of a semi-invalid, and embraced suffering as if it was in itself a comfort.

Louisa's favoured position from which to take tea was reclining on a sofa surrounded by cushions, a smelling bottle at her fingertips, sipping at barely half a cup of a pale tepid infusion, while weakly declining the temptation of a biscuit. Her lustre gone, she resembled an arrangement of *immortelles*, painted porcelain flowers that lived forever under a glass dome as a tribute to the dead. That afternoon, however, Mina found her mother sitting upright by the tea table wielding the heavy silver pot with energy and aplomb. Her companion, Simmons, with a wary and slightly uneasy look, sat silently by, poised for any duty or emergency.

'Mina, my dear, do take some tea,' said Louisa brightly. 'And I would very much like you to meet Mr Bradley.'

Mina entered the room, and a gentleman who had been seated in an easy chair at once started up. He had obviously been warned to expect someone of Mina's appearance, for he adopted a curious pose, his shoulders hunched forward, his hands clasped in front of him like a clergyman about to confer a blessing on the recently bereaved. He was not a clergyman, but Mina could not be sure what he was. A little below middling height and fleshy but not yet fat, he was aged about forty-five and neatly dressed after the fashion of a moderately well-to-do professional gentleman, with a dark rim of hair wrapped like a glossy swollen worm about his balding head, and short trimmed side-whiskers. His features were unremarkable, but when he gazed on Mina his eyes opened very wide, his jaw sagged in dismay, and he adopted a look of sympathy that bordered on the grotesque.

'Mr Bradley is recently arrived in Brighton and I am pleased to say that he has joined the congregation at Christ Church,' said Louisa, with a deft application of the milk jug. 'He is a gentleman of unusual perception and you would do well to pay very great attention to what he says.'

'Oh, you are too kind!' exclaimed Bradley, allowing his body to undulate in his hostess's direction while keeping his attention focused on Mina. 'Miss Scarletti, I must say it is the very greatest pleasure to meet you. Your mother, who is in my opinion a lady of the most extraordinary courage, has told me all about you.'

Mina said nothing, but inclined her head in greeting, then crossed the room to a chair and sat down. All the while Mr Bradley observed her gait as if the very sight of her affliction was causing him the most exquisite pain.

Simmons distributed teacups and plates and offered a platter of fancy cakes, and when they were all settled, Louisa said, 'Mr Bradley, although he is far too modest to speak of it to any degree, has a rare ability, in fact I do believe I have never met another individual with his gift. He is actually able to perceive the spirit of a living person, in quite the most extraordinary detail. Colours and shapes – just imagine! He can in this way ascertain whether the person, be they man, woman or child, is in poor health either in body or mind. But more than this, he can offer comfort for the spirit, and even – yes – *cure* what is ill. We are fortunate indeed that he has decided to make his home here.' Louisa, with a rare flush of her pale cheek, took a mouthful of cake.

'Are you a medical man?' asked Mina, feeling sure that their visitor was not, and thinking that his arrival in a town many of whose amenities were devoted to the requirements of invalids was no coincidence.

Mr Bradley smiled and gave a self-deprecating gesture. 'Medical men attempt to cure only what they can see, and are very imperfect judges of what they cannot. No, I am neither a doctor nor a surgeon, and have never professed to be such. I,—' he said, pressing his palms to his chest, 'am only the poor conduit of a greater power; and I must reassure you, for I am asked this very often, that such little abilities as I have are not exercised for my own advantage. I exist only to be of help to my fellow creatures.' He paused briefly to enjoy the admiration of his audience, most of which emanated from his hostess. Simmons, who had gone back to her chair, looked more afraid than anything else. Their visitor, sensing perhaps that Mina did not regard him with the degree of respect he was accustomed to command, fixed her with a solemn frown. 'There are those, I know, who are so impudent as to demand payment for what they do, but I am a gentleman of independent means and have no need to make myself rich from the suffering of others. I am visiting members of the Christ Church congregation to advise that I intend to start some prayer meetings where those in need of comfort may seek guidance, and where I will do what I can to assist in the Lord's work of the healing of the sick.'

'I declare,' said Louisa, 'I can feel your influence at work already – simply by being in your presence I am better than I was. But Mr Bradley,' she waved a fragment of cake at Mina, 'is there nothing you can do for my poor daughter?'

Mr Bradley sighed, and again he opened his eyes wide, and they were very large and brown and sad, like those of an aged and weary cow. 'If you will allow me?' he asked.

'But of course,' said Louisa, and finishing the cake, gestured to Simmons to bring her another.

Mr Bradley put aside his teacup, dabbed his lips with a napkin, rose to his feet and smiled. 'Do not be afraid, Miss Scarletti,' he said.

'Is there something I should be afraid of?' enquired Mina.

He laughed. 'Oh, no, nothing at all! I merely wish to touch your hand very lightly. You may or may not know this, but touch is one of what we call our five senses, and these tell us all that we need to know. I can use that sense to see and understand what others cannot. When I touch your hand, you will experience an extraordinary feeling, as the divine power, which reaches out through me, a humble vessel, meets your own immortal spirit.' He adopted a more serious look. 'I must first reassure you that we of the Church abhor any suggestion that the healing power we are privileged to convey comes from anywhere but on high.'

'Oh, I had never thought it otherwise,' said Louisa. 'Can people be so envious and so cruel as to say such things?'

'I regret that is so,' said Mr Bradley, with the air of a martyr, 'but you, dear lady, are too kind and too perceptive to think other than what is manifestly right.' He gestured to Mina to rise, then as she eased herself from her chair, he gave a little gasp of dismay, darted forward and offered his arm. 'My apologies, dear young lady. Let me assist you. Your spirit is so strong that I had quite forgotten your – er—'

Mina rose to her feet unassisted, declining to complete the sentence and letting the awkward moment hang in the air.

'Mina, dear, you must do whatever Mr Bradley asks of you,' said her mother, sternly. 'I do not want a repetition of your behaviour before those kind doctors who tried so hard to help you.'

Mr Bradley stood facing Mina, offered her his hand with the palm upward, cupped as if it held a gift, and raised his eyebrows and nodded to show that she must place her hand in his. Mina did not care for Mr Bradley's mournful glistening eyes and neither did she relish the thought of touching his skin, but she complied for her mother's sake, going no further than resting her fingertips lightly on his. He smiled, taking her reserve as an expression of modesty. A few moments passed, but Mina did not experience an extraordinary sensation, which was not a matter of great surprise to her.

Mr Bradley, who clearly needed to demonstrate that something very remarkable was taking place, took a deep breath and tilted his head back, allowing his eyelids to flutter closed. Louisa, one hand pressed to her bosom, stared at him with a look of rapt admiration and just a little hint of excitement. She seemed to be holding her breath. There was a brief pause for the better increase of anticipation.

'Oh but this is most wonderful!' exclaimed Mr Bradley suddenly – his face suffused with an expression of great joy. 'Miss Scarletti, I can see your spirit form most clearly – it clothes you in a beautiful glow, soft like the most delicate amber. And I can tell you, my dear young lady, and I know how much this will gladden your heart – that your spirit form, the one that you will wear for eternity after you have passed the veil, is as straight and tall as anyone could desire!'

'But Mr Bradley,' said Mina, with a mischievous smile, 'why would I wish to be other than I am?'

His fingers moved back quite abruptly, and he looked astonished, then he shook his hand, almost as if Mina's touch had stung him.

'Mina, whatever can you mean by that?' demanded her mother. 'This is so like you, to be wilful and impertinent. Really, I hardly know what to do with you sometimes.'

'Oh, please do not fret, dear lady,' said Bradley, recovering his composure, 'and above all, you must not blame yourself. I can see that your unfortunate daughter labours under an affliction of the mind, one that threatens to eat into her very soul. I do believe that she cannot help what she is saying.'

'But can *you* help her?' asked Louisa.

'The bodily—' he paused, 'deformity, I can do nothing for. Only the Almighty will cure her after she has passed. But I can at least intercede with the Lord to ensure that her case becomes no worse.'

Mina's mother gave a sigh of gratitude, as if he was making a promise that had not already been offered by more human agencies.

'While she remains in the flesh, however, there is a disturbance in her spirit which I may be able to ease.'

'Oh please do try,' exclaimed Louisa. 'I would be so very grateful!'

'I will pray for her,' said Mr Bradley magnanimously, 'but Miss Scarletti must also work to heal herself. I advise her to pray both morning and night, and as often throughout the day as possible. And she must come to my meetings, which I intend to hold every Wednesday afternoon at Christ Church, where my little group of the devout will sit and pray and let the healing powers of the Almighty bathe them in delight. You will be there too, I hope, dear lady?'

'Oh, you may count on my attendance,' said Louisa eagerly, 'and Mina will of course follow your guidance.'

Mina saw that she was about to be encased again, in a device not of plaster or steel, but no less restraining for that. She was not averse to prayer, and already prayed night and morning; for the ease of her mother's sorrows, for the souls of her father and her sister Marianne who had faded away from consumption ten years ago, for Edward's success and Enid's happiness and for Richard to find whatever his butterfly attention sought. Now it seemed that she must also pray for herself, but she could think of nothing she lacked that she might wish to pray for. She did not look forward to joining Mr Bradley's assemblage of the unhappy matrons of Brighton.

Mina, although she did not consider herself to be worldly, was under no illusions as to why her mother's mood would be lifted by visits from a single gentleman of independent means ten years her junior and of moderately acceptable appearance. If she was honest with herself there was nothing about Mr Bradley to which she could object, especially since in one day he had brought about the improvement that Mina had been attempting unsuccessfully for a year. He was not, as far as she could see, trying to woo her mother, neither was he attempting to extract money from her; he was, she thought, a man of little or no talent who lacked occupation, and was trying to court popularity by telling people what he imagined they wanted to hear.

It transpired later that week that the Reverend Mr Vaughan, Vicar of Christ Church, was not amenable to Mr Bradley holding his devotional meetings on church premises. The reverend had heard some of the church ladies talk about promises of healing, and despite Mr Bradley's protestations of Christian piety, had detected a potential whiff of brimstone in the arrangement. Mr Bradley was obliged to look for other situations, and so it was decided that the meetings would be held in the Scarletti front parlour, a simple gathering for which the invitations and planning of refreshments occupied Mina's mother for a full three days of perpetual agitation.

Two

The first meeting was graced by five lady visitors and two gentlemen, who kept Rose and Simmons busy with constant demands for tea, bread and butter, biscuits, sponge cake and fruit, consuming enough to feed a funeral party even before the proceedings had begun. Mr Bradley, bathing in the glow of admiring faces, and thrusting out the suspicion of a developing *embonpoint*, allowed himself to take centre place, and lead the company in prayer.

Having invoked the power of God, and being satisfied that he had not inadvertently summoned a more diabolical spirit, Mr Bradley then proceeded to the healing, which was no more than inviting his little group of devotees to sit in silence and contemplate what infirmity they wished to be cured, while he walked about the circle, allowing his hand to hover over the head of each person. There were a few pitying glances at Mina, the assumption being that she would be asking for divine intervention to straighten her back, something not even Mr Bradley's disciples deemed remotely possible.

Mina was not thinking of herself at all, but was taking advantage of the quiet time to compose a new story about an incubus, which preyed on virtuous widows, and which in her mind's eye looked very like Mr Bradley. Could her mother not see that this man's presence in their house was an insult? Where were Mr Bradley and his pretensions when her father was dying? Where was his healing power when Marianne had lost her fragile hold on life at the age of twelve? It was she for whom Mina had first started writing stories of magic and adventure, stories in which her sister was the golden-haired heroine.

Marianne lived on in print, for unexpectedly, Henry's business partner Mr Greville had offered to publish the stories for a new venture, the Scarletti Children's Library. Mina was invited to visit the office and saw packets of little books piled high on shelves, some of them books that her father had never dared bring home, with stories of brigands and murderers and haunted castles, all illustrated by woodcuts. These appealed to Mina's taste and spirit rather better than pious tales in which the worst sin that anyone might commit was vanity. When Mr Greville suggested that she might like to write him a story about a child who gave her last penny to a ragged boy, Mina was already eagerly perusing *The Goblin's Curse*, and was lost forever to the world of morally improving literature.

The peace of the little circle was broken only by the gurgling of Mrs Bettinson's stomach and the gentle snores of a Mrs Phipps, an elderly lady who was a regular attendee at gatherings of every kind, and slept through all of them, although she always succeeded in being awake when refreshments were served. Mr Bradley then proceeded to what he announced was 'a special healing', which amounted to no more than his going about the circle again, taking each lady briefly by the hand, and placing his fingertips on the forehead of each gentleman. He then led the company in a final prayer, and suggested that they all needed more tea.

One of the company, a Miss Whinstone, was a lady of Louisa's age, but less well favoured by the hand of time. Since emerging from the period of mourning appropriate to the loss of her beloved brother, she had invariably dressed in the same unflattering shade of bronze, which was reflected in her skin and gave her cheeks a sickly yellow cast. Her face was drawn into a permanent frown of anxiety, and she always appeared to be flinching from something. Miss Whinstone had arrived with trembling fingers clutching a copy of the *Brighton Gazette*, which was open at the page of town news, but she did not refer to it until the meeting was drawing to a close.

'Mr Bradley,' she whispered, confidentially, 'if I might seek your advice ...'

'But of course!' he exclaimed. 'How might I assist you?'

She hesitated, then pushed the paper towards him. 'I have read— I have seen—'

'Ah,' said Mrs Bettinson, whose steely gaze missed nothing, 'yes, a most extraordinary thing, but ungodly, I fear.'

'And yet there is the involvement of Professor Gaskin, who I understand is a scientific gentleman of some note,' said Miss Whinstone, meekly.

'He is said to be one of the most scientific men in the world,' Mr Bradley assured her, 'and I am confident that he would not lend his name to anything ungodly.'

Mrs Bettinson looked unconvinced.

'Science,' announced a Mr Conroy, a portly gentleman with a red face, 'is a very remarkable thing.' He hooked his thumbs into his waistcoat pockets, thrust out his lower lip, and stared about the room in case anyone chose to contradict him.

The assembled company agreed to a man and woman that science was indeed remarkable.

Louisa, who did not read newspapers in case they affected her nerves, and had not had one in the house for some years, tried her best to look as though she knew what everyone was talking about, without success. Mina could see the early signs that her mother might be obliged to plead faintness to avoid embarrassment, so she quickly but politely borrowed Miss Whinstone's newspaper, and read the article aloud. The company fell silent. Mina had a sweet, clear reading voice, and no one felt inclined to do other than listen to her.

IMPORTANT ANNOUNCEMENT FROM WILLIAM GASKIN, FRS,
PROFESSOR OF CHEMISTRY AND PHYSICS

Professor Gaskin is honoured to make it known that the noted spirit medium Miss Hilarie Eustace will shortly be visiting Brighton where she will be pleased to offer demonstrations of her powers entirely *gratis*. Professor Gaskin, a founder member of the famous Ghost Club once patronised by the late Mr Charles Dickens, has devoted many years to the study of ghostly phenomena, and his experience enables him to state with considerable authority that Miss Eustace is entirely genuine. She has been subjected to numerous rigorous tests, all of which prove without a doubt that she is a medium of unusually consistent and convincing ability. Miss Eustace has demonstrated on very many occasions the production of spirit rappings and moving lights, all of which occur while she is in a trance. The agent of these manifestations is her spirit guide, Phoebe, a creature of the most extraordinary and angelic beauty who, when conditions are favourable, appears before astonished onlookers clad in glowing raiment. Professor Gaskin has himself seen this spirit rise from the ground, float through the air, and then melt slowly into nothingness, a sight which can only create the most profound amazement in anyone privileged to witness it. Next week's *Gazette* will announce details of where Miss Eustace will be conducting her séances, and how the public might apply for tickets.

'It seems,' said Mr Conroy, with a throaty laugh, 'that you have a rival, Mr Bradley.'

'Not at all,' said Mr Bradley, cheerfully. 'If you imagine that I am jealous of this lady's powers or her ability to command the attention of the public then you very much mistake me. If she can indeed perform all that she claims to do, and it appears that

Professor Gaskin has proved that she can, then I will gladly add myself to the number of her devoted admirers.'

'Then you have not seen her demonstrations?' asked Mina, and there was a general clamour in the room to the effect that Mr Bradley, if he had not already seen the miraculous Miss Eustace, ought to do so as soon as was practically possible.

He raised a hand to speak and the room at once fell silent again. 'I have not seen the lady, and it might be advisable if I was not to. Imagine, if you will, the consequences that would follow if two persons, both of whom are able to act as receptacles of supernatural power, were in the same room and one of them was to enter the trance state, which is a most perilous condition.' He paused dramatically to allow his listeners to consider the dreadful results that might stem from that situation. 'Of course I would do nothing to deliberately harm Miss Eustace, but suppose that by my very presence, I was to quite unintentionally attract forces that were drawn to her in her receptive state, and were more than the delicate frame of a lady could endure.'

'Why, it could kill her!' exclaimed Miss Whinstone, the tea in her cup vibrating like a choppy sea.

'Or at the very least induce catatonia. She might never waken again. Such things have been known.' Bradley shook his head, regretfully. 'No, much as I would wish to witness one of her demonstrations, I dare not, but I can see no objection to anyone else attending. I understand that she created a very great sensation when exhibiting in London only last week. I spoke to a lady who was present on that occasion who was so overcome by powerful emotions when she tried to tell me what she had seen that she was quite unable to find words to describe her experience. You are very fortunate that Miss Eustace comes here now, for if she was here in the autumn season you would not be able to get near her for dukes and earls and countesses.'

'Oh,' said Miss Whinstone, 'but my doctor says that I have a weak heart and a rheumatic stomach – from eating too much, or possibly from eating too little, I forget which – and I think if I was to see Miss Eustace I would catch the most terrible fright. And perhaps it might kill me, so I had really better not go.'

'She wouldn't frighten *me*,' said Mrs Bettinson, and the other ladies suggested that they felt the same, apart from Mrs Phipps who, having finished her tea, had fallen asleep again.

'But isn't it all poppycock and playacting?' said a Mr Jordan, grunting and looking at his watch, something he liked to do every few minutes for no reason that anyone could discern. He was a smartly turned-out gentleman of about thirty who had said very little throughout the afternoon, contenting himself with an expression of deep scepticism.

'If it is, the lady gains no advantage by it,' said Mr Bradley, reasonably. 'Of course there are persons who pretend to be mediums and attempt to play tricks on the public, but there is one sure way of knowing them. It is really very simple, they will do nothing without first being paid.'

Mina's mother had expressed no opinion about Miss Eustace, and after the meeting only commented that she had to wonder if such a person could be wholly respectable. Nevertheless, she told Mina to arrange for a regular delivery of all the popular Brighton newspapers and was later seen perusing them with interest. In a matter of days the dreadful Miss Eustace passed through a process of metamorphosis in which she became by stages the dangerous Miss Eustace, the alarming Miss Eustace, the uncommon Miss Eustace, the fascinating Miss Eustace and finally the astonishing Miss Eustace. One evening at nine o'clock on the hour, a hired carriage arrived in Montpelier Road and Louisa Scarletti and Mrs Bettinson boarded it in a state of very considerable excitement.

'I do not know why this should be,' said Mina's mother, 'but it has been my observation that men who are very clever and whose words repay the most earnest attention are often very ugly, whereas those who have been favoured with a handsome countenance have nothing in their heads worth speaking of.'

'Perhaps,' said Mina, 'men with attractive faces see no reason to cultivate their minds, and men with good minds exercise them so often they have no time to make themselves handsome. But do you speak of Mr Bradley? He seems to me to have neither good features nor a mind that is out of the ordinary.'

Her mother looked displeased, but Mina did not mind that. It was the morning after the visit to Miss Eustace, and Louisa, in command of the breakfast table, already looked plumper and rosier as if, like Brighton, she had been painted for the summer season. Mina wondered if her mother's year of melancholy widowhood that had followed her husband's death had in recent months been less a genuine affliction than a craving for the solicitude of friends. Now, with other things on her mind, she had turned her natural vitality to other projects.

Simmons sat forlornly by, her manner expressing anxiety either that her mistress was about to be enlivened to the point of a brainstorm, or that she would be so restored to glowing health that the services of a nurse and companion might no longer be required.

'I do *not* speak of Mr Bradley, who although not a scholarly gentleman has a reasonably good mind and is not displeasing to look at,' said Louisa severely. 'It is Professor Gaskin, who has been instrumental in introducing Miss Eustace to both London and Brighton society. He is a man with a very powerful brain, and a mind that constantly seeks the truth. But he has a bad posture and very large ears. His wife is a respectable sort of person but she is dreadfully plain, poor creature, and does not dress at all well.' Louisa could not help preening herself.

The previous night's séance had taken place in the parlour of Professor Gaskin's lodgings, and had been attended by eight ladies and gentlemen who were considered to be the very best of the resident Brighton society. Mina's mother said that she felt sure there was a solicitor amongst their number, as well as Dr Hamid who she thought was a very interesting and intelligent sort of person. The company was comfortably seated in front of a curtain that had been drawn across one corner of the room. The professor had then addressed them on the subject of Miss Eustace's wonderful sensitivity; how he had encountered her first with the attitude of a sceptic, thinking to expose deception. On witnessing her demonstrations, however, not only had he become convinced of her genuineness, but he had also realised that she was worthy of serious scientific study. Miss Eustace, he had told the company, was possessed of powers that the most learned men could not as yet explain.

The professor had reassured everyone present not to be afraid of what they were about to experience, and for greater confidence, he had then led them in a short prayer followed by a rousing hymn. 'I think,' Louisa told Mina, 'that that *fully* answers Reverend Vaughan's objections. There was nothing irreligious in the proceedings, in fact quite the contrary. Professor Gaskin says that the spirits are gladdened by our devotion, since they are pure Christian spirits sent by God to guide those who are receptive to His teachings.'

'What sort of person is Miss Eustace?' asked Mina, who was tempted to ask if this creature of the holy spirits had ridden into the room on a sunbeam, but refrained from a comment that she felt would not have advanced the conversation.

'She is a very proper and modest young lady,' said Louisa. 'I have to confess, I was concerned that I might be confronted by a person of coarse manners and appearance, and then I would have been obliged to leave immediately, but that was not the case. She was most tastefully attired, and behaved throughout with great decorum. She was seated on a chair in front of the curtain, facing us, and I am sure that she did not move from her place, yet all around us we saw lights and heard noises that no living soul in the room could have made. Professor Gaskin showed us a bell and a tambourine behind the curtain, also a pencil and paper. All of us heard the bell ring several times and a good hard rattle on the tambourine, then the sound of the pencil moving. None of us was near enough to touch them.'

'All this was behind the curtain, hidden from view?' asked Mina.

'It was. One of the gentlemen present said he wanted to draw the curtain and see what was happening for himself, but Professor Gaskin explained that any disturbance could injure the medium, and so he refrained, but very unwillingly. He was a bad influence and I think he will not be admitted again.'

Mina thought that had she been present she too might have been tempted to part the curtains, and wondered what she would have seen. A bell suspended in the air ringing itself; a tambourine in the grasp of a ghostly hand? Somehow she doubted it. Surely a more earthly and tangible arrangement of wires and black thread would answer the purpose.

'Then, as if that was not wonderful enough, Professor Gaskin announced that he could feel a hand on his shoulder. Of course we all felt somewhat alarmed, but he reassured us that there was nothing to be afraid of, and if anyone should feel the same thing they should not try and clasp the hand, for it disturbed the energy. And then,' Louisa went on, her eyes glowing with excitement, 'I felt it – very briefly – fingers touching my cheek. It was quite extraordinary!'

'It could not have been anyone in the room?' asked Mina.

'Oh no, most assuredly not. We were all, on the strict instructions of Professor Gaskin, holding hands, so no person in the room could have touched my face, and of course Miss Eustace was the furthest away of all. The surprising thing was that I had imagined a spirit hand to be somehow different, less … well, less like a real solid warm hand of a living person. But there was nothing insubstantial about it at all. If Miss Eustace can manifest things of this nature she must have very considerable powers.' Louisa waved a hand at Simmons to attend to her plate, and the young woman, anxious to please, scurried to comply.

'So a spirit hand feels just like the hand of a living person,' said Mina, without a change in her expression. 'That is most remarkable. I wonder how Professor Gaskin can explain such a thing.'

'He has many years of study before him,' said her mother who, if she detected irony in Mina's tone, chose to ignore it, 'but he remains hopeful that one day he will be able to reveal to the world how the spirit powers manifest themselves. Miss Eustace was, as you may imagine, quite exhausted, so that was all we were able to experience on that occasion. We all sang another hymn and then when the gas was turned up—'

'The gas?' said Mina. 'The gas had been lowered? That is a detail you omitted. Was there candlelight? Or was the séance conducted in darkness?'

Louisa looked offended at the question. 'Of course there was darkness; you don't suppose we could have seen the little spirit lights otherwise? But I can assure you that Miss Eustace did not move, or we would have heard her. When the gas was turned up she was barely conscious, and had no memory whatsoever of what had occurred. Then Professor Gaskin drew the curtain aside and all was as it had been before – except for the paper.' She poured more tea, exhumed a warm roll from its napkin and applied a salve of butter and honey. 'You, Mina, have a hard inflexible mind, and will no doubt find this impossible to believe, but there was writing on the paper – clear writing! It can only have been a message from the spirits. It said that all those present would enjoy good fortune.'

Mina had never seen a ghost or experienced anything that suggested the existence of a force outside of the body apart from what was already known to and approved of by science, such as the warmth and light of the sun. The world of paper ghosts she had created from her imagination was, she thought, a great deal more interesting than the commonplace manifestations described by her mother. She was not sure that she even believed in the apparitions of deceased loved ones that fanciful people sometimes reported seeing. Her stories, far from inducing her to credit the possibility of ghosts, did rather the opposite, since they created a vivid impression in her mind that was very different from what she saw around her. Perhaps, she thought, all ghosts, both those in stories and those said to be real, were only the product of the human mind. In her own case she knew they were false and wrote about them to entertain her readers, but for those who did not write, they became not words, but visions.

Still, Mina was obliged to admit that the evening's séance had been considered a success by all present, and her mother said that she would certainly go again, since Professor Gaskin had said that they had only seen a tiny part of what Miss Eustace could do. There were things he had seen with his own eyes that they would not believe until they had seen for themselves. The professor was intending to write a book about Miss Eustace, which, he was quite sure, would cause a sensation not only amongst the public but all the leading men of science.

'She is undoubtedly genuine,' said Louisa. 'She refuses to take any payment at all for her work, although some of those present did press her with small gifts, but she *asked* for nothing! When I go again I will see if Miss Whinstone can be persuaded to come, as I am sure she will benefit. I did ask Mrs Parchment, but really she is impossible. I do believe she may be an atheist, or even one of those horrid materialists who Professor Gaskin says are even worse. How you could have admitted such a person to the house, I do not know.'

'I did not seek to enquire after her religious observation when I accepted her as a tenant,' said Mina. 'She seems perfectly respectable, paid a month in advance without quibble and has given us no trouble and regular rent ever since.'

'Her husband was little more than a peddler,' said Louisa, shaking a copy of the *Gazette* at Mina. 'Do you see this advertisement? Parchment's Pink Complexion Pills, that was he.' She allowed her fingertips to glide over her cheek, as if to demonstrate that she needed no such thing. 'The man must have been a scoundrel, since I believe they once had a fine house in London with a carriage and servants, but I suppose that is all gone now, and the poor woman has to live in one room and pay rent and entertain herself with long walks and fresh air. What a thing to come to!'

Mina was curious as to the nature of the gifts Miss Eustace had been persuaded to accept, but when she asked, her mother replied dismissively that she didn't know, in a manner that entirely confirmed Mina's suspicion that they took the form of money and that her mother had been one of those to part with a 'gift'. Miss Eustace without doubt made a tidy enough income from her activities but then, Mina thought, the lady had provided a few hours of entertainment as one might do at a musical recital and it seemed harmless enough.

As Mina climbed the stairs to her room, trying to ignore the pain that stitched down her back, its needle-sharp point embedded deep in her hip, she began to have second thoughts. Was this new enthusiasm of her mother's really so unobjectionable? Ought she to be concerned about something that might in time become detrimental, either to health or purse? By the time Mina had reached the top of the stairs her worries had multiplied to the point where she felt she needed sensible advice, and decided to write a letter to her older brother Edward.

Three

Mina's room was a quiet place where the ghosts that lived so noisily in her mind were transferred by the medium of her pen to a new life as dark ink bled on to clean paper. Her desk was set before the window where she might take advantage of the clear brilliant daylight, to compose, or read, or sometimes just to gaze out on to the street and think. There were few distractions. The northern end of Montpelier Road was far enough from the seafront to avoid the worst clusterings of excited visitors, the flowing movements and gentle sounds of passers-by affording an unobtrusive and pleasing reminder of the life of the town.

Before Mina settled down to write, she tried to stretch her back, reaching around her shoulder with one hand, pushing her fingertips into the sore muscles there and trying to prise the knots apart. Then she sat, tucking a cushion under one hip to help straighten her posture. She knew that Edward would not come to Brighton. He rarely left his business, or, more importantly, Miss Hooper, a young lady of good family he was ardently pursuing with a view to marriage. Rival suitors of similar persistence, lesser charm but greater fortune, ensured that he dared not be out of the capital for long. Mina started the letter with good news, her mother's improved health and state of mind. She decided not to alarm her brother by revealing that their mother had attended a séance, but wrote instead of the interesting new arrivals in Brighton, Mr Bradley, Professor Gaskin and Miss Eustace, who had recently been in London, and wondered if Edward had heard of them, begging him to tell her all he knew.

She could not help but hope that Miss Eustace would prove to be a nine days' wonder, and vanish like one of her own spirits, to be superseded by some other novelty as Brighton, under its surge of summer visitors, blossomed into life.

Two days later Mina received a small packet from Edward, containing a letter and a booklet, and took them to her room to read. Edward expressed his sincere relief that his mother was so much improved, and reassured Mina that he was in the best of health although hard pressed by business. Unhappily, he wrote that the loveliest girl in the world was sorely afflicted by a cold in the head, which had thrown him into the most perfect anguish. He ended with a stern warning that it would be as well not to meddle in the affairs of people claiming to be in touch with spirits. Mr Bradley was unknown to him, but Professor Gaskin was a respected man of science, the author of many papers on the subject of chemistry and physics, who had lately espoused the claims of spiritualists and had made himself something of a laughing stock amongst his friends and colleagues. The professor had been advocating the claims of a Miss Eustace who had recently appeared in London, claiming that she had triumphantly proved herself to be a genuine medium, and advertised her as such, but the truth, commented Edward, was less convincing.

There was, he added, a new fashion for spirit mediums in London, and the gullible were willing to pay them any sum for the most ridiculous displays of obvious fakery. Professor Gaskin and his wife, shepherding Miss Eustace, had recently removed to Brighton for the early summer season, where they hoped to have fewer rivals and be more successful. Miss Eustace claimed to accept no money for her séances but it was widely believed that she lived on the hospitality of the Gaskins and accepted payments from her sitters. The enclosed booklet, he added, was a recent publication, and an object lesson, but he felt sorely afraid that it was a lesson many would chose to ignore. He urged Mina to read it carefully and take its message to heart.

The booklet, some sixteen pages long, was called *The Claims of D.D. Home Refuted, Containing a Very Full Account of the Lyon Case and His Disgrace*, by Josiah Rand MD. Mr Home, said the author, had been a very active and celebrated spirit medium for a number of years, including amongst his adherents medical men, scientists, barristers, military men, titled personages, and other notable individuals. He was said by many to be the most powerful medium alive, able to levitate heavy items of furniture, cause musical instruments to play by themselves, and touch hot coals without harm, but his most famous achievement was to rise in the air and hover sometimes several feet above his astounded audience.

Scottish-born Home had lived in America from an early age, and was one of many thousands who, after the widespread publicity given to the spirit rappings of the Fox sisters in Hydesville New York in 1848, had suddenly discovered that he too had mediumistic powers. The sisters' exhibitions, which, said Dr Rand, most closely resembled the activities of the almost certainly fraudulent Cock Lane ghost, had themselves attracted allegations of trickery, which had had no deleterious effects on the ladies' continuing fame.

In March 1855 Home had sailed for England, where an ardent believer in his mediumistic powers who also happened to be a hotelier had generously granted him free accommodation. The tall slender youth – he was then only twenty-two – with blue eyes, flowing auburn locks, and the luminous transparency of the consumptive, seemed already to be hovering on the boundary of another world. In repose his face suggested suffering, and this, together with a gentle air of kindliness, was enough to recommend him to ladies, especially those rather older than himself. His natural charm lent him an easy persuasiveness, but it was his undoubted ability to produce powerful spirit manifestations that quickly gained him an entrée into fashionable society and brought many admirers. There were, however, also sceptics who charged him with fraud, and these included the poet Robert Browning who had openly declared Home to be a charlatan. Browning went so far as to satirise Home in a poem as 'Mr Sludge, "the Medium"'. Home was not averse to critical examination, and a distinguished scientist, Sir David Brewster (who was an authority on the nature of light) attended Home's séances. While believing that the phenomena were attributable not to the work of spirits but clever conjuring, Brewster was forced to admit that he was unable to explain what he had seen. The controversy only increased Home's fame, and income.

None of this information was especially troubling to Mina, but what followed was alarming to a considerable degree. In 1866 Jane Lyon, a seventy-five-year-old widow, had asked Home if he could manifest the spirit of her dead husband. Home conducted a number of private séances and received gifts of thirty and fifty pounds. Home then discovered that Mrs Lyon, while living in very modest circumstances, was the mistress of a substantial fortune, and had no relatives. He was easily able to persuade her that her late husband wished her to adopt him as her son, and place him in a financial position in life appropriate to his new rank. Eleven days after their first meeting, Mrs Lyon accompanied Home to her bank and there arranged to sell a block of bonds for twenty-four thousand pounds which she then transferred to her new 'son'. Home next persuaded Mrs Lyon that her husband wished her to destroy her previous will and make a new one in his favour. He changed his name to Lyon, received a further sum of six thousand pounds, and secured his position by having Mrs Lyon create deeds in his favour, which were stated to be irrevocable.

Gradually, however, Mrs Lyon opened her eyes and saw her terrible folly. She realised that had her husband been living he would never have placed her in such a harmful position, and friends advised her that she was being imposed upon by a fraud. There had been a quarrel between the unhappy woman and her leech, which had not resolved the matter, and she went to the law. The court denounced Home as a cheat and an impostor, and the practice of spiritualism as mischievous nonsense, calculated to delude the vain, the weak, the foolish and the superstitious, and assist the adventurer. The supposedly irrevocable deeds were duly set aside and he was ordered to return her property.

Mina read this dreadful litany of crime with a mounting sense of horror. Messages from the dead, tambourines that played themselves and men who flew about the room she could face with equanimity, but the vile behaviour of a heartless rogue who would use an elderly widow's love for her dead husband to dupe her out of her fortune appalled her.

The extraordinary thing, she learned as she read on, was that Home, far from having been put in prison or drummed out of English society, was still residing in England and practising as a medium. He continued to enjoy the confidence of the public and basked in the attention of eminent scientists. Even a claim that he had been detected in imposture at a séance had been swept aside by his adherents who stated that the light on that occasion had been so dim that it was impossible to tell one way or the other whether fraud had been used. Spiritualists, it seemed, saw everything as marvellous, but were blind to the mundane.

Mrs Browning, the poet's wife, who had received wreaths of flowers from spirit hands at Home's séances and had been told that there were rays of glory pouring from a crown over her head that only the medium could see, had to the end of her life remained unreservedly convinced. When Home's critics denounced him as morally worthless, she had riposted that even if he *was* morally worthless it would not impugn his being a true medium any more than her dentist's ability as a dentist would be held suspect if he were caught shoplifting. Mina at once saw the fatal flaws in this argument. Dentistry was a demonstrable medical skill based on knowledge and dexterity, whereas mediumship was a matter of trust and belief. The point at issue was not whether Home was skilled, but whether he was trustworthy, and on the evidence before her, he clearly was not.

A Professor William Crookes was currently subjecting Home to an impressive array of tests, which Dr Rand earnestly hoped would show the charlatan for what he was, but he was not sanguine that this would be the result. Dr Rand felt, and Mina was obliged to agree, that Professor Crookes's interest was probably aroused by a willingness to believe, which would make him an easy dupe for a fraud of more than twenty years' experience. It was often assumed, declared Rand, that frauds most easily deluded the unintelligent, and that the best witnesses were men of science. In reality the man of science was often the easiest mark since he thought too much and tried to find a beautiful explanation for what he had observed that could be fashioned into a scholarly paper while ignoring the sordid and simple truth.

Since the damning episode with Mrs Lyon, Home had not to anyone's knowledge perpetrated a scheme on a similar scale, but memories were short and believers many. Dr Rand ended his document by issuing a warning, especially to women, against entering into any financial arrangements with Home. Rumours were afoot that the adventurer, who still had youth and celebrity on his side, was looking for a wealthy wife.

Mina was still digesting this information when a great deal of clattering and loud exclamations from downstairs announced that her brother Richard had made one of his impromptu visits. Wondering what he was up to this time, Mina eased herself down the staircase, but had yet to reach the lowest step when she was swept up into his arms and lifted from the ground. 'How is my best girl?' he asked, planting smacking kisses on her cheeks.

The question may have seemed no more than a brotherly greeting, but she knew that there lay underneath it a real concern for her health. She reassured him that she was well, which of course meant that she was no worse, and importantly, no shorter.

Richard had been favoured with the willowy height and fair hair and complexion of his mother, and the frank and somewhat raffish charm of his father. He was only a year younger than Mina, and the proximity of age meant that they had, until he was sent to school – or to be more accurate a series of schools – been brought up in each other's company. He deposited Mina very carefully on her feet, held her at arm's length and gazed at her affectionately, then smiled and nodded as he saw that she was indeed well.

With his usual excellent timing he had arrived just in time to enjoy luncheon, and as they ate, their mother talked with some enthusiasm of the rarefied circle of which she was now a member, and the accomplishments of Miss Eustace, who was, she thought, not above thirty and with good connections. Edward, she said, with a very pointed glance in Richard's direction, was in a fair way to achieving the hand of Miss Hooper, who would be an ornament to the family, and she looked to have some happy news from him in the near future. Richard smiled, but would not be drawn, and turned the conversation to his business interests, which he described as in a flourishing state but in need of liquid capital to ensure that he became an established success. He spoke vaguely of partners and offices, and clerks but in insufficient detail to enable his listeners to determine the exact nature of his enterprise. One certainty that accompanied all of Richard's schemes was that they were in want of investment, and his mother promised to transfer funds to him the next day. Unlike the depredations of the egregious Mr Home, Richard only asked for small sums that their mother could easily afford, and Mina comforted herself with the fact that the funds were at least going to a loved and undoubtedly loving son and not a lying adventurer.

Later that day Louisa went to take tea with Miss Whinstone and Mrs Bettinson, and Richard and Mina strolled arm-in-arm along the seafront, where gaily coloured posters were advertising the new attractions on the West Pier. Richard was careful to match his long stride to Mina's short steps, and for a time they were happy just to walk and enjoy the sun and tranquil air.

'Now then,' said Mina after a while, 'you do not deceive me and I want the truth. What is this business for which you need Mother to supply yet another investment? If it is gambling debts I shall be very annoyed.'

'Oh, I have been bitten too many times by that horrid monster,' Richard assured her, 'and have no pleasure in it any more. I am doing what I can to move in the best society and put on a brave show in the hopes of charming myself into a fortune. But it is very costly and dreadful dull work.'

'I despair of you sometimes!' Mina exclaimed. 'Do you really intend to cheat some unfortunate lady of her fortune with winning smiles?'

'Oh, as to that, there will be no cheating. If a rich lady wants a young husband to dance attendance on her then she knows what the bargain is. And I would be a model of the type, and act my part to her satisfaction.' He raised his hat and directed his appreciation to two prettily dressed ladies in a passing carriage, who were unable to resist laughing and blushing in return.

Richard, Mina was obliged to admit, had a curious yet consistent idea of morality. She knew that he would never steal from or blatantly defraud anyone, had never borrowed money without the intention of repaying it, although he invariably failed to do so, and was quite incapable of committing an act of unkindness. 'But you are not yet engaged?' she asked.

'No, and neither is there any prospect of it at present. There are rich enterprises I have in my sights, but I fear that the odds are against me.'

'Have the ladies found you out as an adventurer?' she teased. 'If they are clever they will hold on to their money. If I wanted a handsome face in my drawing room I would purchase a painting. That would be far less trouble than a husband.'

'The London ladies of fortune are like castles moated about with lawyers,' he said gloomily. 'If I have no success there then I might come to Brighton for the high season and lurk around the pavilion, where I might discover a dowager duchess taking the air, and win her hand.'

Mina looked at him carefully and saw that for all the outward show of elegance his garments were not as fresh or as fashionable as they needed to be for such an undertaking. 'I hope you are not in debt for lodgings,' she said, 'or do you remain with Edward?'

'Edward vouchsafes me a corner of his attic,' said Richard. 'He is well, but his talk is all about work. It is a subject for which I feel very little enthusiasm, and I can contribute nothing to the conversation.'

'That does not bode well for Miss Hooper,' said Mina. 'A woman should expect her husband to have more than one subject on which he can talk with some authority, preferably several.'

'I have met the lovely Miss Hooper,' said Richard, 'and I think she will not be very demanding in the area of conversation. I can see why Edward is so much in love with her; her father is really quite rich. But that china doll kind of beauty has never appealed to me. I like the kind of girl who—' He hesitated.

'The kind of girl you could not introduce to Mother?' ventured Mina.

He laughed. 'You have it, my dear.' He squeezed her hand affectionately. 'But Mina, you must be very dull here. Do you really wish to wait on Mother forever? She has Simmons now, and she can do very well without you, you know. You should think of marrying.'

'Oh come, now, who would have me?' said Mina with a smile. 'A miser looking for an unpaid drudge perhaps, who would expect me to be grateful that he has deigned to look at me? No, I shall never marry, and I am perfectly content with that.' She did not say it but sometimes she felt almost fortunate, enjoying unimaginable freedom for a respectable single young lady. No one, seeing the little woman with the crooked body and curious gait, could suppose her to be anything other than honest. No one would press her to marry a tedious man or allow children to command her time and absorb her strength. By not being constrained into the narrow sphere of wife and mother she had discovered that she had the choice of being almost anything else she pleased.

They strolled on a little further. There was a long pause in the conversation, and into the cheerful enjoyment of the early summer weather there crept a grey chill. 'What is it, Mina?' said Richard. 'I am not a fool and I can see that something is making you unhappy.'

They stopped walking, and gazed out across the beach to the distant glitter of the sea. Pleasure boats were drawn up on to the shore like the drying carcasses of stranded porpoises, and there was an almost endless line of freshly painted bathing machines ready to trundle into the water, their large wheels and small bodies making them look like colourful spiders.

Mina looked further, to where the bright water met the soft cloudy horizon, then closed her eyes and thought of sea-spirits and mermaids and kings with green hair and enchanted reefs of pearl and coral.

'Do you still go sea-bathing?' asked Richard. 'I have heard it is very beneficial.'

'So all the medical men say, but I have had my fill of medical men and their opinions,' said Mina. 'I get neither pleasure nor relief from sea-water, warm or cold. There was a time when I bathed once a week when the weather was fine, but that was only to please Mother, and I was able eventually to persuade her not to be too disappointed if I stopped.'

She turned to him. 'I am perfectly well, but if you must know I am concerned about Mother's enthusiasm for Miss Eustace. I am far from convinced that she is not a charlatan preying on the superstitious.'

'Oh, I have no doubt that she is,' said Richard, airily. 'These people are all cheats and conjurers, but they provide amusement and I really think they do no harm. There is a new sensation on the West Pier – did you see the posters? Madame Proserpina the fortune teller. Guaranteed genuine. I am sure the crowds will flock to her.'

'But that is a matter of a few pence, and I have no quarrel with that if folk get enjoyment from it,' said Mina. 'If Miss Eustace asks for a shilling or two, or even half a guinea at the end of the evening, then it is worth it for the improvement in Mother's health and happiness. But there are villains who prey on widows with money, and try to filch their entire fortunes from them.' Mina took the booklet from her pocket and showed Richard the story of Mr Home.

He read it, she thought, with rather greater interest than she might have wished. As he did so, Mina watched a few early summer families trudge out on to the beach, the children bringing fistfuls of seaweed as proud offerings to their less-than-delighted mothers, while distant bells announced the approach of the first caravans of donkeys. The warm, furred flanks of the donkeys and the slippery dark weed could not, she thought, have been more different, yet the weed – while it remained wet – could live on the beach and the donkeys could tread some way into the water. The land and the sea; life and death. Where did one end and the other start? It was not a simple question. Was there a clear-cut boundary like the line of markers where one might go from Brighton to Hove in a single step, or was there a wide borderland of sea-washed pebbles where two worlds became one? Were they really so incompatible that a fleshless spirit could not co-exist with the living?

'Mrs Lyon had a lucky escape from ruin,' said Richard at last. 'Has Miss Eustace tried to persuade Mother that she can pass on messages from Father or Marianne, or demanded large sums of money?'

'Not as far as I am aware, and she may not; after all, Mother has a family to protect her, and poor Mrs Lyon had none. But there are many ladies in Brighton in Mrs Lyon's position, and they may be in danger.'

He looked serious and thoughtful. 'Have you shown Mother this booklet?'

'No, do you think I should? I am not sure it would do any good.'

'I agree. She would only see it as a criticism of her new favourite. And she would tell you that whatever Mr Home did – and he has many defenders – has nothing to do with Miss Eustace. It would not change her mind.'

'Has Mother ever changed her mind?' asked Mina, although she knew the answer.

'Not by persuasion, no. In order for Mother to change her mind she must come to believe that the view she has just adopted is the one she has always held. Mere printer's ink won't do it.'

Mina sighed. 'I fear you are right.'

'And if you say anything to the detriment of Miss Eustace, Mother will have the perfect reply – that you have not seen the lady for yourself and therefore can know nothing about the matter.'

Mina was reluctant to go and see a spirit medium and be ranked with the gullible, but she thought that unless the danger passed it must come to that. She was not, however, as she soon found, the only person in Brighton with doubts. The activities of Miss Eustace had provoked a correspondence in the newspapers in which a number of people who had not been to her séances denounced them as mere conjuring tricks, and others who had been, while unable to explain what they had seen, nevertheless entertained grave suspicions. When Mina's mother read the letters she was scathingly contemptuous about those who talked of what they did not know, or were so closed of mind that they could not see what was before their eyes. There was a strong implication in her tone that she considered Mina to be a member of that offending class. When Mina suggested that she might venture to experience a séance for herself, her mother was surprised but not displeased, and said that it would be easy to arrange. All her friends had gone there or were about to go; even the nervous Miss Whinstone, who was hoping for a message from her late brother Archibald, had finally been persuaded.

Four

Miss Eustace held her séances at the simple lodgings taken by Professor and Mrs Gaskin near Queen's Park. Mina, her mother, Mrs Bettinson and Miss Whinstone travelled there by cab one evening, with Miss Whinstone protesting all the way that she was afraid her heart would stop with fright, and Mrs Bettinson looking as though she rather hoped it would.

They were ushered into a small parlour arranged in unconventional style. Two rows of five plain chairs had been placed in a semi-circle, sufficiently far apart that no seated person could reach out and touch another, but they might, if both extended their arms, hold hands with those on either side. The chairs faced a corner of the room, which was obscured by a pair of curtains of some dark opaque material that hung from a cord fastened to a bracket on the wall at either end, and overlapped in the centre. Mina found herself curiously attracted to the curtains, and had she been alone in the room would undoubtedly have pulled them aside to make a close examination of what lay behind them and determine for herself whether what was supposed to have been moved by spirits showed evidence of a more corporeal hand. The sun had set and the window curtains had been closely drawn, but the light in the room was fairly good from the gas lamps. The only other furniture was a sideboard on which stood a water carafe, a tray of glasses, a candlestick fitted with a new wax candle, and a box of matches.

Louisa introduced her daughter and Miss Whinstone to the Gaskins, who received them with friendly but slightly exaggerated politeness.

The professor was a tall man of about fifty-five, with a cloud of peppery grey hair, eyebrows like the wings of a small bird, and abundant whiskers. One might almost imagine that his head was stuffed full of hair, since it had also sought an exit by bursting through his nostrils and ears, the latter organs being of elephantine construction with undulating edges.

He both walked and stood with a stoop, not, thought Mina, from any fault with his spine, but from a poor habit of posture. It always surprised her to see a person who was blessed with the ability to walk straight but had chosen not to. Either his head was being borne down by the weight of his powerful scientific brain, or he needed to hover over everyone around him the better to impress them with his superior knowledge. Mina's diminutive stature was a particular challenge to him, and he raised his voice as he spoke to her, whether to better cover the distance between them, or because he thought that her bodily deformity meant that she also had some defect of the intellect, she could not determine. His artificially bright, almost simpering smile as he addressed her, drew her towards the latter conclusion. Mina gave him only the most perfunctory greeting, and made no attempt to impress upon him the fact that she was not an imbecile; rather she hoped that he might remain in ignorance of this for as long as possible, as it would give her more freedom to observe the proceedings unimpeded.

Mrs Gaskin, who appeared to be the same age as her husband, was an excessively plain woman, inclining to stoutness and heavily whaleboned. She dressed in an unflattering style suggestive of the most uncompromising virtue and carried herself like a duchess. Her smiles of greeting lacked warmth, and were dispensed by way of charity, serving to enhance her own position. She remained close to the professor, attached by invisible chains of ownership as if his scientific eminence made him a valuable prize amongst husbands. Mina, who thought herself as good as the next person and needed no husband, professorial or otherwise, was unimpressed. More importantly, she had learned long ago that scholarship did not always mean that a man was right in his pronouncements, and neither did it ensure common sense, or knowledge of character.

Two other ladies were also present, Mrs Peasgood and Mrs Mowbray, cheerful widows in search of entertainment, whose confiding manner towards each other suggested that they were sisters. Mrs Phipps, the lady who had slept through most of Mr Bradley's healing circle, arrived leaning heavily on the arm of her nephew, who looked highly embarrassed to be there at all, stared at the curtained corner with alarm, and hurried away as soon as he felt able to do so without appearing to be impolite.

The last visitor to be introduced was Dr Hamid, a quiet man of middling height, about forty-five and very gentlemanly, with black hair going grey and a neatly trimmed beard. All Mina knew of him was what her mother had told her, that he was the son of an Indian physician of great distinction and a Scottish mother, and the proprietor of Dr Hamid's Indian medicated vapour bath and shampooing establishment in Brighton, whose customers had spoken very highly of the relief afforded them from his treatments. The oriental 'shampoo', or 'massage' as it was sometimes called, appeared by all accounts to be a frightful ordeal in which the practitioner pressed and rubbed and sometimes twisted or even stood upon the recumbent form of the patient. Mina had heard about travellers to the East who had submitted to the ministrations of large Turkish gentlemen in the bathhouses popular there, and had later written of their clicking joints and spines cracking like pistol shots. As if to remind her of this, her shoulder gave her a savage pinch.

Dr Hamid wore a dark suit and cravat and carried black gloves. There was a black band around one sleeve and his hat, but Mina saw that this was not the formal fashionable mourning of a man who had slipped easily into an outward show of widowerhood.

As they were introduced she saw an ill-concealed pain in his eyes, the look of a man who was searching for a part of himself that had been suddenly and cruelly snatched away, which he had been unable to acknowledge was gone forever. Just as she was crushed in body so he was crushed in spirit and who could know if his prospect of recovery was any better than her own? There was no trace in his expression of the pity or curiosity with which she was often viewed; rather there was interest, and a hint of recognition.

The company was ushered to their seats, Professor and Mrs Gaskin securing places on the front row, as might have been expected, although they did not sit together but at either end, like sentinels. Mina, her mother and Miss Whinstone made up the centre of the row, but Miss Whinstone, clutching a lace handkerchief and flapping her arms nervously, exclaimed that she did not think she could bear to be so near to the curtain as she dreaded to think what lay behind it, and she really believed that she might faint if she was to see anything at all. Mrs Gaskin did her best to reassure her increasingly agitated guest, but to no avail, and so Miss Whinstone was sent to the back row, and since it was thought best that she be seated with her friends, Mina and her mother were asked to join her, with Dr Hamid and the two widowed sisters taking the seats in front. Mina quietly protested that she was unable to see the proceedings but her mother insisted that she should remain beside Miss Whinstone to attend to her if she should faint. Dr Hamid, overhearing this exchange, at once rose and turned to address them. 'Excuse me, ladies, if I could be of assistance. It would be my pleasure to attend on Miss Whinstone, and Miss Scarletti could then have my place.' It was all done in such a disarming manner that Louisa could do nothing but agree, and Mina returned to the front row.

Before the eagerly expected entrance of Miss Eustace, Professor Gaskin rose to address the onlookers.

'My dear friends, it gives me great pleasure not only to see those who have attended our evenings before but also some new faces. I offer a warm welcome to you all. Some of you may have read criticisms in the press of our gatherings, and I do not intend to respond to them directly as I take no note of anything said by persons wholly ignorant of our proceedings here, and indeed ignorant of anything concerning the world of the spirit. It hardly needs to be said that we have avoided criticism throughout these demonstrations by holding them here and not at Miss Eustace's own lodgings, so rendering it impossible for anyone to claim that she has arranged the room to facilitate deception. Everything in this room may be freely and thoroughly examined by anyone present, both before and after the séance, to satisfy themselves that there is nothing that might invite suspicion.'

But not during, thought Mina, who would have liked to go forward and take up that challenge, but realised that to do so would embarrass her mother in front of her friends, and accepted that such an action should be left for another time.

'You may be interested to know,' added the professor, 'that some of the finest minds in the land have been examining the evidence for spiritualism for over a year and will shortly be publishing their conclusions. The gentlemen, and not a few ladies, of the London Dialectical Society have been holding meetings and séances, and taking the evidence of interested persons of good reputation. I have been privileged to see a copy of the report and I can reveal to you all now that it has concluded that there is abundant evidence for the reality of the manifestations which astound us and which we cannot as yet explain.' He paused for vocal expressions of pleasure from his listeners then held up his hand so he could continue.

'Despite this support from the learned amongst us, there will always be those whose minds remain closed to the truth,' he continued, with a look of great sorrow for those unfortunates.

'It has even been suggested that Miss Eustace carries out her séances under cover of darkness in order to conceal deception, and that the phenomena which many of you have already witnessed are not the work of some force as yet unknown to science but her own hands.'

A little murmur of amused incredulity ran about the room.

'Darkness is certainly essential to our proceedings, but not for the reasons suggested by those cavillers who know nothing of which they speak, but because light can absorb the vital energy of the medium. The phenomena produced by Miss Eustace are not, as we know, the result of any action by her physical hands, but by a force that is as yet beyond our understanding, which extends beyond the periphery of her body and causes vibrations in the ether: a force hitherto unknown to science, the study of which will I am sure reveal to us in time a wholly new branch of knowledge.' He paused. 'However, for your further assurance, and the confusion of her critics, I will ensure that before we begin Miss Eustace is secured to her chair so that she is unable to rise from it or carry out any actions with her hands.'

'It is the greatest insult,' said Mrs Gaskin, loudly, 'to call into question such a virtuous lady, and it says much regarding the coarse and ignorant unbelievers who would subject her to such a proceeding. But their downfall will be our victory!'

'And then,' said the professor in a gentler tone than his good lady, 'we may raise them to greater understanding. Let us take a few moments of silent prayer, in which we give thanks to the Lord God for His miracles as His blessing to the holy, and ask Him to give us the power to save and enlighten those who are even now mired in the slough of prejudice.'

'For they are as children,' intoned Mrs Gaskin, 'and we must lead them.' There were a few moments of quiet reflection after which the professor said, 'Amen!' very firmly, and the company echoed him.

'And now,' said Professor Gaskin, 'I would like to bring before you – Miss Eustace.'

He threw the curtains apart with a brave flourish, as a man might have done who was displaying a marvel of the world or a performing lion, or some such novelty. There was a little gasp of fright from Miss Whinstone, which was soon quelled, for in the dim alcove created by the corner of the room, on a plain wooden chair, there sat a woman, not a spirit, but a real solid breathing woman, in a pose of great humility, her head bowed as if in prayer. She wore a gown of pearl grey silk, embellished with flounces and velvet ribbons, with deep ruffled cuffs, and the hands that peeped out and lay clasped upon her lap were small and very white. Her face, seen as she slowly raised her head, was serene with the kind of regular features that made it pleasing without being beautiful. Professor Gaskin offered her his hand with a proud and gallant gesture, and she took it, rose to her feet in one graceful movement, and came forward until she stood before the curtains. The gathering murmured appreciation, which she acknowledged with a slight bow. Professor Gaskin brought the chair forward into the room, and she was seated. 'If I might have the assistance of any observer who will attest that the bindings are properly done?' he asked.

Mina would have liked to volunteer but she did not move quickly enough, and the ropes, which had lain coiled on a small table behind the curtains, were taken up by Dr Hamid, clearly a gentleman who always endeavoured to be useful, and Mrs Mowbray, who had been gazing admiringly at Dr Hamid, something to which he seemed oblivious. Professor Gaskin supervised the binding, which attached Miss Eustace by her wrists to the framework of the chair. While this was being done, Mina had the opportunity to see what other articles were behind the curtains. The small light bentwood table was barely a foot across, and had no cloth to cover it, so it was impossible for anything to be hidden underneath. On its surface was a pencil, a sheet of notepaper, a small handbell and a tambourine. As far as Mina could see there was nothing else behind the curtain, and the wall covering at the rear of the enclosure was the same as the rest of the room. There was certainly insufficient space to conceal another person or an object of any size.

Once Professor Gaskin's two assistants had pronounced themselves satisfied that Miss Eustace was securely bound, and were back in their places, he lit the candle and turned down the gas. Carrying the candle, the professor returned to his seat – the yellow flickering light casting deep moving shadows in his eye sockets and cheeks.

'I would now like everyone to take the hand of the person sitting beside them,' he said. 'Those who are seated on the end of a row, please take the hand of the person beside you with both of yours. This is for the assurance of all present that no one will be able to move about the room during the proceedings, since the energy of the medium must not be disturbed. I will then blow out the candle, and when I have done so, I ask you all to join me in a hymn. We will have 'Abide With Me'.' This was a popular choice at Christ Church and one to which all the assembled company knew the words.

There was a sobbing whimper from Miss Whinstone, as if she constantly needed to remind everyone in the room that she was not only there, but afraid and in need of attention; however, she did not faint. Miss Whinstone, Mina recalled, had never, as far as she was aware, actually fainted, although she often said that she was just about to. Mina encountered on one side the cold dry hands of Mrs Gaskin, and on the other, the tight clasp of Mrs Mowbray. The candle was blown out, and then Professor Gaskin began to groan out the hymn at great volume, and other voices, of varying degrees of melodiousness, wove around him.

After a minute or two, the singing ceased, and the company was overtaken by a more pleasing silence, and enveloped in an aura of arrested breath and expectancy. As Mina's eyes grew used to the darkness, she saw only very dimly the shape of Miss Eustace still seated, her head moving first forward then back, then tilting from side to side as might be done by a person in a fit, or in a trance, or pretending to be in either state. She felt no fear, only curiosity, and just a trace of hope that something would occur with even a hint of the drama she put into her tales, but her practical mind told her that she was about to see nothing more than pretty parlour tricks.

As the seconds passed, the mood of the company was wound tighter and tighter into a state of anticipation, and then the silence was abruptly broken by the sound of a quiet rap on the wall behind them. One or two ladies gasped, and there was even a little scream. The rapping sounded again, only louder this time, and developed into a sequence of knocks that speeded up until they became almost a rattle. Mina tried to glance about her, but she was unable to turn sufficiently to look directly behind, and Mrs Gaskin held her fingers fast. She could see nothing to account for the noise and as far as she was aware no one had moved from his or her seat. Other raps and knocks followed, stouter and louder, and they were travelling about the room, so they came from the side walls, the ceiling, which of course no one could have reached even if they had tried, and the floor, too. The vibration of the floorboards beneath their feet was apparent to all. It was not a sound that might have been produced by fingers or even a foot or a fist. If Mina could have likened it to anything, it was as if some mischievous and invisible person armed with a stout rod had walked about the room belabouring every surface in sight.

A perfect torrent of raps sounded against the far wall directly behind the company, and then, quite suddenly, stopped. There was a silence, all the more anxious because of what had just occurred, and a nervous apprehension of what might happen next. The next sound was a musical tinkling noise, as if two of the water glasses on the sideboard were knocking gently together. The more Mina thought of it the more she realised that this was exactly what was producing the sound.

She sensed, quite unpleasantly, that there was a presence in the room, something that had not been there when the company had assembled, and it was nothing she could see or hear other than the effects it was producing. She tried to listen for the whisper of feet on the carpet, and the breath of another individual, but Miss Eustace had started sighing and moaning, and the other ladies were giving little excited gasps, so if there were any sounds other than those she could not make them out. Mina, who lived so much in a world of her own creation, was strongly aware of the difference between the things she conjured up in her mind and the real, solid things she saw about her. She trusted her own observation and rejected the idea that there was a spirit in the room that owed its existence solely to her imagination. There was, she felt sure, a being of some kind that was present and apparent to them all, but whether corporeal or not, alive or not, she was unable to tell. More to the point, she wanted very much to find out. Others might be happy to sit holding hands and receive impressions, but for Mina this was not enough.

There was a sudden little squeal from Mrs Mowbray. 'Oh! there was a wind on my face!' and a few moments later Mina's mother exclaimed, 'Oh! I felt a hand touch my cheek!'

Mina was just wondering if these experiences were the product of overheated anticipation, when something like a silk handkerchief caressed her throat. She shivered at the sensation, and would have liked to escape Mrs Gaskin's hands and clasp the thing before it was gone, but Mrs Gaskin had a firm, almost bruising grip on her fingers, and any attempt Mina might have made to break free would have caused some disquiet.

After a few moments, there was another period of near silence, and then the bell behind the curtain began to ring, followed by the rattle of the tambourine. Whatever was in the alcove was extremely lively, and there were either two hands or two entities, since the ringing and the rattling started to sound together until the noise resembled nothing more than the jangling music of the minstrel bands on the marine parade. If this was an example of the music of the spirits, thought Mina, then heaven promised to be a very clamorous and unmelodic place.

All then fell quiet again apart from the sound of panting breath and little gasps from the ladies, then they heard the scratch of a pencil moving on paper. There was another long silence followed by a sudden muffled thud, suggesting that the table behind the curtain had fallen or been knocked over, which caused loud exclamations from the company. Mina longed for a swift movement and a sudden blaze of gaslight, but no one stirred.

The period of silence that followed lasted for a minute or two, and Mina began to wonder if the séance was over. Professor Gaskin must have thought so too, for he was just starting to rise from his chair and say something when he was stopped by the sound of Miss Eustace crying out. Soft moans began to issue from the lips of the medium, and above her head, where her hands could not have reached even had they been free, there appeared a little dancing light. It was not enough to illuminate the room, but very sharp and clear to see, and it hovered above her like a fairy sprite. Another light soon joined it, and then the two danced together about the room, moving about each other, never more than a few feet apart, until first one, and then the other went out.

It was such a pretty display that, strange and unaccountable as it was, no one could be afraid of it, and there was a little sorrowful sigh when the lights vanished. Mina was mystified. These were like no lights she had ever seen; they had neither the yellow flicker of a candle or a spill, nor the sizzling flare of a match, but each was a single bright constant point and they had just appeared without any sign of having been ignited by something else. A professor of chemistry might, though Mina, be able to explain the phenomenon, but then a professor of chemistry was in the room and believed he saw disembodied spirits.

Miss Eustace, who had fallen into a brief silence, began to breathe very heavily and rapidly, with little gasping sounds and groans. Everyone took this as a signal that another marvel was to follow, and there were little murmurs of anticipation and the sound of people shifting in their seats. Mina felt sure that all the onlookers were leaning forward and craning their necks. They were not disappointed, for high above Miss Eustace's head a brightly glowing form began to issue from between the curtains, which parted in the centre just enough to allow it to intrude into the room. There was an exclamation from the audience, and Mina sensed that what they were seeing was a new exhibition that no one, quite possibly even the Gaskins, had expected.

The apparition was hovering about six feet from the ground, and as it pushed forward it grew in both size and brilliance, and began to adopt a familiar shape, until it became apparent to everyone that they were seeing a pair of hands, palm to palm in an attitude of prayer, only so far above the floor that they could not be attached to any living thing. The vision remained still for a while, and Mina hoped that it might perform some act appropriate to a pair of hands, or do anything other than remain stiff as a statue's but it seemed that the hands were simply being offered as an object of admiration. Slowly, they rose up almost to the ceiling, and tilted backwards, still in the same attitude. Then they seemed to be shrinking, although Mina thought that this was an illusion created as they withdrew behind the darkness of the curtains, and finally they vanished.

There were muffled exclamations of pleasurable apprehension as the company waited for what might happen next, and after a few moments, a new shape, veiled in a gauzy glow, peered from the parted curtains. The softness of the outline concealed its form, but as it turned from one side to another there were gasps and cries all around, for it was a face, the face of a man with thick hair clustering on his brow, pools of hollow darkness for eyes and a long black beard. A sudden terrible scream rang out and an exclamation: 'Archibald!' Miss Whinstone rose abruptly to her feet, and there was a loud crash as finally and unequivocally she fainted. There was pandemonium in the room, and someone called for lights and someone called for a doctor, and chairs were pushed back and people dropped hands and stood up. Professor Gaskin pleaded for calm, and relit the candle, and then Dr Hamid tended to the prostrate form of Miss Whinstone, who soon came to her senses and was furnished with a glass of water. Miss Eustace was, saw Mina, still firmly tied to her chair, and appeared to be unconscious, but Mrs Gaskin untied her and dabbed her forehead with a handkerchief, and she raised her head with an exhausted smile.

The disturbance gave Mina the opportunity to go and look behind the curtains, and there was, she had to admit, little enough to see. The table that had fallen was now standing upright with the bell and tambourine in place, and there was an untidy pencilled scrawl on the paper. Mrs Gaskin loomed up beside her. 'Please do look at everything,' she said, triumphantly.

'I didn't intend to intrude, but I am naturally curious,' said Mina. 'I would like to learn more.'

'We are all students,' said Mrs Gaskin, grandiloquently, suggesting that as students went she was at the very least senior in understanding.

Mina picked up the paper on which was inscribed a pious wish for the good health and fortune of those in attendance. 'The spirits have very poor handwriting,' she observed, 'or perhaps they cannot see in the dark.'

'I do not know how the writing is produced,' said Mrs Gaskin. 'It may be that the force exerted by Miss Eustace is as yet insufficiently refined to allow a more elegant hand.'

'Has she given you no clue as to how it is done?'

'None at all. She is always quite unable to recall anything of what has passed, and least of all is she aware of how her powers are exercised.'

Mina, while not wanting to appear to be making an obvious search for trickery, moved about the little alcove, sure that if there were any cords or strings she would encounter them, but she was aware of nothing other than what she could see. 'Miss Eustace is most remarkable,' she said, 'and I profess myself to be full of wonder at what I have seen today.'

Mrs Gaskin smiled indulgently. 'I have seen even more remarkable things, and if you come to us again I am sure that you will see them, too. As our numbers grow and the spirits gain strength from the favourable energies that surround them so they will grant us more powerful manifestations.'

Mina was intrigued by the idea that the spirits were more powerful in the presence of devoted believers. Was Miss Eustace more inclined to perform miracles in front of her most ardent supporters? Or did it mean that believers were more likely to see what they were supposed to see? And what about unbelievers? Supposing someone, a stage magician for example, was to come for the sole purpose of exposing deception? Would he be a source of unfavourable energy, assuming there even to be such a thing? All these were matters that Mina felt she ought not to pursue with Mrs Gaskin; she merely offered her gratitude for the invitation and the hope that she might be allowed to come again. Mrs Gaskin's sturdy whalebones creaked and strained with the sincere humility of Mina's appreciation.

The excitement over, the company had in the meantime settled down to tea and conversation. Miss Eustace had withdrawn, or at least Mina assumed she had done so and not vanished in a puff of smoke, and Dr Hamid had arranged for Miss Whinstone to be conveyed to her home in a cab in the company of Mrs Bettinson. As Mrs Gaskin went to join her guests, Mina crossed the room to where the water glasses on the sideboard had been disturbed, but could see nothing to suggest how they might have moved without human agency. That part of the room smelt slightly of the candle and matches, but nothing more.

'You are new to these gatherings,' said Dr Hamid, appearing by her side.

She turned and looked up at him. He was not at all discomfited by recent events and seemed to be the kind of gentleman that one could always rely upon to deal with any emergency without either fuss or self-aggrandisement. 'Yes,' said Mina, 'my mother has taken a very great interest in them and I determined to come and see for myself.'

'This is my third visit,' he said, 'and thus far all we have had was a great deal of noise and a few lights. You have been favoured with some unusual manifestations.'

There was a hint of caution in his voice, a little doubt, perhaps, thought Mina, or at the very least a desire for further enquiry. Hopeful that she had at last met someone capable of exercising a proper sense of proportion, she was emboldened to make a frank declaration, if only to see what would be the result.

'To be truthful, I am not sure of what I have seen and heard today,' she said. 'Certainly nothing I have witnessed has convinced me of the existence of mischievous spirits or of powers that extend beyond the human form, or the necessity of founding a new principle of science. If someone was to come to me and demonstrate that it was all a conjuring trick I would be neither surprised nor disappointed.'

He was a little taken aback at the suggestion, but not repelled. 'Miss Whinstone informed me that she recognised the shade of her late brother,' he observed.

'Miss Whinstone is in such a state of nervousness she would have recognised a mop wearing a false beard as her late brother,' Mina replied, drawing a smile from the doctor. 'And I for one do not accept Professor Gaskin's reasons as to why the performance had to be held in the dark. If it had occurred in a bright light

I would have been more willing to accept that there was something in it. For all his protestations, darkness is the best means of concealing a fraud, though how it was worked, I cannot say.'

'I think you have the strongest nerves of anyone in this room,' said Dr Hamid, 'and as a man of science, I have to confess that I am still unsure of the foundation for these events, although I would not wish to offend our hosts by saying so.' He slid one of the glasses on the sideboard across the polished wooden surface. It moved with barely a touch of his fingers.

'Where there are simple rational explanations, I prefer them,' said Mina, 'and I am suspicious of anyone who professes to be in possession of a new truth for the good of mankind and then uses it to fill their purse or elevate themselves in society.'

'I hope,' he said, with an unforced humility, 'that you will not see me in that light. I offer treatments for the afflicted, but I must also necessarily be a man of business, since we must all earn our bread or starve.'

'You will not be surprised to know,' Mina told him, 'that I view all medical men with suspicion, and that is not from prejudice, but experience. I hope you are not offended but I must speak my mind on that point.'

'Not at all,' he said, gently, 'and I can well understand what events might have led you to that opinion.'

'But thus far,' she admitted, 'I have heard only good of you.'

'You are too kind.' He hesitated. 'Miss Scarletti, if you do not mind my commenting, I can see that you are suffering some pain.'

Mina frowned. She had no objection to anyone mentioning either her appearance or its consequences; the thing she could not abide was the offer of false hope.

'I am sorry if I have distressed you,' he said, 'but I am very familiar with the presentation of scoliosis. There is an ache which starts in the shoulder from the strain placed upon the muscles – just – if you will permit me –' he reached out and touched her shoulder with his fingertips, 'just here.'

With some surprise Mina was obliged to acknowledge that he had touched the exact spot from which the pain was spreading.

'I trust you will not be offering me a cure?' she said wryly.

'The man who claims he can correct the curvature in your spine is either ignorant or a charlatan,' he assured her. 'But what I can offer is relief for the pain in your back. My sister Anna attends to the lady patients, and would, I know, wish to see you. I promise you that there will be no metal braces, no plaster of Paris waistcoats, no narcotic mixtures and above all no knives.'

Mina was not yet willing to admit this to be a serious conversation. 'And she will not tread on my spine and wrap my arms about my head and make my joints crack?'

'Only if she deems it necessary,' he said solemnly, and Mina realised that he was teasing her. He produced a card, wrote something on the back with a pencil, and handed it to her. 'That is my promise that if you present yourself at my establishment, you will receive your first treatment gratis,' he said. 'Please do come, I know you will feel the benefit.'

Mina did not look at the card; she looked at the man. 'I will,' she heard herself say.

Five

Inevitably, and to a degree monotonously, Mina was often told by well-meaning folk about wonderful 'cures' for her condition. Often, she was not directly addressed; rather the subject was introduced into a general conversation at which she was present, but it was always very clear that the information was being imparted for her benefit. Sometimes these messages would be passed to her mother, who was expected to impose her wishes on Mina as if her daughter was not a sensible adult able to make her own decisions. On other occasions, Mina would be quietly taken aside and advised in an embarrassed whisper to try Brill's tepid sea-water baths for ladies, or drink Dr Struve's German mineral waters. Each of these helpful advisors was under the impression that she – and it was usually a she – was the very first person ever to make such a suggestion.

Mina was also regaled with stories of the wonder cures of the past such as Dr Dean Mahomed's Indian medicated vapour baths and hot and cold douches, which had been vouched for by nobility and even royalty. Dr Mahomed had died almost twenty years ago, and his establishment on the King's Road, whose walls had once been ornamented with murals of richly dressed Moghul Emperors and displays of the abandoned crutches and spine-stretchers of his delighted customers, had fallen into disuse. Only last year it had been demolished for yet another hotel. It was Dr Hamid who was now considered to be Dr Dean Mahomed's natural successor in the provision of oriental medicine, and Dr Hamid who, with some apprehension, Mina was about to visit.

The doctor did not command a large property, but it occupied a good position on the seafront where Manchester Street met the Marine Parade, close to the site of Mr Brill's original bathhouse, a rounded protuberance that had once encroached on to the Grand Junction Road and had gone by the unflattering name of Brill's Bunion.

There were thankfully no bunions or indeed any unsightly signs and posters on Dr Hamid's bathhouse; it was a simple square building that announced itself as 'Hamid's Indian Vapour Bath and Medicated Shampoo'.

Brill's new baths on East Street was a large and prominent presence in Brighton society, much favoured for pleasurable warm bathing, while offering the subtle suggestion that its waters induced a health-giving effect on the skin and organs of the body, but Dr Hamid's baths were different. With mysterious unnamed and specially imported Indian herbs infused in its soothing vapours, it was thought of not so much as a fashionable venue for salubrious repose and dismissing the cares of the world, but as a place of resort for the treatment of diseases such as rheumatism. It was therefore much favoured by invalids, the elderly and the afflicted. Mina had been told – another of those private whispers – that if she went to Dr Hamid's she need have no anxiety that she would be required to share a pool or a vapour room with another patient, as all treatments were given in individual compartments. When she had first been told this she had assumed that the confidence was intended to reassure her that she would not come into close proximity with anyone suffering from an unpleasant disease. On reflection she realised that she was actually being comforted with the knowledge that there would, when she undressed, be no one present who would gaze on her deformity. Mina thought that had she been a person much given to anxiety, which she was not, she would have other things with which to concern herself than whether another lady bather might catch a glimpse of her spine.

As she approached the entrance door, she was surprised to see a familiar figure emerge, Mr Bradley. She was not especially inclined to speak to him, but was somewhat curious as to the reason he patronised Hamid's, since it ran contrary to his claims to be a healer, and did not object when he tipped his hat and stopped for a conversation.

'Miss Scarletti, are you here to take a vapour bath? I did not know you were a patient of Dr Hamid!'

'This is my first visit, Mr Bradley, but I could say the same of you. I trust you are well?'

'Oh, I am in the pink of health,' he assured her, 'but channelling the powers of the spirits at my healing circles can be very exhausting, and I find the vapour quite restores me. You may or may not know this, but herbs are often held to have beneficial properties.'

'Then I must anticipate my bath with some pleasure,' said Mina politely.

He paused. 'I trust that Miss Whinstone is fully recovered from her recent episode? She spoke to me at church and told me all that had happened. I was quite astonished.'

'Miss Whinstone was so alarmed that she has become an ardent devotee of Miss Eustace and means to go again and have still more experiences that will frighten her from her wits,' said Mina, who had been told this at very great length by her mother.

He smiled. 'And what did *you* think of the demonstration?'

Mina was happy to express her suspicions and anxieties to her brothers and a fellow doubter like Dr Hamid, but if she had wanted to share them with another person, that person would not have been Mr Bradley. 'I found it quite extraordinary,' she said guardedly. 'It was impossible for me to explain what I had seen.'

He nodded knowingly. 'I can see that you are also becoming a devotee; as most of Brighton will soon be, so I have heard.'

'I can safely say that Miss Eustace arouses my very keen interest, and I shall be eager to see more of what she does, and learn more about her,' said Mina.

Mr Bradley seemed not to catch her meaning, but then she did not expect him to. 'Would you be kind enough to advise your charming mother that I will call upon her to conduct the healing circle again tomorrow?'

'I will certainly do so,' said Mina, trying to look as if the prospect was one that promised enjoyment.

They parted with the usual courtesies.

Mina paused in front of the doors of Dr Hamid's baths, but did not yet feel ready to enter. If she tried to explore her feelings she did not really know why she was there. It was not in the hope of a cure; that, she knew, was impossible. Perhaps it was because Dr Hamid had not promised her a cure, or even an improvement in her condition, and she therefore felt more able to trust him than any doctor she had previously consulted. She had also sensed that he had a genuine understanding of the restrictions imposed by her twisted body on her daily life. But perhaps she was there simply because her shoulder ached and she would like it to stop aching.

She pushed at the door, and in that moment she was decided. Mina often had a struggle with doors, which were inevitably taller, wider and substantially heavier than she, some of them monstrosities of glass and brass and polished wood, which even a man in full health might find a challenge, but this one, for all its imposing appearance, moved at the touch of her fingers. Some beautiful mechanism had been installed, and whether by a system of gliding counterweights or an oiled machine she did not know, but there could be no invalid or elderly frail person who could not open it.

She found herself in a small but tastefully appointed vestibule, and was greeted by a matronly looking woman to whom she presented Dr Hamid's card. There was a small counter, and behind it a sign listing a scale of charges. A single vapour bath and shampoo was five shillings, but one could purchase six or a dozen at a reduced price, or even an annual subscription.

A visitors' book was open, inviting customers to enter their comments, and a carved wooden box held a pile of printed leaflets listing Dr Hamid's qualifications and the treatments offered by his establishment.

Those waiting for attention would not be required to stand, since there were a number of comfortable seats provided for the repose of ladies and gentlemen, at a variety of different heights, so there was something to suit persons of every size, and there was also a selection of cushions of assorted shapes and varying degrees of firmness. A display of dried flowers and seed heads exuded a subtle and slightly exotic perfume.

Mina had expected something of the Oriental about the interior, portraits of richly dressed and bejewelled potentates, giant decorated urns, painted parasols or statuettes of elephants, and certainly a great deal of gilding, but apart from a colourful frieze that ran around the upper level of the wall, the lover of ornate decoration was doomed to disappointment. Neither was there a poster blaring out in capital letters with fat exclamation marks the wonderful cures that Dr Hamid had effected, or a gruesome display of abandoned crutches. All was peaceful and pleasant, and nothing offended or disturbed the eye.

Three doors led from the vestibule, one for the gentlemen's bathing facilities, one for the use of ladies, and another unmarked door, which was presumably an office.

The lady nodded as she read the card, and operated a bell-pull. 'Please be so good as to follow the signs, and Miss Hamid will be waiting to receive you,' she said.

Mina opened the door to the ladies' baths and found herself at the head of a corridor, where the walls were decorated with prints of tropical plants and birds. A room to her left was a comfortable salon, where some ladies were reposing on couches sipping mineral water and reading periodicals. A large window faced the sea and the room was golden with sunshine. A lady with a spotless white wrapper over her gown, and undoubtedly from her appearance, Miss Hamid, was arranging a pretty bowl of fresh flowers, but as soon as she saw Mina, she came to greet her.

'You must be Miss Scarletti,' she said. 'I am so pleased that you have decided to come. Daniel – my brother – told me that he hoped you would call.'

'I have never experienced a vapour bath before,' said Mina, 'or indeed the shampoo massage, which I think might be more vigorous than is suitable for me.'

'You have nothing to fear,' said Miss Hamid with a comforting smile. 'The vigour or gentleness of the massage is adjusted precisely to the tolerance and the age and health of the patient. Come.' Miss Hamid was, thought Mina, just a little older than her brother, and as tall, which meant that she was above the common height for a woman. She had a round face with a small chin, and very dark eyes, and her greying hair was simply dressed. Mina, aware that the lady performed the shampoo massage, noticed that Miss Hamid's hands were well formed and looked very strong.

As they walked, Mina looked about her, and was obliged to comment that the establishment, while delightful, was not quite as she had expected. Miss Hamid gave a little laugh. 'You refer to the absence of gilded domes, and portraits of eastern potentates?' Mina was obliged to confess that she did mean something of the kind, but Miss Hamid, so far from being offended as she had feared, was amused. 'We believe,' she said, 'that where it comes to Oriental opulence, that Brighton already has a sufficiency.'

By the time they had reached the door of a compartment Mina felt that her companion had somehow seen into and understood the anxieties in her mind, and every discomfort in her body. She was ushered to a small dressing-box where she was to disrobe entirely and wrap herself in a large sheet. A towel fashioned like a turban was provided to cover her hair and there were several pairs of little wooden shoes of different sizes so that she might select the one that would best fit her bare feet. 'Do you require any assistance?' asked Miss Hamid.

'Thank you, but that will not be necessary,' said Mina, who had arranged with her dressmaker to provide gowns specially designed so that she would be able to dress and undress herself.

'When you are ready,' said Miss Hamid, 'enter the next room, where the vapour bath will proceed. After fifteen minutes it will be complete and then I will bring you fresh dry sheets and take you to the massage room. If you require anything at all, please call, I will be nearby.' She left Mina alone.

Mina proceeded to divest herself of her clothing, and then wound the sheet about her body, where it was held in place by linen tapes, and arranged the turban on her head. Any resemblance between herself and the wife of a sultan lounging in an eastern harem, was, she felt, undetectable. Not without some awkwardness, she tried the little wooden shoes, found a pair that fitted, and slipped them on to her feet. She discovered with some surprise that they were very comfortable, being moulded so as to cradle her soles, and easy to walk in. Nevertheless she still felt apprehensive as she went into the vapour room. This was a chamber some eight feet square, lined with pretty blue and white tiles, and with an opening at the top, presumably to allow a free circulation of air. There was one high window, but no danger of being observed, since it was of stained glass with panes of green and blue, admitting only a subdued light. She detected a very faint but pleasing scent of flowers or herbs, which she could not readily identify. In the centre of the room was a simple wooden chair draped in a thick soft towel. Mina sat in the chair and looked about her, but could not see where the vapour was to come from. In just a few moments she understood. The floor of the room, which was tiled in a latticework design, was not a continuous surface but admitted little diamond-shaped gaps, and it was from these gaps that a vapour began to arise. It rose around her like a soft perfumed cloud and gradually began to fill the room. Any apprehension she might have felt was quickly dispelled by the deliciousness of the scent, and the feeling of warmth that stole over her. She closed her eyes, wondering where the vapour, which must already be condensing to spangle the cooler walls, must be going, since she hardly expected to find the room awash with water when she was finished. Wherever the vapour went, she felt sure that there was some ingenious method for its efficient removal. Even the floor had been specially designed so as not to offer a slippery surface underfoot. Dr Hamid seemed to think of everything.

These enquiring thoughts were set aside as she inhaled the sweet medicated cloud, inducing a delightful sense of tranquillity, while a pleasing perspiration bathed her body. The sheet around her became warm and moist; it clung to her skin, infusing her with its own heat and scent. Pain, indeed the concept that pain might even exist, was somehow washed away, time was washed away, and she felt at peace. It was with some regret that she noticed, after a while, that Anna Hamid had entered the room and that the vapour was dispersing. The last threads of moisture were beading the walls and running down into a narrow tiled gully around the perimeter.

'Stand very slowly and I will help you,' said Miss Hamid, and there was nothing in her voice to suggest that Mina might need any more help than another person whose body had acquired a beautiful soft suppleness from the medicinal steam. She wrapped Mina in a warm fresh sheet, and drew her to the next room, which was a haven of scented and soothing heat, and laid her on a couch, then oiled her hands and, with the most exquisite care, ran her fingers over the contours of Mina's back. Miss Hamid was a strong woman with powerful shoulders, but years of applying her hands to the work of untying the knots in strained muscles had given her a perfectly directed firmness and an understanding delicacy of touch. Her hands exerted a gentle pressure on Mina's back, further warming the already relaxed muscles, and her thumbs located the seat of the shoulder pain and began to smooth it away.

'You seem to know exactly where the discomfort lies,' said Mina. 'You must have other patients with a similar condition.'

'There have been some,' said Miss Hamid, 'but the chief of those is my sister Eliza.'

'Oh!' said Mina, startled. 'I have not seen any lady in Brighton who is like myself.'

'Eliza rarely goes from home,' said Miss Hamid, sadly. 'Her case is far more advanced than yours. Her spine became curved when she was a very small child, when her bones were weaker and more pliable, and there was no opportunity for her to obtain the help that a child would certainly receive now.'

'I am sorry to hear it,' said Mina.

'It was her predicament that led Daniel and me to make a special study of scoliosis and other conditions affecting the spine, and devise our own methods of helping patients. Perhaps,' said Miss Hamid, diffidently, 'I could prevail upon you to call on Eliza. I know that she would appreciate your company.'

'Of course,' said Mina. 'I am only surprised that when I met your brother he did not mention her to me.'

'You encountered him at the salon held by Professor Gaskin, I believe?' asked Miss Hamid, her fingers exerting a delicate tapping and fluttering like tiny feet running up and down Mina's back.

'I did. It was a very curious evening.'

'Do you believe that Miss Eustace's powers are genuine?' asked Miss Hamid, with a note of caution in her voice that inspired Mina to take her into her confidence.

'I saw nothing that convinced me that I had witnessed anything more than a clever magician,' she said, boldly, 'and I fear that people are being duped, but I cannot prove it.'

'Daniel has told me that he is not entirely convinced that Miss Eustace's demonstrations are genuine,' said Miss Hamid. 'If you do not mind the question – what drew you to visit her?'

'I think that is a very important question,' said Mina, 'and I have no objection to answering. I went because my mother goes and I do not want her to be exposed to the machinations of a charlatan. My mother goes because she was widowed a year ago and seeks solace, and, I rather think, novelty.'

Miss Hamid began to explore the muscles in the soft angle between Mina's neck and shoulders. 'I think Daniel would not mention Eliza in such company in case they should seize upon her and offer her false hope of a cure,' she said. 'He knows of the terrible machines and even worse operations that a well-meaning doctor will recommend, but someone who claims to be in concert with the spirits can do as much evil.'

'I do not seek a cure,' said Mina, 'since none exists. I am content with that because I must be. Neither do I believe in the kind of spirits that Miss Eustace purports to show us. The world of the spirit is closed to the living; we will meet it soon enough.'

Miss Hamid gently drew Mina's arm across her back to raise her shoulder blade and used her fingertips to seek out clenched and sore muscles with a firm but not unpleasant pressure that made her patient gasp.

'Although Daniel is a man of science, he nevertheless feels some hope, as all of us must do, which induces in him a need to explore and enquire,' said Miss Hamid. 'He is of course aware that there are many things we understand today to have a foundation in fact which only a hundred years ago would have seemed to be impossible. I expect you know that he is not long a widower. He and his dear wife Jane were very devoted to each other. She died three months ago after a painful but mercifully short illness. They had been married for twenty-two years and he feels her loss very keenly.'

'What does he seek?' asked Mina. 'Surely he does not hope to communicate with her spirit?'

'I think,' said Miss Hamid reflectively, 'that he looks only for some sign, some certainty that the spirit, the intelligence, the soul – call it what you will – of an individual will survive entire. If he can be assured of this, he will be content, because he will know that one day they will be reunited.'

Mina thought of her father and Marianne. 'We all hope to be reunited with our loved ones in Heaven,' she said. 'But I do not think the Bible said anything about the dead speaking to the living, or playing on tambourines.'

'The Bible teaches us that we all sleep until the Day of Judgement and then, and only then, do we rise again,' said Miss Hamid. 'I see no reason to doubt it.'

'Then perhaps,' said Mina cautiously, 'your brother should comfort himself with that. Miss Eustace's demonstrations are little more than a sideshow on the pier, like Madame Proserpina the fortune teller, only I fear, very much more expensive.'

'I can see that this worries you greatly,' said Miss Hamid. 'Your neck and shoulders grow more tense under my fingers as you think about it. But now I would beg you to have only pleasurable thoughts.' She anointed her hands with more scented oil and smoothed them over Mina's back. Mina sighed and gave herself up to the sensation. When the massage was done she felt more supple than she could remember ever having felt, with a lightness and freedom from pain that she would have thought impossible.

When Mina was dressed, Miss Hamid brought her a cushion shaped like a door wedge, which she could put underneath one hip to right her posture as she sat, and asked if she had ever been prescribed exercises.

'Only deportment classes,' said Mina. 'I was required to walk in a circle with a bag of shot on my head while juggling oranges. I was not their best student.'

Miss Hamid smiled. 'I believe that oranges are better when the flesh is eaten and the peel dried for its scent. I would like you to undertake some suitable exercises, but I do not wish you to attempt them alone, not yet. Some of the movements, known as callisthenics, would be very beneficial to you, but only if performed correctly. Others, however, are best avoided. If you would like, then the next time you come here I will show you what to do. You need to strengthen your weaker side, but take care not to neglect the other, and also work on expanding the chest to help your lungs and heart. We will begin slowly. You must be patient and avoid over-exertion which can be harmful.'

Mina smiled, because Miss Hamid knew, and she also knew, that she would return. 'I would like that,' she said.

'Young women are often dissuaded from exercising, as if weakness was a desirable state,' said Miss Hamid. 'But it is not. You can be strong; stronger than you might imagine, stronger than anyone would expect of you. Your mind is already very strong, but your body can be as well.'

Mina had never thought of herself as a creature of the body, but began to see that she had spent the last nine years merely trying to exist with her condition, and find an occupation for her mind that would distract her from it. Miss Hamid had offered her not a cure, which was not within her powers, but a means of alleviating the symptoms, and perhaps also making herself into something better than she was.

With an agreement that she would call on Eliza Hamid in two days' time, Mina departed for her home. As she stepped into the open air she felt that she took with her some of the scent of herbs and flowers in which she had bathed and whose delicious savour she had inhaled. The sun seemed brighter, the sky more glowing, the air softer, the people more colourful, the season more charming than they had been before.

She returned to find that an important package, which she had requested by letter from Mr Greville, had arrived. It was an unbound advance copy of the report of the special committee of the London Dialectical Society regarding their investigation into the question of spiritualism, the report that Professor Gaskin had spoken of in such exultant terms.

Six

Fortunately Mina's mother, nesting in the parlour amongst an array of periodicals and pamphlets, was too preoccupied with her own concerns to be curious about the delivery, which did not excite any comment. Mina passed on the message she had been given by Mr Bradley, and Louisa received the news with pleasure and informed Mina that she expected her to attend the healing circle on the following day. It would be a meeting of important and fashionable individuals and quite the most glittering event of the season to date. Mina, expecting no more than the usual gathering of bored widows, quickly agreed and took the parcel up to her room as soon as she was able. The size and weight of the package had suggested to her that it might contain other works, too, since she had expected the report to be a slim bundle of papers, but on unwrapping it she was astonished to find only the report, a work that ran to almost four hundred pages.

It did not, however, take very long for Mina to discover that Professor Gaskin, who claimed to have read the report, had made two very significant errors of judgement. Professor and man of science he might be, but he was as vulnerable to bias as anyone else. He had, first of all, chosen only to see those areas of evidence that might favour his own viewpoint, interpreting them in a manner that supported his contentions, while ignoring not only the other possible and indeed more probable interpretations of events, but also additional evidence and points of view which were not favourable to his cause. The man who pitied the closed minds of others did so, thought Mina, with a mind that was in itself closed. He had also made the fatally dangerous assumption that no one present at Miss Eustace's séance would take the trouble to read the report and compare its findings with his description.

Mina settled herself at her desk, raising her hip with the new cushion, which was a wonderful improvement on the old one, and started to read.

Even a small and seemingly harmless falsehood invited suspicion from the outset. Professor Gaskin had implied that the report was to be published by the Dialectical Society, but this, Mina saw at once, was not the case. The Society had appointed a committee to investigate spirit phenomena in January 1869, which had reported its findings in July 1870, in the hopes that the Society would publish them. The Society had noted the committee's report but had declined to publish, a refusal that suggested to Mina a lack of trust in either the conduct of the investigation or its conclusions. The committee members had therefore taken the decision to publish the report themselves.

During the course of the enquiry, six subcommittees had been created, each of which had held meetings and séances. The committee had also collected statements from non-members, all of whom were believers in supernatural phenomena, having failed, for reasons it was unable to explain, to obtain evidence from anyone who attributed the phenomena to fraud and delusion.

Mina was less interested in opinions than results and so studied the reports of the six subcommittees with especial interest.

Two of the subcommittees reported that no phenomena at all had occurred during their meetings, and another was conducting séances with Mr Home, who, since he was a cheat with money, was in Mina's opinion likely to be a cheat in other things, too. She decided that these three subcommittees had failed to prove anything.

Two subcommittees had heard rappings and witnessed the movement of a table, but this occurred only when certain individuals were taking part. The presence of these persons was undoubtedly essential to the results but whether this was due to their supernatural powers or the ability to deceive was not, in Mina's mind, established beyond doubt.

The most extraordinary performances were at meetings that took place at the houses of two members of the Dialectical Society where, to avoid any suspicion of fraud, the gatherings did not include anyone claiming to have mediumistic powers. Not only did rapping and table moving occur but, by giving the meanings 'yes' or 'no' to numbers of raps, or even spelling out words when one of the party named a letter of the alphabet, it was possible to establish a free communication with the spirits who had produced the manifestations. These cheerful entities expressed a friendly regard for those present and were able to provide correct answers to questions and personal information. The subcommittee members had no doubt that they had been in communication with spirit intelligences, but reported that they had inevitably failed to obtain any manifestations without the presence in the party of the wives of the two members of the Dialectical Society. Mina was left weighing up two possibilities, one being that the party had been conversing with the spirits of the dead and the other that the two ladies had been mischievously providing their friends with some novel entertainment.

The conclusion drawn by the committee from these mixed results was that sounds and movement of objects did occur without having been produced by muscular or mechanical action, and the ability to spell out answers to questions showed that the phenomena were directed by an intelligence.

Further reports revealed that while many members of the society suspected fraud they had been unable to offer any proof. This was unsurprising since once an observer was suspected of being a sceptic who was bent on exposing imposture, the false medium, on being alerted to the danger, quickly arranged matters so as to avoid detection. This was done in a number of ways, the simplest being to produce no phenomena at the séance and then announce that his or her powers were exhausted that day, or that the spirits were being capricious, or even attributing the failure to a hostile influence in the circle. The hostile influence was of course the sceptic, who was thereafter *persona non grata* in the company, since both the medium and the circle of believers would not want that person disrupting their sittings in future.

It was with particular interest, and some amusement, that Mina read a letter written by the chairman of the Dialectical Society's special committee, a Dr James Edmunds. Fending off earnest attempts by spiritualists to persuade him that he himself could be a powerful medium if he would only open his eyes and recognise the fact, he remained unconvinced by the committee's conclusions, and had submitted his personal observations.

In May 1868 Dr Edmunds had attended a public exhibition at St George's Hall, London, given by the Davenport brothers, Americans who were touring England giving demonstrations of phenomena which they attributed to spirits but which many who had seen their performances had denounced as little more than clever, albeit entertaining, conjuring. Mina recalled the Davenports' tour, which had been widely reported and discussed in the London newspapers. The two young men had a large wooden cabinet specially constructed for their performances, which they carried about with them on their tour. Volunteers from the audience were first invited to make a thorough examination of the apparatus, after which two chairs were placed inside the cabinet, to which the brothers were securely bound. A collection of musical instruments, such as tambourines, bells, violins and guitars, joined them in the cabinet and the door was closed. Almost at once the instruments produced a perfect babel of sound, while spirit arms and hands were seen protruding through an overhead aperture. Every so often the door of the cabinet burst violently open and an instrument was tossed out on to the floor. Their most remarkable feat used a coat borrowed from a member of the audience, which was placed inside the cabinet and was later found on the person of one of the brothers, yet when they were examined after the performance the knots and ligatures were found to be as sound and tight as before.

Dr Edmunds was unable to explain away what he had seen that night, which had involved flying violins and the use of his own coat in the famous trick. Later the same month he was invited to attend a private séance, which was to be followed by the Davenports giving their acclaimed cabinet performance. Edmunds, though a natural sceptic, determined to approach the evening with an open mind, anticipating that in a private room he would have a better opportunity to observe and investigate the phenomena. Perhaps his reputation had preceded him, or the company was wary of any newcomer, for when the sitters were conducted to their places he found himself at a large round table that had been pushed close to a corner of the room so trapping him in his place. Had he been inclined to slip off his shoes and creep silently about the darkened room looking for evidence of imposture, something he had thought of doing, he would have been quite unable to do so. The part of the table towards the centre of the room, and thus allowing sitters free movement, was, he noticed, occupied by avowed spiritualists. Edmunds wisely decided not to protest about this arrangement in case he was held to be hostile, in which case he felt sure that no phenomena would occur.

The sitting proceeded in complete darkness for some little time. A few raps were heard but nothing of note occurred, and the company was finding the occasion somewhat disappointing, when it was decided to try and obtain a spirit drawing. The gas was relit and a portfolio case was placed on the table and opened to demonstrate that it contained nothing but a sheet of plain paper, then the case was closed again and a pencil placed nearby. The gas was about to be turned out when Edmunds suggested to a friend, who was also a newcomer to the gathering, that as a further test they should first initial the paper. He opened the case and saw that the paper was not, as he had at first supposed, a plain quarto sheet but a much larger sheet that had been folded. On unfolding it he saw on the interior of one flap a detailed pencil drawing of an angel. He tore off the portion with the drawing and he and his friend wrote on the remaining part of the sheet, which was returned to the case. The gas was turned off and he heard the sound of loud rustling, which led him to suspect that one of the spiritualists at the table had opened the case, and was handling the paper. When the gas was relit there were only a few ambiguous marks on the sheet and the test was declared to be a failure. The spirits, it was explained, were 'capricious'. The sitters were not wholly disappointed by the séance, however, for a basket of fresh flowers was then produced under cover of darkness, which a Mrs Guppy claimed had flown through the walls but which Edmunds thought had travelled from no greater distance than the sideboard. Dr Edmunds was by now finding himself unable to conceal the fact that he thought the whole performance was a deception and was unsurprised to be told soon afterwards that the Davenports would not be performing their miracles as they had no spiritual power that evening.

A Mr Samuel Guppy had later written to the committee to deny that Dr Edmunds's account was correct, but a diligent search through the papers enabled Mina to establish not only that Mr Guppy was the husband of Mrs Guppy but that he was an ardent spiritualist, and his wife professed to be a powerful medium who could shower her devotees with fresh flowers, and even rise up and fly about the room.

Other exhibitions carefully observed by the tireless Dr Edmunds had attributed the sound of spirit raps to nothing more supernatural than the medium's foot. He concluded that during all his investigations he had never seen anything that could not be accounted for by unconscious action, delusion or imposture.

There were other statements in the report, some from gentlemen convinced of the reality of what they had observed, and some from those who felt sure that they had observed something of note but did not believe that spirits of the dead were directing events. The consensus, if such a mixture of differing opinions could be termed such, was that there was something occurring which was worthy of further cautious investigation, a conclusion with which Mina could only agree. She would not wish to prejudge the outcome of such an investigation, but her own feeling was that she was more inclined to believe that a bunch of flowers could be carried across a room by human hands than fly through a wall by spirit power. If that made her a sceptic or even a materialist then so be it.

The difficult question was what she should do next. On the one hand she could not begrudge her mother the pleasure and diversion she gained from the gatherings with Miss Eustace, but on the other it seemed to her that there was a very real possibility that Miss Eustace was a criminal who made money from deceiving the vulnerable. She determined after some thought to discuss the question with the one person she knew who had attended the séances and appeared to have some doubts – Dr Hamid.

Louisa Scarletti was now, in her own estimation at least, well on her way to becoming the hostess of a fashionable salon, and all her talk was of who she might invite to Mr Bradley's healing circle in future, and, more importantly, who should not be invited, and who had attended in the past who ought never to be invited again. She spent much of her time studying the newspapers and directories of Brighton, making lists of her approved guests, and giving orders to the cook.

In one area, however, she remained sorely disappointed. Her efforts, even combined with those of Mr Bradley, to persuade Reverend Vaughan of Christ Church that the healing circle was not irreligious had met with failure. On the Sunday after the first gathering the reverend had taken as his text Matthew 24.11: 'And many false prophets shall rise, and shall deceive many.' While he did not mention Mr Bradley by name, his meaning could not have been clearer, and during his sermon, the reverend cast some very severe looks not only at that gentleman, but at Louisa, Mina and any others whom he had been informed might be members of the circle. Mr Bradley sat throughout with a fixed smile on his face and pretended that the sermon was nothing to do with him, but Louisa made no secret of her increasing fury. According to St Matthew, the false prophets would arrive in sheep's clothing and perform great signs and miracles, but inwardly, they would be ravening wolves. Mina did not think either Mr Bradley or Miss Eustace looked like ravening wolves, but then, on reflection, she realised that this was the very point that St Matthew was making.

When Mr Bradley's healing circle met again, the sceptical Mr Jordan was not present, whether by his own intention or Louisa's Mina did not know, but the two widowed sisters Mina had met at the séance, Mrs Mowbray and Mrs Peasgood, had been added to the company. Mrs Bettinson, Miss Whinstone, Mrs Phipps and Mr Conroy were early arrivals, and to Mina's surprise when she entered the parlour, she saw her tenant, the normally energetic Mrs Parchment, sitting there looking very stiff and uncomfortable, and staring at a platter of iced cakes with extreme disfavour. How Louisa had persuaded her to attend, Mina could not imagine and why she would have wanted her there was an even greater mystery. Mrs Parchment appeared to be labouring under a similar sense of amazement.

Before the proceedings commenced, several more ladies and two gentlemen crowded into the parlour, which was starting to resemble a crush at a society drawing room. Mr Bradley started by greeting all those present with an equal distribution of his charm, although he swiftly moved on to an oleaginous appreciation of his hostess, and an especial welcome to those new to the circle. The ladies and gentlemen present, he declared, might or might not know this, but it was to Mrs Scarletti that he owed the great success of the little circle, which he anticipated might even in time become a very large circle, or even several circles. Throughout the encomium to her mother, Mina could only feel grateful that his attention was thereby diverted from herself. All then proceeded as before, with Mina allowing the peaceful atmosphere devoid of all interruptions to concentrate her mind on completing the composition of her tale of the jewel in the fish.

It was as Mr Bradley conducted the individual healing that Mina's mind came back to what was before her, for when he paused in front of Mrs Parchment he did not, as he had done with the other ladies, touch her hand. Instead he knelt, and rested his palm on her right foot. She started, and almost withdrew the foot, then submitted to the touch with a faint frown.

Mina looked at her mother, and saw her lips curve knowingly. It was too transparent, of course. Mina deduced that the reason Mrs Parchment had not gone on her usual brisk walk that day was because she had some small injury to her foot, something that her mother knew about, and had doubtless communicated privately to Mr Bradley. There was no point in Mina suggesting that there had been any complicity since there was no proof, and both parties would deny it vehemently. The point of the dissimulation was clearly to add to Mr Bradley's fame by demonstrating that his knowledge of Mrs Parchment's injury should be attributed to his special insight. Mina felt disgusted at the imposture, but it appeared trivial enough. If her mother and Mr Bradley thereby felt some enhancement of their status then they should be left to enjoy their shallow delights, and if Mrs Parchment imagined her foot to feel better, why then she had received a benefit. Mr Bradley's healing touch was no worse than the coloured water sold by quack doctors, which so many of their patients declared had cured them.

When Mrs Parchment had limped back to her room, Louisa announced to the remaining company that Mr Bradley had not seen the lady walk before he had arrived, and had not known about the injury to her foot. Nevertheless he had sensed at once that she required a healing and also the precise location of the pain. It was a wonderful proof of his astonishing perception. She also confided that her tenant had barely been able to move at all before the healing, and was therefore now almost cured. Everyone agreed that they had been most privileged to witness the demonstration.

No sooner had the last guest departed than Louisa was busy drawing up a new list of names. Mina had earlier advised her mother that her visit to Dr Hamid's baths had brought her some relief from her accustomed discomfort, and Louisa had initially shown no great interest in this fact, but now she asked Mina if at the next gathering she might take a turn about the room, and say how her pain had diminished.

'But the company will surely form the impression that any benefit I gained was due not to Dr Hamid's establishment but Mr Bradley,' Mina protested.

'Really, Mina, how can you even know that that is not the case?' said her mother dismissively. 'And I do not ask you to do it for Mr Bradley, I ask you to do it for *me*. Is that too great a trouble for you? It seems so.'

'Of course, I will do as you ask,' said Mina, resignedly, wondering how she could possibly avoid it.

'And if Dr Hamid is so very clever,' added Louisa, 'then how has he not healed his own sister, who is, so I have been informed, in a great state? Perhaps I should send Mr Bradley to see *her*.'

Mina clamped her lips shut before she said anything unwise and decided not to mention her invitation to take tea with the Hamids on the following day.

Seven

Dr Hamid and his family lived in a pleasant villa in Charles Street, not far from the Marine Parade. A maid conducted Mina to a parlour where she was greeted by Anna and her brother. It was a house of mourning, but there was a tasteful restraint about the display, which Mina thought was not about outward show or fashion but deep and privately held feeling. The mantelpiece was simply draped in black, and a framed memorial card was placed beside a black-bordered portrait of a lady, undoubtedly the late Jane Hamid, who looked out across the room with a serene and intelligent expression. Other pictures, also in black frames, showed a venerable gentleman of Indian extraction, with a round face and kindly eyes, and an elderly lady, dignified and handsome; undoubtedly Dr Hamid's parents.

On a small table was a collection of pictures in pretty silver frames of three young people at various ages, the most recent one being of two fine-looking youths and a girl.

'I see you are admiring our portraits,' said Anna with a smile, when the usual politenesses had been exchanged, and refreshments served.

'These are very charming young people,' said Mina.

'Jacob is twenty, now,' said Dr Hamid. 'He is in Edinburgh studying to be a surgeon. My two youngest are at school in London. Nathan is eighteen and will soon join his brother in the study of medicine. My daughter Davina is fifteen and, if her wishes can be met, she will also take a medical degree at Edinburgh. There is at present a most unwarranted prejudice in England against women practising medicine, which I hope will be overcome in time.' He looked proudly at the pictures, his eyes naturally moving on to cloud over as they gazed at the portrait of his late wife.

'You are very advanced in your thinking,' said Mina.

He smiled. 'How could I not be with such examples before me? My mother was a very wise and educated lady, as was my late wife, as are both my sisters. I cannot ignore what is plain to see.'

'I am very happy that you have agreed to call on Eliza,' said Anna, warmly. 'She is normally solitary and, although she will protest that she prefers to be so, I am not altogether convinced of it. She hardly ever ventures downstairs but keeps to her room. Of course we spend as much time as we can with her, and there is a maid to see to her wants, but she really has no friends.'

Mina put her teacup down. 'I would be delighted to see her.'

'She has just taken her afternoon nap, and is now expecting you. I will take you to her.' Anna conducted Mina upstairs, and knocked on a door. 'Eliza, here is Miss Scarletti to see you.'

There was a brief wait then the door opened. Mina had prepared herself with a determination to show neither pity nor cloying kindness, both of which she abhorred, guessing that any sister of Dr and Anna Hamid would feel the same. In a moment she realised that whatever the expression on her face, it would have made no difference to the woman who stood before her. Eliza, leaning heavily upon a stout stick, was the only adult Mina had ever seen who was smaller than herself. The little woman's body was so distorted that the curve of her spine had lifted her right shoulder higher than her head, which was forced forward on a downward sloping neck so that its normal position was with the face looking down to the floor. The left shoulder was rotated so that it rested several inches below the right and, while the necessarily loose and shapeless gown concealed it, Mina knew that the left side of Eliza's body must be collapsed and atrophied to a degree that she herself would hopefully never experience. The unfortunate woman's ribs were almost certainly pressing into her lungs and possibly even constricting the action of her heart. Suddenly Mina saw that her own body, her young strong body in which she could achieve all that she wanted to do in life, was a wonderful blessing to her, and that her inconsequential S of a spine could only mock with its comparatively mild displacement the crushed form of Eliza Hamid. Mina had never intended it, but tears started in her eyes. Anna glanced at her, concerned, and Mina knew that if she faltered now she had failed everyone. She took a deep breath. 'Miss Hamid, I am most delighted to meet you.'

Eliza lifted her head with an effort, and for several moments a searching gaze took in the person before her. 'Please do come in,' she said. 'Anna, please ask Mary to send up some refreshments. I do so hope there are almond biscuits.'

'Of course,' said Anna.

Mina followed Eliza into a sitting room, where a small couch, heaped with quilts and pillows, was undoubtedly the only location where the occupant could sleep in comfort. There was a low easy chair, which was provided with a special cushion, angled so that when Eliza was seated her body tilted back and she could see the person who was with her without having to strain her neck. Even so, Mina could see that it would be hard for Eliza to maintain her position without assistance, since her head was of normal size, and the neck not strong enough to support it for long. As she wondered at this, Eliza indicated where she should sit, and prodding the tip of her stick into a groove on the side of the chair, and placing one foot on a low stool, stepped neatly, almost nimbly, into position. When she was comfortably settled she placed a padded collar around her neck, and rested her chin on it. Mina could only admire her hostess's independence, the confidence with which she inhabited her confined yet comfortable world.

From the portraits in the parlour below Mina could see that Anna most closely resembled her father, whereas Dr Hamid and

Eliza both had the oval face and sculpted cheekbones of their mother. Mina had been told that Eliza was fifty, twice her own age, but pain and the constant fight to draw breath had drawn savage lines in her otherwise youthful skin.

'And now,' said Eliza, 'let us talk, and I hope there will be no mention of joints or spines or bones, or any discomfort at all.'

'I agree,' said Mina. 'That can be so tedious.' She looked about her. The room was well supplied with books, and there was a table at Eliza's elbow with an open volume, a pile of newspapers, and a pair of spectacles. 'But I can see that you are a great reader, and we will not want for interesting subjects for our conversation.'

Eliza, it transpired, was an avid devourer of novels, histories and memoirs, and although she rarely stirred from her room, took a keen interest in the world and all its doings. By the time the maid arrived with the almond biscuits there was the unaccustomed sound of laughter in the room. Mina even revealed that she wrote stories of mystery and adventure, which excited Eliza to great admiration.

Eliza tired quickly. Talking and laughing were nourishment to her mind but a strain on her body. Mina had just begun to wonder how she might retire gracefully and leave Eliza to rest, when Anna arrived, announcing that it was time for her sister's massage.

'Please do come again,' said Eliza, eagerly. 'And you must entertain me with your stories, you really must!'

Mina promised that she would, wondering what she might have written that would be suitable. 'If Dr Hamid is not too busy, I would very much like to speak with him before I go,' she asked.

'But of course,' said Anna. 'He is still in the parlour, and you may even find there is a sandwich left, although I very much doubt it.'

There were no sandwiches left, but Mina did not mind that. She found Dr Hamid draining the last of the tea, and looking quietly thoughtful. His was a gentle melancholy, with no room for self-pity, only a contemplation of loss and its meaning.

He looked up as she entered, and rose to his feet until she was seated. 'I am grateful for your visit,' he said. 'I know that Eliza will benefit from your company.'

'It has been my privilege,' said Mina. 'We had so many things to talk about, and I would very much like to call on her again. But if I may there is a subject that concerns us both which I would like to discuss with you.'

'Please do,' he said, surprised. He offered to ring for more refreshments, but Mina said that was not necessary.

'The subject is Miss Eustace,' she said.

'Ah,' said Dr Hamid. He picked up his empty teacup, contemplated its interior and put it down again.

'You know my opinion of these manifestations,' said Mina. 'I believe them to be nothing more than conjuring, and if that was my only concern I would not be so troubled. If the lady can provide a diversion for idle minds or comfort for the bereaved, then I cannot blame her any more than if she was a fortune teller or played the piano. But what if the lady is a dangerous and calculating criminal? Some of those who profess to be mediums are really thieves. They ask for large sums of money in return for supposedly bringing messages from deceased loved ones and their poor dupes are so deep in their power that they give them all that they own. Those who go to séances simply to be entertained will not be vulnerable; no, it is the lonely and unhappy and recently bereaved who will fall victim. Is that not cruel and evil?'

'Of course,' he agreed readily, 'and I believe that Miss Eustace does receive payment in the form of gifts, but these are small and voluntarily given. Do you have any evidence that she is demanding large sums of money?'

'No,' Mina admitted. 'But then if someone is being gulled out of their fortune they are not going to discuss it in company. It might happen secretly and not be discovered until it is too late. And small gifts may over time become large demands.'

He looked unconvinced. 'I cannot imagine that *you* would ever be gulled. Are you perhaps concerned for your mother?'

Mina paused. 'I confess that that was my first thought, and I am sure that she does make payments to Miss Eustace, although she will not admit it to me. But outrageous villains such as Mr Home, the medium who defrauded an elderly widow of thirty thousand pounds, do not prey on ladies who have families to watch over their concerns. My mother may hand over her few guineas but she will not be asked for all her fortune. And if she should suddenly decide to transfer her funds outside the family, our solicitor or our bank will let me know, since I have dealt with the family finances since my father died. There are other ladies, however, who attend Miss Eustace's séances, who have no relatives and manage their own affairs. I am thinking of Miss Whinstone, for example, who was in a highly nervous state even before she had heard of Miss Eustace. Her brother was all her family and he died two years ago leaving her very comfortably provided for. She undoubtedly believes that she has seen his ghost, and who knows what that might lead to.'

Mina could see that Dr Hamid, while not sharing her anxieties, clearly recognised that she was in great earnest and was giving her words serious consideration. 'You are presumably asking for my advice?'

'I ask for advice, or observations or any comment that might assist me,' said Mina, with some energy. 'I wish I did not have to trouble you with this but my brothers are rarely here for me to consult and of course they have not seen Miss Eustace for themselves or formed an opinion of her.'

'I will endeavour to be worthy of your trust,' said Dr Hamid, very solemnly, 'but I find it difficult to imagine what you might do without clear evidence of wrongdoing. You cannot accuse someone of a crime, either to their face or to another person, or, more difficult still, of the intention to commit a crime, without proof. An accusation without foundation is in itself a crime.'

'Yes,' Mina agreed, 'and I am not in a position to acquire evidence, especially without knowing the intended victim.'

'Even supposing there to be one,' said Dr Hamid. 'You must consider the possibility that your fears are unfounded.'

In the face of such undeniable good sense, Mina did consider. 'You are right, of course,' she said at last, in a calmer frame of mind. 'I have been too alarmed by reading about undoubted frauds and have concluded that Miss Eustace is of their number. But as you rightly say, I have no evidence. She may be no more than a sixpenny sideshow after all, and harmless enough. From what I have read it is private séances with a single client where mediums bent on extortion may practise their designs on an unprotected individual, and Miss Eustace does not conduct those.' There was a long thoughtful pause. Dr Hamid looked worried, and Mina, seeing his expression, understood. 'Or does she? If she does, you must tell me.'

'I think,' he said, hesitantly, 'I think it is possible that she may, or at least might do so if asked. There was some talk following an earlier séance; Mrs Gaskin said that Miss Eustace could do a great deal more than produce rappings and lights; she could bring personal messages from loved ones who have passed, but it was harder to do so where a crowd was gathered together, because the energy of many in once place was confusing to the spirits.'

'Did she say that Miss Eustace was willing to conduct private consultations?'

'She did not suggest it herself, but one of the ladies asked if such a thing was possible, and she said it might be.'

'They are subtler than I thought,' said Mina, 'letting the dupes carve their own path. Did anyone actually ask her to arrange such a consultation?'

Dr Hamid looked uncomfortable. 'No, it was just a general conversation, but the information did arouse considerable interest. It did cross my mind that …' He shook his head. 'No matter.'

Mina could only pity the unhappy man before her. 'I don't suppose there was any mention of payment?' she said gently. 'There so rarely is.'

'Not in so many words.' Dr Hamid peered into the empty teapot, and gazed thoughtfully at the crumbs on the sandwich plate, as though considering whether or not to ring for more after all.

'You must tell me everything you can remember,' Mina demanded. 'A hint, a glance, an allegorical tale, there must have been *some* communication.'

He was surprised, but did his best. 'There was a suggestion that only serious enquirers would benefit.'

'By serious I suppose they mean those able to pay more than a guinea, perhaps much more,' said Mina. 'Of course, the Gaskins may be as much dupes as anyone else, lured by the promise of celebrity. At present, Miss Eustace feeds off them, but the professor hopes one day to publish his book, and give lectures, or even found a chair at a university.'

'Professor and Mrs Gaskin will not be amenable to any suggestion that Miss Eustace is a trickster,' said Dr Hamid, 'and those of her devotees who choose to pay large sums for consultations may pronounce themselves satisfied with what they receive.'

'Until they find their bank accounts empty and see what fools they have been,' said Mina, 'and then of course it will be too late, and I for one will regret having stood by and allowed it.' She opened her reticule and drew out the booklet about Mr Home, and the pages of the Dialectical Society report which included Dr Edmunds's statement. 'Please borrow these and read them,' she said. 'It will show you that the dangers are very real, and also how a clever man, a medical man, was not deceived by performances which fooled others. In the case of Mr Home, the law did take his victim's part, but it was only after she herself accused him, and she was fortunate in that she acted quickly and was able to recover her funds. Others might not be so prompt, and what consolation would it be to them if they saw the criminals put in prison but were themselves left destitute? Once you have read this, we will speak again and decide what to do.'

He raised his eyebrows, possibly at the word 'we', but took the pages from her. 'I am really not sure what can be done,' he said. 'You cannot force a victim of a crime to take action if they do not believe there has been a crime. They would undoubtedly defend Miss Eustace against any allegations, and the only person to suffer would be you.'

'You are right, of course,' said Mina, 'and I do appreciate that to accuse someone of a felony without evidence is a serious matter. But what I might perhaps be able to do is demonstrate that Miss Eustace is a false medium. If I succeeded then her dupes would abandon her and she would not be able to part innocent victims from their money.'

'And if her powers prove to be genuine?' Dr Hamid pointed out. 'We must not have closed minds.'

'If she is genuine,' said Mina, 'then she should delight in having her powers put to the test. She should welcome all and every test that there is; she should *ask* to be tested, *demand* it. If she is proven to be true it can only add to her fame, and increase the numbers of her devotees. I would follow her myself.'

'But Professor Gaskin has already been testing her powers and is satisfied that they are genuine,' Dr Hamid objected, 'and he has a world of experience and special apparatus. Could you carry out a test that would be any better than he could perform?'

'Yes, I could,' said Mina, 'because he seeks to measure the phenomena and not to question them. I suppose I could ask if I might move about the room during the proceedings but I feel quite certain that that would never be allowed. In fact the arrangement of the room and the conduct of the séance, the holding of hands, the positioning of Professor and Mrs Gaskin – all these things are designed to ensure that no one can rise from their seat, or even turn and look about them without anyone else knowing about it.'

'Miss Eustace would no doubt protest that such movement would disturb her energy,' said Dr Hamid.

'No doubt,' said Mina, dryly. 'But can you not see that we are tied to our seats as much as she? The conditions she demands are supposedly to ensure that she is best able to produce phenomena, but do they not also aid deception and prevent us from applying unwanted tests?'

He looked down at the papers in his hands.

'The full document is some four hundred pages,' said Mina.

'Which I am sure you have read in its entirety,' he said. 'This will suffice me for the present. Was there anything in the report to suggest how you might proceed?'

'No, only because the authors were too trusting or lacked boldness. I only know that we must expose the fraud in a manner that cannot be denied; act quickly and decisively; give her no warning of what we mean to do.' Mina gave the matter some thought while Dr Hamid looked on silently, his expression suggesting mounting disquiet, if not for the fate of the widows of Brighton then for Mina.

'I think,' she said at last, 'that if there is another apparition we must find some means of seizing it before it disappears. If it is truly the ghost of Archibald Whinstone then it will melt into mist. If it is a mop with a false beard then we will show it to the company for what it is, and Miss Eustace will be quite exploded.'

'But if it *was* a mop with a false beard, which it may have been, it was wielded by no hand that we could see, appeared from nowhere and then vanished again,' Dr Hamid reminded her. 'Can you explain that?'

'I can explain nothing as yet,' said Mina. 'There are too many things that we are not allowed to see or touch. If we were to take matters into our own hands, however, the explanation may become apparent.'

'I think we ought to proceed very carefully,' said Dr Hamid, cautiously. 'I do not wish to insult a lady. Perhaps we might ask her – in the interests of science – if she would submit to a test.'

'Which she would either refuse, or else, since she has warning of our intentions, arrange matters to her own liking,' said Mina, frustrated that he did not share the urgency of her concern. 'We *must* surprise her.'

He shook his head. 'Even if I was willing to consent to such a thing, which, I must make it clear, I am not, since from what you say it seems to involve committing an assault, I think it is impossible to make a plan as we have no means of knowing what we might be presented with. So far each of Miss Eustace's demonstrations has differed from the others. The phenomena we saw on the last occasion were unlike anything I have seen before.'

Mina realised that, while interested in the issue as an intellectual question, he was not as determinedly sceptical as she and quite unwilling to take the bull by the horns. He of course, as a professional man, had far more to lose by making a public demonstration. 'Do you agree,' she said, 'that the matter is of some importance, and that at the very least we should continue to attend Miss Eustace's séances and keep our eyes and ears open and see what more we can learn?'

To that he was more than happy to agree. Mina realised that she had quite a task in hand if she was to bring Dr Hamid unreservedly on to her side. To expose trickery might need a capability for rapid action, and a measure of size and strength, all of which were beyond her. Dr Hamid had these attributes but he lacked her conviction and recklessness.

It was with this in mind that the very next day Mina went to see Anna Hamid at the baths and asked if she might be shown how to do the strengthening exercises. Anna, detecting a fresh and possibly dangerous determination in her visitor, was careful to warn Mina not to try to do too much at once. She demonstrated some simple movements that required no apparatus, the raising and lowering of the arms, or extending and holding them out to the sides. Some further exercises could be carried out while holding a light staff, such as a broom handle. She told Mina that she must not on any account twist her body or make jumps, and if any exercise caused her a moment's discomfort she should stop at once. Only when Mina had mastered these simple callisthenics and could perform them properly and without pain should she take the next step. Mina asked what the next step might be and Anna declined to reveal this in case Mina decided to press ahead with it before she was ready. It was, of course, exactly what Mina had in mind, but she was obliged to accept the inevitable and do as Anna directed her. One day, she promised herself, she would be strong.

Mina returned home to find her mother with a sour and angry expression, drinking hot tea and stabbing at a currant cake as if it had mortally offended her. Louisa's ruse to excite the cream of Brighton society with the accomplishments of Mr Bradley had worked rather too well. The clamour for his healing circle had become so great that he had been obliged to inform her that the Scarletti parlour was now quite inadequate to accommodate all the attendees and he had instead hired a nearby meeting room for his next gathering. Louisa, who had hoped that Mr Bradley's popularity would result in further fashionable salons *chez* Scarletti, was understandably annoyed. Mina tried to soothe her mother by suggesting that she could still hold elegant social events at home, a literary or musical circle perhaps. She was a little mollified and Mina, to her immense relief, soon saw her engaged with new plans that did not involve Mr Bradley.

Mina had learned enough to understand that the next step in her campaign to discover more about Miss Eustace must be to establish a reputation as an unquestioning believer in that lady's mediumistic powers. Her ability not only to be admitted to a séance but to be placed in a position most advantageous for exposing fraud depended entirely on her convincing everyone concerned that she was a true adherent, one who could with confidence be positioned in a place of trust where she could be relied upon to protect the medium from prying suspicious folk. Since so much of what mediums and supposed healers did was to tell people what they wished to hear, Mina found it amusing that she was making Miss Eustace a victim of her own methods.

Even her mother would not be fooled by such a sudden conversion, so Mina began with a careful and humble approach, explaining that ever since attending the séance she had thought long and deeply about what she had seen, had found herself quite unable to explain it away by any natural arguments, and was eager to see more. Louisa looked pleased. She said that Miss Eustace was increasingly in demand, and as well as the séances at the Gaskins' rooms she was also being called upon to give demonstrations in other houses, including some of the most elegant in Brighton. Tickets were hard to come by, but she thought they would always be available to sincere persons. Mina tried her hardest to look sincere, and Louisa melted and said she was sure to be able to get tickets.

Mina was extremely grateful to learn that her mother, who had not forgiven Mr Bradley for deserting her parlour for the bleak space of a meeting hall that could accommodate a hundred invalids, did not think she would be troubling herself to attend any more of the healing circles. In any case the forthcoming meeting was to take place on the same evening as Miss Eustace's next séance at the Gaskins' and she could hardly attend both.

There was one very important piece of information about Miss Eustace which was, felt Mina, being withheld. Whether this was deliberate or not she could not be sure, so she essayed a gentle probe to test the water.

'I understand that Miss Eustace does not lodge with Professor and Mrs Gaskin?' she asked.

'No,' said her mother, 'and that is to avoid any suggestion that she is able to arrange the room in advance. I think that is very sensible. Sceptical people will seize on the smallest thing and make some great difficulty out of it, so she has quite done away with that.'

Mina thought that since the Gaskins were such devotees there would be no difficulty in Miss Eustace asking them to arrange the séance room exactly as she would wish, but she did not mention this.

'I wonder where she *does* lodge?' she asked, with the air of the idly curious to whom the precise answer was not of any importance. 'These sceptical persons would surely complain if they thought that she was living in grand style somewhere. But she does not strike me as someone who would do so. She seems to be a very quiet and modest lady.'

'No, luxury and outward show are not at all to her taste,' her mother assured her. 'Miss Eustace's needs are very few. I believe she has a small and simple apartment where she can retire alone in order to rest and restore her energy.'

'Her peace and privacy are of the utmost importance,' said Mina. 'She must be quite exhausted after her demonstrations, and I am sure she would not want curious persons intruding on her rest.'

'Coarse newspapermen making a great noise, and sceptical persons with their bad thoughts,' said Louisa, with a shudder. 'She must stay well away from them or it upsets her. Professor Gaskin, who of course knows about such things, says that she reminds him of a delicate balance that needs to be perfectly aligned if it is to be true. That is why he and Mrs Gaskin care for her and ensure she is protected at all times.'

It was a small matter but another little clue, thought Mina. Miss Eustace was keeping her address a secret. There might be any number of perfectly understandable reasons why that was the case, but it was also very possible that the lady had something to hide. Quite what it was she might be hiding Mina did not know, but she was now determined that at least some of the lady's secrets would be revealed at the next séance.

Mina had no plan in mind when she attended her second séance, but she had resolved to watch carefully for any opportunity to learn more about Miss Eustace. All she knew was that great wonders were about to be performed in front of her eyes that would convince even the most sceptical person of the divine truth of spiritualism. Either that or there would be a demonstration of blatant trickery that would only fool the gullible. Mina, as a sceptic pretending to be gullible, felt that she was there in disguise, like a spy sent to a foreign court to learn secrets. She was a deceiver, appearing to be of the shining faithful but harbouring deep in her bosom the dark seeds of doubt. It was quite an adventure. She tried at first to conceal her feelings of excitement beneath a calm exterior, but then saw that this was unnecessary. Her keen anticipation would be interpreted by believers as a quasi-religious ecstasy wholly appropriate to the situation.

Dr Hamid was there, and greeted Mina and her mother with a look of deep concern it was impossible for him to conceal.

'Poor man,' said Mina's mother, when they were out of earshot. 'I do so hope Miss Eustace can bring him comfort.' Mina felt sure, however, that the doctor's glance was not an expression of inner suffering, but an unspoken warning that she should not commit an indiscretion. Mina had never committed an indiscretion, but when she came to think about it she was twenty-five and single and independent and might therefore do as she liked. Perhaps indiscretion was something she lacked in her daily life and she ought to try it at least once. She knew that unless something very remarkable was to occur she could not count on Dr Hamid to assist her. Nevertheless his presence as a level-headed scientific observer was of considerable value.

The Gaskins' parlour had been rearranged since Mina's earlier visit. No longer were there two rows of chairs, but a large round table had been brought in and dining chairs in sufficient numbers for the company arranged around it. At least the table had not been pushed close to a wall to trap doubters as the Dialectical Society's Dr Edmunds had been trapped at the Davenports' failed séance; there was more than enough room for a person or disembodied spirit lights or flying violins to proceed about its perimeter. The table was bare, and Mina wondered if this was to prevent breakages in case it was to suddenly tip and tilt, which she knew from her reading that they were, in the right company, prone to do.

Besides Mina's mother, her party of ladies and Dr Hamid, the others in attendance were a young gentleman called Mr Clee, and the two widowed sisters, of whom the younger, Mrs Mowbray, a lady nearing fifty with a very prominent bust, was making her interest in Dr Hamid increasingly obvious, eyeing him as if he was something she might like to purchase and take home. Her face bore unmistakable traces of paint.

Miss Whinstone was making sure, both noisily and repeatedly, that everyone knew she was braving the dangers of heart failure yet again. Mrs Bettinson was almost welded to her side, holding her up with a firm grasp on her arm, as if she had been a life-sized puppet. As Mrs Bettinson moved, so Miss Whinstone moved, and they walked together like a pair of comedy dancers on a stage. Every so often the legs of the puppet seemed to fail and the lady threatened to collapse, or at least claimed that she was about to collapse, and Mrs Bettinson's hand tightened. Mrs Gaskin sailed up with some kind words for Miss Whinstone, assuring her that she was a very important member of the gathering, and expressing the hope that she would not think of going since her presence was an inspiration to the spirits. She must not think, said Mrs Gaskin with a smile like medicinal syrup, that the dear spirits meant any harm; they were a benevolent influence and could do only good. Miss Whinstone, fortified by Mrs Gaskin's praise and a small glass of sherry, decided to remain. Louisa, meanwhile, was watching Mrs Gaskin very closely, and with an unfriendly air. For a moment Mina thought hopefully that she was beginning to have reservations about the séances, and then she realised that her mother, with her nose still very firmly out of joint after losing the opportunity to preside over Mr Bradley's healing salon, was jealous.

The dark curtains that had enclosed one corner of the room had been drawn back and Professor Gaskin was eagerly bustling about and encouraging everyone present to take a look at everything in the recess for reassurance that no trickery of any kind was involved. He spoke mournfully of letters recently published in the *Gazette* written by ignorant, hypercritical and ill-mannered persons. Such people could only serve to upset refined individuals such as Miss Eustace, and he had taken great care that these destructive influences should not be permitted to attend until such time as they became humble enough to receive the truth. Only the other day, he revealed, a man from the *Gazette* had applied for a ticket and had been very firmly refused. The company murmured approbation for this sensible precaution.

Mina joined those who dared to look into the space behind the curtains, but saw and felt nothing out of the ordinary. It might have aroused suspicion of her intentions had she passed her hands over the walls but a pretended loss of balance, which she was sure would have appeared excusable in one such as herself, seemed to force her to put one palm to the wall. She found it solid, with nothing to suggest any recent alterations, and no secret doors or cavities. The little table with the hand bell, tambourine, paper and pencil had been pushed into the corner, and Mina was able unobtrusively to satisfy herself that the paper was a single unfolded unmarked sheet. The only other item in the space was the chair. The carpeting of the room ran right to the edges of the floor, and looked to be well bedded into place.

Mina rejoined the general throng in the room. 'The cabinet is, as you have seen, no more than it appears to be,' observed Mrs Gaskin with slightly narrowed eyes.

'But it is a place of great wonders,' said Mina, with a bright happy smile. 'I confess to entertaining some hope that if I stand there long enough I might benefit from the power of the spirits which must surely be very concentrated on that spot.'

She touched her hand to her shoulder as if it pained her, which that evening, thanks to Anna Hamid's ministrations, it did not. 'Is that too much to expect?' she asked plaintively.

'Not at all,' said Mrs Gaskin, in a more kindly tone. 'Dear young lady, your faith does you credit. The spirits are our friends and watch over us. If you trust in them,' she added with great assurance, 'you *will* be rewarded.'

Young Mr Clee, however, a trim and active gentleman with a sweep of dark Byronic curls, was a bold, even impudent individual, who had no reservations about making a public display of scepticism. Once the recess was empty of other guests, he strode inside and examined the walls minutely, first passing his hands over their surface, hitting them soundly with his fists, and closely examining any marks that excited his suspicion. He next stamped upon the floor as if testing for trapdoors, peered under the little table, scrutinised everything on it, and lifted the chair to look underneath. He even attempted to lift the edge of the carpet, but it was too securely fastened to suggest that anything might be hidden beneath it. Finding nothing untoward, he folded his arms and shook his head with a very puzzled look that was almost comical. Perhaps it was his bemused expression that led the Gaskins not to regard him as a serious threat to the proceedings, and he was not asked to leave, but the professor and his wife, after a long and earnest conversation of which he was undoubtedly the subject, kept him under careful observation.

Professor Gaskin started urging the visitors to sit around the table, and the troublesome Mr Clee was so shepherded that he found himself situated at the furthest location from the corner that had so captivated his attention. Once everyone was in place the curtains were drawn to conceal the recess.

The maid came to the door and announced Miss Eustace, which created a surge of excitement, as if the medium was about to walk in with stars and moons and rainbows sparkling about her head. That lady, with her customary demure and humble deportment, entered the room without fuss. A hush fell as she was conducted to a vacant place at the table, the one nearest the recess, where she reposed with a Gaskin guarding her on either side.

Mina had expected the gas to be turned off as it had been before, but this time the room remained lit. She was not in an unfavourable place, since she could see the curtains to her right. There was no cloth on the table and Mina laid her hands on its surface and found it very smooth and polished. Had she or anyone else wanted to move the table while their hands were in such a position this would have been quite impossible, as they could not have obtained any purchase. It was not a heavy table by any means, and anyone, even Mina, was capable of effecting some movement, but only by grasping it at the edges in a very pronounced and obvious manner. She determined to watch and see if anyone attempted to grasp the table, but this possibility was immediately removed when the company was asked to hold hands. 'We take hands,' said Professor Gaskin, 'to form a complete circle and concentrate our energy. I beg you all not to release your hands until asked. We will now sing 'Praise God From Whom All Blessings Flow'.'

Mina realised that she had omitted to see if the table was upon casters. She would have to do so later. Her mother was holding her right hand very tightly with thin strong fingers like a pair of sugar nippers. Dr Hamid sat to her left, and as he took her hand she sensed a considerable strength from him, but without the crushing muscular pressure that so many gentlemen thoughtlessly inflicted. Perhaps, she concluded, his knowledge of bodily massage, applied to both frail and robust, had given him this rare sensitivity. She looked at Miss Eustace. The medium's eyes were closed, and she had drawn a shawl over her head, and was bending forward as if she wanted to seal herself away from the world and all its corporeal creatures.

Once the badly sung hymn had reached its merciful end, all fell silent. Ten pairings of clasped hands rested upon the table. Nothing moved. They were all seated very close to the table's edge, and while hands and arms and the tabletop were all clearly visible to everyone, there was, thought Mina, no method of knowing what feet might freely do.

It was no surprise to Mina, therefore, when she heard a few light knocking sounds that vibrated through the wood of the table. These were followed, however, by other sounds which she felt sure did not originate from the table and could have been produced by no one in the room, as they appeared to come from the wall. These noises were very similar in nature to those that had been heard at the previous séance although softer, more like a sharp tapping with knuckles than a stick. The sounds seemed to travel along the far wall then briefly stopped, and after a few moments appeared to be coming from a side wall. Everyone followed the noises with their eyes but there was nothing to be seen.

'Spirit, make yourself known!' said Miss Eustace. It was the first time that Mina had heard the lady speak, if one discounted the sighing and moaning that had accompanied her previous exhibition, and it was a melodious voice, which, while soft, suggested that it could, if required, flow thrillingly through a large space.

Three very loud raps came from the centre of the table, which made everyone start. Mr Clee tried to peer underneath but from his position was not able to see to the table's centre, a situation he clearly found frustrating.

'Archibald, is that you?' asked Miss Whinstone, querulously.

There were three stronger raps. It was hard for Mina to tell, but they appeared to be coming from the underside of the table and not its top.

'This has happened before,' said Professor Gaskin, excitedly. 'The spirits always take three raps to mean yes, and one is no. Miss Whinstone, you may question the spirit if you wish.'

Mina wondered what the spirit of Archibald Whinstone might be doing crouching underneath a dining table, something she felt sure he had not been in the habit of doing while alive.

'Archibald – will we meet again in Heaven?' asked Miss Whinstone.

Three raps sounded very emphatically, and the lady could not withhold a sob.

'And when will that come to pass?' she blurted out.

There was a moment of shocked silence as everyone, including possibly the spirit of Archibald Whinstone, took in the enormity of her question. 'Dear lady, the spirits will not answer such a question,' said Professor Gaskin, gently. 'Some things are known only to God.'

The table gave a curious little motion; Mina might almost have said it twitched. It was not attempting to slide or rise, rather it appeared unsettled and Miss Whinstone gave a little scream of fright. 'The spirit is disturbed,' said the professor, but Mr Clee burst out, 'Oh, take no notice! I am sure that Miss Eustace was making the raps with her foot and now she is obviously moving the table with her knee.' Several of the people around the table gasped.

'Sir!' exclaimed Professor Gaskin. 'That is an insult to a very fine and selfless lady!'

'Well, I'll not see any more of this nonsense!' said Mr Clee. 'It is an outrage to the intelligence! If Miss Eustace can make the table rise up in the air without being near it *and* without touching it, why then I might say I'd seen something.'

Miss Eustace raised her head and gazed on Mr Clee with an expression of great calm. Her mouth curved softly into a smile. Even he, with his contemptuous scowl was taken aback, and said no more. She rose slowly to her feet, her face bearing an expression of sublime and intense concentration. She let go of the Gaskins' hands, and stepped back a pace, her chair sliding back from the table's edge, lifting her arms like the wings of a bird. She had the rapt and astonished attention of everyone in the room. With great deliberation, she let her arms sink downwards, until her palms hovered just above the tabletop, and there she stood, eyes closed for a full minute during which no one, even Mr Clee, dared speak or move. She then took a deep breath, and her hands trembled as they gradually rose until they were more than four inches above the table. As she did so, to everyone's amazement, the table rose with her. She was gasping, and there was a flush of moisture on her forehead.

Miss Whinstone moaned, and Mr Clee, who was placed directly opposite Miss Eustace, looked on aghast. He had jumped to his feet, and was holding his hands over the table as if trying to feel the power that was making it rise. Everyone had now taken his or her hands from the tabletop. Mina, still in the circle, could see the table rising before her, but with no idea of how it had been achieved. She was small enough to glance underneath but this only confirmed that all four legs of the table had risen from the floor and there was neither a secret mechanism nor a hidden confederate. The table began to vibrate, and then quite abruptly, it fell back to the floor with a loud crash.

Miss Eustace sat down again. Breathlessly, she took a linen kerchief from her sleeve and dabbed her forehead.

'I don't know what to say!' exclaimed the formerly sceptical Mr Clee. 'I confess that I came here with the express design of proving fraud but now I see that I was wrong – very wrong.' He hurried to the medium's side. 'Miss Eustace, please accept my sincerest apologies.'

She bowed her head. 'Of course.'

'I suggest,' said Professor Gaskin, 'that we all rest for a short while. Miss Eustace, will you be able to continue?'

'I will,' she said. 'I feel a strong connection with my guide this evening, but I need to gather my strength again.'

Miss Eustace was brought a glass of water from which she sipped, then she rose and went to the hidden corner, drew the curtains aside and sat upon the chair leaning forward a little, as one who prayed. There she remained motionless.

Mina and the others left the table and gathered into little knots of eager whisperers to talk of what they had seen. She would have liked to make a close examination of the table, but since she was affecting the manner of an uncritical believer, dared not do anything that might suggest prying. She was able, however, to see with a quick glance that the table was not on casters and its legs were very slender. The amount of force required to move it was no longer an especially relevant question, however, since it had clearly risen while Miss Eustace was not in contact with it.

Mr Clee was in any case doing Mina's work for her, since he started busily examining the table, running his hands over its surface, feeling about its edges, and even getting down on his hands and knees and looking underneath. At last he stood and shook his head. 'I am astonished,' he said at last. 'I had thought I might witness a simple sleight of hand, but I cannot explain it at all, apart that is, from the operation of some supernatural agency.' Mina thought that the gentleman was too easily convinced.

Miss Whinstone was swaying in an alarming fashion, but Mrs Bettinson made sure that she tottered into a seat, and having been prepared for such an emergency, produced a fan, which she used with some energy. 'Dear Archibald!' exclaimed Miss Whinstone. 'I do so hope I didn't offend him!'

'Well, he was a mild enough creature when he was alive so I shouldn't think he'd be easily offended now he's dead,' said Mrs Bettinson.

Mrs Gaskin came and took the suffering Miss Whinstone by the hand. 'Please do not distress yourself,' she said. 'I do not think your brother's spirit was offended at all, rather he was showing a commendable sense of delicacy by not replying to a question of a personal nature while in the company of others.'

'Then – will he answer me while I am alone?' exclaimed Miss Whinstone. 'I have so prayed to hear from him!'

Mrs Gaskin patted her hand. 'His spirit will be directed by Miss Eustace. If you so wish, I will recommend that she make an appointment to call on you. You will be assured then of a result.'

Miss Whinstone burst into tears of gratitude, and even had the strength to wave away Mrs Bettinson's intrusive fan. And now, thought Mina, it was certain; Miss Eustace was offering private consultations, much as Mr Home had done, and the unhappy Miss Whinstone was her dupe. It was useless, of course, to say anything to the lady. Mina could only watch and hope that the comfort of conversation with a deceased brother was not bought too dearly.

After a short while, Professor Gaskin suggested that the next exhibition was about to commence. He could not promise what might occur, perhaps nothing, perhaps a great wonder. He asked Mr Clee to assist him in ensuring that Miss Eustace was securely tied to her chair, and the young man agreed with some enthusiasm. As the knots were tied Mr Clee gazed up into the lady's face with an expression of very pronounced admiration, although her features remained serenely unmoved.

Professor Gaskin asked for volunteers to assure themselves that the knots were securely tied and that it was impossible for Miss Eustace to rise from her chair. Dr Hamid came forward for this duty and Mrs Mowbray almost elbowed her sister aside in her eagerness to assist him. This done, the curtains were drawn, concealing Miss Eustace from view, the candle lit, and the gas turned down, and everyone repaired to the now motionless table, and held hands in a circle. Professor Gaskin blew out the candle, and they were all plunged into the dark.

There was another round of hymn singing, and another silence, but barely a minute later the bell and the tambourine sounded from behind the curtains. Mina kept her eyes on the shrouded corner, looking for the emergence of stuffed gloves or bearded mops, but to her surprise there was a faint whisper of sound as the curtains parted, and a figure, enveloped in a pearlescent glow, was revealed.

There was an intake of breath from all around her. The figure was quite still, like a statue, or a life-size doll. Mina, who thought it might be a doll, although she could not explain where it had come from, was expecting that after it had attracted the admiration of the onlookers, the curtains would simply close and hide it from view, but then the apparition raised its arm towards the company, very slowly and gracefully, and extended its fingers. Mina was still not convinced that the thing before her was anything more than a manufactured object that would have been better employed in a booth on the West Pier, but then it began to come forward, and emerged completely from behind the curtains. It was covered from head to foot in a fine filmy drapery, which shone with its own luminescence. Its form was female, that much was apparent, but it was rather taller than Miss Eustace. The features were indistinct, as if seen through a cloud, and the arms and hands were bare although covered from shoulder to fingertips in a soft mist of light. It was not clad as a lady might decently be clad, but it was a thing of nature, having hardly more than a layer or two of glowing veils covering its form. Even the shape of its lower limbs could be seen as if through a fine gauze. If it resembled anything it was like a marble statue of a Greek goddess, except that it had every appearance of being alive. It walked forward very slowly. It was not, thought Mina, the usual walk of a living creature, and its feet, assuming it had them, made no sound as they traversed the carpeted floor.

'Do not be afraid!' whispered Professor Gaskin. 'But above all I beg you not to touch the apparition unless it touches you. It is Miss Eustace's spirit guide, assembled into a form that we can see using energy drawn from the medium's own body. Any attempt to take hold of it would result in Miss Eustace's death, for it would melt the substance of the form in an instant, and it would not then be able to flow back into her.'

'But where is Miss Eustace!' exclaimed Mr Clee.

'She is still behind the curtain, but she must not be disturbed.'

'I must see!' He leapt to his feet.

'Please, no, that would be very dangerous!' cried Professor Gaskin, but before he could do anything, the apparition approached Mr Clee and extended a hand in a soft fluid movement, laying a light touch upon his arm.

'Oh!' exclaimed Clee. 'It is a wondrous thing!' To his astonishment, the apparition took him by the hand and began drawing him towards the curtained corner, and he, as if mesmerised, followed.

'She approves,' said Professor Gaskin. 'Do not be afraid, but go with her. You may look behind the curtain but you must be very careful and above all, do not disturb the body of the medium.'

Mr Clee approached the recess and cautiously drew back the curtain. The most powerful source of light in the room was the glow of the apparition's garments. It did not re-enter the recess but stood to one side and with a gesture indicated that Mr Clee should go in. Everyone craned forward, and it was just possible to see the form of Miss Eustace, her shawl drawn over her head, slumped in her chair. Mr Clee hesitated, then passed through the curtains, which closed behind him. A few moments elapsed, during which Mina wondered if he would ever return, then the curtains parted once again and he emerged and faced the company, his face, bathed in the glow of spirit light, pale with awe.

'It is she,' he said, in a voice that trembled with emotion, 'undoubtedly she, living and breathing, but in a trance.'

Gaskin rose and took the astonished and visibly shaken young man by the elbow and led him back to his chair. 'The apparition before us is Phoebe,' he said, 'the creature of radiant light, whose brilliance casts out doubt and ignorance. All who see her must believe.'

'I believe!' exclaimed Miss Whinstone, and there was a general chorus of assent, in which Mina joined.

Phoebe seemed to enjoy this approbation, for she showed no signs of wanting to depart. She was an accommodating spirit, and tripped lightly about the room turning her head this way and that so that all present were favoured with her filmy gaze.

'Does she speak?' asked Mrs Mowbray.

'Yes, ask her to speak!' exclaimed Mrs Bettinson.

'She might at least nod or shake her head in answer to questions,' said Mina's mother. 'Or why else has she come before us?' she added tetchily.

'Tell us, Phoebe,' said Professor Gaskin, 'does the spirit world you inhabit have houses and churches such as this one?'

Phoebe slowly nodded her head.

'And will all of the faithful have homes there?'

Another nod.

'Are all those who dwell there happy?' asked Mrs Gaskin.

Not unexpectedly there was an emphatic nod.

'And do they love and worship the Lord God?'

The graceful spirit held her arms open to them all and nodded again as if to demonstrate that they were all embraced by the great love of God. She moved about them once again, holding a hand over the head of each person present, as if imparting a blessing, then she turned and walked back towards the curtained recess.

'She tires,' said Professor Gaskin. 'Ask no more of her, I beg you. This is the longest she has ever appeared and we are truly favoured today!'

As Phoebe walked past Mina she felt a sudden impulse. She rose stiffly to her feet and sighed and groaned aloud as if in pain. She was easily able to slip her left hand from Dr Hamid's clasp and such was the surprise of her movement that she was even able to escape her mother's hand.

'Mina? What is it? Sit down at once!' urged Louisa, and Dr Hamid started up to assist, but Mina staggered, throwing out her arms, and her weight, such as it was, fell against the glowing apparition. She had been hoping to do no more than gain some sense of how solid or otherwise the thing might be, but to her amazement, while she was careful not to fall to the ground, the radiant Phoebe, unbalanced and surprised, toppled and fell to the floor with an audible thump.

Mrs Gaskin cried out, Miss Whinstone screamed, and more importantly Phoebe gave a gasp that sounded very like 'Ooof!'.

'Oh, I am so very sorry,' Mina exclaimed, 'how clumsy I am! Please allow me to help.' She reached out to the figure on the carpet and offered to assist Phoebe to her feet, but before she could do so, an enraged Mrs Gaskin had seized hold of her by both arms and pulled her roughly away.

'Do not touch her!' she cried. 'Who knows what damage you have done!'

Phoebe appeared unhurt; indeed in her fall she had acquired a new nimbleness to her movements and jumping up, she hurried into the recess before anyone else dared to try and help.

The table had been abandoned and everyone was now on his or her feet. Someone turned up the gas, revealing a great many shocked, flustered and angry faces. 'Please, everyone remain calm!' said Professor Gaskin.

Dr Hamid came forward. 'With your permission, Professor, I would like to tend to Miss Eustace and ensure that she is well.'

Professor Gaskin threw up his arms in despair. 'I dare not permit it, sir, I dare not!' he exclaimed. 'No one must disturb her now, not by sight or touch. The form of Phoebe is made from Miss Eustace's own body. While it appears, the lady is in a very fragile and weakened condition, hovering between this world and the next. It takes fully two minutes, sometimes more for the substance of Phoebe to be reabsorbed into Miss Eustace's body. If that process is interrupted then Miss Eustace will surely die.'

'Would it help if we all sang a hymn?' asked Mr Clee. 'Only the Lord can help her now.'

'Yes!' exclaimed the professor, seizing upon a straw of comfort. He addressed the company in a voice breaking with emotion. 'Ladies and gentlemen all, we must sing, sing as loud as we can, as if our lives depended on it, as indeed Miss Eustace's very well might.' He began to bellow out, 'Praise My Soul the King of Heaven,' and everyone quickly joined him.

Dr Hamid, seeing that he was not wanted to attend to Miss Eustace, extricated Mina from the infuriated and painful grasp of Mrs Gaskin and drew her to a seat.

'Was that well done?' he asked quietly when the singing had stopped and Professor Gaskin had sunk into a chair, panting with effort.

'I believe so,' said Mina, calmly. 'Why, even Mrs Gaskin may in time find it in her heart to forgive a poor cripple. My mother will not forgive me, but then she never does. But I know now that Phoebe is as solid as I am, and speaks and breathes.'

'You have taken a very great risk,' he said.

'The greatest risk was damage to myself,' said Mina.

He looked concerned. 'Are you hurt?'

She smiled. 'Only from contact with Mrs Gaskin. I have had worse pain and greater bruises. I will recover without any attention.'

'And what of Miss Eustace? You are not anxious for her?'

'Oh, I am sure she is unharmed and will very soon emerge triumphant.'

Mrs Mowbray hovered nearby. 'That was a very fine thing to do!' she exclaimed, sarcastically, 'but I suppose poor thing, you could not help it. Now we must hope that Miss Eustace lives, but I daresay even if she does, you will not be invited here again.'

'I fear that may be correct,' said Dr Hamid. Mrs Mowbray tried very hard to place herself where he had no choice but to admire her, but on discovering that there was no position where that might be possible, she scowled at Mina and drifted away. She was soon in conversation with Mr Clee.

Mina, resting under Dr Hamid's watchful eye, saw her mother bearing down upon her, and was bracing herself for the consequences, when she was alerted by a great gasp from the other members of the company as Miss Eustace reappeared from behind the curtains. The medium seemed exhausted, and held her hand to her forehead, staggering as though she might fall. Dr Hamid rose to go to her, but Professor and Mrs Gaskin hurried to offer their support, and shunning all other help, quickly conducted their stricken protégée from the room.

Mr Clee took it upon himself to fully pull back the curtains and reveal to the company that the recess was exactly as it had been before the séance, except for the fact that someone or something had written 'Praise be to God' on the paper.

'Well,' said Louisa, staring down on Mina with barely concealed fury, 'you have not killed Miss Eustace, that is some comfort. You silly girl! I had intended to invite her to our house to conduct a séance there, but she will not come now! It would not even do to send you away, she will be sure to say you are a bad influence and that the spirits will not come.'

'Miss Eustace is as we have seen a good and forgiving person,' said Mr Clee, who had a bright and engaging smile when he was not scowling with suspicion. 'Why, I now see that I was most insulting to her when I came here, and yet when I repented she forgave me and granted me the blessing she gives to her most devoted admirers. Perhaps, Miss Scarletti, your sensation of faintness and your fall was only because you were overcome with the power exerted by Miss Eustace, something for which you can scarcely be blamed.'

Louisa gave him a derisive look, but said no more on the subject.

There was a little more desultory conversation, but Mina did not wish to discuss the event with Dr Hamid while others were present, and Mr Clee had taken some of the wind out of her mother's sails. The maid arrived with tea, but the Gaskins did not reappear and shortly afterwards everyone departed.

As they travelled home in the company of Miss Whinstone and Mrs Bettinson, Mina, with the mark of Mrs Gaskin's fingertips still burning on her arms, was enveloped in the thundercloud of her mother's displeasure. Since Louisa did not address Mina directly but spoke exclusively to her friends about her difficult daughter as if she was not there, Mina felt entitled to assume that she was not expected to join in the conversation.

She still felt that she could not believe in the reality of what she had seen. It was not that she did not believe in the existence of the immortal soul, but she could not imagine that the souls of the dead would come to earth and play crude tricks. Perhaps there were genuine mediums who received messages from the dead, but Miss Eustace was not, she thought, of their number. Mina was unable to explain how the table had risen, although she thought it to be a trick within the abilities of a good conjurer. She was in no doubt, however, that the radiant Phoebe, as advised by Professor Gaskin, was indeed composed of material from the medium's own body, though not in the manner he had implied.

Once home, she avoided her mother's lecture by pleading that she was in pain and needed rest. She took two oranges and went up to her room. There, clasping an orange in each hand, she did her exercises.

Nine

Mina did not want to upset her mother, and had deliberately made her attempt to unmask the apparition appear to be an accident, as anything else would have been a far greater embarrassment. Her failure – and she could only see it as such – did, however, give her the opportunity of making one task serve two purposes, both soothing Louisa's displeasure and acquiring more information. She arranged to call upon Professor Gaskin the very next day, and informed her mother of her intention. Louisa was astonished, and protesting that Mina was only attempting to cause more trouble, forbade her to go. Mina explained that her purpose was to offer her very sincere apologies for what had occurred and she was hoping that her contrition would smooth the way to Miss Eustace being admitted to their home. Her mother was temporarily mollified.

Mina was unsure if Mrs Gaskin would intrude upon her interview with the professor and wished that she was strong enough to resist future violent assaults upon her person, but as it so happened, that lady was addressing a meeting of a charitable society and could not be present.

Mina was shown into the parlour of the Gaskins' lodgings, which while not arranged very differently from the way it had been furnished for the séances, nevertheless appeared to be a quite commonplace room. The table was now in the centre and covered by a cloth, and the dark curtains in the corner had been fully drawn back, to reveal that all that had lain behind them had been removed.

The window curtains were open, and since it was a sunny morning, Mina was able for the first time to see the room bathed in a strong natural light that would surely have revealed any imperfections suggestive of trapdoors and the entrances to secret passages. She saw nothing to excite her suspicions, and as she reflected on this she could feel an idea for a new story rapidly forming in her mind.

Mina was not entirely sure how best to present herself, but hoped that all she really needed to do was say little and allow Professor Gaskin to talk freely. He was, she had observed, a gentleman who took enormous satisfaction in imparting his wisdom to others, sometimes at great length, scarcely pausing to allow them to make their own ideas known, since it was with him a predetermined fact that he knew more on his subject than his listeners. He might have allowed another professor to state his opinions, but not a young woman.

They were seated, but Professor Gaskin chose to perch on his chair like a man just about to rise from it, and Mina took this as an indication that their interview would be a short one.

'Delighted as I am to receive you, Miss Scarletti, I can assure you that an apology is not necessary,' he said when Mina had expressed her remorse for the untoward incident. 'I could see that it was merely an unfortunate accident brought on by a paroxysm of emotion to which ladies are so often prone. Mrs Gaskin, I might say, is of the same opinion.'

'You are too kind, professor,' said Mina, who did not believe for a moment that Mrs Gaskin would be so forgiving. 'Might I ask after the health of Miss Eustace? I would be mortified if I have endangered her delicate constitution.'

'She is entirely recovered,' he reassured her, 'and has taken no ill-effects that would prevent her from undertaking further demonstrations.'

'Oh, that is such a great relief to me!' said Mina with an extravagant display of sincerity. 'I would very much like to call upon her to offer my apologies in person. If you could supply me with her address, I will send her a note.'

He smiled, thinly. 'I will make your sentiments known when next I see her, but Miss Eustace does not receive visitors. Even Mrs Gaskin and I do not call on her. The address of her lodgings is therefore not a matter for public information.'

His tone was kindly but firm, and Mina understood that she would receive no further information on that point. 'Please do reassure Miss Eustace that she has in me a most devoted admirer, and one who hopes to be favoured with personal messages from those loved ones who have departed this earthly life. I trust and hope therefore that I will continue to be permitted to attend Miss Eustace's demonstrations?'

The professor's eyes took on a distant look, and he lowered his head so as not to meet her eager gaze. 'Ah, as to that, if it was simply my own wishes I would have no objection at all, but Miss Eustace feels, and my dear lady wife also feels, that in view of what occurred, which of course we all accept was the purest accident, that your presence might induce a certain – anxiety and thereby create a disturbance in the flow of energy which might prevent any future manifestations.'

'I understand, of course,' said Mina. 'I would not want to be responsible for obstructing the proceedings which would be a great hindrance to the truth being revealed. I know, however, that my mother would be honoured to receive Miss Eustace at our home, and I do hope that she will not be disappointed. If I ask her to write to you on the subject, would be so kind as to pass her letter to Miss Eustace?

'I will certainly do so,' said the professor, who seemed relieved that she had taken the rebuff with such equanimity. He afforded her a hearty smile, and clasped his hands together. 'Is there anything else I can do for you?' he added in a tone that suggested that if there was not, the interview was at an end.

Mina thought quickly, realising that if she was to acquire any more information she must direct the conversation another way.

'If I might ask you a question?'

He had been about to rise from his seat, but sank back again, resuming his position. 'But of course!'

'I know that you have seen Phoebe, Miss Eustace's wonderful spirit guide on other occasions but have you ever touched or been touched by her?'

'Well – I –' he puffed out his cheeks with thought. 'She has on one occasion laid her hand on my sleeve, but that is all.'

'I see. And have any other sitters touched her?'

'Er – no – well, Miss Eustace has always said that if any forms should appear it means grave danger to her if they are grasped and so I have always warned the sitters against it in the strongest possible terms. Phoebe does sometimes offer a light touch as she did to Mr Clee, but no more than that.'

'How interesting,' said Mina. 'So it appears that I am the first person to have anything other than the most superficial contact with her.'

He stared at her. 'Well, yes, so it appears.'

'Perhaps,' Mina ventured, 'my experience could be of some value. I have been told that you are making a scientific study of Miss Eustace and her phenomena. I cannot, of course, offer anything more than my humble observations, and you may do with them as you please.'

'I would be most interested to hear them,' said the professor.

'What I felt,' said Mina, 'very fleetingly, was that there was a form underneath the glowing cloud, a form, if you will pardon me, barely clothed, almost in a state of nature, and most undoubtedly female.'

Professor Gaskin's substantial eyebrows gave a noticeable twitch as if they were about to take flight.

'The delineations of the body were quite unmistakable,' Mina assured him. 'A youthful figure, a miracle of both science and art, which I am sure if we were able to see it without its draperies would dazzle us with its beauty. How Miss Eustace was able to produce such a phenomenon in so short a time is quite mysterious to me.'

'Really?' said Professor Gaskin, who was clearly giving the description some very intense thought.

'Now that I have given the events further consideration I can see that, despite my interruption, the evening was a success. I attended quite unsure of what was to be revealed and came away with a most profound sense that something of very great importance had occurred. And of course Mr Clee, who came hoping to expose a fraud, now seems to be utterly converted!'

'As is so often the case, in my experience,' said Professor Gaskin. 'Even the most hardened sceptics will have their eyes opened to the truth if they were only to stop criticising what others report and go and see for themselves. I have to confess that when I first went to see Miss Eustace in London I was not prepared to be convinced, but I was obliged to conclude against all my previous prejudices, that the phenomena produced by Miss Eustace are genuine, and worthy of serious academic study. I have tried to impress this upon many of my friends in the scientific world, but I am afraid so far without result.'

Mina was about to make an observation concerning the findings of the Dialectical Society but stopped herself just in time. The more ignorant she appeared the more she would learn. 'And are you the *only* man of science studying these phenomena?' she asked.

'There are others, but for the most part they are going about it in quite the wrong way and will not listen to my protests. All they try to do is look for trickery, and since there is no trickery to discover, their work is wasted.' He shook his head despairingly. 'I was able to satisfy myself from the very beginning that I was observing preternormal events under circumstances that absolutely precluded trickery of any kind. Having disposed of that question, I then addressed myself to the important concerns. What I hope to do is discover and describe new laws of science that will explain what we are undoubtedly experiencing. I have been corresponding with Dr William Crookes, a Fellow of the

Royal Society, who is, as far as I can see, the only man of note who is willing to entertain the idea that the phenomena are real and should be studied. In the last year he has been conducting experiments with a Mr Home, but has not thus far published his results. He has recently given me to understand, however, that Mr Home has provided irrefutable evidence of genuine psychic phenomena under rigorous test conditions.' The professor was not as pleased with this result as he might have been, and Mina concluded that he would have been very much happier if the success had not gone to another man.

'I have heard astounding things of Mr Home,' said Mina.

'Oh, I think that Crookes has been very fortunate to secure him,' said Gaskin with a grimace that left Mina in no doubt that it was Crookes's espousal of Home that had led him to seek out a rival exponent.

'If you publish your findings first, then the acclaim will be all yours,' said Mina. 'Are you close to success? I do hope so. If you write a book I should certainly want to purchase a copy.'

'Oh, I would like to say that I have made significant progress, but that, I am afraid, would be overstating my achievements to date. Still, I am well aware that a debate that has been raging for many years will not be resolved in a matter of weeks or even months. I am, after all, asking men of science to entirely remould their ideas. Not, I fear, an easy task. All I can do at present is accumulate evidence, but I am confident that there will come a time when it is so overwhelming that truth will triumph.' He sighed. 'But I believe Mr Crookes will have priority. I am told that the next edition of the *Quarterly Journal of Science* will include an article describing his experiments, with findings that will astonish the world.'

'He must be most gratified that such a highly reputable publication has consented to publish a piece on spiritualism,' observed Mina.

'Ah, well,' said Professor Gaskin with a hint of awkwardness, 'you see, there was no difficulty about that since he is the editor.'

Mina made no comment but resolved to obtain a copy. 'I hope that Mr Crookes has discovered the answer to such mysteries as how Miss Eustace was able to lift the table without touching it. What is your opinion on that point?'

The professor, more comfortable now he saw that he was in the presence of a true enthusiast, leaned back in his chair, rested his hands in his lap and stared at the ceiling. 'I call it vital energy, something the medium is able to exert at a distance from her body. It is quite invisible to most people, of course, and even she is unable to explain it. I imagine it to be like a thread, very fine and strong, that she can throw from her fingertips and use it to grasp and control objects.' He smiled indulgently and leaned forward with a conspiratorial air. 'Would you believe that sceptics who have not, of course, been present at such demonstrations, and therefore have no entitlement to comment on them at all, have declared that all those who claim to have witnessed these phenomena have been labouring under a delusion or a hallucination? But such things have been observed times without number by men and women of the best education and highest reputation. The very idea that persons of breeding and intelligence should be suffering from an overheated imagination is patently absurd.'

'Your theory of a fine thread has a great deal to recommend it,' said Mina. 'Has she always been able to do this? I would be interested in learning her history.'

'I have been told,' said the professor, 'that she comes from a respectable family and first discovered her mediumistic powers when she was just fourteen. The phenomena then took the form merely of raps, which appeared not to come from any human intelligence, but as time passed she found that she was able to receive messages and it later became apparent that these came from persons who were in spirit. She did not undertake demonstrations, and her family it seems were ashamed of her and did not court publicity; on the contrary they kept her abilities hidden in case she should be classed as a lunatic and bring shame upon them.'

Mina listened attentively, but did not interrupt the story. If it was true, and even if the rappings had been no more than the product of youthful imagination and a craving for notoriety, she could understand Miss Eustace's wish to escape the displeasure of her family and become greater than she was.

'One day,' the professor went on, '– this was when she was about twenty – a lady who was a stranger to her came and said that she had received a message from a spirit telling her that she should call upon Miss Eustace who she would discover was a very powerful medium, and that the spirit, which was of her late husband, would only fully manifest itself through her agency. Miss Eustace was astonished by this, but the lady entreated her to make the attempt, which was a great success. Even so, Miss Eustace would not go on. She realised that to travel that path would direct her life in a way that she did not wish it to proceed, a way that would be very hard for her. She was then engaged to be married to a young man of good family and felt that her future lay with him. Unfortunately, before they could marry, he passed from this life, and her grief was so profound that her family thought she would soon join her beloved. It was then that Phoebe first came to her, bringing the shade of her intended, who said that she must in future devote herself to opening the eyes of unbelievers.'

'She has certainly opened my eyes,' said Mina, with her sweetest smile.

Mina returned home feeling almost sorrowful at how simple it was for a young woman of no more than the usual education to deceive a man celebrated for his intelligence and learning. Mina assured her mother that she had humbled herself before Professor Gaskin and that Miss Eustace might yet grace their home. Leaving her mother to write the desired letter, Mina wrote to Edward, expressing her earnest hopes that Miss Hooper was fully recovered from her cold, and asking him to send her the next edition of the *Quarterly Journal of Science.*

After luncheon she returned to Dr Hamid's baths, where she found the proprietor in his office, a neat room adorned with portraits of his wife and children, and beautifully scented with a display of dried herbs. He was not displeased to see her, and quickly pulled up a chair, providing it with a cushion so that she could face him across the desk in comfort.

'You will be pleased to know,' she told him, 'that I have just called upon Professor Gaskin to apologise for my error. Nevertheless I am to be excluded from future séances, rather like a disreputable gentleman who has been expelled from his club for improper behaviour; but I knew I risked that, and I may in time be readmitted if I play my part as a true believer. Will you continue to go?'

'I will,' said Dr Hamid, opening a bottle of mineral water and pouring a glass for them both. 'Do try this flavour; it is very good. I am not so determined a sceptic as you, although I do have my reservations, but I must admit, I also have hope.'

Mina sipped the water, which was pink and tasted of berries and spice. '*My* greatest hope is that Mr Home may find himself where he belongs, in prison, instead of as he is at present, deluding another person. This time, it is not a lady being cheated of her fortune but a noted scientist, a Mr Crookes, who is being fleeced of his reputation. He is a Fellow of the Royal Society and editor of a respected journal, and ought to know better.'

'I have read your booklet about Mr Home and can only agree,' Dr Hamid admitted. 'This is not a fellow in whom we can place any trust. But our concern is Miss Eustace. Just because we have reason to suspect one medium of fraud, does that mean they are all dishonest? Can you be sure that Miss Eustace is of Mr Home's ilk?'

'After my adventure last night, I am quite certain,' said Mina. 'It is no wonder to me now why the lady insists that no one must touch her spirit guide. Oh, I know that it is Professor Gaskin who says so but I am sure that he takes his orders from Miss Eustace, who he thinks will make his name as a great innovator. I can assure you that the lovely Phoebe is no more of the other world than I am. I cannot explain the glowing drapery but I am sure a chemist could do so; unless he was, like Professor Gaskin, blindfolded by his own credulity. When I fell against her I knew beyond doubt that what I was encountering was the body of a real, warm breathing woman.'

'But consider,' said Dr Hamid thoughtfully, 'and I am not necessarily disagreeing with your conclusions but merely offering this observation – there have been many cases where persons attending a séance have been touched by spirit hands and reported that they felt something like a solid human hand. I have experienced this myself. That seems to be very similar to what you have described. Could not Miss Eustace have used the vital energy produced by her body to create something warm and shaped like a woman?'

'Could not Miss Eustace have dressed up in a lot of white muslin and pretended to be a ghost?' replied Mina.

'She could, of course,' said Dr Hamid, 'but from my recollection I am sure that Phoebe was several inches taller than Miss Eustace.'

'She was, but I think that has a simple explanation,' said Mina. 'Miss Eustace tends to adopt a slightly round-shouldered posture. She presents herself as the very essence of humility. As we both know, any bending of the spine will make a person appear to be shorter than they are. In order to become Phoebe she had only to stand up straight and walk on tiptoe. That was probably why she lost her balance and fell. You don't imagine that *I* can easily knock another person to the ground?'

'No, but then you surprise me every day,' said Dr Hamid, with a smile. 'But if Miss Eustace did indeed transform herself into Phoebe, she was able to change her clothes in just two minutes. Has a lady been born who can do that?'

'We all can,' said Mina. 'It is a matter of finding the right dressmaker.'

He paused. 'I hope you like the mineral water; it is manufactured expressly for me.'

'It is quite delicious. I will place an order for a dozen bottles if you can deliver them.'

They both sipped their drinks. 'I think,' said Dr Hamid after a great deal of thought, 'and I am reluctant to admit it because to do so would be to relinquish hope – that you may be right about Miss Eustace. Hope blinds people to the truth, makes them see only partial reality or even if they do see it all, they offer explanations that conform to their prejudices and ignore the more probable truth.' He put down his glass, opened a drawer, removed the papers that Mina had lent to him and laid them on the desk before him. 'How can you do it, Miss Scarletti?' he said, shaking his head. 'How can you take away hope? Some of us have nothing else; some of us live for it.'

'I have had false hope offered to me and taken away so many times that I am more content to live without it,' said Mina. 'I prefer the possible and the probable to the mysterious and unlikely.'

'Dr Edmunds of the Dialectical Society, whose observations I have read with very great interest, is a sensible and forthright man,' said Dr Hamid, 'but he admits in his statement that he was a sceptic from the outset, so it might take a great deal to move him, and I suspect that he is not a widower.'

'I think that he is not a man who would let his feelings affect his judgement, and neither, I believe are you.'

He looked dejected and gazed at the portrait of his wife.

'I have lost a darling sister, and also a father who I loved dearly,' said Mina. 'I miss them every day, but they live on in my heart. Neither of them has ever rapped on walls or tables or rung bells or shaken a tambourine, and it is ludicrous to imagine that they might start doing so now.'

He nodded, wistfully. 'Jane could not abide loud noise; she loved sweet music and harmony.'

'The only reason mediums employ bells and tambourines is that they can be played in the dark with one hand and are not expected to produce a melody,' said Mina. 'Let one play a tune on the trumpet and I might be persuaded to listen.'

'You have an explanation for everything,' he replied, with a smile.

'Not everything; far from it. And now that I am an outcast I need your help if I am to expose the fraud. I can see all too clearly that if I simply stood up and said that I did not believe, the opprobrium would fall upon me and not Miss Eustace. We need proof. If you are continuing to attend the séances you must observe them for me and carry back a report. There is no one else to whom I might appeal. All the others who attend are fervent believers in Miss Eustace with not a critical eye amongst them.'

Dr Hamid rested his fingertips on Dr Rand's scathing denunciation of Mr Home. 'There are very many ladies like Jane Lyon residing in Brighton,' he observed. 'Widows or spinsters of means who are as vulnerable as she and have no one to advise them. Well, I will see what I can do.'

That was, Mina feared, the best agreement she was likely to have. Before she left she purchased a subscription and enjoyed another vapour bath and massage. Anna was pleased with Mina's report on the exercises, satisfied herself that her patient was making progress without over-straining herself, and suggested that, if she might like to try it, some light work with dumbbells might be the next step. Mina was eager for the next step. She had hope, a real true hope of something that she could reach out and take with her own efforts, hope that she could build the muscles of her back so that they would support her spine and prevent any risk of further collapse, hope that her lungs and heart would never be crushed by her own ribs. It was agreed that Mina would call to see Eliza again, and bring some of her own stories to read. Mina could see that she was Eliza's hope – not of any change in her body, since that was past any possibility of improvement, but the new friendship had opened a door to another place for Eliza's enquiring mind to explore.

Mina went home and pursued her exercises relentlessly. She spent the rest of the day at her desk. She had completed the tale of the cursed emerald, and her next composition was a story about a haunted castle. Its master was a tall stooping man with elephantine ears who had the command of a whole orchestra of ghosts able to entertain him with the most delightful music. The heroine of the tale, who had been kidnapped for her sweet singing voice, was trying to escape through a maze of tunnels that she had discovered under a trapdoor hidden beneath a carpet in a curtained recess. Chased by ghosts, she had turned and seized one, only to find that it was made of airy nothing and melted away in her arms.

Ten

Miss Whinstone, when she called next morning for a conversation over the teacups with Louisa, was labouring under a fresh burden of barely suppressed excitement, and had made a change in her appearance so substantial that it was hard to know if one should be pleased or alarmed for her. Abandoning the dull bronze gown she had favoured since putting off her mourning, she had found something in light green, which matched the colour of her eyes. It was an old gown, something she had worn before her dear brother Archibald had died and was therefore, she was obliged to admit, dreadfully out of fashion, but she thought that with a little good advice she might have it altered and trimmed and no one would know that it was not just arrived from Paris. It was time, she said, touching her hair, which had had extra attention given to its dressing that day, to do away with drabness and go out and enjoy the summer months. She knew this because she had consulted Miss Eustace at a private séance the night before, and Archibald had come and told her so.

Louisa had grudgingly permitted Mina to sit with them in the parlour, although not without expressing grave concern that her daughter might commit some solecism or random act of mayhem that would hinder or even prevent Miss Whinstone's recall of events. Mina promised to sit very quietly without stirring from her chair, and say nothing at all unless spoken to. She was perfectly content with this arrangement since all she wished to do was listen, and had no desire to interrupt Miss Whinstone's flow of useful information.

Miss Simmons, who with her employer's restoration to vital good health was less of a nursemaid than someone who could be relied upon to fetch and carry, sat in a corner in a dark drab gown, like a piece of old furniture than no one had troubled to discard because it was occasionally useful. Whatever her opinions were of her position in the household, she kept them to herself.

Miss Eustace, enthused their visitor, was a good-natured and kindly young woman, who existed only to act as a channel through which the living could speak to their departed loved ones. Unable to resist inserting a touch of drama into the proceedings, Miss Whinstone felt obliged to mention that she had been very nervous to start with, and required a glass of water and the application of a smelling bottle before she could even consent to begin, imploring Miss Eustace not to summon any spirits that she would find frightening. Miss Eustace had gently reassured her that all would be as calm as possible, and she had nothing at all to fear, rather she would be uplifted and cheered by any communications she received.

Miss Whinstone's private séance had taken place not in the Gaskins' parlour but in the lady's own home, which, she believed was why her brother's spirit had come so readily. Archibald had always had her best interests at heart, and his wise counsel was something she had sorely missed. Through the agency of Miss Eustace, however, she had been able to speak to and even touch him, and had received messages of great comfort.

The proceedings had begun with the medium and her client sitting facing each other across a small table, and after a few minutes of prayer and reflection, Miss Eustace had quietly drifted into a state of trance. Mina would have liked to know if the two women had sat in the dark, but since it was not mentioned, she assumed that they had. Her reading on spiritualism had led her to the conclusion that sitters at a séance only made a point of mentioning the available light when there was any. It was not long, said Miss Whinstone, before the spirit of her dearest

Archibald made itself known by tapping softly on the table. Miss Eustace had whispered to her, asking that she should place her hands underneath the table, and she had felt, very distinctly, her brother's hand touching hers.

'And it was certainly he,' she gasped. 'I know that there are some who might say it was all in my imagination, or that it was really Miss Eustace's hand I could feel,' – here Miss Whinstone cast a very accusing look at Mina – 'but Miss Eustace was sitting much too far away to touch me and in any case it was undoubtedly a man's hand, in a leather glove, very like the ones Archibald used to wear. Miss Eustace has such small, delicate hands and I could not have made that mistake. And there was no one else in the room.'

'Did your brother speak to you?' asked Louisa.

'No, although I am told that if I am patient that may happen in time. It would so please me to hear his dear voice again! But he was able to send me messages by knocking on the table. I asked him questions and he could answer yes or no by the number of knocks, or if I spoke the letters of the alphabet out loud he could show his agreement to them and so spell out words.'

'How very wonderful!' exclaimed Louisa, almost quivering with impatient curiosity coloured by a bitter hint of jealousy. 'Did he have anything of importance to convey?'

Miss Whinstone glowed at the recollection. 'He told me that he is very happy and has a fine house to live in, and worships God daily, but I must not think of joining him for a long while yet as I have my life to lead here first, and good and charitable works to perform. I have missed him so, and he misses me, but the pain of separation will be eased now that we can converse. And he assured me that he is in good company, for he sees Mr Scarletti and Mr Bettinson and many others and they are very friendly.'

'Extraordinary!' said Louisa, as well she might, thought Mina. Archibald Whinstone had died not long after the Scarlettis had moved to Brighton. Her father had only met him once, declared him to be a peevish fellow, and had not expressed any great desire to see him again. 'Was your brother friends with Mr Bettinson?' queried Louisa.

'Oh but that is the marvellous thing!' exclaimed Miss Whinstone. 'They could not abide each other while they lived, and just before Mr Bettinson died they were not on speaking terms. Mr Bettinson, who I cannot say I liked a great deal, was a very quarrelsome man who went to law on the smallest excuse. Archibald wrote a letter to the *Gazette* to complain about a speech that some foolish gentleman had made at a meeting and Mr Bettinson had imagined that Archibald was referring to him. No argument could convince him that he was wrong, and he was on the point of suing poor Archibald when he suddenly fell down and died of apoplexy. But Archibald said that now they are both in the spirit they have quite made up their differences and are the greatest of friends.'

'So the spirit world is a place of harmony where all quarrels may be mended and all wrongs righted,' said Louisa.

'Oh yes,' said Miss Whinstone ecstatically, 'and how happy I am to have been granted even this little sight of its wonders.'

Both women turned to look at Mina as if she might be inclined to say something. Mina was inclined to say a great deal, but was determined to keep to her promise. She smiled politely, took more tea, and was silent.

'I am happy to say that I have now quite lost my fear of the spirits,' announced Miss Whinstone. 'Passing into another phase only makes us better than we were.'

'And – please excuse me for asking this – but you are quite quite certain beyond any doubt that it was your brother to whom you spoke?' asked Louisa.

'I could not be more certain!' exclaimed Miss Whinstone. 'He spoke of his will, which he had signed only days before he died, and how glad he was that he had done so, as it had made matters so much easier for me to manage. He was always so thoughtful.'

'I hope he had good advice for your future,' said Louisa.

'Yes ...' said Miss Whinstone, uncertainly. She paused and her eyes narrowed in concern. 'At least, I think so.' She gave a nervous laugh. 'Of course some of it was not entirely clear to me, it was all a matter of interpreting the little knockings and I fear that there may have been times when I became confused and misunderstood. But Miss Eustace assures me that if we were to try again then I would become more adept at following what is said.'

'What was it you thought he said?' asked Louisa, quickly urging Simmons to bring more refreshments.

'Oh, it was very private, very—' Miss Whinstone shook her head at the proffered plate, and gulped her tea so quickly she almost choked. The brightness of her mood had faded, and her smile became more brittle and then broke. 'Oh, my dear Mrs Scarletti, I really do not know what to do for the best!' Her hands shook and Simmons removed her teacup to the table before there was an accident.

'If you felt able to confide in me,' said Mina's mother, encouragingly, her eyes glistening at the promise of a secret communication, 'I might be able to advise you; and my dear Harriet, if I may call you that, for we have been friends for some little time, I beg you please to address me as Louisa.' She sipped her tea and savoured the sweet taste of a biscuit.

Miss Whinstone looked relieved, and Louisa gave Mina a sharp look and a nod toward the door to convey the suggestion that she ought to leave the room at once. Another glance at Simmons and a peremptory gesture was a command to remove both the tea tray and her daughter. Mina was preparing to depart, when Miss Whinstone abruptly rose to her feet. 'I think – I should go now. Louisa, you are kindness itself, but—'

'Mina and Simmons are both about to leave us, so we will be quite private,' said Louisa quickly.

'Yes, I understand, and perhaps when I am more composed, I will call on you again, and we will speak further. It may just be that I have made a silly mistake – indeed I hope that I have done – and I would regret it if I spoke too soon.'

No persuasion could induce her to remain, and Miss Whinstone made her goodbyes and hurried away before she was tempted to say more.

Mina avoided her mother's accusing look, since she was in no temper to be blamed for Miss Whinstone's decision to go home, taking her confidences with her. She wondered how well Miss Eustace had been rewarded for that private consultation, a question it would have been improper to discuss. It was no mystery to her why Archibald Whinstone had, by coincidence, become bosom friends with two men who had disliked him in life and whose widows just happened to be members of Miss Eustace's circle. The deceased men bound the living relatives closer together in sympathy, and accounts of the private séances would pass very rapidly around Brighton, creating a stir of interest that no one with any pretensions to fashion could afford to ignore.

The reference to Archibald Whinstone's will was, however, unexpected. It was not something that Miss Eustace could have known about; a private family transaction that had taken place almost two years ago, and which was hardly newsworthy. It was a small personal detail that had obviously served to convince Miss Whinstone that she was indeed conversing with her brother, and, Mina was forced to admit, would have weighed somewhat with her had she received similar intelligence from her father.

These thoughts were interrupted by the arrival of two letters, the first of which Louisa read with some astonishment and pleasure. Mina was about to retire to her room, but her mother insisted she remain. 'I wrote to Professor Gaskin as you suggested, begging him to intercede with Miss Eustace about the question of holding a séance here, and would you believe this is a letter from the lady herself. She is extremely generous and says that she does not blame you in any way for what happened, but feels that there may be some disturbance in the vital energy – whatever that might mean – when you are present. At any rate she wishes to pay us a visit, and has also asked that Mr Clee might accompany her as he seems able to bring balance to the energy. Both, it seems, are very eager to converse with *you*. That is quite extraordinary! But I am relieved to say that she does not preclude the idea that we may hold a séance here.' Louisa gave Mina a stern look. 'The entire plan will almost certainly stand or fall on your behaviour. I will issue an invitation forthwith, but I must warn you that you must do nothing to upset the vital energy.'

Mina gave her mother her solemn pledge as to her good behaviour. Louisa's mood was further improved by the second letter, which was from Mr Bradley. He stated that she and Mina had been sorely missed at his new enlarged healing circle, and begged them to accept the honour of being his special guests on the next occasion. Louisa, without troubling herself to consult Mina as to her wishes, promptly replied in the affirmative on behalf of them both.

On the following Sunday, Reverend Vaughan showed no lessening of his endeavours to keep his flock on the true path. He took as his text 1 Timothy, chapter 4: 'In the latter time some shall depart from the faith giving heed to seducing spirits and the doctrine of devils, speaking lies and hypocrisy …' It had come to his notice, he said, that some of his flock were in danger of departing from their faith and heeding these lying, seducing spirits. Some had even dared to compare the demonstrations of mediums with the miracles of Jesus Christ. Reverend Vaughan was uncompromising. These so-called 'miracles' performed under the concealing cloak of Stygian darkness could only be the work of fraudulent false prophets living off the gullible who followed them like so many credulous sheep. He reminded the congregation that when the Lord Jesus Christ performed his miracles he did not do so in secrecy and darkness, but in the full light of day, so that all men might witness the glory of God's goodness. Neither did He use the curious paraphernalia that, so he had been informed, these mediums employed. Jesus did not retire behind a curtain to change water into wine, and He preferred healing the sick to playing tambourines.

When the service was over, there was a great deal of amused chatter from the faithful, but Louisa remained tight-lipped.

When Mina next visited Eliza she took with her a gift of two of her stories. One was the tale of a young sailor, who, when he discovered that his shipmates were vicious thieves, refused to join in their depredations and was cruelly murdered, his body thrown overboard into a stormy sea. It sank to the ocean floor, many miles deep, where the handsome corpse was found by a beautiful mermaid, who entombed it in coral, and then fell in love with the sailor's ghost. But she could not speak to him and he could not see her, so their love was doomed. She pined away and died, and after her death they were finally united. The second story concerned malevolent spirits that lived in a wooden chair. It was discovered that the chair had been made from the wood of a tree used to hang murderers and had absorbed their wicked influence at the moment of their deaths. The haunting, once its source was recognised, was quickly resolved with the aid of a sharp axe and a good fire.

Eliza was eager to know what Mina was currently writing and so she described the tale of the ghostly orchestra, which was as yet incomplete. 'I am not sure how to end it,' she admitted. 'I would like the heroine to escape the castle unharmed, but I fear readers may be tired of the device where she simply stumbles across another secret trapdoor, or a hidden passage, and I suppose it would be too much of a coincidence to have a prince or a good fairy arrive to rescue her.'

'If I might suggest something?' asked Eliza, timidly.

'Oh, please do!'

'Why not have the lady meet a friendly ghost who will show her the way?'

'That is an excellent idea!' said Mina.

'Like you, I do not believe that the spirits of those who meant us no harm in life can mean anything but good after death. But the owner of the castle in your story – is that not meant to be Professor Gaskin? I have never seen him, of course, but Daniel has amused me greatly with descriptions of him.'

'You are very perceptive to notice that,' said Mina. 'Yes, the character is inspired by the professor. Fortunately he is unlikely to read my stories, and even if he did I suspect that he would not recognise himself.'

Eliza studied the engraving on the front cover of the mermaid story. The creature was more fish than woman, and what woman there was peered decorously from a waving mass of seaweed. 'I wonder if I might write a story?' she said. 'I do so enjoy tales of the sea, and often wonder what it must be like to be able to swim so freely. If one was half woman and half fish it would be easy. Oh, but I should not steal your story from you, I must think of something else! An octopus man who can fly, perhaps!'

They both laughed.

The conversation turned to the correspondence in the *Gazette*, which Eliza had been following with considerable interest. 'Daniel says he does not know quite what to make of Miss Eustace,' said Eliza, 'that is to say, is the lady a fraud or not? Have you spoken to her?'

'No, but I will soon have the opportunity as she will be visiting us this afternoon with her new acolyte Mr Clee. He, I think, is one of those energetic young men who like to be at the forefront of everything, and can be neutral about nothing. If he cannot oppose something with all his might then he will propose it with equal force. He seems to admire Miss Eustace; perhaps they will make a match.'

'You must come and tell me all about their visit,' said Eliza, eagerly, 'and perhaps I might even prevail upon the lady to call on me.'

'That would be amusing, no doubt,' said Mina, in a cautious tone, 'but the lady must, I fear, be viewed in the light of a travelling conjurer, or as a kind of Madame Proserpina who tells fortunes on the West Pier for sixpence. The difference being that Miss Eustace plays tricks on the imagination and is more expensive.'

'I will write to her,' said Eliza. 'Perhaps she will call on me, too. I have never seen a conjurer and should very much like to. Do you know where she lives?'

'That is all a part of her mystery,' said Mina, 'I am not sure that anyone knows. If one must write to her then all correspondence should be addressed to Professor Gaskin.'

'Then I will write to him – or better still, would you be so kind as to deliver a note to Miss Eustace this afternoon when she calls?'

Mina hesitated, but knew that if she did not do so then Eliza would find another means of sending a letter to Miss Eustace. 'I will,' she said, reluctantly, 'but only if you promise to heed my warnings, and above all, consult your brother and sister on the matter. If the lady demands large sums of money from you then she is a criminal and should be shown the door.'

Before she left, Mina expressed her concerns to Anna. 'Of course we must protect her,' said Anna, 'and I am very grateful that you have spoken to me, although I did suspect that it would come to this. But she is an adult with a mind of her own, and I would not prevent her from finding a diversion. I will permit a visit, but Eliza has no fortune to lose, so you may rest easy on that point.'

Later that day Mina completed her new story, and the helpful shade that guided the heroine to freedom took the form of a girl of twelve, called Marianne, with long pale hair.

Eleven

Just as it had been an interesting exercise to see the Gaskins' parlour in sunlight, so Mina was grateful for the long bright summer afternoon, which enabled her better to gaze on Miss Eustace.

Soft shadowed gaslight that could be a friend to the vain had previously made the lady appear to be hardly more than twenty-five, but in Brighton's famous white glare Mina saw that she was older, perhaps by as much as ten years. She had a steady gaze, large grey eyes and expressive hands.

Mr Clee, who conducted her in a respectful manner, was not yet thirty, and determined to be cheerful good company whether this was required or not. He had a winning smile and made constant use of it, as if his entire mission in life was to fascinate ladies of all ages. Unlike so many young men whose opinion of themselves far outweighed the opinion of the world, Mr Clee had every chance of success. Louisa returned his smile prettily, and touched a brooch in her hair to ensure that it was still in place, and even the stony Simmons dared to blush, then quickly turned her head aside as if ashamed of her own susceptibility. Mina was immune to the charm of charming gentlemen, not that she had ever known it to be untrammelled by duty and pity.

Mina had the duty of delivering Eliza Hamid's letter to Miss Eustace, which, with some trepidation, she did.

'How grateful I am that you have been so kind as to forgive my poor daughter,' said Louisa. 'The mortification I would have suffered had you experienced the smallest discomfort would have been immeasurable. I was at the time on the very point of inviting you here to conduct an evening séance, and I was afraid, as to some extent I still am, that it might prove to be impossible.'

'No one has anything with which to reproach themselves,' said Miss Eustace, kindly, 'and I see no reason why I cannot conduct a séance here.'

'Then I hope we may agree on a suitable day,' said Louisa eagerly, 'and for your greater confidence, I will ensure that Mina is not present.'

'Oh that will not be necessary,' said Miss Eustace. She turned her dreamy look towards Mina. 'In fact, Miss Scarletti, I would very much like you to be there.'

'Thank you,' said Mina, surprised.

'But does she not upset the vital energy?' said Louisa, frowning.

'Oh, not at all!' exclaimed Mr Clee, with some alacrity. 'In fact rather the reverse. After the last séance Miss Eustace observed to me that the figure of Phoebe has never been more brilliant or more clearly displayed or lasted so long. I have given this very careful thought and I believe that what we experienced was an etheric power that acts like electricity. Some individuals can exert either positive or negative forces and if they are placed in the right position they may become a human battery. The great majority of persons exert no force at all, and negatives are quite common, but positives like Miss Eustace are most rare. I have found that I am a very strong negative, and there may have been other negatives present at the last séance, but you, Miss Scarletti,' he beamed, 'you are a positive and you completed the arrangement. The forces that you were subjected to were too powerful for one so inexperienced, and it was this that made you stumble. It is our belief that you may, unknown to yourself, be a medium of most extraordinary power!'

There was a long silence. Mina was not sure how to react, in fact she was not sure how she was expected to react. Should she show fear, modesty, pleasure? Certainly amazement was called for. 'You amaze me,' she said at last.

'Is that all you can say?' snapped her mother.

'You take the news most calmly, if I might say so,' said Miss Eustace with a smile. 'When I was first told I was a medium I refused to believe it at all.'

Disbelief, thought Mina. That was the option she had failed to consider.

'Are you quite sure this is correct?' she said. 'There was nothing suggestive of this at the first séance I attended.'

'I believe,' said Mr Clee, 'that your abilities have stayed hidden but it was your presence at the first séance that brought them out, only to be displayed at the subsequent event.'

'This is very like what Mr Bradley told me,' said Louisa. 'I don't know if you have met the gentleman, but he conducts meetings for the purposes of prayer and healing, and the spirits make themselves known through him.'

'I have heard him mentioned very often, but we have never met,' said Miss Eustace. 'He has been invited to attend a séance but declined.'

'Perhaps he is one of these positive people,' said Louisa. 'He is of the opinion that were he even to be in the same room as yourself, the powerful forces that he attracts might harm you, and thus with considerable regret he must stay away.'

'He is a gentleman I would very much like to observe,' said Mr Clee, 'and there can be no harm in *my* attending his healing circle.'

'I am sure it would be possible to arrange that,' said Louisa patting the brooch in her hair yet again. 'I suppose you are acquainted with what the Reverend Vaughan has been insinuating about Mr Bradley, that the spirits he brings to heal us come not from Heaven but quite another place. Not that we believe that for a moment. If his eyes could only be opened, what a wonderful thing that would be!'

'All will come in time,' said Miss Eustace, gently. 'Those who commune with God will one day come to understand that the spirits are sent by Him as ministering angels.'

Simmons had gone to the refreshment table and picked up a plate of small cakes to offer to the company. No one had especially noticed her, but she suddenly dropped the plate and gave a little scream, then stepped back with both hands clasped to her face.

'What is it, Simmons?' asked Louisa.

Simmons, trembling with fright, extended a finger. 'The table!' she exclaimed. 'It moved!'

Everyone turned and stared at the table, which looked disinclined to repeat the demonstration.

'Nonsense, Simmons, you have got yourself overexcited by all this talk of séances and probably knocked it with your foot,' said Louisa. 'And now you have made such a mess of crumbs!'

'But it moved! I promise you it did!' insisted Simmons.

'If I might comment,' said Mr Clee. 'It is possible, since we know we have two positives and one negative in this room, that Miss Simmons might be another negative and thus complete the circle.'

Louisa was about to ring for Rose, but turned to Mr Clee in astonishment. 'What can you mean?'

'Miss Simmons, if you could return to your place, and sit very quietly I will see if I can detect any disturbance in the ether,' said Miss Eustace.

Simmons crept back to her chair in the corner but could not avoid glancing at the table as if afraid of it.

'Ah,' said Miss Eustace after a brief interlude, 'yes, I do feel it! Mr Clee, I believe you are correct.'

Louisa seemed very taken aback by this, and not best pleased, since, thought Mina, her mother undoubtedly believed that anything remarkable in the household should repose in herself, not Mina, and most certainly not in her companion.

'With your permission, Mrs Scarletti,' said Miss Eustace, 'we might try to conduct a test. Scientists nowadays are so insistent on tests for everything, and I am sure that I don't mind that at all.'

'Professor Gaskin would be most interested in the result,' said Mr Clee. 'Of course if you are concerned that you might offend

Mrs Gaskin by our making important discoveries here and not within her circle—'

'I am sure that Mrs Gaskin will be happy for the cause of science and is not looking for any credit for herself,' said Louisa quickly. 'What must we do?'

It was soon arranged that for the sake of safety the table should be cleared of any moveables. Louisa rang for Rose who tidied up the spilled cakes and removed the tray. Everyone watched her very carefully as she did so, and there was a tangible sense of relief when she had departed.

'Your maid is neither positive nor negative and she has not therefore created any disturbance in the energy,' said Mr Clee, approvingly. 'I suggest now that the four of us gather around the table.' Louisa stood, but he smiled regretfully and said, 'My apologies, Mrs Scarletti, but in this instance you can only be an observer and not a participant.'

Louisa sat down. 'Very well,' she said, concealing her ill grace as best she could.

Mr Clee jumped up and began arranging chairs so that four persons might sit around the little table, then with a gesture he invited Mina, Miss Eustace and Simmons to be seated.

'Will we need to turn out the lights?' enquired Louisa.

'We will try it in the light first,' said Miss Eustace. 'We should begin by all placing both hands palm down on the table top.'

Mina complied. She was seated opposite Simmons who was staring down at her hands afraid, as if they might jump up and do something she could not control. 'If we close our eyes it will assist concentration,' said Miss Eustace.

Simmons's eyes snapped tightly shut, but Mina simply lowered her eyelids to give the impression that they were closed. The table was so small that she could see from between her lashes not only her own hands but the left hand of Miss Eustace and the right of Mr Clee on either side of her.

'What must we do now?' asked Simmons tremulously.

'We need only wait and pray silently,' said Miss Eustace. 'No one must move, and our hands must touch the table only very lightly so that we cannot unconsciously influence it by muscular pressure.'

Mina feared that her mother was not much given to silence. When not the centre of attention she tended to fidget until she was, and there was a very real risk that she would pretend some spirit visitation in order to prove her credentials and enter the thus far forbidden circle. Fortunately there was not long to wait. The table, which was not at all heavy, gave a little shudder, and then rocked gently from side to side. There were some soft tapping sounds, like little clicks.

'Are you there?' asked Mr Clee, eagerly. 'If you are, dear friends, give three taps for yes.'

There were three soft clicks.

'Do you recognise a powerful medium in the room? You may give three taps for yes and one for no.'

Three clicks and then a pause and three more.

'Is that to mean that there are two?'

Three clicks.

'Is one of them Miss Scarletti?'

Three clicks.

'Miss Scarletti,' said Mr Clee, 'you may ask the spirit a question if you wish.'

'I hardly know what to ask,' said Mina. 'Does the spirit know everything?'

'It does, but it may choose what is right to impart to the living,' said Miss Eustace.

'I would like to know who the spirit was when alive,' said Mina.

'Then ask.'

Mina paused. 'Are you the spirit of my sister?'

One click.

'Are you the spirit of my father?'

Three clicks.

Despite herself, Mina found that she was trembling. Whether this was from the renewed sharp awareness of her loss, or anger that she was being so manipulated, or even the foolish hope that somehow her father was really in the room with her, she could not say.

'Ask him if he is with God,' said Louisa. Her voice was muffled as if she was holding a handkerchief to her face.

'I need no séance to tell me that,' said Mina. 'But how do I know if this is indeed my father and not some false spirit come to delude me?'

'You are too strong for false spirits to work through you,' said Miss Eustace, 'as am I.'

'I cannot be so sure of that,' said Mina. 'And whatever question I was to ask would tell me nothing, since both a true and a false spirit would know the answer.' But not, she thought, a fraud. 'Father dear,' she said, after a pause, 'can you tell me the last words you spoke to me on the day that you passed into spirit?'

The table was obstinately still. Several minutes elapsed, but there was no more.

'Oh, I am so sorry, but the spirit has gone,' said Miss Eustace. 'Do not be downcast, Miss Scarletti, if you try again I know he will come, and better and stronger than before!'

The séance, thought Mina, angrily, had been a charade from start to finish with the table acting under the slender fingertips of Miss Eustace. No doubt the lady had first undertaken to frighten Simmons by somehow moving it with her foot, easily done under the cover of her heavy skirts, or even a carefully laid black thread. The medium dared not answer Mina's question as she did not know the answer, and had employed the pretence that the spirit had left. Henry Scarletti, had he been present, would undoubtedly have seen the bleak humour of Mina's question, and either chided his daughter or made something up. Only Mina and her mother of all those in the room knew that for the last week of his life Henry Scarletti had been unable to speak. There were no words on his last day alive.

'Oh,' exclaimed Louisa, 'it is just too much to bear! Henry was such a dear man and Mina has frightened him away with her silly questions. Miss Eustace, would you consent to see me privately one evening as you did Miss Whinstone?'

'Of course I will,' said Miss Eustace, reassuringly. 'And very soon.'

Mr Clee put the table and chairs back in their accustomed places, conducted Miss Simmons back to the safety of her corner, and then turned his attention to Mina with all the extravagant passion of the recent convert. His new devotion to the cult of Miss Eustace was, she thought, like that of a man who had once been addicted to drink, and had become overnight a champion of and learned authority upon temperance.

'You cannot fail to be curious as to what the spirit world has to offer,' he said. 'So many others with only a small part of your natural ability have been ambitious for advancement, and sought it, yes, and achieved it too. They have striven night and day for knowledge and perfection and purity. They have conquered their basest instincts and become as creatures of the light. You, Miss Scarletti, have hidden faculties that others can only dream of, which have hitherto lain dormant in your soul. Only liberate and develop them, and you will have powers that will grant you unimaginable freedom. You will soar to the dazzling heights, and find true happiness and contentment in the service of the Lord. The path is there before you! Will you follow it?'

In the face of this exhortation, it would have seemed churlish for Mina to make the reply that immediately sprang to her lips which was 'No'.

'I am overwhelmed with wonder,' she said, carefully. 'There is so much for me to learn and understand. Do you really think I am equal to it?'

'I have no doubts! Oh *please* say that you will!' His eyes were very compelling, and the colour of sea mist. She wondered if he was entirely sane.

'I will pray,' she said firmly, 'that is what I will do, I will pray for guidance. I am sure that the good Lord will give me the answers I need. And I will hope also that the spirit of my father will come to me again, perhaps when I am alone with my thoughts, and he will speak to me and tell me what I must do. When he does, I promise that I will listen to him.'

'But will he come again?' said her mother, uncertainly. 'Do we not need all these positives and negatives Mr Clee has told us about?'

'Oh but I may do it alone, now; the power has awakened in me, Mother, I can feel it!' said Mina, with her sunniest expression.

Louisa looked alarmed. 'Please don't go tipping tables, or you will break everything in the house,' she said. 'And if Henry should come again, ask him what I ought to do about Mrs Parchment who I think is an ungodly influence.'

'Our tenant, who my mother suspects of atheism or worse,' Mina explained to Miss Eustace with a smile, 'but she is, I believe, merely a lady who enjoys her own company and walking in all weathers.'

More refreshments were offered, but Miss Eustace and Mr Clee, saying they had other important calls to make in the town, took their leave.

'That was a nonsense question you asked,' said Louisa, before Mina could escape back to her room. 'There could have been no answer as you well know.'

'And there was none,' said Mina.

'I am not a fool,' said her mother, 'although you sometimes appear to think me one. The question was a test, was it not?'

'It was,' Mina admitted, 'but no medium who offers herself as genuine would object to that. Miss Eustace herself said she welcomed tests.'

'I did not mean a test of Miss Eustace who is undoubtedly genuine, but a test of the spirit, to see whether it was Henry's or some imposter. And now I come to think of it, we have our confirmation.'

'We do?' queried Mina.

'Of course we do! Henry was unable to speak. His silence was the reply.'

In the face of her mother's air of triumph there was nothing Mina could say. She was left with the most profound regret that she had chosen to deliver Eliza's letter at the start of the afternoon, for had she left it until later she might very well not have delivered it at all.

Twelve

Mina hoped that by invoking a powerful devotion to prayer she could stave off any repeated attempts by Miss Eustace to turn her into a medium. If pressed she could always announce that the spirit of her father had appeared to her and warned her not to attempt it, as she was too frail for the work. Whether Miss Eustace would renew her campaign in the light of this unassailable supernatural authority Mina did not know, but she hoped that the lady would be perceptive enough to know when she was beaten.

The visit and its curious developments left Mina wondering why Miss Eustace had attempted to make her into a rival for her business, but she could only conclude that what the medium sought was not a rival but a partner, and had lighted on Mina because she thought that her deformity made her vulnerable. So many things, thought Mina, made people vulnerable to this kind of persuasion – grief, illness, loneliness, vanity, greed, boredom, failing mental faculties or the lure of undeserved fame, and who was there who had not suffered from or been guilty of at least one of these?

In the middle of her new concerns she was grateful for a visit from Richard, to whom she could unburden herself freely. He burst in with his usual energy and was discovered in the hallway inspecting a large oriental vase of indifferent attractions, usually employed as a receptacle for umbrellas, which had never excited his interest before. Their mother was out visiting, taking Simmons with her under the pretence that her biddable companion was really that more fashionable appendage, a ladies' maid, so Mina and her brother had the parlour to themselves. Mina regaled him at some length with accounts of the séances she had attended, her actions and observations, and the conclusions she had drawn, while Richard lounged at his ease, in a manner he would never have dared adopt in front of his mother, looking very comfortable and more amused than disturbed at recent events. His scheme to find a wealthy wife had not, he admitted, advanced since their last conversation. The ladies he had approached with protestations of love had had the temerity to compare notes, and discovered that he had addressed the identical words to them all. 'I have no more widows in my sights and must turn to spinsters, or all is lost,' he said, 'but there are few of that number who do not have a kind brother or watchful parents.'

'I hope you will not think of wooing Miss Whinstone,' said Mina. 'She has trimmed her old green dress and gilded her hair. Were you the cause of that?'

He shuddered. 'Oh no, I need to have *some* affection for the lady I marry, and Miss Whinstone is quite beyond me, I am afraid, unless she becomes suddenly very much richer than she is, in which case I might be able to feel a little love for her. But what of Miss Eustace? You say she is young and charming, which promises well. Is she also wealthy?'

'I know nothing of her means,' said Mina, 'but I suspect that if she is not already wealthy then she soon will be. I have asked Mother how much she asks for a private séance but she refused to tell me.'

'I see two courses of action,' said Richard, thoughtfully, 'and they are not incompatible so both may be undertaken at once. The first is that I woo Miss Eustace and make her and her fortune mine, and then she will devote herself entirely to me and abandon her pretence of communing with the spirit world, and the second is that *you* take up the trade of raising ghosts, which will be far less danger to Mother than anything Miss Eustace can do.'

'As to the first I believe you have at least one rival,' said Mina, 'a Mr Clee, who since she converted him to her cause is rarely from her side; and I refuse to do the second.'

Richard took a case of cigars from his pocket but Mina gave him a warning look and he sighed and put it away again. 'Oh, can't you be persuaded, Mina? I'm sure that with practice you could do it very well. It's a good business to get into, it's all the rage and it can only get better. Brighton is a big enough town to stand two mediums, or even more in the high season; why, there are dozens in London. If you start now you would make your name before everyone else sees the opportunity. Then when the notables and the fashionables come in you could name your price.'

'I am glad that I know you are teasing me,' said Mina, maintaining her good humour, 'or I would be very annoyed. It's a dishonest trade and I want no part of it.'

'But everyone knows it's all trickery, don't they?' he said airily. 'A little simple conjuring that wouldn't fool a baby unless it wanted to be.'

'It preys upon the grief-stricken,' she reminded him.

'And it makes them feel happier,' said Richard. 'What can be wrong with that? Would you rather the widows of Brighton turned to drink?'

'That is not the only alternative, and you know it,' said Mina severely. 'Of all the places in the world there are few that can rival Brighton for variety of amusements and worthy causes to pursue.'

He lowered his head, then tilted it and gazed up at her coyly, like a schoolboy who had been caught stealing a bun. 'You will be very angry with me, then.'

'I am always angry with you; only the subject matter changes. What have you done now? I hope you have not come to ask Mother for more money?'

'I only want to borrow twenty pounds,' he said, lightly.

'I will *give* you twenty pounds if you tell me why you want it.'

His face brightened.

'*And* if it does not involve gambling, fraud or immorality.'

His face fell.

'Oh come, now, Richard, tell me everything.'

'Must I?' he complained.

'Yes, you must or I cannot save you if you come to grief.'

'You can't blame me,' he protested, 'it was you who suggested the idea.'

'I did?'

'Well, not exactly suggested, but it was all through you that I thought of it. You showed me the booklet about Mr Home, and I thought, well, here is a fine conjurer and no mistake; now, where can I find one like him and bring him on, so to speak.'

'Are you encouraging someone to emulate Mr Home?' demanded Mina, appalled.

'Oh not the stealing from old ladies,' said Richard, quickly, 'I draw the line at that, but I have some friends who know all the secrets of sleight of hand, illusion, mechanical and optical contrivances and even the art of chemistry, and can dress them up into a magnificent display.'

'I see,' said Mina, 'so you are hoping to employ some conjurer to pretend to be a medium?'

'That's more or less the idea, although the individual who I hope will become the star of the Brighton firmament is a lady – well, near enough a lady; at least she can act the part, I've seen her do it many a time.'

'An actress?' said Mina, to whom this came as very little surprise.

'Actress, singer, dancer, you name it, she will do it,' said Richard, enthusiastically. 'Game for almost anything.'

'Doubtless,' said Mina. 'But why here in Brighton and not London?'

'Ah well, you see, Mother asked Edward to keep an eye on me, keep me off the primrose path, so to speak, and unless he invents a better telescope he won't be able to do it without leaving the delightful Miss Hooper which I know he won't do. And Nellie – that's Nellie Gilden, and the most sporting girl you ever saw – is too well known to London audiences. Also – now, this is in the strictest confidence, you understand – for some years she has been the trusted assistant to the famous magician M. Baptiste who claims to have been a student of the renowned M. Houdin, professor of legerdemain and presenter of theatrical *soirées fantastiques*. She knows all her master's secrets, but he, it has to be said, has not yet discovered the secret of being kind to his assistant so keeping her happy. So Nellie has been looking for another situation, but since M. Baptiste knows every conjurer in the business he would soon find her out if she took up with another man. When she told me her difficulty, I thought of the answer at once. Nellie Gilden of London, artiste and conjurer's assistant, is in the process of transforming herself into Miss Kate Foxton, spirit medium of Brighton.'

He took a card from his pocket and showed it to Mina. 'There! Isn't she the loveliest girl?' It was a photographic portrait of a young woman with a pretty face, a voluptuous figure which the tightness of her costume served only to accentuate, and a great mass of lustrous hair which tumbled past her shoulders to frame a notable décolletage.

'I can certainly see why you find her interesting,' said Mina. 'And this is why you need the money, to set up your – friend with costumes and everything she needs to dupe people.'

'It's only what she did before, on stage,' said Richard, reasonably. 'And it will be the most wonderful entertainment! With all the tricks Nellie knows there won't be a soul who doesn't think they have had value for money.'

'You make it sound almost honest,' said Mina dryly.

'And respectable,' said Richard.

'Oh I wouldn't go that far. So, what is your plan? I am sure you have one.'

'Of course! I will arrange for lodgings and bring Nellie down here and then advertise her as the wonder of the world. The rest will follow.' He took the portrait, looked at it fondly, tucked it in his pocket, which he patted, and then leaned back again with a smile of supreme confidence.

'And what are you going to tell Mother?' said Mina practically. 'If you are living in Brighton she will want to see you often and know what you are doing.'

'Oh, Mina dear, don't make it hard for me,' he sighed. 'All I want to do is earn my living as Mother has always told me I must. She should be delighted that I am complying with her wishes at last. I am sure I will think of something to say.'

'Well, assuming that you are successful we will either have to find some kind of plausible fiction that will not leave her mortified beyond endurance, or you will have to move on quickly to some more acceptable occupation. Whatever happens I do not think it wise that Nellie and Mother should ever meet.'

'Nellie is really the best girl in the world; *you* should meet her, I hope you will.'

'I mean to.' Mina had a new, more worrying thought. 'I don't suppose you intend to marry her?'

He twisted his hands together and gazed at the floor, as his father used to do when admitting to an indiscretion. 'No, that would be difficult.'

'Difficult as well as unwise?' asked Mina.

'Yes, because of M. Baptiste.'

'He is hoping to marry her himself?' she ventured.

'Not – precisely,' said Richard awkwardly.

'He is her husband,' said Mina.

'Well – yes – in a manner of speaking.'

'What manner is that?' she demanded. 'In the manner of holding hands and jumping over a log, or in the manner of going to church and having a wedding service and signing a marriage certificate?'

'Er – the latter,' he admitted, 'although it hardly counts,' he added quickly, 'because he has not loved and honoured her as a husband should. But that is another reason I would rather he didn't discover where Nellie is. He has a very bad temper when crossed, and there is a trick he does with swords. It's really quite alarming, and Nellie says the swords are quite genuine and very sharp indeed.'

Mina shook her head despairingly. 'Well, Richard, because I am so fond of you I shall reluctantly keep your secret, if only to preserve your life. But tell me, since Nellie is such an adept at the magical arts, if she were to attend one of Miss Eustace's séances would she be able to see how her tricks are done?'

'Oh, undoubtedly,' said Richard with a laugh, 'and then do them better herself!'

'Splendid,' said Mina, 'then I am more than ever eager to make her acquaintance.'

'Oh, but you misunderstand my meaning,' said Richard. 'She will of course know the secrets and be able to demonstrate them, but unless you are of the magical trade yourself, she will not impart them to another living soul. What if all magicians were to go about revealing each other's secrets? There would be quarrels and murder done, and business would collapse, and all would be chaos.'

'Well, how interesting,' said Mina, surmising that the world of the theatre was a topsy-turvy place with its own laws and morality quite foreign to what was expected in the parlours of Brighton. Despite this setback she thought Nellie Gilden might yet prove useful, if she could win her confidence.

'I don't suppose you could make that twenty-five pounds?' asked Richard.

Mr Bradley had secured a meeting room at a nearby hotel for his next healing circle, accommodation that could comfortably seat a hundred persons, and was being called upon to do so. There was a small charge for admission, a contribution towards the cost of hire, and simple refreshments. Many of those in attendance were known to Mina: Miss Whinstone, whose green gown had been styled and embellished to her satisfaction, and who, mistakenly believing that she now looked fully ten years younger, had taken to preening herself; Mrs Phipps, accompanied by her nephew, whose main purpose was to prevent her falling out of her chair when she enjoyed her accustomed doze; and Mrs Bettinson, who looked discomfited by the fact that her friends had thrown off their melancholy and was looking around the room in the hope of espying a new project to which to devote her energies. Louisa had brought not only Mina but Simmons, who seemed to be there only so that her drabness could provide a sombre backdrop to her mistress's finery, and Mrs Parchment, whose foot still required Mr Bradley's ministrations.

Some of the assembled throng had, Mina was sure, come simply for entertainment and gossip, but others, as evidenced by the line of bath chairs outside whose occupants, disabled either by old age or injury, were being assisted indoors by attendants, felt in need of Mr Bradley's healing hands. A few eyes were cast in Mina's direction, some of those present perhaps hoping that they were about to witness a miracle, in which her back would straighten and she would announce herself cured, others pitying her inevitable disappointment.

They had hardly taken their seats before Louisa was greeted by an enthusiastic Mr Clee, who quickly attached himself to her party, and declared himself to be bereft of all happiness if he was not permitted to make himself useful.

Louisa was content to accommodate his wishes, and enquired after the health of Miss Eustace. The medium, said Mr Clee, was very tired after all her work, but she fully expected to be restored following a short rest. 'Miss Eustace is so often called upon in the afternoons and evenings that she likes to spend her mornings in perfect quiet and solitude,' he explained.

'She does not seem to go about in society a great deal,' Louisa observed.

'No, she prefers small gatherings if any. I do believe that if she was not called to the service of society she would retreat into some cloistered community of religious and charitable ladies.'

'You do not think she intends to marry?' asked Louisa. 'There are rumours in town that she may soon be betrothed.'

He looked amused at the question. 'Oh no, I cannot think she would ever do so. I have heard the gossip, and I know that there are some who say that I am attached to the lady. I do hold her in great esteem, but as one would a great teacher or a mystic.'

'How interesting,' said Louisa, smoothing the lace on her collar. She had recently emerged from the full deep black mourning appropriate to a widow, and ignoring the slightly less restricted period that would normally have been expected to last until winter, had leaped instead into half-mourning which allowed more elaborate trimming and jewellery and would soon usher her into brighter colours.

For reasons that Mina dreaded to think about, all the ladies present seemed heartened to learn that Mr Clee was not in love with Miss Eustace.

'Miss Scarletti,' he said, 'I trust you have not suffered any ill-effects from your experience of table tipping?'

'I am well, thank you,' said Mina, 'although I am not sure that my being present was in any way responsible for what occurred.'

'Miss Eustace feels very strongly that it was,' replied Mr Clee. 'But if you are uncertain, then perhaps we might make another attempt? I would be delighted to assist. You have only to ask, and it will be arranged!'

'Thank you,' said Mina, preferring not to elaborate on her true preferences while her mother was present. 'I am still hoping to hear more from my father on the subject.'

'Or if Mrs Parchment might like to try?' he said, turning his irrepressible smile to that lady.

'For what purpose?' said Mrs Parchment, with a determinedly unfriendly expression. 'I believe I exhausted all possible subjects of conversation with my husband when he was living, and have nothing further I wish to say to him now.'

'I understand that your husband was a great benefactor to society,' said Mr Clee. 'Was he not the inventor of Parchment's Pills?'

'Oh, yes, that and many other things. He could cure anything and anyone – except for himself.'

The conversation ended when Mr Bradley appeared before the company, and welcomed everyone to the gathering. He was, he said, honoured to see before him the very cream of Brighton society, the most revered and respectable of its inhabitants, who would, he knew, oppose the wholly unfounded suggestions that his humble efforts were in any way irreligious. He made special mention of his honoured guests, and Louisa looked thoroughly displeased to discover that what she had imagined to be her exclusive status was shared with a great many others.

The meeting started with prayers, in which the Reverend Vaughan of Christ Church was especially mentioned, hopes being expressed that the respected gentleman would soon come to appreciate the godliness of Mr Bradley's mission.

He then proceeded to the formal healing. Since the faithful were too numerous to be in a circle, but were seated in rows, Mr Bradley was obliged to walk back and forth along each row in turn, one arm flung out to hover over the head of each person in the room. 'For the power of the Lord is infinite,' he intoned as he proceeded, 'and I am but his humble vessel. Through me He shows His healing power, and such is His goodness that it will soothe and calm the affliction not only of all those present but their loved ones, too; parents and children, husbands and wives, brothers and sisters, even to the husbands, wives and children of their brothers and sisters, all, all will be healed by the grace of the Almighty.'

There was the sound of sighing and even weeping in the room, and it came from all around, as some of the sitters thought about those in their families who were ill and without hope of recovery.

Quite suddenly, and without any warning, Miss Whinstone leaned forward with a cry, and began to gulp and sob convulsively. Everyone around her tried to comfort her, but her body heaved and shuddered uncontrollably as deep groans of misery were torn from her. Someone went to get a glass of water, and someone else suggested she be laid on the floor, and any number of people wanted to call for a doctor, but Mr Bradley stopped and turned to her, laying a hand upon her head. 'Oh my sister in God,' he said, 'be at peace. Only do as the Lord commands you and your conscience guides you and all will be well.' Gradually, the sobbing slowed, and her gasping breaths calmed to the point where she could speak.

'Thank you,' she said, gratefully, wiping her eyes with a handkerchief. 'I must do all that a Christian woman should.'

He smiled at her and passed on.

Miss Whinstone reassured her friends that she was recovered, but despite Louisa's most forceful efforts she would tell no one of the reason for her distress, and it was thought best to take her home.

When Mina next went to Dr Hamid's baths she found Anna anxious to speak with her, and they retired to the privacy of the office. 'I was intending to call, but I am very glad you have come,' she said. 'I am concerned about Eliza.'

Mina was seized with a sudden dread. She and Eliza had formed a bond not only of sympathy but of similar tastes in their two meetings, and she feared that the new friendship was about to be snatched away. 'Oh, I do hope she is not unwell! May I call on her?'

'She is well enough, have no fear on that point, and we hope that she may live contentedly for many years yet, and enjoy your company, but it is another matter I need to discuss. The last time we met we spoke of Eliza's wish to meet Miss Eustace. Daniel and I considered the request and decided that it was unlikely to be of any harm. She has very few visitors, and we thought that a new face would do her good.'

'Did Miss Eustace call on her?' asked Mina, apprehensively.

'Yes, and a Mr Clee. They stayed for some considerable time.'

'Oh, I think I know what you are about to tell me,' said Mina, unhappily. 'And I blame myself, now. I should have seen the danger. I suppose Miss Eustace has tried to persuade your sister that she is a powerful spirit medium?'

'You are right, she has!' exclaimed Anna. 'How did you guess? Has she tried to persuade you, also?'

'Yes, she has, and I am sorry to say it occurred after I delivered your sister's note, and I would have done anything then to have taken it back.'

'I assume that she did not succeed with you,' said Anna.

'No – she cannot – will not!' Mina assured her with some energy.

'I wish Eliza was of the same mind as you,' said Anna, 'but I fear that Miss Eustace has prevailed. Please do not blame yourself, Eliza is our responsibility, and the decision to allow the visit was ours.'

They were both silent and thoughtful for a few moments. 'Would you like me to go and see your sister and tell her that Miss Eustace tries these tricks on everyone?' suggested Mina, although she was not hopeful that this would be of any use.

Anna sighed. 'I hardly know what to do. You see, Eliza is happy, happier than I have seen her in many years. She feels newly favoured instead of at a disadvantage. Ought I to take that away from her? Even if it is an illusion it seems harmless enough.'

'I entirely understand,' said Mina, 'and it is the seeming harmless that is, I believe, the real danger, the thin end of what may be a long and subtle wedge with a bad conclusion. Does your sister propose to go to séances now? Or have them come to her?'

'No, and this is what I meant to discuss. Eliza wants to conduct a séance herself at our house tomorrow evening. There would be only Daniel and myself, but could I ask you to be there also? And if you have a kind friend with a critical eye then by all means bring that friend with you.'

'Of course I will come,' said Mina, 'and if my brother Richard is not otherwise engaged I will ask him to accompany me. Is Miss Eustace to be there as well?'

'No, Eliza asked her to attend, but she has another appointment.'

'That is something,' said Mina with considerable relief. 'If we are fortunate then we will all sit in the dark and nothing will happen and she will give up the idea.'

'Thank you for that comfort,' said Anna.

Once Mina's bath and massage were done she went to see Dr Hamid, who had concluded his treatment of a patient and returned to his office. He glanced up at her with some concern as she entered.

'Please, I know what you are going to say, but Eliza knows her own mind,' he said defensively. 'I can't treat her like a child. The best thing I can do to protect her is let her have her enjoyment but be on hand to keep a watch against any dangers.'

'Of course you can't forbid her to hold a séance,' said Mina. 'At least, you could, but I have given this some thought, and I can see that it would be unwise. If she is determined enough she will do it whatever you say, so it would be best if she did it while you were there. Miss Hamid has asked me to come to your house tomorrow, and my brother Richard, too, who is the most pronounced sceptic, and we will all keep our eyes open.'

'At least Eliza is no Jane Lyon,' said Dr Hamid. 'The man who tries to steal her fortune will have little to tempt him. My father always feared that she could be the target of an adventurer, and ensured in his will that her capital cannot be touched and she has only the income for her lifetime.'

'I am relieved to hear it,' said Mina. She sat down, and they faced each other across the desk, both feeling worried and helpless. 'Something is happening, but I am not sure what,' she said. 'Miss Eustace has tried to make me into a medium and failed. Now she is playing her tricks on your sister. My mother is about to throw off her mourning six months too soon, Miss Whinstone is beside herself but won't say why, and Mr Clee went from sceptic to believer in five minutes. It is as if a disease is rampaging through the town.'

'Sometimes all we can do in these instances is mop the patient's brow and allow the fever to burn itself out,' said Dr Hamid.

'Are we immune to this plague?' asked Mina.

He smiled. 'I think so. I know you are, and Anna is too.'

'But you, I think, like to hope just a little.'

'Just a little,' he admitted. 'And you do not?'

'Oh, I don't deny the existence of the soul,' said Mina. 'We all have to hope for something, but when I die I will not choose to converse with my family through a mountebank.'

He said nothing but his gaze drifted as it so often did, to the portrait of his wife.

'My brother,' said Mina, 'who has a closer acquaintance with the theatrical profession than he would like my mother to know about, tells me it is all done by conjuring, but unfortunately he refuses to give up his sacred secrets.' She shook her head. 'If I was brave enough I would enter Miss Eustace's fold and dare her to do her worst, and then I would find out all about her, but if I did that and then turned around and tried to expose her for what she is, I would only look like a jealous rival, and then she would be more famous than ever.'

'I only want to do what is best for Eliza, but I hardly know what that is,' said Dr Hamid.

'If we all take care of her tomorrow night,' said Mina hopefully, 'she will have a little pleasure followed by a disappointment, but that will soon pass, and she will then be more used to company and so we might find her willing to try another form of entertainment. A ride in the fresh air; views of the sea; a tour of the flower gardens. There is a grand new aquarium being built. I mean to go to it as soon as it opens, and I will ask her to accompany me. She will need a bath chair of course, but she would not be the only person in Brighton to do so; they are a very common sight on the esplanade, so she would not attract the curious.'

'You are a kind friend,' he said, with a sad smile.

'Only promise me that you will not falter in our bid to expose Miss Eustace. There are some who think it is foolish old ladies who are the most easily persuaded, but in reality it is men of education who understand the world and want to understand it better who are the greatest fools.'

He was thoughtful for a moment, then he nodded. 'I promise,' he said.

Thirteen

When Mina next saw her new friend she felt ashamed of herself for even having thought of trying to persuade her that she was being duped. Eliza's shining eyes, her animated nature and sense of anticipation were all too obvious, and if they were doomed to be dulled by failure then Mina promised herself that she would help to avert the worst of the blow and quickly suggest some alternative interest that would be a better direction for this new and otherwise laudable energy.

The tiny woman had been brought downstairs, and was perched on a padded chair in the parlour enveloped with pretty shawls, in such a way that it was not obvious that her twisted body was being carefully supported so that she could sit upright. There she held court, and graciously and smilingly and intelligently conversed with all the company. Richard was his usual handsome charming self, the Hamids were perfect hosts, and the evening would, thought Mina, have been wholly delightful had there been no thought of holding a séance.

'But Mr Scarletti,' said Eliza, to Richard, 'I have not told you or dear Mina – I know we have not known each other long, but I do hope I may address you so – of what transpired when Miss Eustace and Mr Clee called on me.'

'I am all ears,' said Richard, affably. 'I have not so far met these fascinating people, but hope to do so very soon.'

'Oh, they have the nicest manners, and are very kind,' said Eliza. 'Of course we talked at great length about how Miss Eustace was achieving remarkable things with the spirit world and she said that you, Mina, are the most wonderful medium yourself, but you do not know it yet.'

'I am certainly not aware of having any abilities in that direction,' said Mina. 'However, I promise faithfully to use no mediumistic powers at all tonight. The only influence exerted will be yours. That you can depend upon.'

'We dared to hold a little séance ourselves, just the three of us,' said Eliza, 'but at first nothing at all happened. Miss Eustace told me that she was very weary that evening and when she tires all her powers desert her for a day or two and will not come back until she has rested. Then they saw that I was disappointed so they agreed to try once more, and this time there were the most extraordinary raps and knocks, and all coming from a spirit called Joey, who I think is a child and quite a mischievous little fellow. I thought, of course, that he had come through Miss Eustace, but he said he had not, because she had no energy he might use, and it was all my doing!' She beamed with pleasure and excitement, and her breath laboured under the emotion.

Anna and her brother, who had undoubtedly heard this account before, looked at each other sorrowfully but said nothing.

'And did Joey have any messages?' asked Richard.

'Only that he liked very much to play on the tambourine, and he asked if I could procure one for him so that he could play it for me, and if I did then he promised that he would give me some flowers. Is that not extraordinary?'

'If he is a little scamp you must take care he does not steal them from an honest tradesman,' said Richard, 'or pick them from a public garden.'

'Oh, I hadn't thought of that!' exclaimed Eliza. 'Well, perhaps since he is a spirit he can just conjure them up out of nothing; Miss Eustace says that spirits can bring wonderful gifts sometimes. She had a basket of strawberries only the other day.'

'I do not think,' said Dr Hamid, gently, 'that even a spirit may make something like a flower or a strawberry where there was nothing at all before. Think of how long it takes for them to grow in nature.'

'Well, we must try it and see,' said Eliza, with a touch of defiance in her voice. 'Science does not know everything, and if Joey *does* bring me flowers tonight you may have hard work to explain it.'

'You must not be disappointed if he doesn't come,' said Mina.

'Oh no, I won't be,' said Eliza, brightly, 'I don't suppose the spirits come every time, and if he does not then we will try again another day. But let us begin. Anna, please be so kind as to arrange the table for me.'

The table was brought to the centre of the room, and positioned so that Eliza could rest her hands on its surface; chairs were put in place around it, and a tambourine was set in its centre. 'Now where are we to sit?' asked Anna. 'You direct us, Eliza, and we will do whatever you wish.'

'Oh, I suppose we just sit and hold hands,' said Eliza. 'Is there a special way we should be ordered?' She looked enquiringly at Mina.

'I am not aware of any,' said Mina.

'I believe,' said Dr Hamid, 'that Miss Eustace likes to alternate ladies and gentlemen, but due to the preponderance of ladies it has never yet proved possible.'

'Then there are those positive and negative influences that Mr Clee is so clever about,' said Eliza. 'And they must be alternated too.' She looked thoughtful. 'Mina, you and I are both positive, so we must be facing, and not joined. Daniel?'

'Oh I think we can assume that I have no ability in either direction,' said Dr Hamid.

'And of course we can know nothing of Anna or Mr Scarletti,' said Eliza. 'What a quandary! If Mr Clee was here he would know at once. I did ask if he could attend, but I fear he cannot come.' She shook her head regretfully, an emotion which was not shared by her companions.

No one moved and all attention was fixed on Eliza as she considered the difficulty. 'Very well,' she said at last, 'I will have

Daniel and Mr Scarletti on either side of me, and then Mina you may take your brother's hand to your left and Anna's to the right.' Everyone immediately complied with her wishes. 'That is perfect!' she said happily, when everyone was seated. 'I am sure that this is the best arrangement; in fact I can feel the power in me already. Daniel, if you would be so kind as to turn the light out, and resume your place.'

'You wish there to be no light at all?' he asked.

'I do; it is best,' she said authoritatively. 'Light can absorb all the power of the medium and then nothing is possible.'

Mina recalled that the dreadful Mr Home was one of the few mediums said to scorn darkness, which served to explain the devotion of his adherents. Nevertheless she felt sure that there were some tricks equally well performed in the light. A conjurer who demonstrated his tricks on the variety stage but would only work in the dark would not, she thought, enjoy a long and successful career.

Dr Hamid obediently extinguished the gas and made his way carefully back to his seat. The curtains had been closely drawn and not a single thread of light intruded into the room. Everyone clasped hands. 'And now,' said Eliza, the tension evident in her voice, 'I entreat you all to complete silence. Sometimes when the spirits come they are very quiet.'

Silence fell, or what counted for silence in a room occupied by breathing people, and they all sat very still. There would be no trickery this time. Mina had made Richard promise on pain of her great displeasure and a cessation of money supplies that he would only observe and not influence events, and she knew that Dr Hamid and Anna would not want to encourage Eliza into believing she was a medium any more than she did herself. Eliza's belief seemed genuine, in that she truly thought that spirits would come through her supposed supernatural powers, and it seemed unlikely that she would play tricks to convince her companions.

There was a very faint squeaking noise.

Eliza gave a little gasp. 'Joey? Is that you?'

'I am truly sorry,' said Richard, 'I moved and my chair creaked.'

'Was it not the spirit that made you do it?' she asked, hopefully.

'I regret, no.'

The breathing stillness fell again, a calm in which Mina almost thought she could drift into a dream. There in her curious inner life were the stories she found – she never really felt that she constructed them, but that they existed already like gems to be mined, and she lifted out them whole and brought them into the light and polished them. Time passed, five, ten, fifteen minutes or more, she could not tell, maybe as much as half an hour, and she discovered a new story of a gathering such as this, in which everyone waited in the dark silence and nothing came, until, with the company on the point of giving up, there came a ghostly tapping at the door.

She was so lost in her tale, that she did not realise at first that the tapping was real.

'Who can that be I wonder?' said Anna.

'Well, we will find out soon enough, and it seems the spirits will do nothing tonight, Eliza,' said Dr Hamid. 'So let us end the attempt there.'

He turned up the light, and the maid announced that the visitor was Mr Clee.

'Oh!' exclaimed Eliza, clapping her hands, 'that is wonderful! Please show him in, I had thought he was engaged elsewhere. Perhaps we will have some success, now.'

Mr Clee appeared, and was very apologetic. 'Please excuse my lateness,' he said. 'Miss Eustace had asked me to usher the visitors at her séance tonight, and I thought I would not be able to come here, but she has a slight headache and will not be appearing after all; so here I am. I hope I have not inconvenienced you.'

'Not at all!' exclaimed Eliza. 'You are just the man I was most hoping to see.' He beamed delightedly and sat beside her.

'We have been sitting here in the dark holding hands for ever so long, and I am afraid Joey could not come, and we are all very disappointed,' she confessed.

'How were the sitters arranged?' he asked. Eliza described the order of seating and he nodded. 'There was not a great deal wrong in that, but you see the numbers were odd and for the better flow of energy they should be even. '

She gave a little gasp. 'Oh! I was not aware of that – but of course now you are here the numbers *are* even and we may try again!'

'I hope you won't tire yourself, Eliza,' said Dr Hamid, anxiously.

'When I am tired, I will be sure to let you know,' said Eliza with a hint of reproach. 'Oh, Daniel, can we not try just one more time?'

He relented. 'Very well, but a few minutes only, and then I must insist you rest.'

'Oh, we will see if I need rest or not!' she exclaimed, laughing. 'Mr Clee please advise us on where we are to sit.'

'But of course!' said Mr Clee. 'I recommend that I as a negative sit between the two positives.' He took Eliza's right hand and indicated that Mina sit on his other side. 'And everyone else must simply alternate male and female.' Mina took Richard's hand and then Anna and Dr Hamid completed the circle. 'That is an excellent arrangement, I doubt that it could be bettered.'

The lights were lowered again. The air was close and still like ink. Mina could hear Eliza's breath as her constricted lungs struggled under the excitement. Richard to her right was unmoving, but a tremor began in Mr Clee's grasp to her left. It was hard to tell, but it felt as though his entire body had started to shake.

'Do you feel that, Miss Hamid, like a spark or a flame of electricity? It is most pronounced!' said Clee.

'Yes! I do!' Eliza exclaimed. 'Do you feel it Mina?'

'I feel – something,' said Mina, cautiously, 'but I am not sure what it is.'

'Are we all holding hands?' asked Mr Clee. 'No one must let go!'

Everyone assured him that they were holding tight.

Several moments passed during which the quivering and shaking of Mr Clee's body intensified. 'It is the power!' he exclaimed 'I have none myself, but it moves through me!'

'It grows stronger,' said Eliza. 'I can hardly hold on to your hand!'

'You must not let go!' he cried, and Mina for her part was determined not to release her grip on Mr Clee.

The shaking continued for a full minute, then there were three loud knocks on the centre of the table.

'Oh – it is Joey!' said Eliza, joyously. 'He is here! He is here!' There were three more knocks. 'Can you play the tambourine, Joey? I bought one especially for you.'

High above their heads there appeared a glowing light, not the solid brightness of the little dancing fairy points that had appeared at Miss Eustace's séance, but something softer, a little cloud, that hovered over the table, and turned and twisted and revolved, and as it did so, grew slowly larger.

'Oh Joey, my dear, is that you?' gasped Eliza. 'Will you show me your face? I should so like to see your face!'

The cloud changed, as clouds do, and gradually attained a shape that could almost be called a face. There were no eyes or even a mouth, but something like a nose was at its centre and there was a straggly fluff around it that could have been hair. It hovered in front of Eliza, and seemed to nod, as if bowing to acknowledge her, then it swirled about, circling the table.

'Oh Joey, can you speak? Please speak to me!' asked Eliza.

The face danced in an odd jerky pattern, still hovering high above the table, and there were two loud raps.

'Two?' said Eliza, mystified, 'Oh – that was not a yes or a no – perhaps it means that he cannot.'

There were three raps.

'Joey, can you play the tambourine? Oh please do!'

The face bowed again and there was the sound of the tambourine being lifted off the table, and a soft rustling like the wind stirring through metal leaves.

Eliza laughed with joy to hear it. 'Oh Joey, I wish I could reach out and touch your dear face – will you let me?'

There was a louder rattle on the tambourine. 'Do not think of it,' said Mr Clee, nervously, through clenched teeth. 'Keep tight hold of my hand, or all will disappear! Remember it is your own energy that creates the substance of this apparition and plays the instrument. It must not be disturbed!'

In a few more moments the tambourine started a good clattering rhythm, which it seemed to be doing while hanging in mid-air quite unaided by the cloudy shape, which shook itself, and sailed about over the heads of the sitters like a veil caught in a breeze, and there was an eerie sound like the wailing of a whistle.

Eliza gasped and cried aloud, and even with all the noises that surrounded them, Mina could detect a new and disturbing rhythm to her friend's breathing, as if she was finding it hard and painful to inhale. 'Dr Hamid,' said Mina, 'I am concerned for Eliza.'

'As am I,' he said. The scraping of his chair showed that he had jumped to his feet. 'Enough! This is enough! She cannot endure any more! I will not allow it!' His footsteps sounded across the room. There was a loud crash as the tambourine fell to the tabletop, a final strangled scream from the whistle, and the glowing cloud vanished in a trice. As the gas illuminated the scene, Mina saw that no one had moved from the table apart from Dr Hamid, and all other hands were still securely clasped. The tambourine lay on the table, and beside it was a small scattering of fresh flowers. Eliza was pale and struggling for breath. Her sister and brother ran to her at once. Water was fetched, her brow was bathed, and her bent back gently but firmly stroked.

Mr Clee had the good grace to look worried. 'I do hope the lady has taken no harm,' he said. 'The materialisation though a small one was constructed from her own vital energy and it needed at least a full minute to recombine with the substance of her body. The interruption gave it only a few moments. It will have shocked her, like being struck a blow.' He shook his head.

'She was already in danger,' said Dr Hamid, sternly, 'and I would suggest that this is never attempted again.'

'Oh, but it was so beautiful,' exclaimed Eliza breathlessly. 'Please don't blame Mr Clee! And look – Joey brought me the flowers he promised!'

'I blame myself for permitting this,' said Dr Hamid. 'Come now, Eliza, I will take you to your room.' She was too weak to protest. He lifted her effortlessly, and it looked as though it was a child and not an older sister that he held in his arms, then he strode from the parlour.

'There was really no danger,' Mr Clee protested, 'if only—'

'I tell you what,' said Richard, standing up, suddenly, and leaning menacingly over the seated man. 'If you were to leave this house immediately there would be no danger of my striking you.'

Mr Clee took the hint and departed very quickly.

Anna sank into a chair, and Richard, seeing a carafe on the side table, poured a glass of water, which she took, gratefully. 'There was trickery here, tonight, as I am sure you suspect, and Mr Clee was the trickster,' said Richard. 'Miss Eustace has made him her creature, and he is a vile being to prey on your sister in this way.'

'But how was it done?' said Mina. 'I assume he brought the flowers in his pocket, and he could have thrown them on the table at the end, but I had hold of his right hand throughout the sitting, I did not let go for even a moment, all the time the light appeared and the tambourine played, and Eliza had his left, indeed he exhorted her to keep constant hold.'

'Oh these people have their methods,' said Richard. 'It is surprising what can be achieved with a little practice.' He picked up the tambourine and examined it.

'Well, at least Eliza will be safe, now,' said Mina. 'I do not know what they wanted of her, but I am sure that they will not be permitted near her again. And if she tries to hold séances alone she will find that the power has gone.'

Dr Hamid returned, to say that Eliza was resting, but asking for her sister, and also the flowers. Reluctantly Anna put the flowers in a little dish with some water and went up to Eliza.

'We will not intrude on you further,' said Mina, 'but let me know when Eliza is well enough to receive visitors, and if she would like to see me, then of course I will come at once.'

'I am expected at Miss Eustace's séance in two days' time,' said Dr Hamid. 'Should I go? Or would it be better to sever all relations with that circle?'

Richard raised his eyebrows. 'Miss Scarletti asked me to watch carefully at these meetings to see if the sitters were being duped,' Dr Hamid explained.

'I leave the choice to you,' said Mina. 'Of course your sister is your first concern, I understand that.'

'Oh, I think if you need a spy, Mina, that can be arranged,' said Richard. He was thoughtful as they made their way home. 'So is that the summit of these charlatans' achievements so far? Rappings, tambourines, flowers, a shape that could be almost anything and Miss Eustace in glowing draperies?'

'As far as I am aware.'

He was still carrying the tambourine which Dr Hamid, who was glad to see it gone, had presented to him.

'Then I do not think Nellie has anything to learn from her, rather Miss Eustace must look to her reputation.'

'I fear that we must both now be deemed an unacceptable presence at Miss Eustace's performances,' said Mina.

'Oh, I shall find a way around that,' said Richard. 'Leave it to me.'

The following day there were two pieces of news, which were brought to Louisa by Mrs Bettinson. Miss Eustace, she said, was suffering from a bad cold and had decided not to hold any further séances until her health was improved. Mina wondered if that was true, or simply an excuse to avoid possible detection. For all she knew Miss Eustace was even now packing her bags to leave Brighton, something that would happily resolve the difficulty. The second communication was more unsettling. Miss Whinstone, who had refused to tell even her closest friends what was troubling her, had been briefly absent from home on a number of occasions for reasons she would not divulge, and had, according to her servant, recently gone away, her destination, purpose and date of return unknown.

Richard had also departed, and Mina found herself for a time bereft of company. She wrote to Edward, saying as little as possible about Richard's visit, and expressing her hopes that Miss Eustace would not trouble her further.

Miss Whinstone did not appear in church on the Sunday and neither did Mr Bradley. Mrs Bettinson, in a towering mood of frustration, revealed that she still had no idea of Miss Whinstone's whereabouts, although she had called again and been told by the servant that a letter had been received from her employer, giving her instructions and promising to return very shortly. The servant had, to Mrs Bettinson's extreme annoyance, refused to divulge the contents of Miss Whinstone's confidential missive. Mina thought that had such an incident occurred in one of her stories then Miss Whinstone would by now have been murdered for her money, her body, probably headless, hidden in a cellar, and a letter forged to conceal the crime, but she doubted that this was really the case. Mr Bradley's absence was more easily explained. Mrs Bettinson said that he had had an interview with the Reverend Vaughan and as a result had decided to attend another place of worship. She had also been making enquiries after Miss Eustace, and learned that the lady was in better health and hoped to resume her séances later in the week. Mr Clee, she added significantly, was also said to be slightly indisposed.

When Mina returned from church a very troubling note awaited her. Anna Hamid had written to say that although Eliza had recovered from her shock, she had since fallen ill. A heavy cold had settled on her lungs; she was too unwell to receive visitors, and was being nursed night and day. Mina sent a note to express her concern, enclosing one of her stories, which she hoped Anna might like to read to Eliza. The next day she received a reply from Anna who said that Eliza had enjoyed hearing the story and sent her kind wishes to Mina, hoping she would be well enough to see her soon.

Mina's mother had received information that Miss Eustace hoped to be sufficiently recovered to hold another séance in four days' time, and Miss Whinstone was expected home that evening. Mina had heard nothing more from Richard, and was unwilling to rely upon him, since that course of action was more likely to result in disappointment than anything else. For all she knew the delightful Nellie Gilden had decided to return to M. Baptiste, or Richard had thought of another scheme to make his fortune. Dr Hamid and Anna would be devoting themselves to their own concerns and she was left to pursue her worries alone.

Mina wondered if there was, unknown to her, another possible ally. Perhaps one of the ladies who attended Miss Eustace's séances was a sceptic like herself, but had been nervous of speaking out. While she might have visited all the ladies concerned, she decided on a faster and simpler method of interview. It took very little prompting for Mina to achieve her aim, and two days later, Mrs Bettinson, the two widowed sisters Mrs Mowbray and Mrs Peasgood, and Mrs Phipps all came to take tea with her mother.

Their first and it seemed main subject of conversation was Miss Whinstone, who had suddenly taken it into her head to adopt two orphaned children, a boy and a girl, aged about seven and nine. Even the usually sleepy Mrs Phipps was wide awake during that startling revelation. Only Mrs Bettinson had seen the children, and said that they were clean and well behaved. They did not, she said rather too pointedly for politeness, resemble Miss Whinstone. Her friend had refused to divulge her reasons for the adoption, except to say that she had been very selfish of late, and felt that she ought to do some good in the world. The children were to live with her during the summer under the care of a nursemaid, and would shortly be found good schools.

The general feeling of the ladies present, at least the opinion that they chose to speak aloud, was that Miss Whinstone had felt lonely since her brother had died, and was entitled to spend her income as she pleased if it brought her consolation.

Mina was able to introduce the subject of Miss Eustace without difficulty by making an enquiry as to that lady's state of health. All the visitors were pleased to hear that the séances were soon to resume, something they were eagerly anticipating. 'I would not miss one for anything!' said Mrs Mowbray. 'Such a good company there, too! That handsome Dr Hamid is a very fine gentleman, and a great favourite! I went for a vapour bath last week, and I had thought to see him, but the ladies are all attended to by his sister who is very clever lady and I hope to be better acquainted with her.'

Mina thought it best to make no mention of Eliza's illness or Mrs Mowbray would be sure to hurry round and attempt to see her. She did her best to direct the conversation back to the success or otherwise of Miss Eustace's séances.

'All that flim-flam with bells and knockings are one thing,' said Mrs Bettinson, 'and if I hadn't had a private sitting I would be starting to wonder if the lady had any means of speaking to the spirits at all, but when I did, why, that decided me. I heard things she could not have known about. Miss Eustace has never in her life met my brother-in-law, or anyone in my family, but she knew where and when he died and what of. He was always a great one for worrying about his business even when he didn't need to, and through Miss Eustace he told me how happy he was it did so well, and how pleased he was with his partners and how they used their funds. *And* he said he liked the way my sister had arranged the drawing room, but told her not to wind the clock too strong because that made it stop. He was always fussing about that clock. If that wasn't him talking I don't know who it was.'

'It was the same for me,' said Mrs Peasgood. 'Mrs Scarletti, you really ought to consult her when she starts the séances again. I had such good advice from my dear Charles at the private sitting that it was almost as if he stood in the room with me.'

'I have already done so,' said Louisa, 'and I had no doubt that it was Henry who addressed me.' She paused, and sat very straight with a proud look. 'In fact I saw him, standing before me, as clearly as I see you all now, and we conversed, and he kissed me. I would not have permitted such a familiarity had I not been quite sure that it was my own beloved husband.'

This was the first that Mina had known that her mother had attended a private sitting with Miss Eustace. The nature of the revelation left her momentarily speechless, but her silence was not noticed since her mother was assailed by a battery of questions from her friends, which she fended off with a quiet smile. Mina, full of her own concerns, decided that the matter was too personal, too intimate to be aired in company and would have to wait.

'I would like to attend a private sitting with Miss Eustace if I am permitted,' said Mina, when she was able to join the conversation. 'Does the lady give of her time gratis or does she ask for a charitable contribution?'

'You know very well, Mina,' said her mother, 'that the lady does not ask for anything for herself and it is left entirely to the person who consults her if they wish to make their appreciation known.'

'I had thought to consult her, but Ronald is quite against it,' said Mrs Phipps. 'He says that if I want advice I should ask him.'

'You are fortunate in having such a kind nephew,' observed Mrs Mowbray, 'and one who works in the law. We do not all have living relatives to guide us.'

Mrs Bettinson gave a very significant look in the direction of Mrs Phipps. The lady was about sixty-five and had been a widow for so long that no one of her acquaintance could recall a Mr Phipps. Mrs Bettinson had, without any evidence, decided in her own mind that there never had been a Mr Phipps and that Ronald, her supposed nephew, was a son. The idea had become so established that she had convinced herself that it was a demonstrable truth, an opinion from which she was unshakeable.

'But you will continue to attend the séances?' asked Mrs Mowbray.

'I may not go to her again,' said Mrs Phipps. 'According to Ronald she caused a great scandal in London when she held séances there.'

'Surely not,' said Louisa, 'or Professor and Mrs Gaskin would not be so certain of her. They first encountered her in London and if there ever was a scandal, which I doubt, they must have heard of it.'

'Well, they might not know about it, because she was using another name then,' said Mrs Phipps, obstinately.

'And what name would that be?' demanded Louisa.

'Oh, I'm sure I don't know! But it was not Miss Eustace.'

'Then how can he know it was she?' said Louisa, reasonably. 'If the name was not the same then it was probably another woman entirely, and your nephew has made a mistake.'

'Well, I don't think I shall go, all the same,' said Mrs Phipps, firmly. 'Ronald said that she asks two guineas for an evening, and still more if people choose to believe in her. He says that if I want my fortune told I would do better spending sixpence visiting Madame Proserpina on the pier.' She had nothing more to say on the subject, and the other ladies looked on her pityingly as she settled down to her afternoon doze.

When the visitors had finally departed Mina attempted to draw her mother on the subject of her private séance with Miss Eustace, saying that she was eager to learn how her father had appeared and what he had communicated. Louisa was unusually reticent. 'He is happy, of course, and sees Marianne every day,' she said, contentedly. 'He says that her dear spirit was by his side as he passed over and has guided him in his new existence.'

'And you saw him?' asked Mina. 'Really truly saw him? I ask because no one else has made such a claim. Not just a face, or a hand, but a man standing before you?'

'I did,' said her mother calmly. 'Why would you doubt it?'

'You saw his face?'

'Yes.' Her mother grew irritable. 'Why all these questions, Mina? You will make my head ache if you are not careful.'

'Because I am seeking truth and understanding. Was the room in darkness?'

'At first, it was, but when Henry appeared his spirit was bright almost as day.'

'And Miss Eustace was there and you saw them both in the room at once?'

'But of course. I was only grateful that she was in a trance as certain of Henry's communications were of a tender, romantic nature. There are some things, my dear, that must remain forever between a man and his wife, things that no other person may know.'

As her mother reclined with a self-satisfied expression and took another biscuit, Mina could only stare at her, appalled and confused.

Fourteen

It was only a matter of time, thought Mina, before everyone she knew, perhaps everyone in Brighton, took leave of their senses and saw ghosts everywhere. Spectres would stroll freely down the marine parade, drive past in carriages, crowd on to the piers, and even sit down to dine with the living.

With no will to try and investigate the source of her mother's new madness, Mina directed her attention instead to the more tangible fact that her vulnerable parent was being drawn into Miss Eustace's grasp, if only so that she might hand over two guineas or even more for an evening of private revelations and dubious visions. Eager to make some progress, and seizing on the clues revealed by Mrs Phipps, Mina quickly secured an interview with that lady's nephew.

Mr Ronald Phipps was a minor variety of the profession of solicitor, a young gentleman dedicated to making his way in the world through hard work, study and maintaining a spotless reputation. The newest and most junior partner in a larger firm, he occupied an office barely larger than a cupboard and sat behind a small desk, which he had made his own by having everything on it arranged as if by a foot rule. Not having an attractive face, he had compensated for this disadvantage by a dignified bearing and the exercise of perfect grooming.

'Thank you for agreeing to see me,' said Mina, perching awkwardly on a chair and wishing she had brought her wedge-shaped cushion with her. 'I wish to speak to you on the subject of Miss Eustace the spirit medium.'

Deep distrustful furrows appeared on the brow of young Mr Phipps. 'I sincerely hope that you have not come here in order to arrange for the transfer of finances to that person,' he said, sternly. 'If you have, then not only am I unwilling to assist you but I must warn you in the strongest possible terms against such a course of action.'

'I can assure you,' said Mina, hardly able to conceal her delight that she had discovered another ally, 'that I have no intention of transferring a single farthing to Miss Eustace. But I assume from your comments that other clients have come to you with that request.'

'I cannot discuss the private affairs of others,' he said, with some small softening of his expression, 'only your own, but I am relieved that you have no wish to allow Miss Eustace to command your purse. How may I help you?'

'It is my belief,' said Mina, 'that Miss Eustace is a fraud, exercising her profession in order to dupe the bereaved out of their fortunes. I admit that there are many things she does which I cannot explain, but these are surely just conjuring tricks made to appear as if performed by supernatural means.'

His eyebrows jumped almost to his hairline. 'I cannot of course comment, except to say that you would do well not to make your opinions public unless you can prove that what you say is true,' he said.

'That is my intention,' said Mina, 'and I am assembling information for that very purpose. Your aunt recently called to take tea with my mother and I gathered from what she said that you warned her against Miss Eustace on the grounds that she had been involved in some scandal in London but under another name. I was hoping that you might be able to enlighten me on the circumstances. How did you come by this knowledge, and do you believe it to be trustworthy? Did you learn what other name Miss Eustace has been known under?'

'Ah,' he said, nodding, 'I am afraid this is a little awkward. I do know the origin of this story and I was obliged to warn my aunt before she did anything unwise, but it was in the strictest confidence, as there was no proof. I had not anticipated that she would tell her friends.'

Mr Phipps, thought Mina, while a professional man, was very young in experience or he would have known that this would happen with little if any delay. 'From whom did you hear the story?' she asked. 'You must have given it some credence or you would not have passed it on.'

'That is the difficulty,' he said. 'I heard it from an elderly client who I am not at liberty to name. She told me that she had been to one of Miss Eustace's séances, and was sure that she recognised the lady as a medium she had consulted in London some two or three years previously. Unfortunately she was unable to recall the London medium's name but she felt sure that it was not Eustace.'

'What was the nature of the scandal?'

He hesitated.

'I promise that I will not spread any slanders to the gossips of Brighton,' said Mina. 'I am making these enquiries for the protection of my own family but will not act upon any information until I have proof.'

He gave her request some thought. 'Very well,' he said, at last. 'On that understanding I can advise you that there was a rumour, but a rumour *only*, that Miss Eustace had found herself in prison, and that this was connected in some way with her séances. You must appreciate of course that there is a significant possibility that my client was mistaken.'

'I would very much like to interview this lady,' said Mina. 'Can you arrange it?'

He shook his head, regretfully. 'That is impossible, I am afraid.'

'Has she passed away?' asked Mina.

'My client is eighty-six and after a recent fit has become quite moribund,' said Mr Phipps. 'She is not expected to live long.'

'Did she confide this story in anyone other than yourself?' asked Mina.

'Not as far as I have been able to discover. I am sorry but I have no further information.'

Mina, after extracting a promise from Mr Phipps that he would let her know at once if he should learn anything more, was obliged to depart disappointed. Even if the story was true, and this was far from certain, how could she confirm it? She had no date and no name. Supposing she read every copy of *The Times* for the last three years and found a story of a medium who had been sent to prison, how could she even prove that it was the same woman, since the name was different? It was not as if *The Times* carried portraits.

From Mr Phipps's office she went to Dr Hamid's baths, where she learned that he was occupied with a patient. Anna, she was told, was at home looking after her sister. Mina waited in the vestibule, and before long Dr Hamid appeared and greeted her. They went into his office to speak, and he sank heavily into his chair looking weary and worried.

'Eliza is still very weak,' he said. 'Her lungs are badly affected, and Anna is constantly by her side. She speaks of you often, and says how much she would like to see you but she is afraid that she will make you ill, too, and dares not allow a visit.'

'I am very touched by her concern,' said Mina. 'Please do reassure her that I am well, and say that I will visit her as soon as she feels strong enough. And if you could let Miss Anna Hamid know that I have been most diligent with the exercises and already feel some benefit.'

'I shall certainly do so,' he said.

'I have some news of Miss Eustace,' said Mina, 'although what I might do with it I am unsure. It was told to me in the strictest confidence and I promised faithfully not to spread it to idle gossips. I do not, however, count you as such.'

He smiled and poured some mineral water for them both. 'I, too, have news, but please let me know yours first.'

Mina told him of Mrs Phipps's revelations and the visit to her nephew. 'All I can do is keep my eyes and ears open and hope to learn more,' she said.

'That may not prove to be necessary,' he said. 'Miss Eustace resumed her séances last night and although I chose not to go, a patient of mine did, and he has just regaled me with all the circumstances. We may not see that lady again.'

'I am delighted to hear it,' exclaimed Mina. 'Tell me everything!'

'You understand of course that I do not normally discuss my patients, however, in this instance …'

'I will be the very soul of discretion. And of course I need to know nothing as to the reasons he consulted you, or what treatment he received, only what he has to say about Miss Eustace.'

'I think he is intending to make the matter public with a letter to the newspapers, and there were others present too, so what I am about to tell you is no secret,' said Dr Hamid. 'You will just hear it a little before the town does. The gentleman's name was Mr Jordan. I am not sure if you are acquainted with him? He has a habit of rattling his watch.'

'Oh, yes,' said Mina, 'I have met him only once, when he attended Mr Bradley's first healing circle at our house. He made comments of a sceptical nature, I recall, and was not invited back.'

'Mr Jordan informed me that he is a very determined opponent of all things supernatural, and had been trying for some time to gain admission to one of Miss Eustace's séances without success, as his opinions were too well known,' said Dr Hamid. 'He has a friend, however, his business partner Mr Conroy who is a devoted believer, indeed the two men enjoy nothing more than arguing about the subject at some length. It appears that Mr Jordan made a wager with Mr Conroy that if he could only gain admission to one of Miss Eustace's séances he could prove her to be a fraud, and Mr Conroy obtained a ticket for himself and for Mr Jordan who he introduced as his brother.'

'How wonderful! How admirable!' said Mina.

'There was, I think you must admit, some element of fraud in Mr Jordan's proceedings,' said Dr Hamid, carefully.

'I excuse him,' said Mina. 'But what occurred?'

'The deception was complete. No one present recognised Mr Jordan for who he was and so he was admitted. He decided to bide his time, and to begin with he simply observed the table tipping and other phenomena, and then Miss Eustace retired to her chair behind the curtains. Mr Jordan and Mr Conroy volunteered to tie her securely, which enabled him to observe the arrangements closely. The ropes provided were thick and the lady's wrists very slight, and he felt sure that it was impossible to tie her tightly enough to secure her, and she was therefore perfectly able to free herself if she wished. The curtains were drawn and very soon afterwards the figure of Phoebe emerged. As she passed by him, Mr Jordan quickly snatched his hands from the grasp of the ladies on either side, and before anyone could prevent him, he rose up, seized the form of Phoebe in his arms, and pulled aside the veils that covered her face. To everyone's great astonishment – at least I feel we may exempt Mr Jordan from that emotion – Phoebe proved to be none other than Miss Eustace wearing little more than her undershift and enfolded in some brightly glowing draperies. Of course Professor Gaskin and Mr Clee leaped forward at once and tore Mr Jordan from the lady by main force, and she had no alternative but to run behind the curtains and hide. As you may imagine the meeting ended in some disarray. Mr Jordan tried to address the other sitters, but he was prevented from doing so, ejected from the house and told never to return. Mr Conroy, although he had had no warning of what his friend intended to do, was deemed to be a part of the conspiracy, and also found himself *persona non grata* on the pavement very soon afterwards. I am not at all sure if the two gentlemen remain on speaking terms.'

Mina laughed until she was breathless. 'Oh I *wish* I had been there to see it! So Miss Eustace is no more?'

'We may hope,' said Dr Hamid, more cheerfully, despite his other concerns, 'that we have seen the last of that lady, at least in Brighton. I imagine that Professor and Mrs Gaskin are now very disappointed in her and will retreat back to London, sadder and wiser for their experience.'

'Of course there is nothing to prevent Miss Eustace going to another town and promoting herself under another name and finding more dupes, but that is not something I am able to concern myself with,' said Mina, regretfully.

'You cannot be everywhere and be a guardian to the world,' said Dr Hamid. 'We must do all we can to protect our loved ones, keep a careful watch for our friends, and help those in need of charity, but that is all that can be expected of us.'

Mina was obliged to agree. She knew that her mother had not been at the previous night's interrupted séance, but had a ticket for that very evening. It was now, she thought, certain that the planned event would not take place. She decided not to mention to her mother that she knew of Miss Eustace's downfall. She was curious to know whether the news had spread to the faithful who had not witnessed it, and if so, what the town gossips were saying. Her mother, on learning the truth, would no doubt inform her that she had always had her suspicions, and deride the idea that she had been taken in. Mina, who did not want to cause an upset, but simply hoped to lay the unhealthy fashion to rest, determined to use her mother's reaction as the cue for her own response.

Mina returned home to spend half an hour in her room with a new purchase, a pair of dumb-bells. There was as yet no visible difference in her shoulders, but she was confident that that would come as she gained in strength. She emerged to find her mother locked in close enclave with the two widowed sisters, Mrs Mowbray and Mrs Peasgood, who had in all probability arrived carrying the awful news. When Mina joined them, she was greeted with calm politeness and all the conversation was of the weather. The ladies soon departed to make another call, and Mina's mother said that she was tired and took a short nap.

To Mina's increasing surprise nothing was said on the subject of Miss Eustace either at luncheon or at tea. She surmised that her mother did not wish to admit that she had been made a fool of, and, under the impression that Mina knew nothing about it, had therefore decided to drop the subject entirely. Any discomfort would soon pass, and Mina looked forward to daily life returning to something resembling normality. Later that day however, Mina was surprised to see her mother preparing to go out and found that she, together with Mrs Bettinson, Miss Whinstone and Mrs Parchment were all going to a séance at the Gaskins' apartments.

'Is that still to happen?' Mina asked cautiously. 'When I went to the baths this morning I overheard someone say that all future séances had been cancelled. In fact one person advised me that Miss Eustace and Professor and Mrs Gaskin were to leave Brighton. Are you to see another spirit medium?'

'You would do well not to listen to ignorant talk,' said her mother, tying her bonnet. 'They will not be leaving and Miss Eustace will be conducting a séance this very night. We are promised something extraordinary, but the conditions must be exactly right. It is open only to a select few. If you had been more co-operative you might have been of that number, but I am afraid there is no hope for you.'

'Then the rumour about the incident provoked by Mr Jordan is false?' asked Mina. 'It was such a curious story that I could not give it any credit.'

'There was an incident of sorts, although it might better be termed an outrage,' said her mother, angrily.

'Surely not!' said Mina. 'Were Mrs Mowbray and Mrs Peasgood there? What did they say?'

Louisa favoured the hall mirror with an admiring glance. 'If you *must* know, Mr Jordan, who is a highly unpleasant person, obtained entry to the séance by giving a false name. He then nearly killed Miss Eustace by committing a grievous assault on her spirit guide Phoebe. Everyone there was most disgusted by his behaviour and of course he was made to leave. It also seems, and I find this astonishing, that Mr Conroy, who has always appeared to be such a sensible gentleman, actually abetted him in this. Professor Gaskin said that Mr Jordan, who may not be in his right mind, suffers from a hatred of all things spiritual. Such is his intolerance that he is unable to see or even refuses to see what is obvious to others.'

'I was told,' said Mina, 'that Mr Jordan actually claimed that Phoebe was simply Miss Eustace in disguise.'

'Well, that is exactly what such a man would say! I am sure it was nothing of the sort!' said her mother. The carriage arrived with the other ladies and she departed.

Fifteen

Mina was consumed with curiosity about what would transpire at the séance, but had to wait until the following morning to find out. She saw now that she had been excluded from discussion of the event because her mother, imagining that it might be a day or two before Mina heard of it, wanted to learn everything she could, so as to be prepared to offer a complete refutation.

The next morning Mina did not need to prompt her mother to tell the tale, for she was regaled at great length across the breakfast table with an account of Miss Eustace's wonderful triumph. The lady had been surrounded with sympathetic well-wishers, who had applauded her and pressed her with many gifts, and Phoebe had later appeared wearing gorgeous robes and a glowing crown studded with jewels. The spirit had spoken to them all, and even kissed Professor Gaskin's hand. Their host, said Louisa, had offered a full explanation for the events of the previous night, which showed that Mr Jordan had been labouring under a delusion as to what had really occurred. Not only had Professor Gaskin written to all the Brighton newspapers with a detailed account of the incident, but he had also composed a small pamphlet, which was being printed as he spoke and would enlighten anyone who had heard the false accusations.

That afternoon, the professor's pamphlet, its ink barely dry, appeared in newsagents, libraries and reading rooms all over Brighton. The title was 'Miss Eustace, vindicated; an explanation of spirit phenomena.'

It was with considerable curiosity and a heavy heart that Mina obtained a copy and took it home to study.

Professor Gaskin commenced his address to the denizens of Brighton by stating that a certain intolerant hostile and ignorant person, whom he declined to name, but whose character was perfectly described by the fact that he did not hesitate to use violence to endanger the life of a virtuous lady, had suggested that Miss Eustace had been exposed as a fraud. Nothing, he declared, could be further from the truth. Jealous persons, persons who perhaps were interested in promoting rivals to Miss Eustace and hoped thereby to make their fortunes, had tried to destroy her reputation by spreading a false rumour to the effect that the materialised form of Phoebe had been found to be Miss Eustace clad in glowing robes. This was not at all what had occurred, and in the interests of scientific enquiry and progress he felt obliged to set the record straight.

Miss Eustace, he advised his readers, had but recently recovered from a severe cold, which had greatly decreased her available energy, but such was her selfless devotion to the world of the spirit, she had, in order to please her many admirers, recommenced her séances a little before her full powers had returned to her.

It had been determined to secure her to a chair before she entered the trance state, a duty that was always carried out by independent volunteers, and had this been properly done, nothing untoward would have occurred, but it now appeared that the men who had tied her had not carried out their task as well as they should have done. Indeed one of the men in question was the same man who later created the horrid disturbance, and Professor Gaskin suspected that the failure to tie the medium properly was not due to ineptitude at all, but was actually deliberate. His studies had led him to the conclusion that it was always best to tie the medium when a materialisation was to take place, not as a test of her veracity but for her own protection, in case she started to wander about the room while in a semi-conscious state.

When Phoebe's form had been produced on previous occasions it had been made wholly out of etheric matter drawn from Miss Eustace's body to create a complete materialisation. On the night in question, however, because of Miss Eustace's fragile state of health, there had been insufficient matter to create the whole figure. It was his belief, although he had never previously witnessed it, that in order to arrive at a full materialisation, the process had to pass through a stage of transition, which was not usually seen by sitters, since it took place in a cabinet or behind a curtain. Miss Eustace, although in a semi-trance, and therefore hardly responsible for or even aware of what she was doing, was anxious to meet the expectations of her circle, and rather than disappoint them, the process had commenced, but due to her weakness, it had paused during the transition stage and never achieved full materialisation. At this point, she had produced only sufficient substance to produce the outward appearance of Phoebe and had used it to drape her own form. This amazing material can usually be instantly moulded to adopt any shape; however, on that occasion, the shape that it adopted most easily, as causing the least distress to Miss Eustace, was that of the medium herself. The knots about her wrists failing, Miss Eustace had in her unconscious condition emerged from behind the curtains, only to be attacked with great savagery and almost killed.

Professor Gaskin took upon himself the entire responsibility for the unfortunate outcome of the sitting. He had allowed Miss Eustace to conduct a séance when not in full health, had inadvertently admitted to the circle a person of dubious reputation and harmful influence, and had then failed to ensure that the medium was properly secured and protected. The one person who should bear no blame at all for the incident was Miss Eustace herself.

Mina's mother had also obtained a copy of the pamphlet, which she studied with considerable satisfaction. Mr Jordan, so her friends had informed her, was beside himself at this development. Not only had he failed in what was practically an attempt to assassinate Miss Eustace, but the gossip about the incident and the circulation of the pamphlet had only increased that lady's fame, and demand for tickets was more intense than ever.

Mina, in despair over her quarry's triumph, retired to her room to consider what to do next. It was very apparent now that adherents of Miss Eustace and perhaps of all mediums could, in face of the most blatant exposure, explain everything away in terms that would serve to maintain and even reinforce their belief. There was no hope for them, and she could do nothing for them; indeed Dr Hamid was quite right, she had no real obligation to anyone but her own intimate circle as well as the helpless and the needy. It was not her place to save strangers from the consequences of their own foolishness and vanity. She tried to write, but unusually the words would not come. She had thought of composing a new tale, about a medium who turned out to be a thief, but what good would that do? It was after all a story, and anything might happen in a story.

Mina briefly considered asking for a private sitting with Miss Eustace, but even if she could bring herself to part with two guineas to the medium she was sure that any application would be refused, or if accepted, the sitting would have an inconclusive result. It was hardly possible for her to attend a séance in disguise.

Although she had heard nothing from Richard, she soon learned that he had been busy with his new pursuits. An advertisement had been placed in the *Gazette*, in the form of a letter from a satisfied customer of the new and sensational Miss Foxton, who had recently, so it was claimed, concluded a successful tour of all the major cities in the land where she had astounded everyone with her supernatural demonstrations. Miss Foxton was shortly to astonish Brighton, and tickets could be procured at very reasonable cost. A box number was given for enquiries. Mina thought that when she finally caught up with Richard she should at least be permitted to see the demonstration as a guest.

Richard soon swept back into her life like a burst of intoxication. He had the ability to both raise her mood and drive her to despair, often at the same time. He laughed heartily at the discomfiture of Mr Jordan, whom he did not see as a danger to himself. 'Let him come and welcome!' he said. 'Let him do his worst! In fact I shall send complimentary tickets to him and his friend Mr Conroy to ensure their attendance.'

'So you feel that you have nothing to conceal?' asked Mina with some surprise.

'Oh my dear girl, we have *everything* to conceal, but we will make a better job of it than Miss Eustace.'

'I have heard a rumour the truth of which I have been unable to establish, that the lady has been in prison, though under another name,' said Mina.

He laughed again. 'That would not surprise me in the least.'

'But I am afraid I don't know that name,' said Mina seriously.

He made an airy gesture. 'A woman such as she probably has a dozen.'

'I only wish I could find out some way of discovering that name and if the story of her being in prison is true. Do you have any idea as to how it might be done? You always seem to be full of ideas.'

He gave the question a few moments' thought. 'Well, you might waste your money employing a detective, but even if he found out the whole story and bellowed it from the cliff top, what would be the result? Miss Eustace's tribe of followers would refuse to believe it, or see her as a martyr to the cause of truth and a victim of persecution by the ignorant, and they would cling to her even closer. Those who do not as yet follow her would flock to see her and she would be more famous than ever. Those who want to believe will believe. Those who do not will not.'

'Then what can I do?' she pleaded.

He hugged her. 'Oh, Mina, you cannot save the world from itself! I know you are concerned for Mother and that is very good and right of course, but you are not Miss Whinstone's keeper, or even her friend.'

'I am Eliza Hamid's friend,' said Mina.

'And she has a loving family to protect her,' said Richard.

'She has been very ill these last few days,' said Mina. 'I believe that she caught a cold from Mr Clee who is young and well able to shake off such a thing, but it has affected her lungs.'

'Mr Clee will not be allowed near her again,' said Richard, firmly. 'When she is well I will get Nellie to entertain her with some conjuring tricks. Perhaps Miss Hamid can host a salon of magical entertainment that will be amusing but not as tiring as a séance. And she will forget all about Mr Clee's phosphorised handkerchief.'

'Phosphorised?' asked Mina.

He shrugged. 'How else do you think it glowed in the dark? It's an old trick. I am amazed that people are still taken in.'

'Do you recall the Davenport brothers?' she asked, thinking of Dr Edmunds and his mystification at the coat trick. 'They caused a great sensation only two or three years ago. People still talk of their confounding the laws of science.'

'Oh, who can forget the magical Davenports and their cabinet of wonders!' he declared. 'I fear they went to some expense for that. Never trust a medium who has his apparatus specially constructed. Well – never trust a medium. Yes, they had a startling and novel array of tricks but in the end the whole act boiled down to just the one. Only allow that they had some means of getting their hands free, as any good magician can do very quickly and easily, and all is explained. But I cannot fault them as businessmen.'

'Richard,' pleaded Mina, 'don't you think you should consider some means of income which would be more – well –'

'Respectable?' he asked.

'Yes. And less likely to result in your being put in prison,' she added. 'Mother would never forgive you.'

'Oh, you know she would, and so would you! But prison is an uncomfortable place, and I promise I shall make every effort to avoid it.' He jumped up. 'And now, my dear, I have a dozen things to attend to, and you may be sure to receive your ticket very soon.'

'Where is this event to take place?' asked Mina. 'At Miss Gilden's lodgings?'

'Oh no, the rooms are far too small. But I have made some enquiries and found a little band of spiritually minded ladies who like to meet and talk ghosts over their sherry and biscuits, and so I smiled prettily at them. One of their number, a Mrs Peasgood, who has a delightful home in Kemp Town, has been kind enough to let me use her drawing room gratis. There is ample space for both guests and performance.'

'Mrs Peasgood the surgeon's widow?' asked Mina.

'Why, yes, do you know her?'

'She is one of Mother's new friends!' exclaimed Mina, in alarm. 'Will you be there?'

'But of course! I am the master of ceremonies for the evening.'

'Richard, you cannot do this!' said Mina. 'Supposing Mother goes, or Mrs Bettinson or her other friends who all know you, as they very well might! What then? Mother would never be able to hold her head up again, and she would find some reason why it was all my fault.'

Richard was unperturbed, and planted a kiss on the top of her head. 'Have no fear, my darling girl! I have thought of everything!'

It was some hours after he left that Mina noticed that the oriental vase in the front hallway had vanished.

Despite accepting the fact that there was nothing further she could do for Miss Eustace's dupes, Mina was still curious enough to pay a visit to Mr Jordan. A Brighton directory and a few discreet enquiries soon provided the information that he was the proprietor of an emporium supplying suits of clothing to young men of fashion. He and Mr Conroy, who dealt in ties, cravats, cummerbunds and hats, had once had separate establishments and had long glared at each other from across the way, but one day they had met by chance, struck up a crusty sort of friendship and gone into partnership. This had flourished so well that they had recently taken another shop next door for ladies apparel, the supervising angels being Mr Conroy's wife and Mr Jordan's sister.

Mr Conroy was a bluff uncomplicated gentleman, with a talent for putting his customers at their ease, but Mr Jordan adopted a manner that was both imperious and condescending, as if to suggest that while the customer he was serving was neither noble nor royal there were others who were. He employed a hard-pressed assistant, but was always in evidence, looking on with a hard critical eye and making sure to give the wealthier customers his personal attention. The word in Brighton was that Mr Jordan was little more than a jumped-up tailor, although no one would have said it to his face.

The shop was redolent with the acrid, nostril-stinging scent of new freshly steamed wool, with a citrus hint of gentlemen's cologne. When Mina entered she found Mr Jordan overseeing his assistant, who was showing a gentleman a display of fabrics. His watch was in his palm as if he was timing the exercise, but when he saw Mina he snapped it shut, and put it in his pocket. 'Miss Scarletti, how may I assist you?'

'If you have a moment, Mr Jordan, I would be interested in discussing your encounter with Miss Phoebe – or should I say Miss Eustace, since I understand that you claim they amount to one and the same person.'

He grunted, and beckoned Mina away to one side of the shop, out of the earshot of his customer. 'You are not one of her acolytes?' he said with an unattractive sneer.

'Not at all,' said Mina, choosing to ignore the rudeness of his manner in the interest of extracting information. 'In fact I had a recent experience when I stumbled and fell against the spectre, and was thereby convinced that it was a living person, and female. It can only have been Miss Eustace. I understand that you went further than this and deliberately clasped her.'

'I did,' he said with some dignity. 'May I assure you that it is far from my nature to treat a lady in such a rough and indelicate fashion, but then Miss Eustace, whatever her pretensions, is not a lady. I cannot be sure quite what she is, or indeed who she is, but honest and selfless as she likes to claim, she is most assuredly not.'

'And you were quite certain that Phoebe is just Miss Eustace in draperies?'

'Oh beyond a doubt,' he assured her, with a short barking laugh. 'The supposed spectre struggled and kicked me most unmercifully as I took hold of her. She has all the good manners of a fishwife. I will admit that I cannot explain the mechanism of the imposture, but that is not my business.'

'Do you intend to take any further action against her?' asked Mina.

'No, none,' he declared. 'I have written to the newspapers of course, but my efforts are swamped by those of her credulous adherents, and she is now unassailable. Really, if these people wish to be parted from their money then I can only leave them to their fate. And now, I understand that there is to be a new sensation in town, a Miss Foxton and her – well, I hesitate to say what he might be – her theatrical manager shall we say, a Mr Ricardo. Are you acquainted with these people?'

'I am not familiar with anyone of that name,' said Mina, truthfully.

'He has sent me a letter today with a free ticket, and of course I shall attend and they must look to it or I will show them up to be the cheats and charlatans they are, and if I can see them both in prison I will consider my work well done.'

'I may well attend myself, as a matter of curiosity only, of course,' said Mina. 'And what of your partner Mr Conroy? Did your actions convince him that Miss Eustace is a fraud?'

'Mr Conroy prefers not to speak of that night,' said Mr Jordan, shutting his mouth with a snap no less firm than his watch.

Mina was naturally abiding by Eliza's instructions not pay her a visit, although she was anxious for news, and after leaving Mr Jordan's she turned her feet towards Dr Hamid's baths, which was not far distant, hoping that someone would be in attendance who would be able to let her know how her friend was progressing. Although Mina's exercises, which she continued with a dedicated determination, concentrated on developing her shoulders, back and chest, there were some that strengthened her legs and Anna had encouraged her in her usual habit of taking short refreshing walks. Mina still limped, and accepted the fact that she would always do so, but at least she could now limp faster and for longer and without pain.

As she approached the baths she noticed two gentlemen standing outside the building peering closely at something in the window but making no attempt to enter. Initially she supposed that it was an advertisement, but as she drew closer she saw that the interior of the establishment, seen through the glass, was in darkness although it was well within its usual hours of opening. A sensation of cold dread settled over her.

The gentlemen stood aside as she approached and she saw that they were looking at a notice bordered in black. 'It's closed up today,' one of them said, and they turned and walked away. Mina, her eyes clouded with emotion, could barely read the sign, which offered apologies for the fact that the establishment was closed due to a family bereavement, and promised that it would reopen on the following day. For several minutes she leaned against the door, making no attempt to control the tears that were coursing freely down her face, and ruminated on how cruel life could be. She thought of Eliza's sweet face and quick mind, and their lively conversations. She thought of how much she had looked forward to writing stories for her friend and encouraging her to seek new amusements. As she stood there several people came up and read the sign and went away, and some asked her if she was well and needed any assistance, but she said that she would recover, it was due to the shock of the bad news. One kind lady, who was a friend of Anna's and had known of Eliza's illness, confirmed what Mina had feared, and they talked for a few minutes until Mina felt able to leave.

She did not want to go home unless she could be certain of being able to escape to her room in order to be alone with her grief, and that was far from sure. She thought it likely that her mother would be entertaining her friends that afternoon and did not feel equal to feigning politeness in the company of Mrs Bettinson and her like; neither did she want to carry the tragedy home as if it was simply another piece of town gossip to be bandied about by chattering ladies. She walked instead towards the seashore, where she could best think about the muddled uncertain line between two worlds, and what might happen when crossing from one to the other.

Brighton was beginning to welcome the first of the new season of visitors, but on the eastern side of the town it was not so busy. A great swathe of building work had cut through the approach to the old Chain Pier and carved it away to make room for the new aquarium, but the new truncated entrance to the pier was not unpleasing. Close by, one could stand and take in the sight of the great iron structure that seemed to power its massive way into the sea like a steam train, and see the waves beating against its supports. In mild weather, as it was that day, the waves appeared to be caressing the pier with a firm but approving affection, but Mina knew that they could suddenly turn to rage and resentment. She saw the figure of a man standing alone and looking out to sea, and recognised him as Dr Hamid. She hesitated, then approached him.

'I have just come from the baths,' she said. 'I saw the notice. I don't know what to say. I am so very sorry.'

'I must apologise for closing the business today,' he said quietly.

'Please, there is no need for any apology,' she reassured him.

'There are patients who rely on us for regular treatment; some are elderly, some in great pain. I have a duty to them.' He sighed. 'Anna is at home making all the arrangements, and I would help her but I think I am not very useful at present; at any rate she suggested I go out and take the air for a while.'

'Do you mind if we talk?' she asked. 'If you would rather be alone, let me know, and I will go at once.'

'No, please stay. You were Eliza's friend, and even in such a short while you came to know her better than most. Towards the end, she said what a comfort you were to her and how she hoped that when she was well you would meet again. She liked the stories you sent her.'

Mina hardly dared look into his eyes, the irises like fractured marble, with splinters of pain. 'I was so looking forward to seeing her. She helped me with a story I was writing, and I thought perhaps we might write one together.'

'When she was a child,' said Dr Hamid, 'my father was told that she would most probably not live past her twentieth birthday, but we gave her the best care we could, and she had a not unpleasant life, filled with interest. She inspired me, she inspired Anna and by her example we became better than we might have been and more able to help others.'

'That is her monument,' said Mina. 'She will live on through you and your sister. Please let me know when it would be appropriate for me to call.'

'Of course. I know Anna would like to see you.' There was a long silence as they both looked out across the rolling sea.

Carriages rattled past, like ships full of merriment and the promise of delight.

'Too many losses,' he said with another heavy sigh. 'Too many people taken away before their time. Eliza might have lived another twenty years, Jane another thirty. It is so cruel and unnecessary, when there are evil people in this world who live long and good people who do not. I wish I knew why that was! I can only pray, and …' For a few moments he looked as though he was biting back tears. Not so long ago they had sat beside each other in a circle and clasped hands, and she felt she wanted to reach out and touch his hand as a friend, but it would not have been right. 'When Jane died it was like a light that had illuminated my life going out,' he said. 'I would like to think that somewhere, somehow, that light is still burning, and that one day I will be able to see it again and go towards it. I need to believe. Surely we all do?'

Mina waited for him to say more but he did not. 'I hope,' she said, 'that you are not considering going to see Miss Eustace again?'

'And why should I not?' he demanded with sudden ferocity.

'You know why not,' said Mina, trying to speak as gently as possible.

He shook his head. 'One of my patients told me that he went to her for a private reading and received information that could have come from no one other than the deceased.'

'So some people claim,' said Mina, 'but I am not convinced it is so.'

'Well, you can hardly blame me for seeking the truth,' he said obstinately.

'No, I cannot, but this is not the time to do it, when you are in pain and wanting to believe anything that will give you comfort. Please tell me you will wait awhile.'

He closed his eyes as if to shut out the world and be alone with his misery.

'I would like to walk a little way,' she said. 'Will you assist me?'

'Yes, of course.' He offered her his arm, and they turned and walked along the Marine Parade with the sun reflecting off the bright white hotels to their right and the sea crashing like shards of blue-veined jasper to their left.

Sixteen

Mrs Peasgood was a lady nearer in age to sixty than fifty and nearer in weight to fourteen stones than thirteen. Her late husband had been a well-regarded surgeon and had thus left her in extremely comfortable circumstances, with an annuity, a property, three grown sons, and as many grandchildren as any woman could decently want. She lived in a very pleasant villa in Marine Square, the upper part of which she had converted to make a roomy apartment for her sister Mrs Mowbray, whose husband had left her with neither family nor fortune but a great many attentive callers asking for the urgent settlement of their accounts.

On the ground floor of the villa was a magnificent east-facing drawing room, where twenty-five people might easily assemble in comfort, or thirty if they were more determined and less particular. As if one drawing room was not enough, the house had provided a second smaller one, behind the first, the two rooms being separated by a pair of heavy damask curtains, and both accessible quite separately from the hallway, while the back room led through a set of double doors to a beautifully maintained garden. Mrs Peasgood was a lover of music and often gathered her friends for a recital, the main drawing room serving as a kind of auditorium and the smaller as a stage for the performers, so transforming her home into a theatre in miniature.

It was this enviable space into which Richard had somehow cajoled himself and his protégée the extraordinary Miss Foxton.

Mina, to her great relief, had discovered that her mother had no intention of attending the new sensation's séance. Not only did Louisa feel that patronising Miss Foxton impugned her loyalty to Miss Eustace, which had become immeasurably stronger since the unfortunate incident with Mr Jordan, but she had heard rumours that Miss Foxton was not all that she seemed, and could not imagine what Mrs Peasgood could be thinking of to admit such a creature to her house.

As the ladies assembled in Mrs Peasgood's drawing room, Mina looked anxiously about in case her mother had changed her mind, but fortunately she had not, and neither Mrs Bettinson nor Miss Whinstone were present. Mr Jordan and his friend Mr Conroy were there, and while the ladies were engaged in conversation the gentlemen dedicated themselves to the more businesslike task of obtaining the best possible seats. Mina wondered if another wager had been made, and feared that Mr Jordan was planning an assault upon Miss Foxton and an exposure of the dastardly Mr Ricardo. She could not imagine how she might protect Richard from such an attempt, which could well prove violent. If Richard brought disgrace on the family she could quite see her mother packing him off somewhere to manage a ranch or plant tea, and realised that she would miss him dreadfully.

Thus far, Mina felt confident that no one in the room knew Richard by sight, but then she saw a familiar figure enter discreetly and slip though the crowds to find a seat near the back. It was Mr Clee, and Mina surmised that he was there to see what the other medium in town was doing and report his findings to Miss Eustace. He avoided engaging anyone else in conversation, and seemed anxious not to draw attention to himself. Mina was unable to decide if it was more important to protect Richard from Mr Jordan or Mr Clee, but could not see how either feat could be accomplished. She sat where she could see them both, hoping that she would not find it necessary to create a scene.

At length, Mrs Peasgood suggested that those of the company who had not yet taken their places might like to do so. There was an unexpected difficulty when two ladies discovered that

Mr Jordan and Mr Conroy had taken what they considered to be their seats, presumably because they always occupied those places at the musical evenings. Mr Conroy was all for giving up the seats to the ladies but Mr Jordan, claiming priority, was not, and incurred his hostess's grave displeasure by sitting with folded arms and stolidly refusing to move. It took all of Mr Conroy's tact and a promise of silk ribbon to enable the gentlemen to keep their places without a quarrel.

Mr Clee, Mina noticed, was watching Mr Jordan very carefully, although he was also pretending to read Professor Gaskin's pamphlet. She feared that even from the back row of seats Mr Clee would recognise Richard both by features and voice, as any man might another who had threatened to knock him down. She was uncertain what he might choose to do about it, and hoped she would be able to delay him if he made a sudden rush.

Mrs Peasgood glanced at her maid who turned down the lights. There were little exclamations of nervous anticipation as the room was plunged into semi-darkness, not the deep black demanded by many mediums, but a soft accommodating shadow. A moment or two passed during which the sea of onlookers rippled and settled into a pool, then gradually two hands pushed between the curtains and eased them apart. The draperies made a pointed arch in which stood an enigmatic figure, the faint light to which all eyes were becoming accustomed suggesting the form of a tall man.

'Good evening, ladies and gentlemen!' he announced in an accent that was very nearly Italian. It was Richard, of course, and since no member of his family had ever met the great-grandfather whose surname they bore, the attempt was more theatrical than convincing. 'Allow me to introduce myself. I am Signor Ricardo, and I have come before you to introduce a great wonder the like of which you will never have seen before.' He stepped into the room, allowing the curtains to fall together behind him. They could now see that he was in evening dress, but around his shoulders there swirled a long cape with something on it that glittered like stars. His hair had been brushed back, its unruly waves smoothed with an oily dressing that made it shine and appear darker than it was, and he sported a false moustache of evil aspect and a half-mask of black velvet edged with gold lace. It was a guise in which he might have personated Mephistopheles on the stage and wanted, thought Mina, only a blood-red waistcoat to be complete. She breathed a sigh of relief as he continued to speak.

'Newly arrived in this country from her triumphant tour of the Continent of Europe where she appeared before the crowned heads and nobility – soon to be the honoured guest of a Very Exalted Personage – I bring you the beautiful, the astonishing, the unique Miss Kate Foxton!'

He threw his arms wide and gave a deep bow, then drew back the curtains on either side. The space behind them was nearly bare, and appeared to have been darkly draped. All that could be seen was, to the right, a deep armchair, and in the centre of the stage a tall oriental vase, which looked very similar to the one that had until recently stood in the Scarlettis' hallway. Not only similar, reflected Mina, but identical – in fact it was the one that had stood in their hallway, and she was in no doubt that it was Richard who had, under some pretext or other, managed to abstract it.

Signor Ricardo strode across the stage with an attitude appropriate to a tenor at the opera expressing his undying love for a mature soprano, extending his hand towards the space that lay behind the fall of draperies to his left. He then moved backwards, with the lithe tripping gait of a dancer, leading with him the figure of Miss Foxton, whom he conducted to the centre of the stage for the examination and admiration of the audience.

Miss Nellie Gilden, for it was certainly she, was attired quite differently from the revealing costume in which she had posed for the *carte de scandale* which Mina had seen. She wore a plain drab-coloured costume so voluminous as to conceal her pronounced womanly form almost entirely, and neat little gloves and boots. Her hair, which the photograph had suggested might be gold with more than a hint of amber, had been transformed into a knot of glossy brown curls heaped high and surmounted by a wide hat trimmed with feathers. Mina, knowing that Nellie was an actress and therefore a woman who had abandoned all claims to respectability, looked in vain for anything in her features that might reveal a disreputable mode of life. The portrait, she was obliged to admit, had not done the lady justice. Miss Gilden might have graced any drawing room, any court even, and carried off the guise of a lady with complete success. The freshness of her complexion, which if painted was done with such subtlety that it appeared to be entirely natural, the brightness of her eyes, the curve of her lips, gave her a discreet yet alluring charm. All around, the audience gave a soft murmur of approval.

'Do not be concerned at this lady's youth,' said Mr Ricardo. 'True, she has not seen eighteen summers, but her abilities have been strong since she was but a small child. When only seven years of age she dreamed of the tragic death of a beloved royal personage. Just over six years ago she was in America and begged to be allowed to send a message to a very great man to say that he should not think of going to the theatre that evening. But the words of a young girl carried no weight – would that they had!' He shook his head sorrowfully.

'But now!' he exclaimed, with a suddenness that make everyone jump, 'to happier thoughts! Miss Foxton will shortly enter a state of trance and I beg you all to strict silence and contemplation.' He escorted Miss Foxton to the armchair and there she was seated, taking more care, thought Mina, than one might expect over the exact arrangement of such a simple costume. He then held his hands over her head, and moved them about in circles, to suggest that he was subjecting her to mesmeric influence. After a minute or so, Miss Foxton's eyelids drooped, then closed, and her head sank forward, so that her face was hidden underneath the brim of her hat and the plume of gently quivering feathers. She appeared to be asleep, yet it was more than that, as he demonstrated, since he carefully raised her hand, and allowed it to fall back limply into her lap.

Mr Ricardo then removed his cloak and after swirling it about his head a number of times, for no apparent reason other than to add a touch of drama and perhaps also distract the audience's attention from anything Miss Foxton might be doing, he draped it carefully over the somnolent medium. When he stepped back, all that could be seen of Miss Foxton was a small gloved hand, a tiny foot, and the feathers on her hat.

'The lady is in a trance,' he confided to the audience in a hushed whisper, 'and while she is in this state of unconsciousness the vital energy will begin to flow from her body!'

Mr Ricardo began to make extravagant passes over the recumbent figure, then he stepped away, with gestures suggesting that he was pulling at an invisible cord.

Abruptly, Mr Jordan rose to his feet. 'If I may be permitted,' he said in a voice more suited to a public announcement than controlled reverence, 'I wish to take the lady's pulse.'

'Mr Jordan!' whispered Mrs Peasgood. 'Kindly moderate your voice! And will you please sit down!'

Mr Ricardo paused, and smiled at Mr Jordan, who was standing in a very rigid and determined posture, his hands clenched into fists. 'I understand your concern for the lady's state of health,' he said. 'Do be assured that she is in no danger.'

'That I would like to see for myself,' said Mr Jordan, making no attempt to speak more quietly. 'Or are you one of those charlatans who prevent others from going near to the medium so as to cover imposture?'

'Sir!' insisted Mrs Peasgood, 'do please be seated. I fear you are making a disturbance!'

'I do not intend to cause a painful scene while a guest in your house,' said Mr Jordan with great dignity, clearly recalling his peremptory ejection from the Gaskins' parlour, 'neither do I accuse you of being a part of their confederacy,' – there were appalled gasps at the effrontery of even mentioning the idea – 'but I do ask, before we proceed any further, to satisfy myself that the lady is well. You cannot object to that.'

'I have no objection at all,' said Mr Ricardo, generously. 'Please do come forward, sir.'

Mr Jordan had clearly not expected to be so accommodated, but after an involuntary start of surprise he approached the covered figure in the armchair. Mr Ricardo drew back the cloak and then carefully lifted the brim of the hat to reveal the peaceful face of the medium. 'A veritable sleeping beauty in the flesh,' he said.

The sceptic paused, and after a moment, took Miss Foxton's hand in his, drew back the fabric of her glove, and pressed his fingertips to her wrist. There was half a minute of expectant silence.

'Are you satisfied now, sir?' asked Mr Ricardo.

Mr Jordan granted him a strange look. 'Hmm – yes – for the moment.'

The glove, hat and cloak were replaced as they had been before. 'Then if you would be so good as to return to your seat.'

There was nothing more that Mr Jordan could do, and unwillingly he turned back and resumed his place.

'And now,' said Mr Ricardo, addressing the audience, 'you will see before your very eyes, something that has never before appeared on any stage, or in any house in all this land. You will actually witness the stream of vital etheric energy as it flows from the lady's body. Prepare yourselves to be amazed.' He waved his hands over Miss Foxton again, but this time he gradually stepped closer, and at last a small gesture enabled him to catch in his fingertips the end of a bright wisp of something that was so light it was almost nothing at all emerging from underneath the cloak. Slowly, then with increasing speed, he pulled and lifted it away. It was a long strip of delicate transparent material that glowed in the semi-darkness and floated in the air as if it had no substance. He stepped backwards away from the recumbent medium, drawing out the banner of light until it extended for several feet, getting wider and brighter as it flowed, and then he carried it across the room to the vase and guided it inside. More and more it came, ten feet, twenty, it was impossible to measure, until far more had come than would have seemed possible, and still it piled softly into the vase. The audience was utterly silent, and as Mina gazed about her she saw that eyes were wide and lips parted in amazement.

The ethereal production at last glided to a conclusion and all was laid in the vase. Mr Ricardo hurried over to the still figure of the medium and touched her wrist. 'She lives,' he said, in a reassuring tone, and there were some sighs of relief.

Mr Jordan rose to his feet again, 'If you will permit me—' he began.

'Really, sir, I will not permit you!' exclaimed Mrs Peasgood testily. 'You have been given liberty once and pronounced yourself satisfied. Now either be seated or depart.'

Mr Jordan sat down again, but with very ill grace.

Mr Ricardo returned to the vase and walked all around it, allowing his hands to hover over its rim, moving them in circles with great deliberation, then he suddenly stepped back with a gesture as if throwing something inside. There were little sparkles in the air, like a cloud of dust motes reflecting all the light in the room. For a few moments he stood still, both arms extended, and then there appeared underneath his fingers little bright darting blue flashes like tiny flames.

There were gasps from the assembled company: partly wonder but mainly alarm. Several people glanced toward the exit as if calculating how easy it would be to escape if the house caught alight. A few looked pityingly at Mina, convinced that she would be unlikely to survive such a catastrophe. Smoke began to rise from the vase, a column of luminous silver blue mist that ascended to the ceiling like a fountain of fire. Fortunately there were no roaring flames, and Mr Ricardo's confidence so near to the display suggested to the onlookers that there was not, after all, any danger of their being roasted alive.

All eyes were on the shining feathery apparition, when gradually a shape began to form behind it, a shape that seemed to have risen from inside the vase and was coalescing into a figure of human stature. The eyes of the onlookers, which had become accustomed to the semi-darkness, were now partly blinded by the fierce blue glow, and for a time it was hard to determine what was being displayed, but eventually it was possible to make out a figure rising up, until it was above the rim of the vase and hovering in the air. As the smoke gradually dispersed, they saw that the form was female, and it was as well that it was a spirit and not a human creature, or its state of undress might have caused outrage instead of wonder. She was youthful, with a face white as a pearl and a great cascade of yellow gold hair. Her graceful form seemed to be quite naked, although she might have been clothed in a substance that resembled a second skin, glowing brightly and glistening with silver spangles, but revealing the outline of her tiny waist, rounded bust and hips, and long graceful limbs. Some delicate gossamer material that hung from her shoulders and wrists appeared to be wings and the undulation of her arms was all that held her in place. Unlike so many ghostly apparitions it was impossible in the presence of this heavenly creature to feel any fear, and the sighs of pleasure and approbation at the vision spoke of the onlookers' sense of privilege to have been there to witness the sight.

So intent was the gaze of everyone in the room, including Mina that it was some moments before she realised that Richard had vanished. Not that she imagined anything supernatural had occurred, rather that he had slipped quietly to one side while all eyes were on the lovely Nellie. After some graceful movements of her arms, the beautiful sprite, who might have been thought to have done quite enough to ensure her lasting fame, began to float away from her position above the vase from which she had apparently risen, and fly slowly about the little stage. She might have been merely swaying from one side to another, but the illusion that she was actually circling in the air around the vase, but several feet from the floor, was very compelling. Nothing like it had been seen in Brighton before, or possibly anywhere, and some of the ladies were actually sobbing quietly.

Slowly, the delicate sprite flew down to alight on the floor, and then she turned towards the side of the stage and with all the grace of a ballerina extended one arm. There was a small movement of her fingers, which produced the soft rattle of a tambourine. She beckoned, and from behind the curtains the instrument appeared, bathed in an opalescent light, and hovering in the air. Slowly it rose in an arc, like the sun ascending the heavens, and all the time it quivered and sounded. Higher and higher it rose, as if being guided by her gestures, until it reached a peak, and then declined again, finally disappearing behind the curtain on the other side.

The lovely apparition advanced a little, and stood before Mr Jordan, slowly beating her wings, and fixed him with a very enigmatic expression. Mr Jordan, who, if his eyes had started out from his head any more than they were, would have found himself blind, recoiled in terror. He had had no compunction about roughly clasping the figure of Phoebe in his arms, but as he gazed on the fairy creature before him, he was both struck dumb and too afraid to even think of reaching out to touch her. She laughed, and it was a sound like bells. Then, she began to dance.

It was a sight more appropriate to a gentlemen's private booth at a fairground than the drawing room of a respectable widow; still, since the dancer was not after all a living creature, the display of sinuous movements could be excused as unconscious innocence. Her arms were so like serpents that one expected them to turn into silver snakes and snap and hiss, while the undulating motion of her upper body supported by a supple spine pronounced her at once to be other than human.

Her dance done, she swirled lightly around, and tripped back to stand beside the vase, then turned and faced the throng in all her pale star-like glory. Her fingers moved as though she was casting a spell, and slowly she rose up into the air. The silvery smoke began to flow from the vase again, and she slowly dissolved into it and was gone. Just as everyone thought they had seen enough wonders, so the form of Mr Ricardo appeared in an instant before their eyes.

The audience burst into spontaneous applause, which he received with great humility. When the room was silent once more, their host said, 'And now it only remains for the etheric power to return to the body of Miss Foxton.' He circled about the vase once more, and a little wisp of light appeared in his hand. He guided the glowing trail carefully back across the stage to the sleeping body of the medium, and after urging it back below the covering cloak, he needed to do no more than stand by, making encouraging gestures as the material flowed in of its own volition. When the last of it had gone, he went to the vase and, tilting it, demonstrated to the audience that it was empty. He then made what Mina assumed to be counter-mesmeric passes over the form of Miss Foxton, who awoke with a sigh, threw back the cloak, took the hand of her gallant magnetiser and rose to her feet. Both made courteous bows to the company before Mr Ricardo came forward and closed the curtains once more.

As the lights went up the room was awash with conversation and everyone stared accusingly at Mr Jordan, who seemed uncertain as to whether he had received a blessing or a curse, since his face alternated between the pallor of fear and a flush of embarrassment. He utterly declined to describe his feelings – even Mr Conroy could get no words from him – and they hurried away, although Mina saw them pause in the hallway and Mr Jordan take a one-pound note from his pocket book and hand it to his friend. Mr Clee also left the house taking care not to speak to anyone on the way.

Seventeen

Mina had already told her mother that she would not be dining at home that night. Louisa had probably assumed that there would be sufficient refreshment at Mrs Peasgood's but Mina had other plans, a table she had reserved in a nearby restaurant at which she would entertain Richard and Miss Gilden, an invitation which they had accepted eagerly and for which Mina expected to pay.

She was joined at the table at the appointed time, Richard having doffed the mask and moustache, and scrubbed the oil from his hair, while Miss Gilden, her cascade of amber curls neatly dressed, was wearing a charming costume in a shade of blue that was only a little too bright. Whatever her origins, she was clearly experienced in restaurant etiquette and handled the silver and glassware with delicacy and assurance. Even viewed across the table, and with powder and paint so subtle that it was hard to be sure if she had applied any or not, she was a very lovely young woman, although unlikely to be as young as the claimed seventeen. Richard naturally took command of the table and ordered food and wine like a lord.

'I must congratulate you both on an extraordinary demonstration,' said Mina, as they waited for their soups and beefsteaks to arrive.

'Yes, it went mightily well,' said Richard. 'Mind you, I thought we were in for some trouble at the start when Mr Jordan decided to put his oar in. Nellie had already done what was needed for the next part and had to undo it, if you see what I mean. Fortunately Mrs Peasgood's observations gave her a few moments and all was well. It helped us, too, that he started up so early when we had not yet drawn out the etheric force, or he might have demanded to look into the vase. I think that was what he had in mind the second time he spoke but by then our hostess had had enough of him, as we all had, and put him in his place.'

'About the vase …' said Mina.

'Oh I popped in to see Mother and told her it needed repair,' said Richard, helping himself to buttered rolls. 'Don't worry, I'll put it back.'

'I suppose,' said Mina, 'that neither of you will tell me how you achieved such startling effects?'

Miss Gilden sipped wine and smiled sweetly. 'Oh, we like to keep our professional secrets,' she said.

'All I can say,' said Richard with a wink, 'is that I have been at great expense for a large roll of black velvet.'

Mina decided not to remind him of whose expense it had actually been.

'All the other materials and costume we required I already had in my possession,' said Miss Gilden, carefully omitting to mention how they had come into her possession or the opinion of M. Baptiste on the matter.

'We have been engaged for three more evenings,' said Richard, 'and this time, we may command five shillings a ticket. It will be a rather longer display but I am sure we are equal to it. Once we have our funds in place Nellie has some marvellous ideas about new sensations, which will need very little additional expense. In time we may even be able to hire a theatre and see what wonders we can perform in the mode of Professor Pepper.'

'He creates the most beautiful apparitions,' said Miss Gilden, with a dreamy look, as if seeing herself as a veritable ghost.

'But surely people know it is all a trick?' said Mina.

'Professor Pepper makes no secret of it, but there are some who like to hope that it is not a trick at all but real,' said Richard.

'Did you know that there are those who try to expose mediums by performing the same tricks and then explaining how they are done?'

'Do they have any success?' asked Mina eagerly, wondering if she could engage the services of such a person.

'None at all,' said Richard with a cheerful shrug, 'the mediums simply say that their accusers are themselves mediums and hiding their powers either knowingly or unconsciously under the guise of conjuring. And, of course, the dispute only adds to the fame of all concerned.'

'I wish someone would expose Mr Home,' said Mina, with some feeling. 'He is little more than a thief.'

'He is a slippery fellow and no mistake, but a clever one, and therefore very rich,' said Miss Gilden. 'But even if he was shown to be a fraud it would make no difference.'

Plates of hot soup were brought to the table, and they all ate, although Mina had less appetite than her companions.

'Have you ever seen the Davenport brothers?' asked Miss Gilden.

'I have read of them,' said Mina. 'They sit inside a cabinet and make musical instruments fly about and have a trick with a coat.'

'Some five or six years ago a watchmaker called Maskelyne witnessed one of their performances, saw how their tricks were done, and promised that he could do them as well. He and his friend Cooke constructed their own cabinet, advertised an exhibition and did all the Davenports' tricks and more, but in full light. They have since gone into the conjuring business themselves.'

'But the Davenports still command an audience,' said Mina. 'They were in London in 1868.'

'Oh yes, Mr Maskelyne did them no harm at all,' said Nellie. 'Just because their tricks could be performed by conjuring does not prove to the spiritualists that this was how the Davenports actually performed them. And the public wants, indeed prefers, to believe that they are communing with the spirits of the dead. It makes the evening more exciting.'

'Would you be willing,' asked Mina, hesitantly, 'to go to one of Miss Eustace's séances and observe how she carries out her tricks? There are some things I think I can guess. I believe she clothes herself as her spirit guide by untying her hands and having some means of changing her garments very quickly.'

'Undoubtedly,' said Miss Gilden. 'Tell me, is there much hymn singing at her séances?'

'Oh yes, Professor and Mrs Gaskin make a very great thing of it; they wish to be thought of as holy.'

Miss Gilden laughed her little bell-like laugh. 'Religion is no more than another disguise. Remember, everything has two faces. When something is shown to you openly and its purpose explained, it really has another secret one. I am sure that Miss Eustace asked very particularly for the hymn singing, as proof of the godliness of her endeavours. The true effect is, of course, to create noise, to conceal any sounds she might make such as the rustling of silk as she slips out of her costume.'

'Something you did not require,' said Mina.

'Ah, well,' said Miss Gilden archly, 'I have my own methods, which, of course, I cannot describe. My experience is of the stage, where we do not perform in darkness, and neither does our audience sing hymns. I will certainly attend one of Miss Eustace's assemblies, but I do not feel it would be appropriate for me to reveal how she accomplishes her feats.'

Mina was disappointed, but felt she must accept this. Although Miss Gilden might have regarded Miss Eustace as a rival, she would also have seen her as a member of the same profession. Theatre people living on the borders of respectable society had formed their own circle where they would be freely accepted, and assist fellow members in times of difficulty. To reveal the professional secrets of another would have been an act of betrayal, not only of an individual but a class.

The soup plates were cleared, and their steaks and potatoes arrived. Richard, looking pleased at the free and friendly conversation between his sister and his mistress, attacked his meal heartily while Mina and Miss Gilden ate with more decorum.

'Have you never thought,' said Miss Gilden, 'of going on the stage yourself?'

Mina was shocked by that question, not so much by the idea that she might enter the theatrical profession, but the thought that she might be in demand as some kind of novelty for audiences to stare at. Miss Gilden sawed neatly at her steak with no idea that she might have said anything disturbing, and Mina realised that for her, such displays would not be unusual. 'I am not at all sure what I might do upon the stage,' she said. 'I am certain that no one would part with money to hear me sing or see me dance.'

'But you may personate a child very convincingly,' said Miss Gilden, 'and you have a good speaking voice. If there is no role already written for you I am sure one could be done. Could you dress as a boy? You would be a great success as Tiny Tim.'

Richard gave a concerned glance at his sister, unsure of how she might react, but Mina could only laugh. Used to the pointing fingers of children, or pitying stares of adults who quickly turned away, or the embarrassed whispers of miraculous cures, she had not encountered anyone who was so bold as to comment unashamedly on the practical applications of her unusual appearance.

'Thank you,' she said, 'but my energies are directed another way.'

'Mina writes stories for children,' said Richard, hastily.

For a moment Mina regretted that she had not yet revealed the nature of her endeavours to her own brother, but reflected that if she did so his lack of caution might lead to unwanted disclosures.

'I accept,' said Mina to Miss Gilden, 'that since I am not of the theatre you will not reveal Miss Eustace's secrets to me, but would you be able to comment on whether what she does is a manifestation of the supernatural or conjuring tricks?'

'I can do that without seeing her,' said Nellie, calmly. 'It is the latter. But I am curious to see her, all the same.'

'The rapping noises for example?' said Mina, hoping that by addressing specifics she might draw out more information. 'I recall that at the first séance I attended, Miss Eustace was bound to a chair, but the noises were all about the room; the walls, the floor, even the ceiling.'

'There are a hundred ways in which that can be done,' said Miss Gilden, 'whether the medium is bound or not.'

'Tilting of tables?' Mina persisted.

'One of the easiest tricks there is. A child could do it.'

'And making the table rise up from the ground without touching it? Without anyone touching it. It left the floor completely, I saw it myself.'

Miss Gilden paused and looked reflective. 'Ah, now that is interesting. Was Miss Eustace alone at the table or was she part of a circle?'

Mina described what she had seen, and Miss Gilden gave it some thought. Richard ordered another bottle of wine and stared at his pretty companion with open admiration. 'You see, Nellie is both beautiful and clever!' he announced. 'Our demonstration was all her invention. But my lips are, of course, sealed.'

'Not only did the table trick astound us all, but the effect of it was to turn an avowed sceptic into her devoted acolyte,' said Mina.

'Oh, please explain!' said Miss Gilden eagerly, and Mina told her the story of Mr Clee's conversion, his appearance at her house and his part in the séance at Dr Hamid's.

The steak plates were removed, and Richard called for a list of iced puddings, which he studied with interest.

'I cannot imagine how the trickery at Dr Hamid's was effected,' said Mina. 'Obviously I must suspect that Mr Clee was somehow involved as nothing at all happened before he arrived, but both his hands were held fast the whole time. I had hold of one of them myself.'

'Oh that would pose no difficulty for an adept in the business,' said Miss Gilden.'One might easily free a hand to perform tricks while making it appear that both were being held. Everything you have described to me is simplicity itself if the practitioner has had sufficient time to master it.'

'But he is not an adept, unless he achieved mastery of the art in a few days,' Mina said.'Is that even possible?'

'To learn sleight of hand and have the confidence to carry it off alone, with no confederate, in such a short time?' Miss Gilden shook her head.'No, that would surprise me.'

'Well, that's a conundrum,' said Richard, beckoning the waiter, but Mina, with a sudden flash of understanding, thought that she had the answer, an answer that would explain not only how the lifting of the table had been done but everything else. It was, however, impossible to prove that her idea was right. Denouncing or even plainly demonstrating fraud was, she now saw, no obstacle to the medium and would not deter passionate supporters who clung to their admired favourites and their beliefs. Miss Eustace and her kind remained unassailable.

On the following afternoon Mina was able to study the most recent edition of the *Quarterly Journal of Science* in which its editor, the notable Mr Crookes FRS, had published his own contribution. She could not help but wonder if any other journal would have been so accommodating. The very title, 'Experimental Investigation of a New Force', seemed to tell the whole of the story she needed to know; nevertheless she read on. Mr Crookes had begun his work fired with a belief in phenomena that he thought were inexplicable by any known natural laws, a position which from the point of view of scientific disinterest seemed to Mina to be a poor one. The most remarkable exponent of this force was, he declared,

Mr D.D. Home, and it was on the basis of his extensive work with that gentleman that he was able to affirm so conclusively his belief in that force. The marvels which Mr Home had performed before the astonished eyes of Mr Crookes and other observers, who were friends of his, consisted of extracting a tune from an accordion while holding it in his fingertips at the opposite end to the keys, and later while it was being held by another person, and affecting the weight shown by a spring balance by lightly touching the end of a board to which it was attached.

Mina could not explain how Mr Home performed his tricks, and did not expect to be able to do so. If Mr Home had fooled learned men in front of their faces, she was unlikely to be able to devise an answer. She noticed, however, that Mr Crookes was wont to describe the force as 'capricious' and that even the miraculous Mr Home was subject to its unaccountable ebbs and flows. This was his explanation for a number of earlier failed demonstrations, Mr Home's power being 'very variable and at times entirely absent'.

Mr Crookes, thought Mina, was, like Professor Gaskin, too ready to explain away these difficulties in the light of his own prejudices. How likely was it that this supposed force of nature could be present one day and not the next? Did gravity vary from day to day? Did the tide sometimes choose not to appear? She thought not. Mr Crookes, in presenting his own case, had also, however, unintentionally pointed out its flaws. Everything, as Miss Gilden had said, had two faces. Whatever methods Mr Home had used to produce his results, he must have been unable to perform his tricks or chosen not to attempt them when the conditions, which had nothing to do with any supernatural force, were not right. He might even have used those failed attempts to familiarise himself with the equipment and artefacts provided, and learn how he might achieve success in future.

A gentleman called Cox had been present and he had been sufficiently impressed by the phantom accordion and the beam balance trick to suggest that the force used by Mr Home should be given a name. He proposed to call it 'Psychic Force', and suggested that those in whom it manifested itself should be termed 'Psychics'. Personally Mina preferred the word 'charlatan'.

Eighteen

Over the next few days Mina's pressing anxiety over her mother was alleviated; that lady had abruptly departed for London to visit her eldest daughter and family, saying that her assistance was needed with a domestic difficulty that she declined to describe. This inevitably created a new anxiety for Mina over her sister Enid, although she could not help wondering if the 'domestic difficulty' was the robust good health of Enid's husband, the desperately dull but worthy Mr Inskip.

With time on her hands, Mina was able to complete her story of the ghostly orchestra, although the helpful shade that had guided the heroine to freedom had transmuted since her first imagining of the tale from a young girl with long pale hair to a very small lady with a sweet face. Her next literary endeavour had as its heroine a mother who was obliged to assist her daughter in disposing of the corpse of her son-in-law, who had succumbed to a dose of arsenic in his soup.

She composed her story as she exercised, or took gentle walks in the gardens and on the promenade and piers. She didn't mind the crowds or the noise, or the quick stares that flickered away, or even the assumption made by worried onlookers, when she looked over the pier rails into the crashing sea, that she was contemplating ending an unbearable existence, rather than trying to calculate how long a man's body would take to be washed up on shore. It was a harsh ending for Mr Inskip, his mouth full of seaweed and teeth battered by pebbles, and dead, dead eyes. If only, she mused, all difficulties could be addressed so easily, but her thoughts brought her no answers, and she was even tempted to waste sixpence on a visit to Madame Proserpina, but decided against it.

She saw nothing of Richard, and assumed that he was busily engaged establishing his new career as an impresario of supernatural entertainment, although she was not sure if she should be glad of this or not. It was, admittedly, a source of income, and provided that he did not squander it, as he seemed to do with every other item of value that came into his hands, might make him independent of their mother. After all, M. Robert-Houdin had made a very respectable living on the stage for many years. Their father would in all probability have thought it a wonderful joke and made eyes at Miss Gilden. One afternoon, while Mina was out having her steam bath, the oriental vase reappeared in the hallway, with only a small crack on its rim that had not been there before.

The arrival of Miss Foxton in Brighton had not, to Mina's great disappointment, created any difficulty for Miss Eustace. Each lady had her own coterie, and as Richard had predicted, there was ample room for them both in the town. There was no suggestion in any of the prevailing gossip that the two were rivals. If anything, the excitement regarding Miss Foxton had merely served to increase the general interest in spirit mediums, and while Nellie Gilden quickly acquired a large number of admirers, Miss Eustace's fame also advanced. Mina had not heard a great deal of Mr Bradley, but saw from the newspapers that he was continuing to advertise his healing circles and assumed that he still prospered. While she was prepared under sufferance to accompany her mother to his pious demonstrations, she had no intention of going of her own volition.

With no new scheme in mind with which to end the career of Miss Eustace, Mina could only wait and hope that the craze would end, or that some other opponent more powerful than herself, another Mr Maskelyne perhaps, would appear, or that Miss Gilden's observations might provide some clue that would assist her.

The clue, when it did appear, came, however, from another source.

The newspapers had recently reported the death of a Mrs Apperley, a long-time resident of Brighton who was well known for her charitable work. As Mina read a lengthy appreciation of this selfless paragon, a detail that particularly caught her attention was that the lady had been eighty-six. This was the age mentioned by the young solicitor Ronald Phipps as that of the lady who had denounced Miss Eustace. Could Mrs Apperley have been the lady to whom he had referred? He had been silent as to her name, since she was a client, and Mina wondered how she might discover more. The only obstacle to this lady being the one Mr Phipps had mentioned was that the visit to the medium had taken place in London and Mrs Apperley had never, to Mina's knowledge, lived in London.

The next time she visited Dr Hamid's baths Mina mentioned Mrs Apperley and her sad demise, and learned that the lady had been a regular customer. Mina was quite open with Anna Hamid about the reasons for her interest, and found her forthcoming, since none of what she had to say was in any way confidential information or related to her patient's medical condition or treatment. On the last visit before her final illness Mrs Apperley had mentioned Miss Eustace, asking if Anna had ever been to one of her séances, commenting only that she had been once and would not trouble herself to go again. Mrs Apperley had never lived in London, but she did, it transpired, have a niece, a Lady Dunkley, who resided there, and a great-nephew of whom she was very fond.

Following Eliza's death, Anna and her brother had determined to devote themselves wholly to each other, Dr Hamid's children and their patients. Both lived with a grief that was weighty and relentless, but they had been able to take comfort from the fact that what they did for others was inspired by their sister.

The energy that Anna had once directed to the care of Eliza had now been transferred to Mina. There was a new kind of steady and concentrated focus on building Mina's strength and endurance, something with which Mina was more than happy to comply. They often worked together as she learned and refined her exercises, and the benefits were becoming apparent. Mina could see a new firmness in her muscles, which were beginning to achieve a defined shape quite out of keeping with what might have been thought womanly. It was pleasing to have such a secret, to have hidden power in her tiny frame. Anna was also experimenting with new ideas for exercises to benefit scoliosis patients for which Eliza would not have been sufficiently robust and Mina was her willing subject. One room in the bathhouse premises was now devoted to assisting patients with careful exercise, and was furnished with all the items that one might need, including a ladder of wooden bars that had been fastened to the wall. Mina had to perform a set of stretches while holding on to the bars, and under Anna's eyes found the heights that were best for her, sometimes grasping with one hand a little higher than the other to try and align her obstinate spine. In time, said Anna cautiously, she might even progress to lifting her feet from the floor and hanging her full weight from the bar, but not yet, she warned, and not without supervision.

The date and location of Mrs Apperley's funeral had been announced in the newspapers, and at the appointed time Mina joined the large throng who attended the service at St George's Kemp Town to give thanks for a long life spent in the service of others. It was not hard to identify the small grouping of people who were the family of the deceased, and Mina's request to be allowed a brief interview with Lady Dunkley was quickly agreed to, it being assumed from her appearance that she was one of Mrs Apperley's charitable cases who wished to offer her personal appreciation.

'Lady Dunkley,' said Mina humbly, 'it is very kind of you to spare a little of your time to speak to me.'

'Not at all,' replied that lady, who had a ready smile. 'Were you well acquainted with my aunt?'

'It is my great regret that I was not,' Mina admitted, 'but of course here in Brighton, she was generally famed and revered for her devotion to the poor and afflicted. There was, I have learned recently, another more unusual matter that concerned her, and I hope to be able to continue her work in that area.'

'That is very good of you, and it would be much appreciated,' said Lady Dunkley, supplying a small card. 'Please do let me know if there is any way in which I can assist.'

'Thank you,' said Mina. 'For the moment, I require only one small piece of information. Mrs Apperley very recently expressed her doubts about the activities of spirit mediums here in Brighton, who she felt were preying on the bereaved and doing great harm. In the case of one such lady whose name it might not be politic to mention, she thought she had encountered her once before, in London. Did she perhaps mention this to you?'

'I am afraid not,' said Lady Dunkley. 'We have been abroad for the last six months and I have not seen my aunt to speak to her in that time. In London, you say?' She shook her head. 'My aunt did not in any case visit London very frequently. After she passed eighty travel was very difficult for her. The last time to my knowledge that she was in London was almost two years ago for the christening of my grandson.'

'If I may be so bold,' asked Mina, 'when precisely did that take place?'

Lady Dunkley was clearly a little startled at the way the conversation had turned. She hesitated, and the ready smile faded, but after a few moments, as Mina had anticipated, accommodated the wishes of the little woman with the misshapen body who stood before her. 'It was in the early part of September 1869.'

'Do you think it possible that your aunt did go to a spirit medium during that visit?' Mina asked.

Lady Dunkley was even further taken aback by that question, and Mina feared that her boldness had made her venture too far. 'I can only say,' replied the lady, carefully, 'that it was a subject she did once mention to me as a great curiosity, in that it was a subject of conversation in society, but I am afraid I cannot advise you further.'

Mina thanked the lady warmly and departed. Once home, she packaged up the manuscript of her recently completed story to send to Mr Greville, and included a letter advising him that she had been reading about spirit mediums with the idea of writing a new story to feature one who was guilty of a terrible crime. She had been told of a scandal in London regarding a lady who had been conducting séances in the capital, most probably in September 1869 and had been detected in fraud and sent to prison. Unfortunately she did not have the lady's name, but hoped Mr Greville might know of, or be able to discover something about the incident.

Since Eliza's death Mina had not seen a great deal of Dr Hamid, although they occasionally met briefly when she visited the baths. After the confidences they had shared, which had seemed to add warmth to their friendship, he had made no more attempts to initiate a conversation, and she wondered if he had regretted his openness. On her next visit to the baths Mina mentioned this to Anna, saying that she hoped she had said nothing to offend her brother. Anna smiled sadly.

'The fault is not yours,' she said. 'I am sorry to say that Daniel has been receiving visits from Miss Eustace, two so far and I believe another is planned.'

'You mean he has paid her for private consultations?' said Mina, both concerned and disappointed.

'I am afraid so. I would prefer it if he did not, but I could not dissuade him.'

'Do you feel he takes any benefit from these consultations?' asked Mina. 'They may all be fraud, but if he finds some comfort in them then maybe – just for a short while –'

'It is hard to be sure,' said Anna, although her worried expression betrayed her feelings. 'You may imagine how it was for him to lose both a wife and a sister within months of each other. He looks for hope and it is hard to reason with him. He knows I do not approve and declines to speak to me on the subject. I think he knows very well that you would be of the same opinion as I, and it is for that reason he avoids speaking to you.'

'I am pleased to hear it,' said Mina, after some thought. 'It shows that he still retains a healthy doubt in what he is doing. Had he been convinced that he was right he would have been so armoured with certainty as to be impregnable to all argument and would be eager to try and convince me, too.'

'I am wondering if he has been warned that you are a bad influence best avoided,' said Anna, awkwardly.

'Oh, I do hope so!' said Mina. 'What could be more fascinating? I shall see him at once.'

'What will you say?' asked Anna.

'If you will permit me, I will be bold with him and ask what messages he has received,' said Mina. 'Miss Eustace in her private consultations convinces people that she is genuine by providing personal details of the departed, things which it would seem only their closest family and friends know. Everything else Miss Eustace does, be it ringing bells or raising tables off the floor, can be put down to conjuring tricks. Even the believers in such phenomena who put them down to a supernatural force are not convinced that there is an actual guiding intelligence causing them; they think it is some form of energy produced by the medium, and not the actual spirits of the dead. The private séances, however, leave us with only two possibilities – that

Miss Eustace is genuinely bringing messages from the departed or that she is an outright fraud with some secret means of finding out information. Perhaps there might be something in what your brother has experienced that will help us decide.' She paused. 'I do not wish to add to his burdens; only tell me I am wrong and I will go.'

'You are very welcome to try,' said Anna. 'What you learn may do good. Sometimes people will confide in friends what they will not tell their most intimate family.'

'That is true,' said Mina. 'My mother claims to have seen my father's ghost and received messages from him of a private nature, but will tell me no more than that. Perhaps I should interview her great friend Mrs Bettinson, or her dressmaker, who will no doubt have all the details.'

When Mina knocked on the door of Dr Hamid's office she was careful not to speak, since if he was avoiding her, hearing her voice would have given him the opportunity to plead some other appointment. She knew that he was kindly and would not thoughtlessly turn anyone away even if he was busy, and as she expected, he bade her enter. As soon as she saw him, his little guilty hesitation tainted with poorly concealed dismay showed that her surmise was correct; he was ashamed of himself for consulting Miss Eustace, but was unable to give up the visits, and thought that Mina was there to scold him.

They made the usual polite enquiries after each other's health and Mina asked about purchasing some mineral water. He tried to divert her to the lady at the reception desk, but Mina said, 'I will see about it on my way out, but I have more important matters to discuss.'

'If this is to be a long consultation, then perhaps—' he began.

'No, this cannot wait for another time,' she said. 'You know, I think, some of what I have come here to say, but I beg you to hear me out. I understand that you have attended private consultations with Miss Eustace, and I do not blame you for that, neither do I ask you to do anything other than what you feel will benefit you.'

'But you have a mission in mind, or you would not be here,' he said, folding his arms and leaning back in his chair.

'Of course I do,' said Mina, 'and an important one. You may hold in your hands the whole secret of whether or not Miss Eustace is genuine.'

'But supposing,' he said, 'I do not care whether she is or not?'

'Today you may care nothing at all,' said Mina. 'Today, if someone was to offer you conclusive proof that she is a fraud you would prefer not to know. Another day may be different, and then we may talk of this again. The difference between us is that I care very much, but I promise you that whatever the answer is, whatever the truth may prove to be, I will accept it.'

There was a long pause as he stared at his pen, which he had laid aside when Mina entered. He looked as though he very much wanted to take up the pen again and work on his papers, anything other than engage in the conversation she so earnestly wished for. He needed to choose, thought Mina, between his previous accepted view of the world, untrammelled by emotion, and a comfort that he knew in his heart was really an illusion; but he was not yet ready to make that choice. He seemed on the verge of taking the easy path and saying that he did not want to speak on the subject that so consumed his visitor, but as he gazed on Mina, there was a very slight sad smile, the capitulation of a man who saw his inevitable fate.

'I – received a message from Eliza,' he said at last. 'She said that she was in no pain, and I was grateful for that. I know that any charlatan might have invented such a message, but there was one detail about the seat and the nature of the pain that suggested to me that the message could only have come from Eliza. It was something she only ever spoke of to Anna and myself. What more can I say?'

It was a small point, but a convincing one, and she had to admit it took some of the energy from her campaign. He looked so dejected that she decided not to press him further, and wished him well.

She returned home to study the most recent edition of the *Gazette* and found that the arrival of a new medium in Brighton had encouraged a renewal of correspondence on the subject of spiritualism, some of which was from Professor Gaskin, and some from Mr Bradley, who wholeheartedly supported the world of the spirit as a very real, holy and beneficial phenomenon.

One correspondent, who declined to mention his or her name but hid behind the *nom de plume* of FAIR SPEECH, advanced the theory that only some of the manifestations at séances were honest but that proving one instance of fakery did not mean the medium concerned was a fraud. Even genuine mediums might find their powers failing them on occasion, and having to meet the expectation of their admiring audiences they were sometimes obliged to resort to a little trickery in order to provide a performance. This, thought Mina, was yet another argument that meant that even a medium caught out in a blatant cheat could escape exposure. The poor hard-pressed and exhausted medium, anxious to please the public, was thereby transformed from a charlatan to an object of sympathy.

In this curious war between the believers and the sceptics, the medium, she realised, was always bound to win. Even a temporary setback could be overcome and the beloved of the spirits would rise again stronger than before. The reason was obvious – the sceptic was a creature of the intellect, using sense and calm reasoning, whereas the supporters of the mediums were led by their emotions; more than that, their passionate need to believe in a more immediate afterlife than promised by scripture, the continued happy existence of loved ones they had lost, and their own immortality. Attack that, and one attacked the fundamental human desire to deny death, a fortress that appeared unassailable.

The one thing that might weaken the power of the mediums was the thing that Mina had been told would never happen – war within their number, which might lead to incaution and therefore revelations that might not otherwise have been made. But mediums, like conjurers, knew each other's secrets, perhaps even exchanged them, and supported each other when needed, and an attack on one was an attack on them all. A betrayal could easily rebound to the detriment of the accuser. Mina realised that if she wanted a war between the mediums she would have to start one herself.

Nineteen

It was a difficult path to tread, but after some thought she felt she had the answer. It was useless to make accusations of fraud, she could see that now, unless she had some very compelling evidence, which was not as yet in her possession, but there was another course she might take. Mina took up her pen and wrote a letter, which she decided to send to all the Brighton newspapers.

> Sir
> I have been a spiritualist for many years and have followed with some interest the correspondence on this subject in your pages. There are, as your readers will be aware, two ladies currently residing in Brighton who have been conducting séances. Both have impressed the populace with their sincerity, and the manifestations produced have been of the very highest order; nevertheless I feel strongly motivated to express my concerns regarding the demonstrations by the most recent arrival in this town. The medium who has been holding séances during the last few weeks is a lady of unquestionable respectability, who has always conducted herself with great modesty, and there has been nothing in either her deportment or her exhibitions that could arouse concern. The same, however, cannot be said of the lady who is newly arrived. The apparition which comes at her command and flies about the room in such a remarkable way may well be clad in a manner appropriate to the regions of the spirit, from

which she comes, but such a sight is not to be tolerated in a drawing room, especially where there are ladies of quality present. Rumour has it, and I earnestly hope that this is rumour and nothing more, that these demonstrations are largely patronised by single gentlemen, and not a few married gentlemen who ought to know better. Is this true? I hope your readers will enlighten me.

Yours truly

A SPIRITUALIST

Brighton

Mina thought the letter to be of sufficient interest, provoking without being actually actionable, to be taken up by at least one if not all the newspapers in Brighton, but that was only the first part of her plan. She carefully prepared two more letters, which she would send once the first was published.

Sir

I read with considerable concern the attack upon the character of Miss Foxton, who although not named, was undoubtedly the subject of A SPIRITUALIST's letter in your last issue. The writer claims to have been interested in spiritualism for many years but is quite ignorant of the manifestations that with the natural innocence of the newborn babe may appear. He – or is it a she? – with no understanding of these phenomena, chooses to insult Miss Foxton, who cannot be at fault in this matter. I suggest that A SPIRITUALIST write at once to withdraw the unfounded remarks, which include the vilest of rumours. I do not profess to know who the author might be, but do I perhaps detect a motive for the attack – i.e. professional jealousy?

Yours truly

BRIGHTONIAN

Kemp Town

Sir

I feel I must protest in the strongest possible terms against the tone and insinuations of the letter from A SPIRITUALIST published in your recent edition. The identity and motives of the author are no mystery to me. A fawning acolyte of Miss Eustace, seeking to enhance his own fame by attaching himself to the lady, has misguidedly sought to add to her reputation by insulting another medium. Should material of this nature be tolerated in a respectable publication? I do not believe it should.

I have personally attended the séances of both the ladies referred to and consider them to be of equal merit and interest.

Yours truly

A BELIEVER

Brighton

Mina posted the first letter and awaited developments. She had no concern about mounting an attack on Miss Foxton, which could only add to that young lady's fame, and she might make of it what she could. Miss Eustace, if she read the newspapers, which Mina felt sure she did, if only to be well acquainted with events and personalities in Brighton, would not appreciate until the second letter was published that it was she who was suspected of having written the first. Whether or not Mr Clee would recognise himself as the 'fawning acolyte' of her third letter she did not know. The accusation of indecency had a second purpose for Mina; it ensured that her mother, and quite probably those of her friends who knew Richard by sight, would continue to avoid Miss Foxton's séances.

Mina received a kind letter from Mr Greville, who thanked her for her new story, which he agreed to publish, but could not immediately recall having seen any item of news about the imprisonment of a medium for fraud. It was the kind of event that might have received only a paragraph, if that, in any reputable paper. He promised, however, that when he had the opportunity he would look into it further.

Mina's mother returned home, reporting that Enid was fully recovered from a mild attack of hysteria. Curiously, the natural disappointment that must have followed her daughter's recent discovery that she was not, as she had thought, about to become a mother again, had aided rather than delayed her return to health. Mr Inskip, confident that Enid was now well, had just gone abroad to undertake the negotiation of a property purchase by a reclusive nobleman, a loss which the abandoned wife was facing with commendable fortitude.

By the time Louisa Scarletti was preparing to plunge back into Brighton life, the letter denouncing Miss Foxton had appeared in the *Brighton Herald*, and was read with the triumphant declaration that she had always known there was something not quite right about Miss Foxton.

'I have heard,' said Mina, who was rather enjoying stirring the bubbling pot of suspicion, 'that the two ladies are deadly rivals and dislike each other intensely. I would have thought that there was room enough in Brighton for two spirit mediums, but they do not see it that way. I believe that the letter was written by an admirer of Miss Eustace – not the lady herself who I am quite certain is above such things – who misguidedly seeks to harm Miss Foxton's reputation in order to elevate his or her favourite. And you may not yet have heard this, since you have not been in town, but there is a rumour being spread about Brighton that Miss Eustace has once been in prison for fraud. It surely cannot be true!'

Mina waited for her mother's shocked reaction to this news, but to her surprise she only said, 'And what if it were? That is just the kind of thing that might be an endorsement rather than proof of fraud.'

It took Mina a moment or two to understand that her mother had already heard the story, and dismissed it. 'Do you mean to say you already knew of it? Is it true?'

Louisa smiled. 'I really have no idea. But why should it matter, in any case? Why should it not be true, and no blemish upon the lady? Just because a martyr has been burned at the stake or torn apart by lions it does not make their cause any the less holy, indeed, it becomes more so. I had heard the story from somewhere, and did not trouble myself to enquire further.'

Mina was content. She knew that the seed she had planted would grow, and perhaps in time bear fruit.

Richard did not trouble himself to write to the newspapers in defence of Miss Foxton, but it was with Mina's second and third letters that interest in the rivalry between the mediums was fully aroused. Professor Gaskin, in his role as Miss Eustace's patron, wrote to deny in the strongest possible terms that she had written the first letter. Its composer was unknown to him, as was Miss Foxton, and his protégée was too kind and gentle an individual to become embroiled in such unpleasantness. His was not the only letter, however; there were several others supporting A SPIRITUALIST's contention that Miss Foxton's exhibitions were indecent, some who agreed with BRIGHTONIAN that the author of the first letter was undoubtedly from the phrasing, female, and a rival who had chosen to offer anonymous insults, and others who agreed with A BELIEVER that the production was that of the 'fawning acolyte', who was known to creep into the séances held by his favourite's rival. While the debate raged through the mails, this was as nothing to the rumours that flowed around Brighton borne by that most ephemeral and rapid means, the spoken word. Mina soon heard her own rumours return to her, but this time she was told with great certainty that Miss Eustace and Miss Foxton had met in the street and almost come to blows, and that the cause was not so much professional jealousy as the fact that both ladies were in love with Mr Clee.

Her mother felt impelled to add her voice to the general furore, and decided that the best mode of protest was for the adherents of Miss Eustace to compose a joint letter to the newspapers and possibly even present the lady with a memorial to show their appreciation. It was for this purpose that a small assembly was arranged in the Scarletti drawing room, to which all interested parties were invited.

Miss Eustace, being the subject of the meeting, was not present, but the throng included Mrs Bettinson, Miss Whinstone, Mr Clee, Mrs Parchment and Mr Bradley, who while prevented from attending séances had expressed himself an admirer of the lady in question. Miss Simmons occupied her usual corner, but instead of the downcast eyes and humble demeanour of a servant, she attended to the proceedings with some interest, as if she was one of the invited guests.

'You may or may not know this,' said Mr Bradley, evoking a strong desire in Mina to take one of her dumb-bells and throw it at his head, 'but spirit mediums are often denounced by the ignorant, who envy their abilities and their fame.'

'We cannot educate those whose minds are closed to the truth,' said Mina's mother, 'rather I wish to console Miss Eustace that those of greater understanding support her unreservedly.'

The persons of greater understanding populating the room all nodded with expressions conveying relentless wisdom.

'I hope,' said Mrs Parchment, 'that we will be able to dispose of that foul slander on Mr Clee.'

'Oh indeed!' said that gentleman with a laugh. 'Why, I have never even met Miss Foxton, and you are all aware that my admiration for Miss Eustace is as pure as it is sincere. I have no attachment to either lady.'

'There are also some unpleasant rumours in town concerning an incident in London,' said Mina, 'events which are attributed to Miss Eustace, but which must have concerned another person entirely. I know nothing of the detail but it seems to have involved a spirit medium being sent to prison.'

'Well, I can assure you,' said Mr Bradley, with a broad smile, 'that I have never heard anything to the lady's detriment.'

'Nor I,' said Mr Clee. 'And recall that I have been until recently a most pronounced sceptic concerning mediumistic powers. Why, I used to read everything I could to support that prejudice. I was living in London at the time of that incident, and would most certainly have heard if Miss Eustace had been accused of any wrongdoing.'

'But these rumours will persist,' said Mina, 'and I am concerned that they may do harm to the lady's reputation. It is nothing short of slander, and must be stopped. I would suggest that our best course is to discover all we can about what occurred in London, and then when we know for certain the identity of the person involved we can publish our proof of Miss Eustace's innocence, and demand that the whispering stops.'

There was a slight pause, during which Mr Clee seemed about to say something, but restrained himself.

'That is not an easy thing to do,' said Mr Bradley, maintaining his smile with an effort. 'You may or may not know this, but—'

'Well, since you have both resided in London,' interrupted Mina's mother, 'perhaps you can tell us all if indeed there was any such incident as has been rumoured.'

'I am not aware of it,' said Mr Bradley, firmly.

'Nor I,' said Mr Clee, with equal conviction.

'Then that is our proof,' said Mina's mother. 'There is no need to try and find out more if the thing did not happen at all.'

'I think,' said Mr Clee, 'that anyone who is acquainted with Miss Eustace will know that she is incapable of carrying out a dishonourable act. That, I think, should be the whole tenor of our message.'

This was agreed and the meeting fell to discussing the wording of a letter to the press, and whether there should be a memorial or even a pamphlet.

Mina made no contribution to this, since she had her answer. When spreading the rumour of Miss Eustace's imprisonment she had said nothing about the date of the incident, yet Mr Clee had said he was living in London 'at the time'. It was a significant slip, which showed that he knew more than he was telling.

The next day Mina visited the reading rooms where she knew that a set of post office directories was kept, including those of both Brighton and the capital. Here she was able to discover a listing for the London business of the Theatrical Novelties Company, proprietor Benjamin Clee, costumiers and suppliers to the trade. Mr Benjamin Clee had been in this business for over twenty years and Mina wondered if he could be the father of Miss Eustace's new young admirer.

On her way home she thought carefully about the first séance at which Mr Clee had appeared, and the levitating table, and as soon as she was at her desk she drew a circle representing the table on a sheet of paper and marked on it from memory where all the members of the company had been seated. She thought that a great many conjuring tricks were effected by means of black silk threads and thin wires, but the table trick, because it had risen vertically and not tilted, could not be done by a single person. It followed that Miss Eustace had had an accomplice, and that both of them had come prepared with the apparatus they needed, perhaps hidden in the cuffs of their garments. Mr Clee had been seated exactly opposite Miss Eustace, at the furthest distance from her, supposedly to protect her from the interference of a sceptic, but this had actually positioned him where he needed to be to help her. When the table rose, the other sitters had moved back in alarm, but only Mr Clee, the very person who had suggested the test to begin with, had appeared to be holding his hands over its surface.

Mina was now certain that Mr Clee had never been a sceptic; he had been Miss Eustace's creature from the beginning. The two had probably been acquainted and in compact for some little time. The scepticism and the sudden conversion had been a pretence meant to add a touch of drama to the evening and increase the medium's fame. Mr Clee, Mina felt sure, was an accomplished conjurer, which explained how he had been able to perform all the mysteries that had appeared at Eliza Hamid's séance.

The next morning Mina received a letter from Mr Greville. He had found a small paragraph in a newspaper in October 1869 stating that a spirit medium and her husband had both been imprisoned for three months after claiming to have produced the ghost of a client's deceased child, which had proved to be a real child in white draperies. The fraud had been discovered because the tiny phantom had been unable to maintain the composure proper to such an occasion, gone into a fit of giggles, and dropped the spirit 'baby' he carried, which turned out to be a bundle of cloth. The client, outraged at the cruel deception for which she had parted with the sum of five guineas, would not be mollified by any explanation and had brought a prosecution. The medium had practised under the name Madame Peri, but her real name, the court had been told, was Clee.

Mina was unsure what to do with the new information, but decided, after some thought, to take it to Dr Hamid, whom she hoped had not lost his ability to reason. It was some encouragement to her that after she had described her discoveries and the conclusions she had drawn from them, he thought long and hard and even noted down what she had said.

'So,' he said at last, 'it is your contention that the lady called Clee who was sent to prison, presumably a Mrs Clee since the article states that she is married, is none other than Miss Eustace.'

'Yes,' said Mina. 'And since I can make a convincing case that she was well acquainted with and in collusion with Mr Clee long before they went through that theatrical ploy of his conversion to her cause, he must be her husband.'

'You have no portrait of this Mrs Clee,' Dr Hamid pointed out,' so the identification rests solely on the word of Mrs Apperley, and neither do you have the name of the lady she saw, but even if she did see this Mrs Clee, and that is far from certain, she last saw her two years ago. Mrs Apperley was then eighty-four years of age. More recently, when she was in a state of failing health that led to her death soon afterwards, she concluded that Mrs Clee and Miss Eustace were one and the same. I cannot see a court accepting evidence of that nature. And, of course, Mrs Apperley cannot now be consulted on the matter.'

Mina was tempted to mention that Mrs Apperley's standing as a recently deceased person ought not in some people's minds be an obstacle to the lady being questioned, but restrained herself from commenting. 'But is it not a remarkable coincidence,' she said, 'that the medium who Mrs Apperley said resembles, indeed is Miss Eustace, was actually called Clee? That is not a common name. And then we have Mr Benjamin Clee of London, who is in the very profession that suggests the family has an intimate knowledge of the stage.'

'It is certainly possible,' admitted Dr Hamid, cautiously, 'that Mr Clee is a member of that family, but the connection may not be a close one. Even if he is the son of Benjamin Clee, that proves nothing. He may well once have been a sceptic but later became convinced. And this Mrs Clee need not be a wife, but a cousin or some other relative, or even not related at all. You don't know if it is her real name.'

'But Mr Clee has lied to us,' said Mina. 'Whatever the connection he has with Miss Eustace, he has concealed it, represented himself as a new acquaintance and colluded with her in a piece of trickery which they had arranged between themselves before he even came to the séance. If he has been engaged in that dishonesty, what else is he hiding from us?'

Dr Hamid nodded, and for a while Mina hoped that her arguments were having some effect. She could see in his face the struggle that was taking place in his mind. 'I can understand what you are saying,' he said. 'If the levitation of the table was done as you suggest, with some apparatus concealed in the cuffs, then it does need two people standing opposite each other to perform it, and we might view it more as a theatrical demonstration than a communion with the spirits.'

'Exactly!' said Mina.

'But,' he continued carefully, 'I would maintain that what we see at the séances performed before an audience is different from what takes place at a private consultation.'

'In what way is it different?' asked Mina. 'We have caught them out in a deception. I know that some people claim that mediums sometimes perform conjuring tricks to please the faithful when their powers temporarily desert them, but do you really believe that?'

'Perhaps,' he suggested, 'we might regard the public séances as if they were only a means of advertising the private ones. Perhaps we cannot blame the medium too much for a little – I would not go so far as to call it fraud –'

'I would,' said Mina. 'The rappings and rattling tambourines and spirit faces made of nothing more than rags dipped in some phosphorus material are all trickery which Miss Eustace wants us to believe proceed from the spirits of the dead.'

He shook his head. 'I don't believe she has ever made that claim,' he said. 'Even Professor Gaskin thinks that these phenomena come not from some spirit intelligence, but are a manifestation of the medium's own powers; some force within her own body which she can mould and use.'

'But the lifting of the table –' Mina protested.

'I can see that it is possible that Mr Clee did assist in that, and you may be correct, he may be a relation, but even if he did help, he might have done no more than augment the powers that were already there. Perhaps Miss Eustace was unable to perform it alone. Mr Clee has said he is a strong negative and he might have been needed there to complete the circle.'

Mina stared helplessly at the unhappy man before her. 'What does Miss Eustace charge for a private séance?' she said at last.

He looked startled. 'She asks for nothing,' he said.

'Not directly, perhaps, but I know that she does receive payment from grateful clients. I have heard the sum of two or even five guineas mentioned. That is a goodly fee for an evening's work. Miss Eustace is on her way to becoming a rich woman. How much do you give her?'

He frowned. 'That is a private matter,' he said.

'Then you do give her money.'

'What I choose to give,' he said, with some annoyance, '– voluntarily you understand – is my concern. Now, if I may, I must return to my work. I have a patient I must see in a few minutes.'

'I don't wish to argue with you,' said Mina, sadly. 'I have had losses too and know how you feel. We may disagree strongly on this matter but let us at least be friends.'

He looked relieved that the questioning was over. 'Yes, of course. I am sorry if I spoke harshly. I did not mean to.'

'After all Mr Jordan and Mr Conroy can be friends and even business partners despite their differences.'

He gave a faint smile. 'If I might change the subject of our conversation,' he said, 'Anna tells me you have been very diligent in your exercises, and I can see that you move more easily than you did.'

'Yes, I shall soon be like an ape who hangs from the branches, or a man in a leotard who lifts weights, and astonishes the crowds. I shall take a booth on the West Pier and charge sixpence a show like Madame Proserpina.'

He laughed, and it was the first time she had seen him do that in some while.

Twenty

Mina's next call was on Mr Jordan, who with his watch-cover snapping like a hungry alligator, was bustling with energy, supervising an extended display of fashionable garments and fabrics in the recently opened ladies' emporium. Mr Jordan was, as ever, a smartly dressed and perfectly groomed man, but that day Mina detected something more. He had made himself into a walking advertisement for gentleman's summer clothes, and all about him was new and fresh. He wore a flower bud in his buttonhole, a sparkling pin in his cravat, and there was more than a sufficiency of cologne.

'The very latest fashions for the summer months,' he said, proudly. 'French-woven striped silk is all the rage, and there can never be too many bows or flounces. The court train, too, is quite the thing just now; there is nothing better to be had in London!' He drew her quietly to one side. 'I can assure you of our utmost discretion. Our ladies are very highly skilled in fitting every variation of the female form, and I know you will find something to please you. We also, of course, have a mourning department and our demi-mourning fabrics are both pleasing and tasteful.'

'That is very kind of you,' said Mina, 'and I will pay great attention to your display. But my visit today was on another matter. May we speak privately?'

He looked surprised, but after another consultation of his watch he agreed to allow her a few moments of his time and conducted her to a small office.

Mina explained to Mr Jordan the discoveries she had recently made about Miss Eustace, and asked what he thought ought to be done. She had expected him to be very interested in what she had to say, excited that his initial suspicions had been borne out, and eager to progress his campaign. To her surprise and disappointment he was none of those things, and instead appeared worried that some action was expected of him that he was unable or unwilling to perform.

'Mr Jordan,' said Mina, 'please tell me that you have not gone over to the spiritualists!'

'Oh no, not at all,' he said hastily, 'but you must know that my business partner Mr Conroy and his lady wife are very firm in their belief, and my opposition has caused some unnecessary friction between us. I have decided therefore to withdraw from the fray, and attend to my business. If people wish to be duped then they must take the consequences. I have done all I can, but I believe nothing can save them from their own folly.'

Mina decided to waste no more time on Mr Jordan and returned home, to find a scene of chaos. Rose met her at the door as soon as she arrived. 'Oh Miss Scarletti, I am so glad to see you – I didn't know what to do for the best! Mrs Scarletti rang for me and she is in such a state! She's in the parlour now.'

'Is she unwell?' asked Mina, hurrying as best she could to attend to her mother. 'Where is Simmons? Have you fetched her?'

'I think she is more upset than unwell,' said Rose, 'and Miss Simmons is upstairs packing her bags.'

Mina's mother, whose studied fragility had provoked a dramatic collapse under shock, was draped on the chaise longue like a discarded shawl, while the more robust figure of Mrs Parchment stood over her, alternately flapping a lace kerchief in her face and offering whiffs of smelling salts. 'Oh, Mina!' exclaimed her mother, extending her hand as if the weight of her arm could be supported only with a struggle. 'Where were you when I needed you?' Mrs Parchment, looking even grimmer than usual, stood back and allowed Mina to sit by her mother. A rapid glance showed Mina that there was, thankfully, no black-bordered envelope or telegraph message nearby.

'Whatever is the matter?' asked Mina, with the uncomfortable feeling that her mother's distress was in some way connected with the curious mania for the spirits that had so recently gripped the town. 'Has someone upset you? Have you been to a séance? Please do tell me if there is anything I can do.'

Her mother shook her head as if speech had become difficult, and making little choking sounds in her throat, snatched the kerchief from Mrs Parchment's hands and clasped it to her eyes.

'Mrs Parchment,' said Mina. 'Please tell me what has happened. Do I need to send Rose for the doctor?'

'No, no,' murmured her mother, 'it is just –' she gulped – 'I have been so terribly betrayed!'

Rose was standing in the doorway and Mina, seeing that this was an emotional shock rather than the onset of disease, sent the maid to fetch brandy, and set about chafing her mother's cool papery hands. 'Now then, Mother, you mustn't be anxious, I am here now, and if you like I will see if I can find Richard, and bring him here to see you, I know that will cheer you up.' Mina paused, suddenly fearing that that had been the wrong thing to say, and it was Richard and his adventures that had provoked the scene before her. Fortunately there was no reaction from either her mother or Mrs Parchment. 'Only tell me what has occurred and I will do my best to set matters right.'

Mina's calming words seemed to have some effect. 'It is that young person Simmons,' said Mrs Parchment. 'She seemed such a quiet sensible woman, but I am afraid that she deceived us all. She has had a fit of hysterics, and said some very unkind things to both your mother and myself which I will not repeat.'

'She is to leave at once,' said Mina's mother, pleadingly.

'Of course,' said Mina, firmly. 'She must. Mrs Parchment, please look after my mother and I will go and see to it that Miss Simmons quits the house immediately.'

Before either of those ladies could say another word, Mina left the room and with as much energy as she could muster, took the stairs up to Miss Simmons's room, which was at the top of the house. By the time she had made the climb she was grateful indeed for the exercises she had been doing, as a month or two ago she might not have achieved her object without some pain. The newly developed strength in her grip was both a surprise and a pleasure.

Miss Simmons, who was unusually red-faced, was in her bedroom, throwing unfolded garments into a small trunk, where they lay heaped upon each other in great disarray. She looked around in astonishment when Mina appeared, and while labouring under feelings that seemed to approach anger, had the hard defiant look of someone who thought she was about to be scolded and didn't care.

'Please calm down,' said Mina, 'and tell me all that has happened. Don't worry yourself about the trunk, I will get Rose to come and help pack your things. Do you have anywhere to go?'

Simmons breathed more easily and nodded. 'Yes, I have a sister in Brighton. I can go to her.'

'Well, that is something. Now sit down. Neither my mother nor Mrs Parchment will go into any detail about the reasons behind this upheaval, and since it was I who initially employed you, I feel I should know everything before you leave. You have been very efficient in all your work, and unless there is some compelling reason not to, I am prepared to give you a character so you may find another position.'

Miss Simmons sat on her bed, her eyes sparkling with unshed tears. 'It is Mr Clee,' she said.

'Oh dear!' said Mina. 'What has he done?'

Miss Simmons gave her an anxious look. 'You do not like him?' she said.

'My opinion of him is of no consequence,' said Mina. 'I am only interested in learning what has so upset my mother.'

'He is a very charming and clever and nice-looking young gentleman,' said Miss Simmons defensively.

Mina had a horrible suspicion where the conversation might be tending but said nothing.

'I had never thought for a moment that I might receive the admiration of a young man such as he,' Simmons went on, 'but some weeks ago I chanced to encounter him one afternoon as I was going to see my sister on my half-day, and he engaged me in conversation. We struck up a pleasant acquaintanceship, and after that we used to meet as often as we could. My sister always walked with us for propriety's sake, only she was a little way behind so that that we could talk alone. He never – I mean, there was no – he was always very respectful.'

'I am glad to hear it,' said Mina, 'although my mother would undoubtedly have disapproved, especially as these assignations seem to have been made without her knowledge.'

'That was the reason we could tell no one,' said Miss Simmons. 'James – Mr Clee – said he wanted very much to meet me more often, but he knew that I might lose my place if it became known.'

'Did he speak of his intentions towards you?' asked Mina.

'Oh, yes, and they are the most honourable possible,' said Simmons, happily. 'Marriage, of course. But he has no fortune and cannot think of it at present. He is, however, the favourite and sole heir of a great-aunt, who is in poor health and unlikely to live long, so he is sure to be a rich man very soon.'

'I suppose my mother found out,' said Mina, certain that the wealthy great-aunt would prove to be as illusory as any ghost. She declined to mention her suspicions that Mr Clee was already a married man, as she felt that Miss Simmons was quite upset enough without that suggestion.

'Yes, and I am sorry to say it was Mrs Parchment who told her. She must have seen us walking together and reported it. I think that is very petty-minded, to so destroy the happiness of another.

I am not sure the lady approves of marriage at all. From the things that she has let slip, I have gathered that she disliked her husband, perhaps dislikes all men. When I said that Mr Clee and I were intending to announce our betrothal as soon as he came into his fortune, she was very rude to me. She said I was deluded. She accused me of throwing myself at him, and said that it was quite impossible he could have any affection for me. I am afraid I was not at all polite when I replied, and I said a great many things I ought not to have. Still, it is in the open now, and at least your mother knows the truth behind the séance, though it cannot have pleased her.'

'The séance?' said Mina. 'Do you mean the one that took place here?'

'Yes, James asked if I might help him. He said he feared from some incident that had occurred recently that you had lost your faith in the spirit world and he wanted to restore your belief. He hoped very much that the spirits would be able to do all that was necessary, but sometimes, in the presence of an unbeliever, their powers fade and they need help.'

'So when you said that the table had moved –' said Mina, understanding at last.

'James said that Miss Eustace would try to get the spirits to move a table or a chair if they could, but if not, he would give me a signal and I was to pretend that something had happened. That would increase the energy in the room and after that the spirits could do all that was necessary. And you did hear rappings, which gave you a message from your father. I had no part in that, it was quite genuine.'

Mina saw that there was no hope for Miss Simmons, who would have to discover the hard way that Mr Clee had no interest in her, and had only courted her with a view to having an accomplice in the Scarletti household. How many other women he had duped in a similar way for the same purpose she dreaded to think.

It took all afternoon to restore the household to some semblance of calm. Mina dispatched a note to Richard, hired a cab for Miss Simmons and her trunk, and wrote a character for her, but not before obtaining her new address in case she might wish to speak to her again. Her mother was settled in a darkened room with her smelling salts and a carafe of water, and Mrs Parchment, whose foot had been restored to its accustomed strength, went out on one of her long walks.

There was very little point, thought Mina, in discussing the revelations concerning the séance with her mother, especially since Simmons, knowing that some of the events had been trickery, persisted in her belief that the rest were not. She could only hope that her mother, lying alone with her thoughts, would make her own conclusions, and come to her senses.

As Mina exercised alone in her room she reflected on the fact that Mr Clee and Miss Eustace had both been very eager to bring her on to the side of the believers. She recalled that Dr Edmunds in his letter to the Dialectical Society had mentioned that when he had expressed scepticism, the spiritualists had tried to persuade him that he was a medium. It appeared to be a common ploy to convert sceptics into believers by promising special powers, but in this case there had been particularly strenuous efforts to persuade her, and Eliza as well. As she pondered the mystery, Mina suddenly realised why both she and Eliza would have been valuable associates to a fraudulent medium, and it was Miss Gilden who had unknowingly supplied the vital clue. Both Mina and Eliza were adults in child-size bodies. Mrs Clee in London had used a child to represent a child's spirit and as a result had been found out and put in prison. She cannot have wanted to risk such an exposure again, yet the ability to produce the form of a child was one that would add greatly to the demands on her services. An adult who could masquerade as a child, smuggled in under cover of darkness, the sound of hymn singing masking any telltale noises, was a considerable asset.

Now that she thought about it, the smuggled confederate was probably the source of the phenomena at the very first séance she had attended. She had sensed another person in the room, and with good reason; there had been one, a very human presence. A figure cloaked in black, moving silently about on stockinged feet, tapping on walls and clinking glasses, while the onlookers, commanded to stay in their seats, had to clasp hands so they found it impossible to turn and look about them. The confederate, in all probability Mr Clee, had then disappeared behind the curtains to wave the glowing apparitions on the end of sticks. There was nothing he had used that could not be hidden under a cloak or in a pocket or up a sleeve. At the second séance the raps on the walls had been more distant, and must have come from someone knocking from the hallway or the next room, but these had occurred when Mr Clee was in plain sight, so there must have been another confederate, the maidservant, perhaps. Phoebe's voluminous draperies must have been made of some soft gauzy material like the delicate wisps that had formed so many yards of Miss Foxton's etheric powers, something that could be rolled up and made very small and carried under Miss Eustace's skirts.

In the middle of these deliberations, Mina was surprised by the sudden arrival of Mr Bradley, and found that unknown to her, her mother had asked Rose to send for him. Mina was unwilling to allow him to sit with her mother alone, and was obliged to remain in the darkened sickroom and listen to that gentleman's sympathetic and uncontroversial mutterings, which pandered to her mother's sense of outrage and were therefore well received. Mr Bradley said that while having only limited acquaintance with Mr Clee, who had occasionally attended his healing circles, he had been impressed by the young man's sincerity, good taste and intelligence. The entire blame for the upset was therefore laid firmly at Miss Simmons's door, that lady having had her foolish head quite turned by Mr Clee's natural friendliness, which she had misunderstood as protestations of love. It would have been useless for Mina to make any mention of the supposed wealthy great-aunt. Since she had originally employed Miss Simmons she was in no doubt as to how such an intervention would have been received, and for peace and quiet decided to remain silent.

Her reflections led her to the conclusion that Dr Hamid in their most recent conversation had been correct in one very important respect; there was a significant difference in what was performed at the public séances and the private ones. While it was easy to provide explanations for the simple phenomena produced in front of a gathering, everyone who had been to private consultations had reported being given personal information that could not have been known to anyone but the deceased and their intimates. It was with some reluctance that Mina decided that the only way she might gather more information was to obtain a private consultation with Miss Eustace. The chances that Miss Eustace would agree to such a thing were, she realised, extremely slender, but she felt that she at least had to try. Once Mr Bradley had departed, she wrote a letter to Professor Gaskin asking if she might make an appointment.

Mina remained sure that the Gaskins were as much dupes as anyone else, that the professor had embraced spiritualism as a means to enhance his standing, hoping to make great discoveries in science, while his wife bathed in the sunny glow of celebrity and the knowledge that she held a great truth which it was her duty and pleasure to convey to the ignorant. If the Gaskins' apartments were arranged so as to facilitate Miss Eustace's deceptions then it was done in innocence at her behest. Mina still did not know where the medium lodged, a location where presumably she stored all the items that were necessary to her performances.

Richard breezed in, and said he thought he could have his mother sitting up and drinking tea in a trice. He had good news; his business was prospering and he had no need to borrow money.

'Please do not tell Mother that you are appearing on stage with an almost naked actress,' said Mina.

'Oh, I will find some story to tell her, don't fear!' he said, hurrying upstairs.

Richard returned after an hour announcing that their mother was vastly improved, and would almost certainly not need nursing, although she had announced her intention of never employing another companion. 'I am afraid that will be your duty from now on,' he said. 'It is not what you might have wished, but I see no way to avoid it.'

'Nonsense,' said Mina. 'I would gladly tend my mother night and day if she really needed me, but this is no more than one of her airy vapours. Rose shall see to her wants, she has been with us for five years and my mother likes and trusts her, and I will engage a daily woman to take care of the cleaning.'

He smiled. 'You have it all planned. Now then,' he said rubbing his hands together, 'Mother declares that she has no appetite for anything except a little broth, so that means there is a dinner in the house that should not go to waste!'

Mina rang for Rose to order dinner and a suitable tray for her mother.

'I really do think that it will benefit my mother far more if I was free to go about my business and put a stop to Miss Eustace, than sitting chained to her side,' said Mina. 'I don't suppose Mother has mentioned Miss Simmons's confession that she was Mr Clee's accomplice in the séance they performed here?'

'She has not, although that doesn't surprise me. Simmons is a good young person and deserves better than Mr Clee, but unfortunately she can be easily persuaded of the reverse. Plain young ladies with no fortune can be made to do almost anything on a promise of marriage.'

Mina gave him a hard look.

'Oh, no please, Mina,' he said hastily, 'whatever I have done, I can assure you that I have never given any lady cause to complain of me. Does Nellie seem unhappy? But I know that other men do not have my scruples.'

'Has Miss Gilden attended one of Miss Eustace's séances?' Mina asked, avoiding any further conversation on the subject of Richard's scruples.

'It has been hard to get tickets,' said Richard 'as the gatherings are so well patronised, but yes, by dint of calling herself Lady Finsbury and having an expensive calling card not to mention one of Mrs Conroy's new Paris gowns, she was one of the congregation last night, and created quite an impression. She is all bows and lace and fans, and looks quite the thing. I think the Gaskins were very taken with her and, of course, Miss Eustace who thinks of nothing but money and how she can get it, has noticed her particularly.'

'Was Mr Clee there?' asked Mina, concerned that even from his seat at the back of the room he might have recognised Nellie from the séance at Mrs Peasgood's.

'Not in the flesh, but there were some rappings and knockings that might have been him. And if he had stood before her, he would not have seen the dowdy Miss Foxton in the elegant Lady Finsbury. As to her etheric and finely shaped friend,' he added with a knowing smile, 'I do not believe there was a man in the room who could have described her face.'

'And what were the noble Lady Finsbury's conclusions?' asked Mina.

'Exactly as we suspected, the effects are purely conjuring and chemistry and not very skilled at that. M. Baptiste is a hundred times better and he performs in full light. But then he does not pretend to be anything other than he is.'

'And you, Richard? What are you pretending to be to please Mother?'

'I am the manager of a theatre,' he said, proudly. 'A large theatre, patronised by Brighton's most fashionable society. Respectable entertainment only, of course. Mother never goes to the theatre so I think she will not demand to know more, although if she asks to be driven past the establishment so she can see my name on the posters I will have to make some excuse.'

'I might have wished you to be a private detective,' said Mina, 'then I could have employed you to discover where Miss Eustace lives.'

'Oh, that shouldn't be difficult!' said Richard.

'Excellent,' said Mina 'then I expect the answer within the week.'

Twenty-One

Not unexpectedly, Mina's letter to Professor Gaskin was favoured with a prompt reply to the effect that Miss Eustace was unable to grant a private séance as her energies were fully occupied with her present clients. Miss Eustace, thought Mina, would be occupied for as long as was necessary to prevent her ever having such a consultation.

She also received a letter from Miss Simmons, revealing that Mr Clee, the man who she regarded as her future husband, had somehow omitted to tell her his address. She had only ever met him in the streets or gardens of Brighton, and on each occasion they had made the appointment for their next meeting. It was essential, she wrote, that she should advise him of her new position, but unaccountably, at their most recent rendezvous, he had not appeared. Thinking that there might have been some mistake, she had gone to all their usual haunts, but he was nowhere to be found. Miss Simmons was by now consumed with fear that her betrothed had been taken ill, and was unable to send for help. She had called on Professor Gaskin for information, but he was unable to assist, other than assuring her that when he had last seen Mr Clee a few days previously, he was in perfect health. He promised to pass on a message to Miss Eustace, and shortly afterwards a brief note was received advising that although Miss Eustace understood that Mr Clee was resident in Brighton, she did not know his address. Miss Simmons had then attended one of Mr Bradley's healing circles, which she knew Mr Clee occasionally patronised, but Mr Clee was not there, and no one at the gathering knew where he lived. She had applied for a ticket to Miss Eustace's next séance, feeling sure that she would see Mr Clee there, but was told that the séances were fully subscribed and would be so for some time to come. In desperation she had taken to standing outside Professor Gaskin's lodgings in case Mr Clee should enter, but without any result.

Miss Simmons begged Mina to tell her if she knew her betrothed's address, but, of course, Mina did not. Mina wondered if Dr Hamid had found anything in Eliza's effects to suggest where Mr Clee lived, but on enquiring there, found that all Eliza's correspondence had been sent via Professor Gaskin, his lodgings being the address on the calling card left by Miss Eustace, and Mr Clee had not been a client of Dr Hamid's baths.

The desperate efforts of Miss Simmons to try and find Mr Clee, who, she was eager to advise anyone who wished to listen, was her intended, did eventually produce one result, a letter, postmarked London, the envelope printed with the name of a firm of solicitors, addressed to Miss Simmons at the Scarletti address, which Mina was obliged to bear to her former employee, now residing with her married sister Mrs Langley in Dorset Gardens.

Miss Simmons received the missive with great excitement and relief, for while she had never seen Mr Clee's handwriting she felt convinced that the letter was addressed in his hand, while the stationery he had employed proved that he had been attending to urgent business matters in London. Although she did not state it outright there was more than a hint of hope in her voice that the long and worthy life of his great-aunt might have drawn peacefully to its natural close.

Mrs Langley, a capable-looking young woman, was bearing up admirably under the requirements of a baby whose teeth seemed to erupt every five minutes. There was barely time for Mina to be introduced to her before a squeal of renewed outrage from the nursery sent the attentive mother hurrying away. Mina decided it was best to offer to withdraw so that Miss Simmons might enjoy her letter in private, but was reassured that this was unnecessary. 'You have been a better friend to me than anyone other than my own family, and you must share the good news.' Mina sat at the parlour table, while Miss Simmons went to fetch a letter opener. Even with the aid of the little silver knife, used carefully so as not to harm the precious contents, her hands were trembling so violently that it was a close question as to whether she would tear the envelope or stab herself in the hand.

There were two sheets of paper in the envelope, and although Mina could not see what was written, she observed that they were business notepaper, the top one with a printed heading. Miss Simmons read, at first eagerly, then with her eyes opening wide in disbelief, and by the time she reached the bottom of the first page, she almost fell back into a chair.

'Is it bad news?' asked Mina. 'Would you like me to fetch your sister?'

'I don't understand,' she said. 'There must be some mistake.' She glanced at the letter again, but this time her eyes flooded with tears and she was unable to read it. She held it out to Mina. 'Please, look at this, I can't see.'

The letter was not written by Mr Clee, but by a solicitor employed by Mr Clee. This gentleman had been instructed to advise Miss Simmons that he was aware that she had been spreading the rumour in Brighton that she was affianced to his client, a circumstance which had caused considerable distress and annoyance not only to his client but to the young lady of fortune and good family to whom Mr Clee was actually affianced and whom he was due to marry very soon. Miss Simmons was accordingly instructed to cease at once from spreading the untrue story, with the assurance that if she complied, then no unpleasant consequences would ensue. Should she continue, however, his client would have no alternative but to take further action to force her to desist.

There was nothing for Mina to do but go and fetch Mrs Langley at once, and show her the letter. Mrs Langley's expression as she read revealed that the contents, while unpleasant, were not, to her, wholly unforeseen.

Miss Simmons, heartbroken and wretched, was taken to a darkened room to rest. Mina naturally supposed that she ought to leave, but Mrs Langley asked her to remain. Her sister, she said, had spoken very highly of Mina and she would appreciate her advice.

Mrs Langley was a lady of very strong beliefs as to what was right and what was wrong. Proposing marriage to her sister and then pretending that the event had never occurred was a wrong that was not to be accepted lightly or without compensation. Making threats against her sister, who had done nothing more than tell the truth, was not to be tolerated.

Mr Clee had made a very grave error, said Mrs Langley with the steely look of someone bent on revenge. He had assumed that when he and Miss Simmons had gone on their romantic perambulations while she had followed at a discreet distance, that his words could not be overheard, but he was mistaken. She had been suspicious of his intentions from the start, and being blessed with unusually sharp hearing, she had been able to remain within earshot the whole time, and had heard every word he spoke. Mr Clee, she confirmed, had made her sister an honourable offer which he claimed could only be realised when he came into his fortune. Whatever his motives might have been, it was clear that he now had no further use for her, but by communicating through a solicitor, he had now supplied an address at which he could be reached. If her sister was willing to bring an action for breach of promise of marriage – and she would strongly encourage her to do so – she was fully prepared to go to court and give evidence of Mr Clee's guilt. It only remained for the family to appoint a legal advisor, and Mina suggested that she approach young Mr Phipps who she thought might be the very man.

Since Mrs Langley was a level-headed lady and not given to attacks of emotion, Mina decided to lay before her everything she had thus far uncovered about the medium who had been committed to prison in 1869. If Mr Clee was already a married man, most probably the husband of Miss Eustace, then unless his claim to be affianced to another lady was a lie to extricate himself from any association with Miss Simmons, he had been planning to commit a very serious crime, and had some questions to answer about his conduct. She saw a fresh light in the lady's eyes, the light of a huntress who had sighted her prey, noted its weaknesses and was in determined pursuit. Young Mr Phipps was about to be presented with a case that would shock and scandalise Brighton, and perhaps even bring a sudden end to the career of Miss Eustace.

Mina and Mrs Langley, seeing that they had a shared concern, promised to keep each other acquainted with developments. A few days later, however, Mina received a somewhat disappointing letter from her new friend.

Mr Clee, she learned, on being confronted with the newspaper report of 1869, had denied that he had any acquaintance with the lady named therein, declared that the newspaper must have made an error in the medium's name, and asserted that he was a single man, had never been married, and anyone who attempted to prove otherwise was free to try it, but would inevitably fail.

The confidence with which he made these denials made Mina pause. Either he knew that no proof of a marriage could be found, or he was gambling that no one would trouble to make enquiries. Mina did not feel equipped to challenge him on this point, but at least Miss Simmons's suit still remained.

There was better news from Richard, which Mina thought well worth the inevitable price of the dinner and wine she provided for her brother and Nellie. Richard had discovered that Miss Eustace was living in a lodging house in Bloomsbury Place. As he had promised, the secret had not been a hard one to uncover; he had simply hired a messenger boy to loiter outside the Gaskins' rooms on the night of a séance and then follow the medium to her lair. The lady, it was reported, on leaving the house had stepped quickly into a cab that had been ordered in advance, and it had been a delicate balance between speed and concealment to keep up with her progress unseen. The cab had not paused to take another person on board and Miss Eustace had completed her journey and slipped into the lodgings alone. A careful watch had been kept for some hours but no one else entered the premises. The house boasted a basement, a ground floor, and three upper storeys, but how these were divided and how many tenants were accommodated was unknown.

'Perhaps Lady Finsbury might pay her a visit,' suggested Nellie, who was resplendent in another new gown and a necklace that sparkled rainbows like broken glass. She patted the jewels occasionally as if wishing that they were real. 'I am sure Miss Eustace would be very amenable to that. The only slight awkwardness would be explaining how I came by her address, which she has clearly been at some pains to conceal.'

'I don't suppose she has thought to try to discover if Lady Finsbury exists,' said Richard, easing open a button on his waistcoat and puffing at a cigar. 'These lying types are so easily taken in, you just have to play them with their own tricks.'

'That's it!' said Mina. 'Her own trick! Of course!'

'Oh you have a perfectly wicked imagination, Mina,' said Richard, appreciatively. 'We are all ears.'

'All that Lady Finsbury needs to do,' explained Mina, 'is say that she was given the address by a spirit. Miss Eustace can hardly argue with that, as it is her stock in trade. Even if she is a conjurer, there may be some shred of belief in her that the things she pretends are real. I suggest, Miss Gilden, that you go there in your finest gown and best jewels, present Lady Finsbury's card, and insist on an immediate interview. She is bound to see you.'

Nellie nodded, thoughtfully. 'I can carry that off without any trouble; and perhaps I should offer some reason why the interview cannot take place at my hotel; a disapproving or invalid husband, perhaps. But what reason should I give for the urgency of my request?'

'There is only one thing that tempts Miss Eustace and her kind, and that is money,' said Mina. 'Perhaps the spirit has spoken of buried treasure or a hidden will, at any rate something of great value, and has directed you to Miss Eustace as the only means of discovering its location.'

'But would she agree to that?' said Richard dubiously. 'She can produce messages that make sense to the listener, but finding some hidden object would surely be beyond her. She might fear losing her reputation if it is not found.'

'If the customer is eager enough and willing to be duped, she will agree,' said Mina. 'Only make it clear that she will be paid well whatever the result. All we really want is the opportunity for Miss Gilden to visit Miss Eustace, and note anything in her apartments which might offer us clues as to her mode of life and business.'

Miss Gilden smiled. 'That should be easy enough. I shall even provide her with a picture of the spirit.'

'A picture?' said Mina.

'Oh, I have any number of portraits of theatrical persons. What about Rolly?' said Miss Gilden, turning to Richard

He laughed. 'Oh yes, Rolly Rollason, the master of mirth. He has this thing he says—' Richard adopted a curious pose with his arms wrapped about his head, and affected a villainous grimace – 'I ain't, though! Ain't I?' he said gruffly, and chuckled. 'Very droll.' He paused. 'Nellie, dear, I didn't know you had his picture?'

'Oh, a great many gentlemen give me their pictures,' said the charming Nellie, without even the hint of a blush. 'Yes, there is a very characterful one of him which would do extremely well. He is in evening dress, wearing a monocle and a full wig and staring at a rose. I shall tell Miss Eustace that he is my late uncle. If she manages to produce his ghost that would be most amusing.'

'You will be very convincing, my dear,' said Richard. 'Perhaps, to demonstrate your grief concerning the deceased relative, your personation from *The Wayward Ghost* would be suitable?'

'Oh yes,' said Nellie with a smile. 'It was a burlesque of the tragedy of Hamlet,' she explained to Mina, 'I played Ophelia and sang and danced and went mad and tore my clothes to ribbons.'

'There were gentlemen in the front row in tears every night,' said Richard. 'I think Lady Finsbury might aspire to a slightly more modest exhibition of distress, but if Miss Eustace hesitates to assist then you might open the floodgates a little. Yes, let us make the attempt tomorrow!' He signalled the waiter and ordered a glass of brandy.

'And what of Miss Foxton, how does she prosper?' asked Mina.

'Well, we have not quite reached the heights of the Theatre Royal or the Dome,' said Richard, almost as if that was a possibility, 'but we have played extensively in some very prestigious drawing rooms, and just lately we have been reaching an altogether wider audience by taking our turn at the New Oxford Theatre of Varieties in New Street.'

'We appear just after the Chinese sword-swallower and before the one-legged gymnast,' said Nellie.

'How wonderful!' exclaimed Mina, thankful that her mother was as likely to patronise such an establishment as she would a hospital for infectious diseases.

'Only sixpence for a seat in the gallery and packed to bursting every night,' said Richard. 'We are in place for the whole of the summer but we might look for something more elegant in the high season. Mind-reading, perhaps.'

'Can you do that?' asked Mina.

'Oh yes, I used to be the Ethiopian Wonder when I was with M. Baptiste,' said Nellie. 'I had to be Ethiopian so I could wear paint and wouldn't be recognised. It was a wonderful costume.'

'It is all a trick, though,' said Mina.

'Everything is a trick,' said the former Ethiopian Wonder. 'The secret is making it look as if something is happening before your eyes that you know to be impossible. Of course in a séance it's still impossible and it's still a trick, only then people believe it. And, of course, they pay more to see it.'

'I don't expect you to tell me how these things are done,' said Mina, 'but there are some things that I can't explain, and it is those that trouble me most, the things that Miss Eustace tells people at the private séances. Everyone who has been to one says that they are told things, quite personal things unknown to anyone else, things that Miss Eustace could not possibly have known and which therefore must be messages from the deceased. It is those messages that convince people she is genuine. I applied for a private reading myself, but she will not grant me one. That fact alone tells me she is a fraud. If she was genuine she would have nothing to fear.'

'People who want to believe in the spirits are too ready to dismiss something as impossible by natural means,' said Nellie. 'They say that the medium could not have known this or that, but there is always a way. How many secrets are there that are known to only one or two people?'

'Dr Hamid, whose sister died very recently, claims he has received messages from her that convince him,' said Mina. 'Miss Hamid would not discuss the pain she suffered except with her own family, yet Miss Eustace was able to say where it was.'

'It is like every such trick,' said Nellie. 'When you do not know the secret it is mysterious and inexplicable. Once you know, it seems so simple, so obvious, you would swear that a child could do it. Remember, Miss Eustace does not work alone. She is like a spider with a web, and she spins it all around the town and draws people in. I am sure that if you took a single example of something she has said and found out how she learned about it, you would discover a great deal more about the lady and how she deceives people, and perhaps then some of her followers would see her for what she is.'

'Only some, not all?' asked Mina, although she knew the answer.

'Only some,' said Nellie.

Twenty-Two

Not for the first time Mina was tempted to put her case before the police but on reflection, realised that she had nothing to go to the police with. She had not been fooled or paid over any money, so had nothing personally to complain about, and anything she said would be opposed by a chorus of voices extolling the virtue and probity of the medium.

The next time Mina exercised at Hamid's she expressed her continuing anxieties to Anna. Anna now had quite a number of lady patients who went to her to exercise, often for diseases of the spine. She did not believe in the wearing of stays during these activities, indeed she confided in Mina that she did not approve of the wearing of stays at all, since she thought that a lady's own body ought to be developed to create and support her shape and not pulled into some distortion dictated by fashion in order to please men. She had therefore devised an exercise costume consisting of a loose blouse and pantaloons which ladies might either purchase or hire. Mina had ordered a set made to her own dimensions, and it was beautifully comfortable. If she had one exercise that she especially enjoyed it was a simple side stretch, not so much because it was in itself pleasurable, but because she knew from what she was told that when she placed her left hand on the back of a chair and leaned to one side, raising her right foot from the ground, this was the one position in which, perversely, her spine lay perfectly straight. How she wished she had known that some years before, when, ordered to straighten her back by her mother, she could quite simply have adopted this pose.

The exercises with the dumb-bells had in the last few weeks so strengthened her upper arms and the muscles of her chest that Anna had deemed her ready to advance to the next stage, which was hanging by both hands from a bar. Mina first stepped on to a low stool then grasped the bar, and Anna slid the stool away, and carefully supervised her so that the stretches were applied in the correct place. It was too soon, she warned, for Mina to attempt this at home, for an exercise incorrectly done was worse than none at all. The weight of Mina's small body seemed to pull through her arms and shoulders and back, lengthening and warming her muscles, but without pain, although the effort made her want to gasp. As Anna eased Mina to the floor, she looked concerned, and asked if all was well, but Mina's slight breathlessness was a good feeling, and she felt tired yet exhilarated, having achieved more than she had ever thought possible.

Dr Hamid, Mina learned later as they were enjoying a tisane, had been visited by Miss Eustace three times for private séances, and planned another. He had now told Anna about the communication regarding Eliza's pain, and Mina asked if Eliza had ever described this to another person.

'Daniel and I were the only persons she ever spoke to on the subject,' said Anna. 'I believe she did not even talk about it to you.'

'That is true,' Mina admitted. 'But both Miss Eustace and Mr Clee came to see her. Might she not have disclosed something then?'

'I very much doubt it. She preferred not to discuss the subject at all, and had they pressed her on the matter she would not have wanted to see them again.'

'And she has not been examined by any other doctor?'

Anna paused. 'We did receive a visit some months ago from Dr Chenai, who Daniel has known for a number of years. He had been making a study of the spine and asked if he might see Eliza. We persuaded her to allow him to examine her, which I think she did only because she thought that it might help others, but I was there and she did not speak a word all the time. I think she was very relieved when he left, and did not need to tell us that she preferred not to see him again.'

'I suppose,' said Mina, 'that Miss Eustace could have read a book about scoliosis and guessed where the pain might be.'

'I had the impression from Daniel that he was told more than that, something very peculiar to Eliza.' She sighed. 'I shall ask him again and see if he will tell me what it was, but he thinks that I only ask him in order to destroy his belief, which of course I do, and he prefers for the moment to cling to it.'

'I am hoping that Mr Clee's fame in Brighton will be of short duration,' said Mina, and revealed the impending suit of Miss Simmons and her own suspicions that he was secretly married to Miss Eustace.

There was a very marked change in Anna's expression. 'I have only encountered that young man three times and was not impressed by him,' she said, almost angrily.

'Three times?' asked Mina. 'The first was when he visited Eliza, and the second was the séance. What was the third?'

Anna put her cup down very deliberately, and on her pale fawn cheeks there was a glow of red. 'He came to offer his condolences after Eliza died, and to express the hope that he was in no way to blame. Of course he was, in a way, as he brought the infection to the house, although it was hardly deliberate and he may not have had the first symptoms himself, so I reassured him that we did not hold him responsible. He then—'

Mina waited.

'He then attempted to woo me.'

Mina hardly knew what to say and decided to remain silent.

'When I was much younger,' said Anna, after she had taken a moment to calm herself, 'I did, from time to time receive expressions of admiration and even offers of marriage from gentlemen, and I rejected them all. My life is not destined that way, and never has been. I am now forty-eight years of age and well aware that a man who proposes marriage is interested not in me, but in my private fortune, which is of some value. Daniel and I jointly own this property, and any husband I chose would at once acquire half the business as well as all my funds. I have no doubt that Mr Clee has been making enquiries about this and therefore has a proper understanding of my worth.'

'What did you say to him?' asked Mina.

'I told him very plainly that I knew what he was up to and wished never to see him again. I thought it as well to be blunt, and he removed himself at once.'

'I am quite sure,' said Mina, secretly wishing that she had been present at that scene, 'that he had no intention of marrying Miss Simmons and wooed her only in order to gain a confederate. The wealthy great-aunt whose heir he was supposed to be would have been a long time dying. I am only wondering if he was being truthful when he said that he was engaged to another. How many victims can this man have?'

'There are too many adventurers of his kind,' said Anna, bitterly. 'They assume that all a woman wants is marriage, and they seek out the vulnerable: women who they assume have little or no chance of marriage because they are plain or middle-aged, and then they marry them and take all their property and neglect or even abuse them.'

'Well, let us hope that Miss Simmons will stop his game for a while,' said Mina. 'I wish I could prove what I suspect to be the case about Miss Eustace. If she and her acolyte and Mr Bradley could all be drummed out of Brighton I would be very much happier.'

'I do not like Mr Bradley,' said Anna. 'He sometimes comes to inhale the vapours but spends most of his time lounging in the gentlemen's salon reading the newspapers and telling our other customers how important he is. I don't believe he is here for his own health at all, but to drum up custom from among our clients for his own healing circle. After all, if one wants to find people who might seek his services then where better to go? They are all here in one place. For all I know he goes to Brill's Baths as well.'

'Mr Bradley started by offering his services gratis, but now he charges for tickets to the larger meetings,' said Mina. 'He says it is only to pay for the hire of the room, and he takes nothing for himself, but I don't know how true that is.'

'I suspect it is untrue,' said Anna. 'The gentleman whose rooms he uses is a customer here and he is a profound believer in Mr Bradley's healing abilities. I would not be surprised if Mr Bradley used the rooms for nothing and makes a tidy income, while his friend also profits by selling refreshments.'

Mina could only feel grateful that Mr Bradley showed no inclination to woo her mother, although she had an unpleasant suspicion that if he were to do so, he might prove successful.

Richard came to see his mother again, a trying visit, since her sole subject of conversation was the terrible betrayal she had suffered at the hands of Miss Simmons. Louisa Scarletti now spent much of her day reclining in her parlour being fetched morsels of food by Rose. Richard smiled a great deal and patted his unhappy parent's hand, and agreed with everything she said, before she declared herself exhausted and retired to her bed.

'I suppose it is still all my fault,' said Mina, when he came to her room. She was at her desk, where Mr Inskip was busily decomposing. She had not yet decided how to end the story, as it was contrary to popular expectation for a murderer to escape conviction.

'And will be until the end of time,' said Richard. 'We must be content with that, I am afraid. Still, she does admit, albeit reluctantly, to feeling a little better; has the wondrous Mr Bradley been here working his magic?'

'It would appear so. Really I would prefer him not to enter the house at all if it was not for the fact that Mother has taken to him, and seems to improve after his visits. He has not been courting her, has he? She has said nothing to make you think that?'

'No, never a suggestion of it.'

'Well, that is something. And how is Miss Gilden?'

Richard, who usually looked cheery every time his beautiful inamorata was mentioned, appeared instead to be slightly discomfited. 'She is very well, and even now is being fitted for a new gown, something I have been assured will take a whole day. Why do fashions have to change once a week?' he said petulantly. 'I am sure it is only to give ladies something to talk about.'

'Has she been to see Miss Eustace?'

Richard threw himself down on Mina's bed. She wondered what he might say if he saw her dumb-bells packed away in a box at the bottom of her wardrobe, although the exercise staff might easily be mistaken for a walking cane.

'She has indeed, and with an interesting result. Miss Eustace was, of course, astonished to receive a visitor, but as you correctly anticipated was willing to admit a titled lady. Miss Eustace occupies an apartment on the second floor of the house, which seems to comprise only two rooms, and received Lady Finsbury in a parlour, which did not contain anything exceptional. Lady Finsbury explained that the ghost of her beloved great-uncle Sir Mortimer Portland had appeared before her, and implored her most earnestly with tears in his diaphanous eyes to see Miss Eustace without delay. Sir Mortimer, said Lady Finsbury, was reputed to have hidden a fortune in jewels in his mansion, Great Portland Hall, which was about to be torn down, and she thought that he was afraid it would be stolen or destroyed before his great-niece, who is his only heir, could take possession of it. The ghost was struggling to describe where the fortune could be found, and finally it gasped that only Miss Eustace of Bloomsbury Place could enable him to materialise sufficiently to draw the treasure map. Miss Eustace, on being assured by Lady Finsbury that any failure to produce her uncle's spirit would be regarded as evidence only of the natural capriciousness of the etheric force, and that she would be paid generously whatever the result, agreed to make the attempt. Nellie showed Miss Eustace Rolly's character portrait, which she asked to retain, saying that it would help her to concentrate on her task. There the matter was left.'

'You said there was an interesting result,' said Mina.

He sat up. 'Yes, two of them, in fact. When Nellie was shown into the parlour, Miss Eustace was closing the door to the adjoining room, but Nellie was able to catch a brief glimpse inside, and saw several large trunks, the kind theatrical people use to transport costumes and properties. Then part-way through the interview, there was a sound in the next room, and Nellie felt sure that there was another person in there. It was too loud to ignore, and so she commented that there must be a spirit in the house. Miss Eustace agreed, and said that spirits often visited her with messages, but sometimes they were just playful and made noises to say that they wanted company. Nellie decided not to press the matter, or it might arouse suspicion, and it was not thereafter alluded to.'

He patted his pockets for a cigar, but desisted at a look from Mina. 'Are we thinking the same thing?' he said.

'I believe so,' said Mina. 'We need to find out what is inside those trunks, but I cannot imagine how that might be done.'

'I agree.' He adopted the attitude of a consultant, and gave the matter his earnest consideration. 'I am reluctant to engage a burglar to carry out the plan—'

'I am most relieved to hear it,' Mina exclaimed.

'They can be expensive, I understand and not necessarily reliable. And much the same can be said of bribing the maid. After all, we have no intention of taking anything; all we want to do is observe what may be there. A common thief or a maid that will take bribes may not be able to resist helping themselves, and where would we be then?'

'Under arrest as accomplices to a robbery I believe,' said Mina.

'Precisely. So I shall do it myself.'

'Richard! You cannot mean that!' she said, horrified. 'Please tell me this is one of your jokes.'

'No, I have thought it all through,' he said calmly. 'I will find some means of entering Miss Eustace's apartments while she is absent, and simply look for the evidence we need, but take away nothing. Can that be against the law?'

'If you force an entry into the house it is,' said Mina. 'And if you were caught, you would never be able to prove that you were not there to steal. Please, Richard, this is a very foolhardy scheme. You must think of something else.'

'If I am caught, I will just say that I am a devoted admirer of the lady and am there to present her with a gift,' he said, with an easy shrug. 'Perhaps I shall take a little nosegay or sweetmeats or my portrait. I shall appear romantically reckless, perhaps, but that is all. But I shall not be caught, and it will be an adventure.'

'Richard, I would very much rather you did not attempt this,' urged Mina. 'You must find some other method. After all, Lady Finsbury managed to gain entry without committing a crime.'

'And having done so I think Miss Eustace will now be doubly suspicious of a new unexpected visitor,' said Richard. 'Oh, I could try to woo the lady, I suppose, but she is reputedly impervious to any such attempts, so it might take me a week or even a fortnight to win her over. No, my plan is by far the best.'

'I cannot condone this,' said Mina. 'How would you even achieve it? You can hardly slip into the house through either door without being seen by the servants.'

'Oh, it's perfectly simple,' he assured her. 'There is a balcony below the windows on the first floor; I can easily climb up and then get a foothold up to the next one. It shouldn't be hard to get in. Nellie says she thought the window was unlocked, so I shall just prise it open and slip inside. The important thing is to work under cover of darkness, and choose a time when

Miss Eustace and her friend or husband, or whatever he might be, are away, and to have the means to depart quickly. Nellie will hire a cab and wait for me nearby, and when I am done, I will just jump aboard and fly away in moments.'

'But if you are seen!' Mina exclaimed.

'Did you see me on stage, when I carried the airy sprite about on my shoulders?' he said with a knowing smile. 'Black velvet, Mina, a wondrous material that can deceive the eye. I will be quite invisible!'

All Mina's entreaties were in vain, and Richard pulled a cigar from his pocket and swaggered away to make the arrangements.

Twenty-Three

Mina was so preoccupied by this new development that she did not pay great attention when first Mr Bradley then Miss Whinstone and Mrs Bettinson called later that day to commiserate with her mother. She was only thankful that her mother had suitable company and demanded little of her, since she needed to retreat into her own thoughts. Mrs Bettinson was looking remarkably satisfied that the new flourishing Louisa, who had no longer needed her, had been replaced with the invalid she had always known her to be, and was busily buttering her charge with sympathy. Miss Whinstone, who was looking faded and unhappy, even in her green gown with its extra flounces, could only speak of the cost of maintaining the two children she had adopted, and the constant demands by their school for the payment of 'extras'.

Mina had no information concerning when Richard might make his foolish attempt at housebreaking, and was half-expecting to hear that he was coming up before the magistrates and needing to be bailed, but the next morning he arrived in a rush.

'Mina dear, I have come to entreat your help,' he exclaimed.

'If you have escaped from the police cells I will not shelter you,' she said severely. 'I must take you straight back there.'

'Oh, it is nothing of the sort, and in any case I have not attempted the enterprise yet, but it must be tonight. Miss Eustace is engaged for a séance at Professor Gaskin's and will be from home, and I have everything I need, but Nellie cannot help me with the cab, so you must do it.'

'I must? Richard, might I remind you that I do not approve of this scheme and want nothing to do with it,' she said, crossly. 'In fact, since it has not yet been attempted, I beg you to abandon it at once.'

'But who else can I trust?' he pleaded. 'Mina, my darling sister, all you have to do is wait for me in the street, and if we are questioned then you can say that you have been in my company all evening, so you may save me, too.'

'And what of Miss Gilden? Is she unwell?'

'No, she has gone to London. Have you not seen the newspapers?'

Mina shook her head, dreading to think what she had missed.

'There has been some shocking news,' Richard informed her. 'M. Baptiste – and I think in spite of everything Nellie still retains some affection for him – has been shot and wounded in the street by a madwoman. So, of course, as his wife, and in all probability his sole heir, Nellie has rushed to his side. It's understandable of course, but my plans are now in disarray, and who knows how long she will have to stay there, mopping his brow, or whatever it is that ladies do.'

'And, of course,' Mina observed, 'not only Nellie but Miss Foxton and Lady Finsbury are absent from Brighton.'

'Yes, and the Ethiopian Wonder, and whole host of fascinating ladies besides. But please promise me you will help.'

'It is a very dangerous scheme,' said Mina.

'But your help will make it less so,' he said with his most persuasive smile. 'I am asking such a little simple thing, and you will not be in any danger at all. If needs be you can always say that all you did was hire a cab at my request, and knew nothing of my reasons for wanting it.'

'And what of the cabman?' she reminded him. 'Will he also be your alibi? Or a witness for the prosecution?'

'The cab will be at the end of the street, so he will see nothing.' He hugged her. 'Please, Mina, darling Mina, you are the only person clever enough to help me.'

It was with considerable reluctance that Mina, accepting that she could not dissuade her brother, agreed to help, if only to protect him from disgrace, and her mother from shame.

Mina felt bereft of proper advice. She dared not approach anyone connected with the law, but felt that at the very least she should speak to someone sympathetic and sensible. After a great deal of hesitation she decided to speak to Dr Hamid, who, she thought, at least needed to know of the grave doubts that had arisen from Nellie's visit. She felt sure that underneath the grief and the hope there was still a man who remained settled in his appreciation of the world and how it was formed and worked.

It was a fine day and he agreed to take a walk with her on the Chain Pier, where he seemed to be not so much contemplating the land and all that moved on it, or even the cool waters and the constantly changing place where the two met, but gazing instead into the air, as if looking about him for evidence of spirits. They walked slowly, not only due to Mina's preferred speed of gait, but because the gentleness of the stroll pleased them both. They passed under the cast-iron arches, which housed little kiosks selling toys, sweetmeats and novelties, going toward the old landing stage at the end, where the packet boats arrived from Dieppe. Being of purely commercial use it was the least attractive part of the pier, and it was no coincidence thought Mina that the most popular portraits of the pier seemed either to be facing away from it, or with its slime-blackened supports in the misty distance. They stopped briefly for refreshments, and passers-by looked on the pair with approval, seeing a kind gentleman assisting a poor crippled lady.

'I don't know if you have heard about the scandal regarding Mr Clee,' Mina said.

'No,' said Dr Hamid, 'but nothing would surprise me about that individual. Anna has told me about his attempt to win her, and a more transparent fortune hunter was never known. Anna is a fine, honest and loving woman, and I hope even now that she may find someone worthy of her, who will add to her happiness, but that person is not Mr Clee.'

'He may well be married already,' said Mina, 'and he appears also to be engaged to two other ladies, one of whom, my mother's former companion Miss Simmons, is taking an action for breach of promise.'

'The scoundrel!' he exclaimed, shaking his head in dismay. 'And this is the creature who has attached himself to Miss Eustace, no doubt with hopes of winning her, too. Thankfully Miss Simmons's action will alert her to his true nature. I, like you, have become convinced that he is simply a conjurer, and his object has been from the start to conjure Miss Eustace from her fortune.'

'The lady has many admirers, yet seems to entertain none of them,' said Mina. They walked on. There was little enough to divert them on the pier, other than the sea and the sky, but that was all to the good. 'My brother Richard has recently told me he wishes to court her, but I have told him he is unlikely to be successful.' She looked at Dr Hamid carefully as she spoke, but he seemed unconcerned at the news, and she was reassured that he at least had no tender interest in Miss Eustace. 'But Richard can be impulsive and reckless, and I fear that he may do something foolish,' she went on.

'He did recklessly offer to knock down Mr Clee unless he left my house, something which I must admit did commend him to me,' said Dr Hamid, with a smile.

'He wishes to make Miss Eustace a gift to express his admiration, but he disdains to deliver it in the usual way,' said Mina. 'He plans to make a bold gesture by placing it in her apartments without her knowing, so it will seem to have appeared by supernatural means.'

He stopped walking and stared at her. 'Goodness – how does he propose to do that?'

'I am very sorry to say that the means he is adopting may place him in danger of arrest,' said Mina.

Dr Hamid looked shocked. 'You must try to dissuade him!'

'I have done my best, truly I have, but he insists on making the attempt. He has asked me to wait with a cab at the end of the street – Miss Eustace lodges not far from Professor and Mrs Gaskin – and I am to be there to make sure he can make his escape.'

'Oh, this is very wrong!' said Dr Hamid, clapping one hand to his forehead and pacing up and down. 'Not only does he risk his own liberty but he draws you in as an accomplice! But you say that he only wishes to leave something, and intends to take nothing away?'

'Oh, Richard is no thief; I can assure you of that. I only hope that if he is caught it will be put down to a youthful escapade and he will have learned his lesson. What do you think I should do?'

He sighed. 'Is there anyone else whose opinion might sway him?'

'Only Mother, and I prefer her to know nothing of it, in fact I dread her finding out. She is very unhappy over the business with Miss Simmons and I will not add to her worries.'

He looked at her sympathetically. 'I can see that you are very fond of your brother. You would not have harm come to him and whatever he does you will not abandon him. I can only advise you to do your utmost to dissuade him from this foolhardy plan, and if you cannot then no advice I or anyone else can give will prevent you from assisting him. Of course, if he is only intending to leave a gift then it may take just moments to achieve his aim, and you may then hurry him safely away; only do make him promise faithfully that any future gifts are delivered by more conventional means.'

'I will do as you suggest,' she said. 'Will you be at Miss Eustace's séance tonight?'

'That is my plan, and now I can see where I might be able to help you. On my way home I will look to ensure that you and your brother have departed safely before Miss Eustace returns. Where does she lodge?'

'Bloomsbury Place. I will have the cab wait at the northern end.'

'Then I very much hope that we will not meet there.'

The séance was due to start at eight o'clock, although how long it was likely to last was unpredictable. Mina hired the cab for eight, but Richard, with his customary sense of urgency, arrived late and then insisted on stopping on the way to purchase cigars. It was therefore well after half past the hour when they arrived in Bloomsbury Place, and stopped at the end furthest from the seafront, where the road took a turn into College Place and the cabman would not be able to see where Richard was going. The sun was dipping towards the horizon, and the summer light was fading as Richard drew his black velvet cloak about him.

'Did you bring a gift for Miss Eustace to act as your alibi?' asked Mina.

'Oh, no, I forgot,' said Richard. 'Well, it's too late now, I suppose.'

Mina handed him a lace handkerchief. 'Oh, my wonderful sister!' he exclaimed, pocketing it, 'What would I do without you!'

'Please be as quick as you can,' she urged.

He laughed affectionately at her worried expression, kissed her cheek, and then jumped down from the cab and sauntered down the street disappearing around the corner. 'Am I to wait here, Miss?' asked the cabman.

'Yes, my brother is just delivering a gift to a friend, he will return soon,' said Mina. Time passed, and she could imagine Richard climbing up to the balcony, swinging his long legs over the railings, then, more perilously, using the narrow window ledges, ascending higher to Miss Eustace's rooms. She hoped that he would not fall, hoped also that when he reached the second floor that he would find the windows had been securely locked, give up the enterprise, and return to her with a rueful expression. He did not return, and after a while she began to worry that he had indeed fallen and was lying injured in the street, or worse still, had become impaled on the iron railings that surrounded the basement area. Perversely, she thought of a story – the ghost of a man who had died in that horrible way, haunting passers-by with the great iron spike through his chest. It was a dreadful image and she almost disliked herself for thinking of it. She was about to ask the cabman to turn around and move closer when there was a knock on the door. Her first happy thought was that it was Richard, thankfully safe, but to her surprise she saw that it was Dr Hamid.

He climbed in, and though it was now growing dark, she could see that his face was grim and drawn.

'Did you walk up Bloomsbury Place?' she asked. 'Did you see anything? I was so worried that Richard had fallen, and I was about to go and look for him.'

He shook his head. 'No, no, I saw nothing.' Suddenly he leaned forward, hid his face in his hands and groaned. 'I have been such a fool!' he said. 'Whatever will you think of me?!'

'What has happened?' asked Mina. 'Is the séance over? Is Miss Eustace on her way home?'

He raised his head and his face was a picture of misery. 'No, it is still in progress. I made an excuse and left early. I needed to think about what I had been told.' He made a little gulp that was almost a sob. 'How could I have been so taken in?'

'Because she caught you when your grief and pain were fresh and you would have done anything, grasped at any hope to relieve them,' said Mina, gently.

He nodded. 'You are right, of course. But at first it seemed so very real, so full of hope! Tonight, we were just a small circle, receiving messages through rapping noises that spelled out words. Eliza – only, of course, I now know it cannot have been Eliza – said she was sorry if she had caused any offence to Dr Chenai when he met with her. He is a friend of mine, and some months ago she agreed with some reluctance to allow him to examine her, but I saw at the time that she regretted it and would not answer his questions. The message stated that she found herself unable to look at or speak to him as she was unsettled by his appearance, something for which she now felt profoundly sorry. Dr Chenai had been stricken with a palsy, and one side of his face was drawn up. But the mere idea that Eliza would have made a comment on a person's appearance could only be entertained by someone who had never met her. And then – and then I recalled that Dr Chenai was not afflicted until some weeks after he examined Eliza. She never saw him again, and his case was not reported in the newspapers and I thought it best not to mention it to her, so she never knew of it.'

'Did you challenge Miss Eustace?' asked Mina.

'No, I needed to walk about in the air and think, so I just pleaded another appointment and left, but even if I had, I am sure that some clever explanation would have been forthcoming.' He peered through the window. 'Where is your brother? He seems to be a long time about his mission.'

'He is,' said Mina anxiously, and ordered the cabman to turn and move around the corner into Bloomsbury Place, stopping a few yards nearer to Miss Eustace's lodgings. She peered down the street, but there was no sign of Richard. They waited in silence for a while, and Mina was wondering if she ought to admit her deception to Dr Hamid and reveal the true nature of her brother's mission, when her companion leaned out of the window.

'There is a carriage approaching,' he said. 'It is stopping and a lady is getting down. It is Miss Eustace! Is your brother still there?'

'He must be!' said Mina. She thought she saw a slight movement at the window of Miss Eustace's apartments. 'I can see him!' she gasped. 'He will be discovered!'

In a moment, Dr Hamid had leaped down from the cab and was running down the street. 'Miss Eustace!' he called out, and she looked up in astonishment.

'Dr Hamid!' she said, 'whatever are you doing? Are you well?'

'Yes, and I must apologise for accosting you in this fashion. I happened to be visiting a patient who lives nearby, but my thoughts have been in some disarray since attending the séance tonight. I could think of nothing else – my poor dear sister! I need to know more! Would you allow me the favour of a few moments conversation? Let us walk down to the seafront and view the sunset.'

'Perhaps it would be better to wait until you are calmer,' she advised.

Mina, trying her best to see, was sure now that it was Richard at the upper window but he was unable to descend without grave risk of Miss Eustace seeing him.

'Oh, but I must speak with you now, or I will never be calm again,' pleaded Dr Hamid. 'One minute only, I beg of you, and we will walk just a little way down the street and then up again, and I know it will refresh me. And I will engage you for another private séance – I will do anything, pay any price if I can hear from my dear sister just once more.'

'Very well,' said Miss Eustace, dismissing her cab, 'let us walk.' Dr Hamid took her arm and they strolled down the street towards the seafront.

As soon as their backs were turned, Richard began his perilous descent, his cloak flowing about him so he looked like a gigantic leathery bat crawling down the wall. 'Do you see that, Miss?' asked the cabman, suddenly. 'On the wall of that house. There's something funny going on there! I think I should get the police!'

Mina peered out of the window. 'I can see nothing,' she said. 'But the lady who lives there is a spirit medium and is often visited by ghosts. Perhaps you are seeing a ghost?'

'Oh my word!' gasped the cabman. 'And you say that you can't see it at all?'

'No, it is quite invisible to me. I think your best course is to turn the cab around, so it cannot see you.'

'Oh! Yes! Right away!' he said, complying with some energy.

'And it might be best if you do not speak of this incident to anyone. You would only be accused of drunkenness which would be very unfortunate.'

'I haven't taken a drop,' he declared, 'but I can see that there are those who wouldn't believe me.'

A minute later, the door of the cab opened and Richard climbed breathlessly inside. 'That was good work by Dr Hamid,' he said.

'Did you deliver the gift?' asked Mina, holding out her hand.

He dug in his pocket for the handkerchief and returned it to her. 'Oh yes, with great success.'

Dr Hamid soon joined them. 'Mr Scarletti, I am pleased to see you are safe, but let that narrow escape serve as a warning never to attempt such a dangerous escapade again.'

'I understand there are men who make a living at it, but the work is too hard for me,' said Richard, as Mina signalled the cab to move off. 'Still, if my business partner fails to return from London I may yet be obliged to take up house-breaking as my new career.'

Dr Hamid frowned, not sure if Richard was joking or not. 'And there is another thing of great importance I must say to you. I am sorry if you will be disappointed in the lady who so commands your affections, but it must be said before another moment passes. My eyes have been opened tonight. I have received evidence that has convinced me she is a fraud.'

'Now, it is strange that you should say that,' said Richard, 'because I have just found out the very same thing. It is no wonder that she tries to keep her address a secret, for she has items hidden in her lodgings that she does not want the world to see.'

'You have searched her rooms?' said Dr Hamid, astonished.

'Oh, one thing led to another and I confess that out of a natural curiosity I did, but very carefully. She will not know that anyone has been there. The lady has boxes of costumes, including masks, wigs, false beards, stuffed gloves, rag babies and the like, as well as oil of phosphorous and everything she needs to create her spirits. But there was something else, too, a great many items cut from the newspapers, notebooks with intimate details of the residents of Brighton, culled from who knows where. She is a squirrel for gossip and lays her store aside for when it is needed.'

'I am sure,' said Mina, 'that all the private revelations she passes on will be found there.'

'But there was another thing,' said Richard. 'I saw personal effects and clothing, which suggests that she does not live alone, or at least that she is visited by another who sometimes sleeps there. A man.' He smiled. 'Well, that was hungry work, and I can quite fancy a bite of supper!'

'It would be my great pleasure for both of you to be my guests,' said Dr Hamid, directing the cab to his home.

'The question is,' said Mina, 'what can we do with the information we now have? We may express our suspicions to the police but that is all. We have no evidence, no facts with which to persuade them to take action. And Miss Eustace has too many supporters for our voices to carry any weight. We most certainly cannot tell anyone what Richard saw in her lodgings tonight or they will want to know how we came by that information.'

'I suppose we could ask someone to keep watch over the premises and see if Mr Clee slips in of an evening and then departs in the morning, but that would prove nothing,' said Richard.

'In any case, I do not think Mr Clee is even in Brighton at present,' said Mina. 'There is the breach of promise action to be heard, and he has engaged a London solicitor. He may well be staying there until the trial. I suspect he will want to keep well away from Miss Simmons and her sister Mrs Langley who may be tempted to box his ears if she sees him, as might the other ladies he has addressed.'

A gloomy atmosphere descended as the three conspirators pondered the difficulty. It was agreed that if any one of them came up with a plan, then that individual would share his or her thoughts with the other two before taking any action.

The next morning Mina was pleased to see that her mother was feeling a little better. Part of the reason for Louisa's recovery was her recognition of the fact that Miss Whinstone was even more miserable than she was, and she did not enjoy competition. Miss Whinstone's wailings about her expenditure on the two orphans was becoming tiresome. They seemed to need a dozen suits of clothing each, and books and equipment for every activity the school offered, including lessons in riding, sailing and languages. She received letters from them once a week, which usually asked for money, and described the appurtenances of wealth that other pupils enjoyed with the strongest possible implication that they would be desolate if they did not acquire the same. All questions as to how she had selected the children or even why she had suddenly taken the course of adoption were met with silence.

Mina was busy with her writing when there was a knock at her door and she opened it to admit Mrs Parchment. 'Miss Scarletti, if I might have a word?'

'Yes, of course, is there anything the matter?'

'Not at all, I am entirely satisfied with my accommodation here. However, I need to inform you at once that I intend to leave Brighton in the very near future. There is family business I must attend to, and it is such that I might be absent for many months or even be obliged to make my home elsewhere.

My rent is paid to the end of the month, and I am content with that arrangement. I will inform you of the date of my departure as soon as I know it myself.'

'Thank you for letting me know,' said Mina. 'I hope you have enjoyed your stay here in Brighton.'

Mrs Parchment gave an uncharacteristic smile. 'I have, thank you.'

'Might I ask one thing?'

'Please do.'

'I hope – I trust – that your departure is not connected in any way with the difficulty concerning Miss Simmons? Her behaviour was unacceptable, as of course was Mr Clee's. I would not like to think that in making the error of employing her I created some dissatisfaction with the arrangements here.'

Mrs Parchment's back achieved a sudden rigidity. 'I do not blame you in any way, Miss Scarletti. Miss Simmons's masquerade of innocence was skilfully done and would have convinced anyone. When the truth is known, she will be exposed for what she is, a conniving and deceitful woman. I know all about her plans to extort money from Mr Clee under false pretences, but I also happen to know that she and her sister, both of whom have told lies to the police, will fail.'

'May I ask how you know this?' asked Mina. Both Miss Simmons and her sister had struck her as truthful, and she did not like to think she had been so categorically deceived.

'You may, but I am advised that that is a matter best aired in court.'

'Will you be giving evidence?'

'I will, since it was I who observed them and reported what I saw.'

'But did you overhear their conversation?'

'That,' said Mrs Parchment with a smirk, 'remains to be seen.'

Mina saw nothing in Mrs Parchment's manner to shake her trust in the veracity of Miss Simmons and her sister. 'I wonder,' she said, 'if the young lady of fortune to whom Mr Clee is shortly to be married will appear to give witness to his good character. That would cause quite a sensation.'

'It would indeed, if such a lady existed.'

'You think she does not?'

'Do you have any evidence that she does?' said Mrs Parchment confidently. 'I have heard this rumour, of course, but I do not give it any credit.'

'But it is not simply a rumour,' Mina advised her, 'the engagement was mentioned in the letter Mr Clee's solicitor sent to Miss Simmons. She showed it to me. Where can the solicitor have obtained the information except from Mr Clee himself?'

Mrs Parchment gave a curiously brittle laugh. 'Oh, there is nothing in that. Young gentlemen, especially handsome young gentlemen like Mr Clee, always imagine that all the ladies are in love with them. Only wait for the trial and she will not appear.'

She swept out, her nose tilted in the air. Mina was left wondering if the young lady of fortune was a myth for quite another reason, because she had been invented by Mr Clee as a means of escaping the consequences of his engagement to Miss Simmons.

Mrs Parchment was kept very busy over the next two days with her preparations for removal from Brighton, and then, quite abruptly, she announced that she would be away on business until the hearing, packed a small travelling bag, and departed.

Twenty-Four

Richard, in the meantime, had been saved from the necessity of undertaking burglary as his new profession by the reappearance in Brighton of Nellie Gilden, bringing with her all her many personalities. M. Baptiste was well on the way to recovering from what had proved to be a trivial flesh wound; however, the lady who had shot him was not after all, as had first been supposed, a mad woman, but his lawful wife. These two states were not, Nellie suggested with some acerbity, entirely incompatible. The would-be murderess, who had arrived in London accompanied by her three small children, had come armed not only with a revolver but a French marriage certificate, which pre-dated the conjurer's nuptials with Nellie by ten years. After some harrowing scenes, M. and Madame Baptiste had become reconciled, M. Baptiste had announced that he would not bring any charges, and Nellie had left London, her main regret being that the lady had not been a better shot. Her only consolation was a generous gift from her former employer and supposed husband to ensure that his bigamous marriage was never mentioned. After telling Richard the sad tale, Nellie had gone to Mrs Conroy's emporium to console herself with a new parasol.

Pleased as Mina was that M. Baptiste had survived and been reunited with his devoted if rather desperate wife and innocent children, and that Richard could now continue his theatrical career, which was at least preferable to burglary, Mina saw another danger. Nellie was a free woman, a single woman, and it was therefore more than possible that she and Richard might marry. Mina only hoped that if this did occur, Nellie might choose to do so as Lady Finsbury, having presumably first found some acceptable method of disposing of Lord Finsbury.

'You will never guess who I encountered in London,' exclaimed Miss Gilden, as she, Richard and Mina enjoyed a quiet supper after the reappearance of Signor Ricardo and the Mystic Beauty on the Brighton stage. 'None other than Rolly! He was hoping to be at the Gaiety for the season, but is now without employment, and it is such a shame, as he does do such amusing eccentrics. I especially admire his Caledonian Marvel, in which he rides a velocipede while wearing a kilt and playing the bagpipes. So I suggested he comes down here to see what is doing.'

'Why not?' said Richard. 'He can even become Signor Ricardo if he wishes.' Richard looked a little subdued. Mina wondered if he thought Nellie's old friend might be a rival for her hand; either that or his ardour had waned since he had discovered that his mistress was not, after all, a married woman.

Nellie produced some portraits of Mr Rollason in his favourite characterisations, which included the Caledonian as well as the King of Siam and a one-eyed sailor. It was very hard to imagine that all these were one and the same man. As she gazed at them a tiny seed of an idea began to take root in Mina's mind.

Two days later, at Brighton Police Court, Mr Clee appeared to answer the charge of breach of promise, the object being for the magistrates to consider whether he should be committed to take his trial at the assizes. As Mrs Parchment had so confidently predicted, there was no betrothed young lady to give evidence on his behalf. Miss Simmons declared that Mr Clee had paid court to her, and that they were secretly engaged to be married, the event depending only on the inheritance he was due to receive from his great-aunt. Mrs Langley also appeared to testify that she had overheard all the conversation between Mr Clee and her sister and entirely supported the prosecution's evidence. A gentleman then appeared and, stating that he was Mr Clee's cousin, he told the court that Mr Clee had no great-aunt living, and neither did he have any relative wealthy enough to provide any expectation of inheriting a fortune. The replies were couched in such a fashion that it suggested that it was Miss Simmons and her sister who had invented the story.

The final witness was Mrs Parchment, who stated that she had reported Miss Simmons's behaviour to Mrs Scarletti on witnessing the companion walking out with a young man, who she readily identified as Mr Clee. She might not, she said, have revealed what she had seen had the conversation been innocuous. If she had believed for an instant that Mr Clee had been making unwelcome overtures to Miss Simmons she would have stepped in and warned the lady. The situation, however, had been quite different. She had been shocked to hear Miss Simmons throwing herself shamelessly at the young gentleman, who had been trying to persuade her that she was deluded about his intentions.

In vain did Miss Simmons weep and Mrs Langley exclaim angrily. The court, taking the balance between the plain young woman of humble origins demanding compensation from the handsome young man with the Byronic curls and the respectable widow declaring that the claim was founded on lies, dismissed the suit. Miss Simmons, distressed almost to the point of collapse, was half carried from the court by her sister.

'I can well understand Mr Clee's interest in Miss Simmons,' Mina later told Richard. 'She was an intimate of my mother and could provide all kinds of information to establish Miss Eustace's credentials, and, of course, she was a willing confederate in the séance. If it were not for the fact that Mrs Parchment has no fortune I would almost suspect Mr Clee of making her an offer. As it is, she has appointed herself a moral guardian and that seems to be the basis of her actions.'

'But Mrs Parchment does have a considerable fortune,' said Richard. 'At least, her husband died a wealthy man. She may choose to live simply, but that is no clue to her means.'

'How do you know this?' asked Mina.

'True,' said Richard, 'how do I know it? I have read it somewhere very recently.' He thought for a moment. 'Oh, yes, I recall it now. When I was searching Miss Eustace's rooms I found a notebook recording the names of wealthy residents of Brighton, and their worth. Mrs Parchment's name was there, with an extract from a newspaper showing that her husband's estate was worth above forty thousand pounds.'

'Was Mother's name there?' Mina demanded in alarm.

'I don't know, I didn't have time to read all of it.'

'Should I warn Mrs Parchment?' asked Mina.

'Would the lady be prepared to hear anything to the dishonour of Mr Clee?' asked Richard.

'I don't know, but I should at least make the attempt,' said Mina.

On her return home, however, Rose told her that Mrs Parchment had left the house after taking an early breakfast that morning, and a carrier had later called to remove her effects. She had left no forwarding address. Mina was just pondering what to do when Mrs Bettinson appeared, full of news. Mrs Parchment and Mr Clee, she said, had gone straight from the courtroom to the register office where they were married by special licence.

Mina could do nothing but abandon the lady to her fate and hope that her eyes would be opened to her dreadful situation before too long.

The morning post had brought with it an interesting packet from Mr Greville. His enquiries about the fraudulent medium in London had not ended with his discovery of the brief newspaper account. Realising that the sensational papers might provide better detail, he had obtained a copy of the *Illustrated Police News*, and sent it to Mina, observing that its report was undoubtedly culled from other newspapers, but the quality of its woodcuts was excellent. The artist had chosen to depict the sensational exposure of the medium, and the likeness, taken from a portrait photograph, was unmistakable. 'Mrs Hilarie Clee', whether or not that was the lady's real name, was undoubtedly Miss Eustace. The article corrected an impression that had been given previously, in that the imposture had been detected because of the unruly behaviour of not one child, but two, a boy and a girl, said to be the medium's own children. Both she and her husband, Mr Eustace Clee, had been arrested.

Mina realised that there was no time to lose. She told Rose to summon a cab and went to see Miss Whinstone. That lady was looking most forlorn, and despite the unexpected arrival seemed grateful for the company. She was clutching a handkerchief in one hand and a framed portrait in the other, but on Mina's being admitted to the room, she replaced the portrait on a side table with fingers that trembled so violently that the object fell over. Mina retrieved it for her and replaced it, seeing, and this was no great surprise, that it was a photograph of two children.

'Are these the children you have adopted?' she asked.

Miss Whinstone nodded, miserably. 'They are good children, but I had no idea that it was such an expense keeping them at school.'

'I beg you, Miss Whinstone,' said Mina, very determinedly, 'not to pay another farthing for whatever luxuries they demand. You have been the victim of a callous plot.' She proffered the newspaper. 'Take a look at this picture. Do you recognise the lady?'

Miss Whinstone stared at the illustration. 'Why, it is Miss Eustace! The likeness is very marked.'

'I cannot say what her real name is, but she is married with two children, a boy and a girl, the same ages as the ones that have been foisted upon you.'

'But—' Miss Whinstone looked confused.

'Please, you must be open with me. How were you prevailed upon to adopt them? Was it a spirit message? Where did you fetch them from?'

Miss Whinstone uttered a piteous wail. Mina went and sat close to her. 'Please tell me,' she begged, but the unhappy woman shook her head.

'Were they living in an orphanage, or a boarding school or a charity home?' Mina persisted. 'What are their names? Do you have their birth certificates? What papers have you signed?'

Miss Whinstone flapped her hands in confusion at so many questions. Mina rang for the servant to fetch a glass of water and allowed the distraught woman to calm down enough to speak.

'I don't know where they were living,' she said at last. 'The children were brought to me in the Pavilion Gardens by a lady who was a stranger to me. I do not have their certificates; they are called John and Mary, but I believe the births were never registered.'

'Did the lady tell you who they were?'

'No. Really – I can say nothing about it.' She gulped water so rapidly she almost choked, and it splashed down the front of her dress unheeded.

'What papers have you signed?' asked Mina.

Miss Whinstone shook her head. 'None, it was thought best not to.'

'Why was that?' asked Mina. 'For the sake of secrecy?'

There was a long silence.

'Miss Whinstone,' said Mina. 'I think that you have been told lies, by unscrupulous people determined to part you from your fortune, and then made complicit in your own downfall by being manipulated into keeping a secret.'

'But—' whispered the lady, meekly.

'Yes?'

'But Archibald would not have told me a lie.'

'I have no doubt that your brother was a good and honourable man,' said Mina soothingly, 'but any messages you have received from him through Miss Eustace may have been nothing more than an invention to entrap you.'

Miss Whinstone hesitated, and Mina put the newspaper before her again. 'Only read here about her arrest for fraud. Can you continue to trust her?'

'I – I don't know,' said Miss Whinstone, in a voice that seemed to echo from a deep pit of wretchedness. 'I was so happy when she brought me messages from Archibald, happy, that was, until …'

'Until he demanded that you adopt two children?' said Mina. 'On what pretext? Can your brother who cared so much for you really have intended you to be as unhappy as you clearly are now? I cannot believe it of him!'

Miss Whinstone sobbed, and was for a time incoherent, but was able after a while to say with an effort that good as her brother had been, one could never tell what secrets a man might have.

'I understand,' said Mina. 'You need say no more; I can see that it pains you. But it is my belief that your brother was as virtuous a gentleman as you have always known him to be, and that the real transgressor is Miss Eustace.'

Slowly, Miss Whinstone recovered her composure, and dried her eyes. 'Do you really think so?' she asked, hopefully.

'I am certain of it!'

'But what shall I do? I have been sent an account for another quarter's schooling, and they both need new clothes and books.'

'This is my advice,' said Mina. 'Pay nothing to these criminals. You will not be challenged unless you show weakness. Go to see Mr Phipps the solicitor without any delay, and put the whole matter into his hands. Any further demands for money can then be redirected to him. Ask him to make enquiries about the antecedents of the children. Once you have proof of what is suspected then the police can be informed. Will you do that?'

Miss Whinstone was drowning under waves of indecision. On the one hand, there was the shame of admitting that she had been made into a fool, and sucked dry of her income. The shame of her brother's transgression was on the other hand, something that she could bury deep and with it came two children, supposedly of his and therefore her blood, a family she could never have hoped for. She looked at the newspaper again, sighed, and took Mina by the hand. 'Will you accompany me?' she asked. 'I do not think I have the strength to go alone.'

Mr Phipps, though a busy man, was happy to find time to see Miss Whinstone and was understandably shocked at what she had to reveal. He promised to commence enquiries immediately.

'Well, here is a to do!' said Mina's mother on her return. All of Brighton, it seemed, was buzzing with the news of Mrs Parchment's nuptials, and the general view was that she had lied in court to extricate Mr Clee from Miss Simmons's suit, and gained a husband as her price. The happy couple were spending their honeymoon at the Grand Hotel. 'What can the silly woman have been thinking of? And he seems to have got a very poor bargain.'

'He has a wealthy wife,' said Mina, 'and for some men that is all that matters.'

'Nonsense, Mrs Parchment doesn't have a penny to her name. I told you so myself, Mina, but you cannot have been listening to me.'

'I thought – I believed that her late husband died a wealthy man,' said Mina. 'Was I mistaken?'

'No, he had made himself rich on the vanity of others. But he and his wife were on bad terms and had separated long before his death. He left all his fortune to a nephew, who out of charity made a small allowance to his aunt. Now that she is married,

I expect that will cease. If Mr Clee expected to live in luxury from the proceeds of Parchment's Pink Complexion Pills he is in for a very unpleasant shock.'

With the possibility that Mr Phipps might take several weeks to obtain firm evidence of the duplicity practised upon Miss Whinstone, and Mr and Mrs Clee about to leave town, Mina realised that she had a very short period of time to put her plan into action. She wrote two notes and the next day there was a meeting.

'The thing that makes it especially difficult to expose fraud is that if it takes place it does so before hardly more than ten people, most of whom are devotees of the medium,' said Mina. 'Whatever happens and whatever is said, the thing that counts is how the event is represented to the wider public. The only advantage we have is the fickleness of popular opinion. Just as people may flock to the latest fashion so we may also expect that they will be as quick to abandon it and find the next sensation to amuse them.'

'But if what you say is true,' said Dr Hamid, in whose parlour the co-conspirators were assembled over a pot of tea and a large plateful of Eliza's favourite almond biscuits, 'as soon as Mr Phipps has his evidence Miss Eustace will be found out.'

'I cannot help but think that she will find some way to extricate herself,' said Mina. 'There are any number of people who would lie or blind themselves to the truth in order to protect her. And we must catch Mr Clee, too, and soon, or he will disappear. We can't wait for Mr Phipps to complete his enquiries.'

'Then what do you suggest?' asked Richard. 'I suppose I could always break into her apartment again and declare my undying love. That should work. I'd have all her secrets in an hour!'

'Promise me that you will not,' said Mina. 'No, we must engage that great and noble personage, Lady Finsbury.'

Nellie, who had been admiring her new pair of lace gloves, laughed.

'Lady Finsbury,' Mina pointed out, 'is an admirer of Miss Eustace, so much so that she wishes to be her patroness, and use her influence to enhance her protégée's fame. Lady Finsbury will hire a hall, she will engage a man to sell tickets and keep undesirables from the door, pack the room only with the most dedicated believers, guarantee that she will purchase a dozen or more tickets for herself and her fashionable friends, and she will promise Miss Eustace a generous extra payment if she can only produce a full form manifestation of her beloved great uncle Sir Mortimer Portland.'

'Do you expect Miss Eustace to personate a man?' said Richard.

'Not at all. I expect her to get Mr Clee to personate Sir Mortimer. Mr Clee is well known by sight to all of Miss Eustace's circle. Only unmask him and the imposture will be apparent. Remember, in her previous séances, Miss Eustace, through the Gaskins, had full command of all the circumstances. She will imagine that on this occasion she enjoys not only the approbation but the protection of Lady Finsbury. Miss Eustace will undoubtedly make many conditions for her appearance, and Lady Finsbury will agree to them all, but it will be we who have the control.'

'If she should suspect anything …' said Dr Hamid.

'I know,' said Mina. 'If she does then the event will be a failure. She dare not risk a complete failure before such a large gathering, and will produce some slight effects to please the crowd, but there would be nothing we can use to prove fraud beyond a doubt. She has escaped so many times, she knows what to do. The important thing for our purposes is the production of the spirit form of Sir Mortimer Portland. Lady Finsbury must make a very valuable offer to tempt her to do that.'

'Has she brought out a male spirit before?' asked Richard. 'I mean a whole body that walks about, not just a mask and a false beard on a stick.'

'It seems she has. Mother swears that at a private séance she saw Father actually standing before her in the room, and conversed with him and even touched him. It is my belief that it was Mr Clee, as they are of similar height and build, perhaps with a scarf or shawl around his face, as they do not look very alike, but Mother insists that she saw Father clearly and cannot have been mistaken. Lady Finsbury has provided Miss Eustace with a portrait of her great-uncle, and if asked about his height and build, she should mention something very like Mr Clee. That will be enough to tempt them to try the imposture, if, that is, Mr Clee can bear to leave the arms of his new bride.'

It took several days to make all the arrangements. Mina hired a suitable meeting hall, and hoped that with the sale of tickets, which were deliberately priced at a very reasonable level to encourage the maximum possible attendance, she would not be greatly out of pocket. Fortunately Miss Eustace's circle was so well known that there was no difficulty in securing considerable interest in the event, which it was promised would be the most astounding séance that the renowned medium had ever conducted, with the added relish that it would be graced by a noble lady celebrated for her beauty and taste, and her glittering entourage.

Mina, though not Miss Eustace's most favoured person, was fully intending to be there to both witness and oversee the course of events, and since Richard was acting as doorkeeper there would be no difficulty over her gaining entry, but she thought it best to conceal herself at the back of the room in case Miss Eustace was to spy her and take alarm, which would give her the opportunity of casting the blame for any failure on Mina's bad influence. Once the room was in darkness, Mina intended to creep forward and secure a better position in a seat reserved for her at the front.

On the day of the event another package arrived from Mr Greville, and Mina was just about to open it when Richard, who had hired the cab to take them to the hall, arrived with a downcast expression.

'What is the matter?' asked Mina. 'Has Miss Eustace taken flight? That would be almost as good a result if we were never to see her again.'

He shook his head. 'No, she is here and Lady Finsbury is fawning on her and promising the most astonishing wealth, but I do not think we will see Sir Mortimer, in fact without her accomplice it is doubtful that anything of note will happen, and we will have spent our money in vain.'

Mina ignored the suggestion that he had had any share in the financial arrangements. 'Has Mr Clee left Brighton?'

'Oh, he is still in Brighton,' said Richard, 'very much so, and unable to leave it if he wished, but he and his lady wife have had a disagreement which took quite a violent turn. I am surprised that it did not echo all over town. The subject of their dispute was, I believe, which one of them was able to pay the bill at the Grand Hotel, and the only thing they could agree upon was that it was neither of them. Mr Clee has by now discovered that his wealthy bride has not a copper coin to her name. There was a great deal of shouting and epithets and some broken furniture, and the manager had no choice but to call the police. The two lovebirds are currently cooling their heels in the cells, and will come before a magistrate tomorrow. What shall we do?'

Brother and sister sat together and considered the sad wreckage of their plans.

'There is nothing we can do,' said Mina, eventually. 'All is arranged and must be paid for, but I think now that we will get little result from it. It is my fault, I am afraid, I have been too ambitious. Well,' she said, folding the unopened package and pushing it into her reticule, 'let us go.'

Twenty-Five

They arrived at the hall shortly before the main crush was expected. Richard and Dr Hamid, while reserving for themselves seats on the front row, had taken on the role of doorkeepers, supposedly to ensure that pressmen and other undesirables were refused admission, but actually only to make Miss Eustace believe that this was taking place. The medium had also been reassured that when a volunteer was asked for from the company to check that all was genuine, the person who would step forward would be a friend of Lady Finsbury who was a firm believer in spiritualism.

Professor and Mrs Gaskin were early arrivals. Although they had relinquished their supervision of Miss Eustace to Lady Finsbury and her agents, they remained close by the medium's side, perhaps hoping that some of the glamour of her noble patron would touch their garments, and brush them with a little glossy stain. Nellie was impeccable in her role; her dress, deportment, manners, and mode of speech were exactly as someone who had never met a titled lady would imagine one to be.

Mina took care to make herself inconspicuous, which for the most part meant sitting behind a person of a larger stature, there being more than sufficient to choose from. As the audience arrived, in a steady but powerful stream, all chattering with excitement, Mina was able to see each individual as they entered; her mother, Mrs Bettinson, Mrs Phipps and her nephew, Mrs Langley, Miss Simmons, Mrs Peasgood and her sister and friends, Mr Jordan and Mr Conroy. The crowd was, she knew, salted with representatives of every leading newspaper in Sussex, and there was a local artist specially hired by the *Illustrated Police News* to record the event, and several plain-clothes detectives. The unfortunate Miss Whinstone had, Mina had recently learned, gone away on a sea trip to recuperate from her upset. Mr Clee and his wife were presumably still incarcerated, and did not make an appearance.

As the room filled she remembered that she had not yet looked at the item she had received in the post from Mr Greville, and so pulled it from her reticule and opened the packet. It was another copy of the *Illustrated Police News* from October 1869, and this one included a small picture of Miss Eustace and her husband on trial. It was cruder than the paper's usual portraits, and the likeness of Miss Eustace was only fair while the man in the dock beside her looked nothing like Mr Clee. Mina wondered if the artist had been in court at all.

A theatrical-looking gentleman with a colourful cravat and a flower in his buttonhole strode into the hall and looked about him with an air of aristocratic confidence. He clearly expected to be and indeed was directed to one of the reserved places. Mina was a little mystified at first as to who he might be, although there was something a little familiar about his appearance. He clearly knew Lady Finsbury for he greeted her in a warm but respectful manner. Mina suddenly realised that this must be Rolly Rollason, the man who had posed for the portrait used for Sir Mortimer Portland. In his own person he was a remarkable-looking individual, a giraffe of a man, well above six feet in height, with a long neck and prominent Adam's apple but without the bushy hair and long nose of the character he had portrayed. He seemed to be formed almost entirely of arms and legs with prominent knees and elbows attached to a small body. Mina felt some curiosity to see him as the Caledonian Marvel.

It was time. The hall was filled and the doors closed. Richard and Dr Hamid came forward to take their reserved places, and Richard took Lady Finsbury by her tiny fingertips and drew her to face the assembly. All grew silent in anticipation of her words.

'My dear friends,' she began, in a queenly voice, 'for I do most sincerely believe that we who have come together today to celebrate a great truth are friends; how happy I am to see you all! You may be wondering how it was that I came to meet Miss Eustace, and the truth is quite as astonishing and wonderful as any story you may have heard of her powers. Some days ago I received a visitor in the form of a spirit, the spirit of my dear departed great-uncle, Sir Mortimer Portland. I was not afraid, for in life Sir Mortimer was the dearest, kindest and most generous of men, and one who always had my welfare at heart. He had a message for me, one of very great importance, but since I am no medium it was hard for him to express what he wanted so urgently to say. At last he said that I must go at once to see Miss Eustace, who alone was able to receive his words, and this, at the very first opportunity, I did. I have been privileged to witness her powers myself, privileged too, to become acquainted with Professor and Mrs Gaskin whose intelligence and perceptiveness I must applaud. I ask them now to stand and receive your appreciation.'

The Gaskins both rose and faced the audience and bowed without any attempt at humility. There was polite ripple of approbation.

'They,' Lady Finsbury continued, 'better than any of us here know the foundation of Miss Eustace's powers, and it is to them that we should be grateful for first bringing her to the notice of the public. I would urge you all to study carefully anything they may say or write on the subject.

'I have now determined to do everything in my power to ensure that the fame of Miss Eustace will spread. Her wonders must not be confined to drawing rooms, and seen only by a fortunate few. All the world must know of Miss Eustace. She has astonished Brighton, and next she will astonish London, and all of Europe. Soon, she will conquer America. But today, I know, she will win all your hearts.'

There was enthusiastic applause for Lady Finsbury as Richard escorted her back to her place.

There was no curtain to conceal a stage, and no cabinet. The hall was generally employed for meetings at which a long committee table and chairs were used, but the table, which was draped with a thick dark red cloth, had been moved back against the far wall, and all the chairs but one assimilated into the rows laid out for the audience.

The assembled company therefore sat facing nothing apart from an open space with the table at the back and a single chair on which lay a coiled rope. 'May I please have a volunteer to inspect the arrangements?' asked Richard, and before anyone could move Rolly Rollason had leaped energetically to his feet and darted forward. Rolly was a whirling windmill of activity. He picked up the rope and examined it carefully along its length, then, with the ends wrapped around his fists, tugged it hard and loudly declared it to be unbreakable. He picked up the solitary chair, lifted it above his head and looked underneath it, then he drew back the red cloth and showed everyone that nothing was hidden under the table. He next walked about stamping on the floor and pronounced it solid. He was quite an entertainment on his own, and did everything except dance.

Finally, he spotted that there was a door to one side of the room, and hurried over to it, but after making a great display of trying and failing to open it, he told everyone that it was securely locked.

Richard thanked Rolly warmly for his efforts, and asking him to remain, offered his hand to Miss Eustace, who was sitting at the end of the front row. She rose with her customary gracious manner, and came to sit in the chair, then Richard and Dr Hamid tied her in place, and Rolly inspected the knots and said that it was utterly impossible for the lady to escape. Rolly then returned to his seat while Richard and Dr Hamid went to turn down the lamps, allowing Professor and Mrs Gaskin to lead the company in a hymn.

Mina, having already determined her route, left her seat and crept forward into a better place, covered by the darkness and the sound of singing.

The hymn droned to a close, and everyone waited for wonders. The audience, thought Mina, was not only larger than Miss Eustace was used to, it was also, unknown to her, differently composed, being made up partially of those who had seen Miss Eustace's tricks before and were hoping for something novel, those who had seen Miss Foxton and were unlikely to be impressed by anything Miss Eustace could do, and unbelievers. The atmosphere was therefore less one of expectancy than impatience. Believers, thought Mina, were better able than others to endure a long wait for a manifestation. Time ticking away brought them to a state of heightened emotion, the better to appreciate what loomed out of the darkness. Time ticked, but nothing happened. Someone had a coughing fit, someone else giggled, and there was a silken rustling of people shifting in their seats, a creaking of leather shoes, and even some subdued muttering.

At length, after what seemed like an unusually long wait, there was a rap on the far wall. A few moments later another rap sounded from the right. There followed a soporific silence, and then a rap on the wall to the left. It was an unimpressive performance. The dancing lights were next to appear, but while they were attractive enough, they had been seen before, and were not what people had paid their ticket money to see.

A noticeably disgruntled whispering arose, and Mina caught the words 'Miss Foxton', since it appeared that Miss Eustace was being compared unfavourably to her rival. It was apparent to Mina that Miss Eustace, robbed of Mr Clee who was her usual accomplice, had been obliged in some haste to engage another rather less adept. Mina was tempted to turn up the lights and reveal the imposture, but she knew that Miss Eustace would only claim ignorance of what was being done, and it would be impossible to prove that the medium was directing the fraud. The only result of such an action would be an angry audience demanding a refund of their ticket money, a heavy loss to Mina and the closing of the ranks of the faithful about poor ill-used and maligned Miss Eustace.

Even the appearance of the praying hands and the glowing mask from under the tablecloth did little to pacify the crowd, especially when the mask fell off the end of the stick, and had to be retrieved by an invisible, presumably black-gloved hand. This time there was no Miss Whinstone to claim it as a relative, and the result was a mixture of dismay and amusement.

Mina turned to Richard beside her. 'I think we should call an end to this soon,' she whispered. 'Could you make the announcement, and then stand by the lights with Dr Hamid?'

'Right you are!' said Richard. 'It's all a bit lame, I'd say. Sorry, old girl.'

He was about to creep away, but before he could move there was another development, and this one more promising. Mina put her hand on his arm and he stayed.

From underneath the heavy draped tablecloth there came a little extrusion of light, quite formless, but slowly growing. The audience fell silent, as the cloudy shape pushed forward, and became the size of a large pudding, and then a pillow, and then a hound, and then a chair. Having decided on its preferred width, it started to grow in height, and gradually rose to the size of a man. At last it was unfolded, and raised its head and lowered its arms, and stood before them. It was undoubtedly a male figure, dressed as for a fashionable assembly, but covered all over with pale glowing draperies. Through the phosphorescent gauze few of its features were distinct, but there was a luxuriant shrub of wild hair and the thrust of a long nose. A glassy sheen suggested that a monocle adorned one eye and in an outstretched hand it held a single rose.

Bathed in the phantom's pale radiance, Miss Eustace flung her body back in her chair and uttered a great sigh. 'Spirit!' she cried. 'Identify yourself!'

The form slowly turned to face the assembled crowds, some of whom cowered back, while others leaned forward and peered with interest. There was, from the body of the hall, the scratch of busy pencils. 'I have no name, for I am part of another world,' it intoned, in a guttural voice. 'I live in heaven above with the angels, but when I was alive and walked the earth in fleshly form, I had a name, and a history, and loved ones.'

'What was that name?' demanded Miss Eustace. 'And do you have a message for anyone here present?'

'I was once known as Sir Mortimer Portland,' said the form, sonorously, 'and I was the master of Great Portland Hall. I hid a great treasure there, in gold and jewels, which should by rights belong to my heir, Lady Finsbury. The place where it is to be found I will communicate to the lady privately very soon.'

'Let the lady step forward and say that she knows you for her dear relative,' said Miss Eustace.

'Well, here's a pretty thing and no mistake,' came a man's voice from the front row, speaking very loudly. 'Fancy that, to be so personated! It's a disgrace!'

'Be quiet, sir!' urged Professor Gaskin. 'You must let Lady Finsbury speak!'

'I won't be quiet!' said the new voice. 'I will have my say!' There was the sound of a chair moving back.

'Sit down at once, or you will be removed!' snapped Mrs Gaskin, who had forgotten who was in charge of the proceedings.

There was a great deal of annoyed muttering about the interruption, and Mina seized the opportunity and quickly told Richard and Dr Hamid to turn up the lights.

As the yellow glow of the gas lamps flowed through the hall, it could be seen that Rolly Rollason, for it was he who had called out, had got to his feet, but he was no longer Rolly. Under cover of darkness he had donned the elaborate wig, false nose and monocle of his portrait, and was holding the rose he had removed from his buttonhole. 'You, sir,' he said, pointing the rose at the startled spirit, 'are an impostor! I am Sir Mortimer Portland, and I am very much alive, so you can't be my ghost.'

The spirit, which in the glimmer of gaslight resembled nothing more than a man draped in a grubby grey shawl, hesitated. Miss Eustace did not move. During the commotion she had slumped forward so that her head rested almost on her knees, and in that uncomfortable position, her face hidden from view, she remained, to all appearances unconscious.

Professor Gaskin rose up with a cry. 'Oh, please dim the lights! Do so at once or Miss Eustace will surely die!'

'Turn up the lights?' exclaimed Richard, deliberately mishearing, 'All hands to the lights! Let's have more light, here!'

'More light! The professor wants more light!' called Dr Hamid. Several men in grey suits bustled forward, and all around the hall more lamps jumped into flame.

'No! No!' cried the professor, burying his hands in his hair, and clawing at it in desperation; but he was being ignored, for what was visible was very hard to deny. Mrs Gaskin looked unsure whether she should scream or faint. Neither was a strong item in her repertoire, and instead she looked about for someone to insult.

'This is a trick!' she growled at Lady Finsbury, but the lady faced her with some swift and pointed words that should never have left a lady's lips, and Mrs Gaskin retreated, too shocked to speak.

It was the great final scene in the melodrama, and Nellie played it as only she could. She stepped forward, then looked first at one Sir Mortimer and then at the other, as if making up her mind which was the true one. Since Rolly was a full nine inches taller than his impersonator the choice ought not to have taken as long as it did, but Nellie knew how to create and build rapt anticipation in her audience. Finally with an emotional gesture she flew, sobbing wildly, to Rolly and laid her head on his chest. 'Uncle! Dearest uncle!' she cried, 'I thought you were dead!'

Rolly gave a great smirk to the audience and wrapped his arms about his head. 'I ain't dead, though! Ain't I?'

There was a burst of laughter.

'No, it was just a nasty cold in the head, that's all,' he went on, giving his 'niece' a fond hug. 'You must have had a dream and imagined it. And there's no treasure, I'm sorry to say. Never was any.'

'Then who is this?' exclaimed Nellie, turning to the other Sir Mortimer, who had dropped the rose and was backing away, lifting the shawl to try and cover his face.

It was Mr Jordan who strode forward, and before the figure could protest, he whipped away shawl, wig, false nose and monocle, to reveal the shiny pate of Mr Bradley.

There were gasps of recognition from the audience.

Mina, suddenly realising why the picture in the newspaper of Miss Eustace's husband did not resemble Mr Clee, came forward, while Mr Jordan stood by Mr Bradley preventing his escape, and Richard called on everyone for silence, which was not an easy thing to achieve.

'My friends,' said Mina, as soon as the hubbub had subsided sufficiently that she could be heard. 'Not only are these two persons frauds and deceivers, they are also husband and wife and have been practising their wiles for some years. Both have served a prison term, and the proof of that is in my hand.' She raised the newspaper; although there was no chance that anyone could see the illustration, the distinctive page made it very clear as to which paper it was.

'That is a lie!' exploded Mr Bradley. 'And that newspaper is a rag from the gutter! This person is an unbeliever! An imp! A demon! A monster! Why, just look at her, she has the stamp of the fiend himself in her form!'

Louisa Scarletti marched forward and slapped him hard across the face. 'How dare you! She is my daughter!' She burst into tears and hugged Mina, then inevitably appeared to feel faint, and was rescued by Mrs Bettinson and taken back to her seat where Dr Hamid tended to her.

The next person to emerge from the throng was Mr Phipps, who addressed the audience with a packet of papers in his hand. 'Lady Finsbury, Sir Mortimer, ladies and gentlemen,' he began. 'I can confirm that Miss Scarletti has spoken the truth. Here are some legal documents, received by me only an hour ago. They are proof that Mr Bradley and Miss Eustace are indeed husband and wife, and also the parents of two children, who they foisted on to an unsuspecting lady under false pretences and from whom they have been stealing ever since. They have been plying their fraudulent trade for some years and have both served terms in prison.'

Two men in grey suits appeared on either side of the discomfited spirit healer, and took him firmly by the arms.

'You may or may not know this,' said Mina, to Mr Bradley, 'but you are under arrest.'

Mr Bradley, all defiance vanished like the ghost he had pretended to be, was taken away, to the loud hisses and imprecations of his former acolytes, and with missiles of compressed paper bouncing off his head.

The Gaskins stared after him in grotesque dismay, exchanged horrified glances, and then, very quickly and quietly, left the hall.

There was a sudden movement near Mina. Miss Eustace had decided to give up the pretence that she was asleep and use the distraction caused by her husband's arrest to make her escape. She was free of her bonds in an instant, and that feat alone brought a gasp from the audience as they realised how adept she was at such tricks. Only Mina's slight form lay between her and a free route to the door, and she tried to push the trifling obstacle aside, but Mina dropped the newspaper and seized Miss Eustace by both wrists. For a moment or two they struggled, as the medium tried to break free and amazement spread over

Miss Eustace's face as she found herself being immobilised by a tiny, seemingly frail woman who was very much stronger than she looked. Mina knew she could only hold on for a short while before her wrenched shoulder and lesser weight allowed her quarry to prevail, but help was at hand.

'I'll take her, thank you,' said Mrs Bettinson, striding up to grab Miss Eustace from behind, pinning her arms to her sides. 'Now then, Miss Cheat, Miss Hoodwink, let's see if you can melt yourself out of this!'

As Miss Eustace was hauled firmly away to join her husband at the police station, Richard came to stand by Mina. 'What a wonder you are!' he said. 'And the best of it, no one will be asking for their money back!'

Twenty-Six

Mr Phipps later advised Mina that he had turned over all his documents to the police, who now had ample material with which to mount a search of Miss Eustace's apartments. The very next day the couple attracted a different audience from the one they had recently entertained, when they appeared before the Brighton magistrates. The case was adjourned for the accumulation of new evidence, but it was thought to be certain that they would in due course be committed to take their trial at the next assizes. The couple had asked for bail, but Mr Phipps had argued strongly against this and won.

Mr and Mrs Clee also appeared before the Brighton magistrates, where they were bound over to keep the peace, ordered to pay costs and released. During the entire proceedings they neither looked at nor spoke to one another. On leaving the court they went their separate ways, but Mr Clee was immedi ately rearrested and charged with conspiring with the Bradleys to commit fraud. The new Mrs Clee announced her intention of applying for a legal separation from her spouse, something he did not seem averse to, although he was less delighted by her demand for a regular allowance.

Professor Gaskin and his wife were briefly taken into police custody, and for a time they were strongly suspected of having abetted Miss Eustace in her deceit, but it was eventually accepted that they had been little more than unwitting dupes. They regained their freedom, though not their reputations, and agreed with a singular determination to give evidence for the prosecution.

Over the course of the next week, and at the resumed hearing, new facts were made public.

Mr Clee, it was discovered, was Miss Eustace's brother, and an accomplished stage magician, card sharp and occasional spirit medium. He had been attending Brill's Baths and learning all he could about the citizens of Brighton, while Mr Bradley had been doing much the same at Dr Hamid's.

When Dr Hamid's friend Dr Chenai was questioned he admitted that while relaxing after an Indian steam bath he had spoken to Mr Bradley and made some incautious comments that had formed the basis of Miss Eustace's supposed communications from Eliza. While Eliza had never told him of the exact position of the pain in her back, he had learned all he needed to know from his examination. There were a dozen other examples of gossip being passed on in this way, all of which had later been recorded in Miss Eustace's extensive notebooks. There were also articles taken from the newspapers about important Brighton figures: their families, illnesses, accidents, deaths and legacies; even information that had been copied from tombstones.

The committal hearing ended as Mr Phipps had anticipated. While awaiting the trial of Mr and Mrs Bradley, the Gaskins, who were not seen in public after the arrest of their protégée, gave up their apartments in Brighton and returned to London, where Mrs Gaskin founded a girls' school and Professor Gaskin devoted himself to studying the chemistry of radiant matter.

As the summer blossomed and the sun broiled the town and its people to a turn, fashions moved on, and the spirit mediums and mystic healers departed. Even Madame Proserpina no longer told fortunes for sixpence on the West Pier, and it was a curious coincidence that she had vanished on the very same day that Miss Eustace had been taken into custody.

Mina was hopeful that there would be no more work for her to do, but Dr Hamid was not so sure. 'Those who want to believe will never be shaken,' he said. 'It enhances their idea of themselves, and in some individuals it will be central to it. Their belief is everything to them; it can become them. If they abandon it then they will be nothing. Even those who have seen the truth about Miss Eustace and her associates may yet believe that another medium will be the true article, forget how they have been made fools of, and take up the next arrival with just as much enthusiasm.'

'Well, we know all their tricks now, and if they try us again we will be ready for them,' said Mina, confidently.

Dr Hamid looked apprehensive, but whether this was at the prospect of the mediums returning to Brighton or Mina commandeering his assistance to deal with them, he didn't say.

There was a new arrival in town, which brought pleasure and meaning to Louisa Scarletti's life. Enid descended upon her mother with the twins and a nursemaid, saying that she planned to stay for several months. She had received a letter from Mr Inskip saying that the property negotiations in distant Roumania were taking longer than he had anticipated and he might well be absent for another six months; indeed, if the snow on the mountain passes next December was as deep as it had been last winter, he might not be able to come home until the spring. Enid, enduring her husband's absence with a fortitude that approached joy, embraced the pleasures of Brighton like a starving person faced with a laden table, while encouraging her mother in a new pastime that she took to with alacrity – spoiling her grandchildren.

There was more good news for the Scarletti family when Mina's brother Edward arrived, bringing with him the delightful Miss Hooper who had at long last consented to become his bride.

Richard was no longer in the theatrical business. It was not so much that mediums were out of fashion, for what Miss Foxton had to offer the eager eye would never be out of fashion, but he had not, as he had hoped, found it to be profitable. Such money as had come in from sales of tickets for private shows or remuneration from the New Oxford Theatre of Varieties had somehow found its way into Mrs Conroy's emporium where it had been transformed as if by a conjuring trick into Paris gowns, and lace gloves fit for a queen.

It was with some hesitation that Richard had suggested to Nellie that the business should be given up, and to his surprise she readily agreed, and they parted as friends. Soon afterwards, there was an elegant society wedding, when Nellie Gilden, in her real name of Hetty Gold, became Mrs John Jordan. The event was only marred by one unhappy incident, when the bride, admiring her new husband's favourite timepiece, accidentally dropped it on the ground and stepped on it.

Only one thing still puzzled Mina: her mother's continued insistence that at a private séance conducted by Miss Eustace, she had seen and conversed with her dear deceased Henry, and even clasped him in her arms. No man, she declared, could ever personate him, and she derided the very idea that she could have been mistaken. Mina, recalling that the claim had first been made in front of Mrs Bettinson and Miss Whinstone, could not help but wonder if the entire story had been made up to impress her mother's friends and even make them a little jealous.

'Mother,' said Mina, one day in frustration, as they were alone apart from a beribboned baby bouncing on the proud grandmother's knee, its twin having been removed by the nursemaid for feeding, 'I must know the truth of this. When you were at the private séance hosted by Miss Eustace, did you truly see Father, as solid and real a figure as you see me now? Or was it just a story to tease and amuse? No one would think the worse of you if it was the latter. Come now, surely you can tell me, and I promise not to breathe a word of what you say.'

Louisa waved a teething ring in front of the baby's chubby fingers. 'Oh Mina, how can you ask such a thing?' she said. 'Would I tell a lie?'

'Of course you would not,' said Mina.

'Well then, that is settled.' She gave a wistful smile. 'Dear Henry, I think of him every day, I miss him every moment. No woman could have had a better husband. Yes, Mina, I saw your father as clear as can be. I saw him as I see him always, as I see him even now: in my mind's eye.'

About the Author

LINDA STRATMANN is a former chemist's dispenser and civil servant who now writes full-time. She lives in Walthamstow, London.

Also by the Author

Chloroform: The Quest for Oblivion

Cruel Deeds and Dreadful Calamities: The Illustrated Police News 1864–1938

Essex Murders

Gloucestershire Murders

Greater London Murders: 33 True Stories of Revenge, Jealousy, Greed & Lust

Kent Murders

Middlesex Murders

More Essex Murders

Notorious Blasted Rascal: Colonel Charteris and the Servant Girl's Revenge

The Crooks Who Conned Millions: True Stories of Fraudsters and Charlatans

The Marquess of Queensberry: Wilde's Nemesis

Whiteley's Folly: The Life and Death of a Salesman